HI LOVE, YOU JUST DROPPED YOUR GLOVE

A McCUSKER MYSTERY

PAUL CHARLES

HI LOVE, YOU JUST DROPPED YOUR GLOVE

Praise for the McCusker Series

"A welcome return for Brendy McCusker... Charles crafts with such a careful eye on the sparks that can fly—some of them charming, some witty, some downright menacing—between characters who don't happen to see eye to eye, or sometimes even to be operating in the same galaxy. Once again, it's hard to resist a hero who realizes, 'He just had a habit of opening his mouth and not knowing what was going to come out."—*Kirkus Reviews*

"Charles's skillful depiction of the many sides of love and its strange bypaths lifts this clever novel well above the genre average."—*Publishers Weekly*

"Paul Charles is an outstanding author of crime fiction novels. They are models of character development and powerful observations of people the detectives meet. I enjoy reading his books."—*Irish American News*

"Charles's skilful depiction of the many sides of love and its strange bypaths lifts this clever novel well above the genre average."—*Publishers Weekly*

"Charles has a wealth of experience in the crime genre from his past Kennedy and Starrett novels and the McCusker series delivers the same blend of mystery and engaging protagonists. The characters have an authenticity that Charles has fine-tuned throughout his writing career. Charles ability to weave real-like details helps bring the story full to life. A Day in The Life of Louis Bloom is both a love letter to Belfast and a gripping thriller."—**Aoife Bradshaw**, *Hot Press*

"Charles In Full Bloom With Novel... a thrilling page-turner."—*Sunday*

Chapter One

I was born here and I'll die here, against my will.
—Dylan

'Hi love, you just dropped your glove.'

When she turned to face him, he was amazed. He remained totally in shock to the extent he became a blabbering idiot.

'Just now as it fell from your coat pocket…' he continued, 'I caught it before it hit the wet ground… Honestly it didn't get wet. I mean it's a little wet, but only from the rain and not the pavement…agh…' and mid-sentence he reluctantly turned and chased after his two mates.

She was the most beautiful creature he'd ever set his eyes on during his seventeen years on this earth. When she'd passed him a few life-changing seconds beforehand, she was walking, arms interlinked in the midst of two friends with her head bowed to the pavement. Consequently, he'd missed her green eyes, hidden by her long black hair, and he'd missed her quiet demeanour, but, most of all, he'd also missed the chance to make a connection.

He insisted his two mates, Brendan and Lefty, continue walking around the streets of Portrush with him until darkness fell ninety minutes later. He was working on the theory they'd bump into the three girls again. They'd discovered, to his cost, the only thing more difficult than finding someone in Portrush in the peak holiday season was finding someone on the deserted streets of Portrush during the off-peak season, when Ulster's number one tourist centre reverted to its more comfortable status of winter ghost town, aka Ghostrush.

Thomas Barry—Tommy to his acquaintances, Tom to his good friends—minus his two mates was back on the streets the following morning, just before eight o'clock. He walked the short distance from his parents' house in the sedate Antrim Gardens to the nearly (but not quite) refurbished railway station in Eglinton Street, passing the moth-balled Barry's (historic) Amusement Arcade on the way. It was a journey just like he'd done most days of his life. Most other days of his life. though, he'd just taken Barry's (no relation) and every other local landmark, for granted. That Sunday morning in October 1976 though he'd studied every nook and cranny around the streets of the Port as if his life depended on it.

He felt it did.

When his friends met up with him just before lunch time, he admitted to them he'd already had tea and toast in Portrush's Holiday Hostel, with its ultra-colourful rooms; the once elegant Adelphi Hoteland The Atlantic Hotel, with its spectacular views, in the vain hope the three girls were out-of-towners. The other hotels and guest houses were all closed for the winter, he claimed. Still, he'd tried them all, "just in case, you understand." He also, for one who'd always gone to great trouble to keep the majority of his feelings inarticulately to himself, articulately explained he felt for the sake of his well-being, if not his life, he needed to find this girl. He also admitted that, not only did he not know what he was going to say to her when, and if, he met her, but if such an accidental, on purpose, meet happened he'd be so tongue-tied again, he might even need to walk on past her. He just knew he really needed to find her. He told them he'd been awake all-night thinking about her. Lefty put him out of his misery by offering to take him to some of the out-of-town hotels. The two of them hopped on Lefty's trusted red Vespa 125 scooter and headed off out past Kelly's trailer park and bar and on to Castle Rock, Portstewart, Portballintrae and even Bushmills.

They returned just over an hour later with the Vespa's petrol tank empty and their four arms all the one length.

Thomas Barry admitted to his two best friends he'd never felt so convinced about anything before in his life. A real-life girl had never ever had such an effect on him before. Isabella Adjani on the silver screen yes, but a real live human, certainly not. He most certainly accepted the fact he was never ever going to meet the long-haired, green-eyed girl again in his life.

He admitted how weird this feeling was to him.

Nonetheless he continued his search.

He thought of all the things he could have done, should have done. Perhaps all of them were things capable of scaring her off for life. But what did it matter now? He'd most certainly lost her for life.

The lads wanted to go to the Old Harbour Bar. Even with the new glitzy restaurant extension, accessed by a half a flight of wooden stairs, it was still the cosiest bar in the winter and their favourite watering hole. He declined, suggesting he might join them later. Once again, he took to the streets of Portrush. The same familiar streets he had taken for granted all his life, but which now took on major importance due to the fact they may be keeping him from finding the green-eyed girl. He tried chastising himself for feeling sorry for himself. It didn't work. How could it possibly work when someone, something, a God even, if such a spirit existed, had allowed him to experience this special creature and then not equip him properly about how to approach her? He chastised himself further for not considering what he'd say to her if, or when, he met her. He'd already let himself down once by blabbering away when he had the perfect excuse to greet her. Equally he felt if he had something rehearsed it would have sounded too false, stifled, insincere and a chat up line. He kicked himself over his rap about her glove being wet not because he had let it fall on the wet pavement but because it had gotten damp in the rain.

He'd never been one for the chat up lines. They'd left those to Lefty. Funny enough this approach hadn't worked out for their lead wingman either. Thomas Barry had often wondered if they'd become mates, "blood brothers" just so they could hang out together and look for girls. Anyway, they had launched their little gang, the BLTs. They even had their own unique motto: *May the Sauce be With You.* It was funny at the time. They'd picked it over a meal together in Morelli's as they simultaneously chased the food-saving flavouring known as HP. They'd also debated using: *Life is a Beach and Then the Tide Goes Out,*. Considering their endgame objective, they had unanimously voted against this option on the grounds it was too negative. As he wandered around the deserted streets, now it had gotten down to the nitty-gritty, he wasn't so sure about their motto either, or even about their gang in the first place. Lefty was always complaining three wasn't a good number to hang out in. If they met two girls and got through the even more complicated task of chatting them up, then the girls would surely feel sorry for the additional boy they would have to exclude due to the mathematical impossibilities. He reckoned maybe they could possibly have made the problematic maths work down in the more liberal Belfast. In the meantime, they had agreed they would figure out such a scenario as and when it arose. Lefty had claimed the girls would probably make their preference known and they, the boys, would just have to deal with it. They'd been happy to leave the tactics to Lefty. Even though Lefty's tactics had, so far, been 100% unsuccessful, they still left him in charge. The alternate didn't bear thinking about.

Tommy wondered if it would be any easier if, and when, one of them found a girlfriend and peeled off their gang as it were. He wondered who'd be the first to find a girl. He thought if you were a betting man and you followed the odds, then Lefty *should* be the first to find a girl. But then what would they do? They'd surely be lost without the tactics man. Or would they?

'At least the rain has stopped,' he said aloud, as he rounded the corner of the forsaken Mark Street Lane and into the desolate Atlantic Avenue.

'Hi Love,' he thought he heard a ghostly breathy voice say, not much above a whisper, 'you haven't found another glove, have you?'

There she was, there right in front of him on what would now become the hallowed, Atlantic Avenue. His green-eyed girl's green eyes were smiling straight at him.

He was so intent on finding her he pretty much nearly walked straight into her. He knew if she hadn't spoken first, he would have walked past her. Lucky enough before he'd a chance to figure out what he was going to say she spoke again.

'What am I like?' she started, 'I'm forever losing a glove, thankfully never both at the same time, mind you, always just the one at a time. The one you picked up for me I…'

'I've been looking for you all day,' he admitted, his voice sounding a lot calmer than he felt.

'Mmmm,' she replied, studying his face and sounding like she knew, and accepted, such an admission wasn't as weird as he feared, 'you'd look good with a moustache.'

Of all the things he'd imagined her to reply, and most of them also included her rushing off as quickly as her shapely legs would carry her, this was not even in the top 1000. It wasn't as though he had actually come up with more than three possible replies.

Before he knew it, they were involved in a natural freewheeling conversation.

She seemed inclined to linger rather than to walk away.

At a very brief lull in the conversation, they both silently acknowledged they didn't want the conversation to be stifled, so they spurted out their next questions simultaneously.

'Do you live here?' Tommy asked.

'Who were you talking to as you walked around the corner?' she asked over the top of his question.

'No, I'm at the University of Ulster in Coleraine and one of my course mates invited me and another friend over to her parents' house for the weekend. Her parents own a wee guest house over by the West Strand,' she said in response to his question.

'I was talking to myself,' he admitted, 'what's your friend's name?'

'Gilly Hutchinson.'

'Oh,' he said, without even meaning to.

'You know her?'

'Well I know of her,' he replied, 'I know her sister.'

'Which one?

'Gilly would have been a few years ahead of me,' Tommy replied.

'Right,' she replied, without allowing him to finish, 'so you'd know the youngest, Emmi Mae.'

'Yeah we were really good friends when we were…oh 13 ish and then she outgrew me.'

'Ah yes, it happens at 13 or even 13-ish.'

'Tell me about it,' he offered more to himself, 'so was that Gilly the blonde-haired girl with you yesterday?'

'No, Gilly was swotting, you saw the eldest sister, Adele, who's just great craic altogether.'

'Okay, figures, I don't know her at all,' he replied.

He looked at his green-eyed girl out of the corner of his eye. He couldn't see her as well as he'd seen her yesterday when they'd met face to face. She still looked stunning even though her long dark hair covered the side of her face. He couldn't see those amazing green eyes though. On the upside what he'd missed yesterday was her personal scents. She smelt of a blend of soap, shampoo, mixed with little hints of a heather based perfume. The combination was totally intoxicating. 'I'm Tommy,' he offered, extending his hand, and knowing it was an excuse to steal another glimpse of her stunning emerald eyes, 'Tom Barry.'

'I know,' she said, offering her own hand in return.

'You know?' he said, surprised while noticing two of her top teeth protruded a wee bit to the extent it looked like her top lip was going to have trouble covering them.

'Yes, Adele told me,' she said, as she smiled, 'she also said you weren't part of the *other* Portrush Barry family.'

'Yeah, sorry about that,' he said, still holding her soft skinned hand and shaking it gently, determined to never let it go again if he could get away with it. ''Fraid it also means I'll not be able to get you free rides on the dodgems.'

'I'd be more of a Barry's Big Dipper kind of girl, anyway.'

'Ditto on the Big Dipper, although I can't pull any strings there either,' he offered regretfully, while thinking he didn't see her as being a Big Dipper kind of girl. All that screaming seems so alien to one so reserved and private. 'I could get you a pony ride on the beach though if you wanted?'

'Accepted,' she replied, seeming content to leave her hand where it was, she leaned towards him, her nostrils wriggling the more they bridged the gap to his ear, 'but not being part of the amusements also means you won't smell of petrol and grease and candyfloss.'

'Or Daulse and Yellowman,' he added, attempting to complete her list and praying it was a compliment, 'oh look…' he continued and pointed with his free hand to the cuff of her red duffle coat, 'there's your missing glove, stuck up the sleeve of your coat.'

Sadly, for Tommy, this gave her an excuse to break away from him.

'I'm Isabella,' she said, retrieving her glove, 'Isabella Scott and the pleasure to meet you on this wintery weekend, is all mine. That's twice you saved me, Tommy, which means I'll never forget you.'

And that, was how Tommy Barry and Isabella Scott first met.

Neither Isabella, her two friends, Gilly Hutchinson and Jane Murray nor Tommy Barry's two friends, Lefty Kelly and Brendan 'Brendy' McCusker, would ever forget Tommy Barry. This fact was even more definite now that forty-three years later (bar three months) on Wednesday July 17th, 2019, the very same Tommy Barry died a very unnatural death.

Chapter Two

'Do you still have a property up at the Port?' Superintendent Niall Larkin asked McCusker, as he casually strolled into his office in the historic Customs House, a building designed by Sir Charles Lanyon in the Italianate Palazzo style and built in 1854 on the mud of the west bank of the River Lagan. McCusker made a point of checking his watch, not so much for his own benefit, as for his Super's. Larkin was casual with his permanent staff over timekeeping. McCusker however was an agency cop from the nearby Grafton Agency and Larkin was keen McCusker was not only on time clocking in and clocking out but was also *seen* to be on time clocking in and out, if only to avoid the naysayers such as DI Jarvis Cage, making an issue over the employment of agency staff. McCusker was ten minutes early as he always was. He would also ensure he was always well turned out. Today he was in a subtle blue linen suit with a crisp white shirt, no tie and clean shaven. There wasn't much he could do about his copper-coloured hair though, apart from the occasional finger-comb through. Initially McCusker needed the job, he really did, thanks in no small part to his wife doing an Amelia Earhart and disappearing to America with the proceeds from the sale of their retirement property portfolio. In fairness this wasn't the whole story. His ex-wife, Anna Stringer, had met someone else while in the USA and had returned to Belfast earlier in the year to tidy up her business with McCusker. He'd received a very tidy cheque (albeit belatedly) for his share. But no-one, particularly the Jarvis Cages of the PSNI Custom's House branch was aware of the windfall because they'd then have another gripe to target at one of the Yellow Packs. The Yellow Packs was a derisory nickname given to the agency cops by the permanent and less well paid (they claimed) staff by comparing them to the cheaper, inferior (they boasted) yellow-coloured boxes and jars of household products currently available in the supermarkets around Belfast's fair city. Actually, staff in the PSNI not knowing about his windfall was not exactly accurate. McCusker's girlfriend Grace O'Carroll knew for sure, as did her sister, Lily O'Carroll, who was also a detective inspector of the PSNI, and his partner.

'Funny you should mention this,' McCusker said, following his boss into his office one flight up. 'I've just been offered the house my wife and I lived in for nearly twenty years at a very good deal. The person who my wife sold our house to never actually moved in and now needs a quick sale, as her husband, who works for PetroChina, has been posted to SFO.'

'What did they do, stick a postage stamp on his forehead?' Larkin offered, as he busied himself about his desk. As ever he was in his trademark three-piece brown pin-striped suit, the jacket of which was on a coat-hanger dangling from his antique hat and umbrella stand.

McCusker felt tempted to develop the theme but then thought better of it. He didn't exactly give his boss the details of the deal and admit he'd been offered the house for less than half what his wife had received and (eventually) shared with him, which in effect meant, even with his 50% pay-off, he'd make a profit on the deal. On top of which all the original furniture was still in-situ. The steal of the century (as McCusker saw it) was just due less to the quality of the property and due more to a need for a cash buyer in a big hurry, than the down turn in the property market in Northern Ireland in general and Portrush in particular. Although all the property heads were talking up Portrush—or Portmagic as they were now referring to it—mainly due to the fact the 148th UK Open Golf Tournament was being hosted at The Royal Portrush during July 2019. Allegedly a lot of Government money had been pumped into giving the wee toon a big facelift.

'Anyway,' McCusker started back up again, wondering where this was going. 'I've been offered the house for a couple of weeks to try and persuade me to take it. The Chinese couple, who bought it, bought it sight unseen, thinking Portrush was in the south of Ireland and not the wee North or maybe not even aware there was such a thing as a border in the first place. Anyway, it now transpires they cannot, for tax reasons, own a property in the UK, and so the Estate Agents have been accordioning the deal to facilitate a quick sale—'

'All very interesting McCusker,' Larkin cut in, looking at his diary while checking his watch, 'but I have my barber coming in shortly so…am…'

'Of course, Sir,' McCusker replied, a little put off. 'The quick answer is yes, well maybe… More like maybe, why do you ask?'

'I just needed to check because your old Super, my good friend Ivan, who persuaded me to take you on in the first place, has requested you to work on a murder investigation for him and he's fighting budgets, as we all are, so we both needed to make sure there wouldn't be an accommodation issue. You see your benefactors, the Grafton Agency, feel just because this would technically be seen as overnight work, they'd have to charge 175% of your normal rate plus accommodation plus travel plus blah blah blah!'

'Okay I see,' McCusker offered, 'look this'll be totally fine, whatever I need to do for you and Super Valley…-well…just count me in.'

'Good,' Larkin said, shaking his head in a satisfied manner, 'Correct answer!' he announced, sounding like a headmaster McCusker once knew, 'this accommodation of yours,' he continued, trying unsuccessfully to make it sound like an after-thought, 'it's good for two, yes?'

'Well yes, two? Why?'

'Well you'll still be representing the Customs House and I need to ensure our reputation will be well taken care of, so I'm going to have to station you with DI Jarvis Cage.'

'You've got to be kidding. No way, just not possible. Sorry Sir I just couldn't.'

'I thought you might say something similar, so I came up with plan B,'

Larkin offered, looking at his watch again. 'So, it seems to me if I put you with Cage, you'll complain, or if I put you with O'Carroll, she'll complain. So, I'm going to leave it with you McCusker; if you can persuade O'Carroll to go to Portrush with you, I'll live with it. However, if she won't go then I'm afraid you and I won't have a choice in the matter, it'll have to be DI Jarvis Cage.'

'But she's off on leave at the end of today's shift, Sir,' McCusker protested.

'Is she really?' Larkin offered faux sympathy, while throwing up his hands and rolling his eyes in a "Well that's that then" gesture.

'Really?' McCusker protested.

'Really!' Larkin offered in a "I'm the leader" voice.

Mind you, McCusker thought, Paul Francis Gadd was the last person to make such a claim and look what happened to him. McCusker knew his solution needed to be an immediate one.

'Leave it with me,' McCusker sighed, 'let me speak to DI O'Carroll. When do we need to go?'

'I told Superintendent Valley you'd be there by lunch time.'

'Ah come on Sir, DI O'Carroll is going to need to pack. We're not talking about a chap chucking a few clothes in an overnight bag. DI O'Carroll is a woman, Sir.'

'Is she really?' Larkin said, kicking the ball dangerously close to McCusker's goal.

'Well yes she is actually,' McCusker replied, hoping he wasn't making his answer sound like it was a debatable point; a point O'Carroll would certainly never debate with him. More importantly, a point O'Carroll would never forgive him for. 'It's just never going to happen.'

'Look on the bright side, McCusker,' Larkin said, rising from behind his desk to show the interview was over.

'And what's this illustrious sunny side you talk of, Sir?' McCusker asked, the sun now very much missing from his morning.

'She'll have already packed her suitcases for her holidays, so she'll be able to leave immediately. Please give Superintendent Ivan Valley my very best wishes.'

Chapter Three

'Remind me again, McCusker,' DI Lily O'Carroll groaned as they drove, well as she drove. She was really a very bad passenger, and he was a very absent-minded driver. He was okay with the steering wheel and accelerator, but he kept forgetting what all the other bits and pieces of the controls were for. They were heading up the M1 towards the North Coast in general and Portrush in particular, '*How* did you manage to talk me into this?'

'I think what might have swung it for you, was when I told you Rory McIlroy was going to be up in the Port for the next week or so.'

'Ah that would be a big fat no on that one, McCusker,' she replied, noisily changing gears. She seemed to insist on grinding them, perhaps it was her way of ensuring the gears had truly changed. On the positive side, her engine was most likely going to outlast the clutch. 'What actually swung it for me was the fact you said there would be a lot of sun-bathing. Well added to the fact you promised not only was Rory going to be in Portrush, but you'd also introduce me.'

'Well, I think what I actually said was I used to play golf with a certain Gerald Mannering who had now become the Captain of the Golf Club, The Royal at Portrush, and Rory was going to be playing at the open and so I'd…'

'…introduce me to Rory.'

'What I actually promised,' McCusker insisted, 'was that I would introduce you to Captain Mannering and the good Captain might introduce you to Rory…'

'I don't remember the word "might" ever being used in the conversation,' O'Carroll replied, sounding like (McCusker hoped) she might be toying with him.

McCusker had planned to drop DI Lily O'Carroll off at his former house in Portrush, so she could settle in while he visited the PSNI station, meet up with Superintendent Valley and the rest of the team and catch up on the case.

O'Carroll felt it was just too cosy for her to stay and settle in; they were not here on holidays, but to help solve a suspicious death.

'You never know, McCusker, with your local knowledge—you know, who sells the best coffee—and my powers of deduction we might wrap this case before darkness and get back to Belfast before dawn without even having to unpack my holiday suitcases.'

She wouldn't hear of "settling in" at his house and insisted they persisted through the heavy traffic to the PSNI Station House.

They, eventually, arrived at 21 Lansdowne Crescent, the Ramore Head PSNI headquarters. It was pebble-dashed, with a run-down grey hue, in complete contrast to the neighbouring yellow painted house at the end of the crescent. McCusker explained it looked like nothing from the outside and Super Valley let it stay this way so the robbers will at least miss out on one house, the PSNI house, while on their nocturnal route. O'Carroll thought the PSNI sign would keep everyone away for sure. 'Hah,' McCusker chuckled, 'you don't know the firms around here then for sure.'

Around the corner from 21 Lansdowne Crescent was Tracey's Diner, one of McCusker's personal favs, he claimed. Both the station house and the diner overlooked the sea. Just across the sloping green was Lower Lansdowne Road. McCusker noticed O'Carroll seemed besotted by the views and so he walked her down towards the sea. Just off the seaside edge of the footpath, there were several park benches on a slab-stone viewing area. O'Carroll clocked the area, clearly guessing this was where PSNI officers came when they wanted to enjoy a bit of privacy.

O'Carroll looked around the roof tops, noting there was at least one seagull perched atop the chimney stack or on the peak of the slates of every roof visible from where they stood. Two obviously privileged apartment blocks enjoyed an entire row of seagulls on sentry duty.

'You boys made great time,' flush-faced, chubby-cheeked, bubbly Superintendent Ivan Valley said by way of greeting. He was wearing an immaculate dress uniform. McCusker assumed it was the one the Super usually wore at official functions. Valley checked his watch as he said those words and his facial expression seemed to suggest he was thinking better of his greeting and didn't really think it was all that great a time, after all.

'This is Detective Inspector *Lily* O'Carroll, my senior, Sir,' McCusker offered, feeling he really did need to emphasise the fact that Lily was not a boy.

Valley led them through to the incident room, a small, coffee-scented, incident room, but an incident room nonetheless, as proven by all the notice boards with notes and photos.

'So, you're the one we have to thank for taking the quare fella here off our hands,' the Super offered, as he shook O'Carroll's hand vigorously. McCusker noticed how his ex-boss was clocking his current partner. As usual she was impeccably turned out in her dark grey, shiny, trouser suit, vibrant blue, linen crew neck top and white and grey Nike trainers. Her fair hair was centrally parted and tucked behind her ears. She wore very subtle, but effective, make-up and a smile was never very far from her face.

Valley had given O'Carroll a gift of an opening to set up McCusker for a fall. McCusker prepared himself for the worst.

'Well I'm also here to thank you and to advise you, you won't be getting him back anytime soon,' O'Carroll started, surprising McCusker as much as his old Super. 'I've learned to stop looking over my shoulder because he's always one step ahead of me on our cases.'

'Augh, sure I was only kidding you,' Valley admitted, 'Brendy here didn't come up the Bann in a bubble. He knows me well. I told him all he needed to do was get out from behind his desk and back into cases again. Working live cases is what he excels at. As a pen pusher he was a brilliant window-cleaner.'

O'Carroll seemed totally thrown at the Super's turn of phrase.

McCusker's mid-moment of glory evaporated when his eyes spotted several photographs of the remains of the victim.

McCusker totally went into shock, so much so he had to sit down.

The victim, whose case he'd been brought back to Portrush to work on, was none other than his former, fellow teenage BLT gang member, Mr Thomas Barry.

Thomas Barry.

If anything was needed to focus McCusker out of his joy at being back in Portrush, it was these several images.

'I didn't know…' McCusker started, trying to come to terms with the body blow while appearing professional.

'Obviously Superintendent Larkin didn't give you any details on the case,' Superintendent Valley, offered gently,'

'There just…there just wasn't time,' McCusker apologised, 'I mean I hadn't been in touch with Thomas for quite a while.'

'I'll be okay, it's just such a shock. Okay, Sir,' McCusker started, shaking his head briefly in order to clear it. 'It's time for us to get stuck in. When can we meet the rest of the team for a catch-up?'

'McCusker for heaven's sake, catch yourself on man, the 148th UK Open Golf Tournament opened this morning at The Royal. It's the first time it's been here in sixty-eight years. Did you not notice the stationhouse is all but empty,' Valley guffawed. He reached over to one of the desks and picked up a phone and punched in a few numbers. 'The practice rounds started last Sunday. We've got a quarter of a million visitors in town. So, what I'm saying to you is most of our boys,' he paused and looked at O'Carroll, 'and girls, are on high level security details around town and up at The Royal. Put another way…' He paused to speak, in a less friendly tone, into the phone, 'Could you c'mon in please?' he said, and as he was setting the phone down, he continued to McCusker and O'Carroll, 'youse two *are* the team, well along with, D.S. Melodee Johnson. And here she is in person.'

'Hi, DI McCusker, I've heard so much about you.' Johnson offered, over a friendly energetic handshake.

'All of it true if she's talking about the examples I gave her, about what it is best to avoid in her police work,' Valley offered, 'and this is his colleague, DI Lila O'Carroll.'

'DI *Lily* O'Carroll,' McCusker offered in a polite correction.

'Sorry…sorry Lily, I won't get it wrong again,' Valley apologised, 'now I've got a quick meeting up at The Royal at 7.00 with Captain Mannering so I need to scoot. DS Johnson here will get you up to speed on the Thomas Barry case,' he concluded, as his pace belittled his weight on his exit.

DS Melodee Johnson was as good as her Super's word and led them straight over to the largest of the notice boards.

The Detective Sergeant was about five foot-ten, perfectly groomed white (rather than blonde) hair but with jet back-eyebrows. The contrast in hair colours switched on something in McCusker's memory banks. Her blue eyes made her look like she was permanently smiling, and her natural country girl complexion benefitted immensely from her light make-up. Her tight royal blue skirt showed off her hour-glass figure while the matching suit jacket was permanently opened, revealing a perfectly laundered gent's white shirt with button down collar. Even though she was originally from Belfast there was not the slightest hint of an Ulster accent in her voice. Her ID tag attached to a PSNI lanyard, confirmed her first name was spelt "Melodee" and not "Melody" as McCusker had originally thought.

'Mr Thomas Barry was discovered on the massive rocks, which enclosed the harbour in the early hours of this morning, Thursday 18th July at 05.50. He was found, at the foot of the Pilgrim's Steps, by a local man out walking his dog.'

McCusker only heard the words spoken but, to his eyes, O'Carroll seemed more preoccupied with the person who was delivering them.

'The man was called Mr Hugh Costello, a grumpy old man, who was more interested in trying to persuade me you could cure diabetics by drinking sea-water. His dog's name is Oliver.'

All this was lost on McCusker as he focused on the largest of the photos. The photos featured a male dressed in tan chinos, black and silver checkerboard, slip-on Converse trainers, no socks and a crimson Ralph Lauren polo shirt. The man had fashionably long, salt and pepper hair and a medium length bushy beard. He looked familiar to McCusker and of course the detective had guessed the victim was indeed his former friend, Thomas Barry. However, McCusker hadn't seen him for years and so he also acknowledged to himself, particularly with the new beard, if he had passed Thomas on the street or met up with him at a party, he knew he would have felt he looked similar to someone he once knew, rather than have recognised him outright. The former Portrush detective was overcome with a tidal wave of sadness by this realisation. He regretted losing touch and accepted at least half of the responsibility.

In the photograph Thomas Barry's left hand rested on the rocks on a higher level to his body. His right hand was by his side and his right leg had crossed over his left leg at the ankles.

McCusker started to ask a question but backtracked immediately, deciding it was best not to interrupt DS Johnson, until she'd completed her script.

'I checked with Mr Barry's office, Ramore Investments, this morning. They are located a 13a Ramore Avenue. I spoke with a Mrs Maude Hughes, Mr Barry's P.A. for several years, and she said the last time she saw Mr Barry was when he left the office at 16.30 on Wednesday afternoon. She didn't know where he was going in the evening, explaining she was not his personal secretary but his business secretary. Mr Barry did not have a personal secretary. There is one other employee at Ramore Investments, a Mr James Lamb. Mr Lamb is on official annual leave this week for the Open. He also took in the practice rounds at The Royal. Mrs Hughes gave me his home number. I expect you'll want to speak to him as soon as possible and I'll set it up for you. Mrs Hughes also advised me Mr Barry was healthy both mentally and physically.'

'Good, yes, let's set up an interview with Mr Lamb as soon as we can,' McCusker said, 'Anything else?'

'The original officer felt it was a suicide...'

'But?' McCusker prompted, feeling O'Carroll was too distracted to be paying attention.

'But Superintendent Valley knew the victim, thought he was in good health, solid mind, stable, owner of a very successful business and so, even though we were up to high doh at the station house, with all The Open carry-on, he thought we needed to investigate it more to ascertain if it really was a suicide, an accident or indeed, as he said he suspected, a murder.'

'So where are the remains now?'

'They are with Dr Aynesworth over at the University Hospital in Coleraine, shall I take you over there now?' DS Johnson asked.

'Maybe you could take *me* over there?' O'Carroll suggested. 'We need to cover as much ground as quickly as possible and McCusker knows his way around "The Port" and I don't.'

'Good idea,' McCusker agreed, 'I'll go and check in with Lefty Kelly…'

'Ah…another member of the BLT gang, the original Three Amigos,' O'Carroll cut in.

'From what I've heard maybe they were more like the Three Stooges,' Johnson added.

'Oh, I like you,' O'Carroll said, blossoming from her concerned stern face to a large smile, and following DS Johnson out of the incident room, 'I like you a lot.'

'…he'll give us an update on what Tommy's been up to for the last few years,' a completely ignored McCusker offered to their heels as O'Carroll literally skipped out after DS Melodee Johnson.

McCusker couldn't be sure, but he thought he heard O'Carroll say something along the lines of, 'I still don't get what it is my sister sees in him.'

Chapter Four

Lefty Kelly, just like Thomas Barry, had aged to the degree where McCusker at first mistook him for his father. McCusker wondered if he looked just as much older to Kelly. He certainly didn't feel it, but he worried this might be simply due to the fact he believed, in your mind's eye, your spirit never ages.

Unbelievably Lefty Kelly still lived in the same house. Yes, in the exact same house on Craig Vara, he had lived in when McCusker had originally known him in the early 1970s. The main difference was that Lefty now owned the house. Sadly Mr Tim Kelly, Lefty's father, and his mother, Geraldine, had long since passed. So long passed in fact, Lefty addressed their deaths as though they were one and the same without an ounce of regret. Nonetheless the end result was that Lefty—whose grandfather Tim, the original, had built the two-story, four bedroom house, with amazing uninterrupted views of the East Strand in the foreground and the Atlantic Ocean in the background—was now the sole owner and occupant of the house.

As McCusker knocked on the mostly glass fronted door he thought it was funny the once wingman of the BLT gang had turned out to be the only confirmed bachelor in the trio.

So acute was the angle between Lefty Kelly's neck and his chest, that he looked like he had been a drummer in a marching band. He looked like his mum had dressed him (a la Alan Bennett) in his blue, button-down-collar, shirt and blue tie; red sleeveless, V-neck, jumper; black cords; tan cord jacket and perfectly shined, light brown shoes. He was clean shaven and his shoulder length, white hair, was tidy and well combed. Really this had always been his preferred look from his teenage years. He still hadn't changed apart from substituting the jumpers to green and blue and, in the winter months, swapping his jumpers to the version with sleeves, and rotating his cords with pairs of green or blue or brown. He was so comfortable in his uniform he hadn't felt the need to heed the varying fashions of the passing decades.

'Sad about Mister Barry,' he said, as he offered McCusker a large, slightly shaky, red-purple hand. McCusker immediately remembered how Lefty always referred to men not in present company as Mister.

'Aye,' McCusker offered in exchange, finding no suitable additional words.

'Com'on in Brendy,' Lefty said, pulling McCusker by the hand he was still feebly shaking, into his narrow hallway and led him through to the lounge.

McCusker was surprised by how house proud a man Lefty Kelly had turned out to be. On second thoughts he felt "shocked" was a more apt word than surprised. He remembered the trio would just always hang out either in Thomas Barry's house in Antrim Gardens or McCusker's parent's house up on Blackrock Road with incredible panoramic views of the Port. Up there, on a clear day with still waters, he was always close enough to Barry's to hear the excitement of those screaming while on the big dipper. The stunning views from up on Blackrock Road, he had taken for granted when he was younger. However, when he married Anna Stringer he found himself finding more and more excuses to escape up to his parent's house, just to sit in their cosy lounge and greedily drink in the life inspiring views at times when he felt his life needed inspiring. He eventually came to realise his wife had skedaddled for two reasons. One, he had taken early retirement as part of the Good Friday agreement, and she feared she was about to become a golf widow. Two, and more importantly, she'd accepted, but never shared with him, the fact they were both withering away in a loveless marriage. He also realised if she hadn't left him, drastic though it was at the time, he would never have returned to his passion of detecting and consequently he most certainly would never ever have met Grace O'Carroll.

'A strange time for you?' Lefty continued when they'd settled into the comfy chairs in the masculine decorated and furnished room.

'How so?'

'Well of all the times, to come back to finalise buying back your house…'

'Oh, I see what you mean,' McCusker replied, joining the dots. The estate agents bush telegraph was obviously in full cry and he'd forgotten Lefty still dabbled a bit in buying and selling properties himself. 'No, I'm here on official PSNI business.'

'How so?'

'Well with Rory and Tiger in town for the Open, Super Valley and his team were already fully stretched and so…'

'So, they sent for Colonel McCusker and his Cavalry… I must say I much preferred you with the longer blonde hair, it was quite becoming,'

'Ach aye, but a bit of a devil to wash and dry,' McCusker started, falling into one of their routines and then pulled himself up short when he remembered the reason behind his visit.

'So it's Mister Barry you're here about?' Lefty offered. 'Sad affair, very sad affair.' 'When did you last see Tom?'

'The last time I saw Mister Barry was the spring of zero five.'

'No?'

'Well when was the last time *you* saw him?'

'Yes, but I didn't live a few streets away from him,' McCusker protested, sounding like he was trying to shore up his own defence a little bit too much.

'None the less you could have at least made it up for his wedding?'

'I did,' McCusker protested.

'I'm talking about his important marriage, the first one, not the one…the one responsible for destroying his life.'

'I was…I was…'

'You were away on a golfing holiday in Portugal,' Lefty Kelly stated, for the record but somehow managed to ensure it didn't sound accusatory.

'He didn't come to my wedding.'

'Miss Anna Stringer made it very clear to all of your mates, me included, we were not welcome and if in possession of this knowledge, we still chose to attend, we had to behave ourselves and not show her up in front of her family and friends.'

McCusker prepared himself for a stormy half hour or so of his former wingman moaning about his former wife. It started with a simple enough question.

'Tell me this Brendy, why did you always, but always, even when you were married refer to your wife, as Anna Stringer? She was your wife for heaven's sake.'

'Well, I did it automatically and never really thought anything about it until she left me and then I came to realise I'd never really thought of her as…' McCusker paused searching for a word.

'…as Mrs Anna McCusker?'

'Exactly Lefty, exactly, I couldn't have put it better myself, even if I tried,' McCusker smiled at the pure simplicity and accurateness of Lefty's suggestion. He prepared himself for the possibility he wasn't going to get off so lightly with the next question.

However he was totally shocked when Lefty Kelly diverted off from the expected mini-rant with, 'Look shall I make us some tea, nothing fancy, just a wee cup of tea in your hand and I do have a couple of Paris Buns fresh from Tom Tom's Bakery this morning. You don't like yours warmed up do you?'

'Yes, yes of course,' McCusker replied, his relief transparent, perhaps too transparent, particularly when he should have remembered Lefty Kelly didn't do strife well, and so he was never going to keep the pressure up for too long. 'And I do prefer my Paris Buns heated up but equally, if they are to be served cold, I quite like the process of the tea warming up the Paris Bun as I eat it.'

Lefty Kelly was only six years older than McCusker, yet, like all older men rising from a comfy low seat, he was a bit unsteady for the first few steps of their journey.

McCusker followed him out to the kitchen where the view through a fairly large (very clean) window, had drastically changed from the beauty of the beach and ocean to an uninviting concrete jungle window of Lefty's small back yard.

Lefty Kelly's neck was sufficiently bent to the perpendicular to ensure he could pay perfect attention to his tea making process.

Water boiled; tea pot heated; a spoon and a half of Barry's Gold Leaf tea leaves (no relation to either the deceased or the Amusement Arcade family and imported from across the border in Donegal) added to the warm pot; tea wetted with boiling-hot water in pot; tea allowed to settle in the pot for a few minutes; milk added to the white, translucent, bone, china cups; tea poured in same cups; sugar added; tea solution stirred and steam still rising from two delicious looking cups of perfectly prepared tea, which Lefty Kelly insisted McCusker carry while he took sole responsibility for transporting the treasured stash of three Paris buns through to the living room.

'I saw Mister Barry last in April 2005,' Lefty Kelley said, after they'd tasted their tea and tore into their Paris Buns. 'I'd had enough of him by then.'

McCusker kept quiet while considering the mathematical possibility of three Paris Buns and two people.

'Did you have a big falling out?' McCusker asked.

'What do you mean, a big enough falling out where I'd consider ending his life?'

'No, sorry, of course I didn't mean that Lefty.'

'Well you know Brendy, I'll say this, I watch a lot of these cop TV shows—both true crime and fiction—and I know you can't rule me out until you can definitely rule me out.'

'If you want to go down this route then you could have just offered those words to give the impression you couldn't possibly be the killer as you'd raised the subject by drawing attention to yourself first.'

'Yep I'll give you that,' Lefty Kelly replied as he rose from his chair and once again wobbled his way into the kitchen returning a few seconds later with a very large and shiny kitchen knife shaking precariously in his right hand.

'Jez Lefty, you're not meant to produce this weapon until the final scene when we've got rid of all the other suspects and we've narrowed it down to just yourself.'

'Sorry? What?' Lefty wheezed, looked at the sharp knife in his shaky hand, looked at his friend growing more and more anxious by the second, and then broke into an uncontrollable fit of the giggles. McCusker couldn't help but joining in and pretty soon there were tears running down both their faces. The tears were maybe not so much from the humour but from the unbearable sadness of losing the third member of their gang.

When they'd regained their composure, Lefty sat back down again and commenced the important business of neatly dividing up the third and final Paris bun. The sharp kitchen knife ensured the absolute minimum of wastage in crumbs.

'It's not by accident I didn't marry,' Lefty started up again after he'd refreshed their tea. 'Aye and it wasn't due to lack of offers Brendy. But let me tell you this. I'd one girl I dated, and she insisted on trying to sing along with Crosby Stills & Nash's, *Suite: Judy Blue Eyes.* I mean how could she attempt to hit those notes and not hear what I was hearing? Now don't get me wrong, I know I have a list of faults as long as my right arm and I really don't want to be responsible for inflicting them on a person for the duration of my lifetime. Equally I don't want to…no…"don't" is not strong enough…I *can't* bear to have a fourth harmony on *Suite: Judy Blue Eyes* inflicted on me on a daily basis. In her case the only alternate solution I could come up with was to stop listening to *Suite: Judy Blue Eyes.* Sorry, this performance is as close as were ever going to get to witnessing the sound of angels singing, so mothballing the record was never going to happen. I think it was with Miss Annie Hull. What am I talking about, of course it was Miss Hull. Yes, it was towards the end of my relationship with Miss Hull I decided I was just never going to get married. I decided I didn't want to spend my life trying to change someone and have that same someone trying to convert me to their version of who they wanted me to be. It seems to me the only constant in most people lives, is their need for change. I am not one of those people. I mean don't get me wrong, I continued to enjoy female relationships as in the sexual nature. Let me tell you Brendy I very quickly discovered that when sex is not being used as an enticement or a bargaining ploy, but purely for the pleasure a non-emotional physical relationship can only deliver, then you start to realise why we were put on earth. Equally I discovered I could have brilliant relationships with women if I wasn't after the other. It was around this time I started to have some amazing lady friends. So, all told I was fine with my decision to never marry and really enjoy my life. Then, after a while, I realised yes, of course, I had removed the anxiety factor from my life by reaching this agreement with myself. I soon discovered my decision had been in my own personal best interest. Don't get me wrong, I accept it's perfectly fine for me but not for everyone. Some people don't become the best version of themselves until they meet and marry their life mate.'

'I wouldn't disagree with your there, Lefty.'

'Then having successfully kicked into touch all my own romantic stress, didn't I only go and discover I was starting to inherit even more transferred strife from Mister Barry's life. I found his stress over his relationships was becoming a bit like passive smoking on me. I mean it got to the point where, unlike in my own disastrous relationships where I could just dump the problem partner, and move on, I couldn't just dump my friend's partner or wife. Next, I came to the realisation that if I couldn't dump my friend's partners then at least I could get rid of all the inverted stress by dumping my friend.'

'You mean Tom?'

'The very same Mister Barry.'

'And this was in 2005?'

'Aye.'

'So, you didn't really have a big fight?' McCusker asked.

'To be perfectly honest, when I told him I really didn't see the point in us being friends any more...'

'Wow.'

'He was so preoccupied with his romantic predations he didn't even notice. Neither did either of us put any energy into attempting to resurrect our friendship.'

'That's sad.'

'Well you were the same really.'

'And I'm truly sorry, Lefty, but after I met Anna Stringer…'

'When you and Anna Stringer split up, Mister Barry said to me, he said, "what the hell did Miss Stringer ever put in his drink to get the big man to marry her?" And I said to him, "well whatever it was it must have been very strong because it's only just worn off."'

'You know the fool I am, I'd still be married to her if she hadn't just up and left me and disappeared to America.'

'Yes…didn't she have a relation over there?' Lefty asked, seemingly happy to have speculation turning to fact, and direct from the horse's mouth as it were.

'Aye a sister, Gwendoline.'

'Gwendoline Stringer. I remember her. I pulled her once at the Arcadia in the summer of '75. I was only young, and she wanted to go the whole way before I'd a map of even the first steps of this mysterious and enticing journey,' Lefty Kelly the man, admitting what the boy never would have.

'So, what about Tom?' McCusker asked, after a few seconds break in the conversation allowed him to change gear.

'Well I can only tell you what I know.'

'But of course.'

'No, I mean I owe it to Mister Barry not to indulge in gossip,' offered the man who had put the L in BLT while leaving McCusker to imagine there must be a lot of gossip about on Thomas Barry.

'Okay sounds fair to me. Do you think you also might owe it to Tom to share any suspicions of your own about the case?'

'Well let me tell you this. I don't know anything about his business dealings of late, and we all know where that path can lead us, but you wouldn't have thought his other weaknesses could have been dangerous to his health. On reflection, I suppose it would depend on who the husbands of the ladies in question were?'

'So, Tom was having affairs? McCusker asked.

'Oh, c'mon, Brendy sure wasn't he always falling in love with everyone who walked around the corner and into his life?

'But then he got married?'

'Yes indeed, three times…and twice to the same woman!'

'I know,' McCusker started, 'but…'

'At least he'd the decency to keep it in the family.'

Just then the doorbell chimed.

'Look am…this is a wee bit awkward… I'm expecting someone. By any chance could we continue this later?'

McCusker knew the PSNI business trumped previous arrangements but he felt Lefty could be invaluable on the information front.

'Of course, I've a lot to do anyway and I need to pick up the keys to the house before the estate agent closes…'

'And no doubt knowing you, you'll be nipping over to The Royal,' Lefty said, leading McCusker out to the door. 'Come around in the morning and I'll treat you to brekkie, say 9.00 a.m.?'

At which point he opened his front door for McCusker to discover the rain had started to fall as only the rain in Portrush can fall after a cloud burst. He also discovered a stunning, beautiful, very tall, well-dressed woman, who was protecting herself under a pink umbrella and hopping from foot to foot very dainty like. When she smiled at McCusker, he thought she had the widest mouth he had ever witnessed; all the better to see her two rows of perfect molars by.

Lefty stepped out into the rain and placed his shaky red purple hand in the small of her back and gently guided her towards his hallway.

'C'mon in, Barbara, this is a friend of mine, Brendan, Brendan, this is Barbara.'

A few hellos were grunted but before he knew it, the door had closed, and Lefty Kelly and his mysterious friend Barbara had disappeared and McCusker was left standing in the rain with both his hands the same length.

Chapter Five

Meanwhile O'Carroll and Johnson were pulling up in the public-to-pay-for carpark at University Hospital, in nearby Coleraine. So nearby in fact was the university town that one of Portrush's precious heirlooms—a 5.5 metre grandfather clock—now resided in the office building of the Coleraine Coast and Glen Borough Council. This was one of McCusker's hobbyhorses. He passionately felt it was about time the giant clock, which was designed and built by Sharman D. Neill of Belfast for the original Portrush railway station opening in 1893, was returned to the people of Portrush and displayed in either the Causeway Street Library, the wonderfully refurbished Town Hall or even the new ultra- modern railway station itself?

By the time the two PSNI officers had negotiated the complex disinfectant stroke insulin scented corridors to Dr Aynesworth's cubicle he had already conducted his preliminary examination of the cadaver, which was once a healthy Thomas Barry.

'Well,' Aynesworth, who was extremely chubby and minus all facial (and head) hair but wearing a very expensive looking pair of bi-focal, blue, thick framed, glasses, which contrasted loudly with his green bursting-at-the-seams, scrubs, started, 'You know I've always thought living your life is a wee bit like playing a game of cricket or baseball. You concentrate intensely on not getting caught, or bowled, out. The biggest concern you experience,' he paused to nod at the remains of Thomas Barry, 'is the duration of your innings is not always within your control.'

'Interesting,' O'Carroll said, in a tone implying she didn't really mean it but wanted him to get on with some details. 'So, what can you tell us about our victim?'

'Well I can tell you he didn't meet his maker due to a Portrush Kiss,' the doctor replied, looking very pleased with himself.

'A Portrush Kiss?' O'Carroll asked.

'Yes, back in the day,' DS Johnson started, rolling her eyes behind Aynesworth's back, 'before the railway brought the tourism industry to this neck of the woods, employment was thin on the ground but every autumn, boats from Donegal would stop off at various points on the north coast picking up men, and ferrying them over to Donegal for the pratie gatherin'. Portrush was the last stop before they headed off to Donegal and so by the time the boats reached here, they would be jam packed. This meant the men would have to fight for a place on board. Understandably enough, the men would prefer to head to the Harbour Bar instead. So, the wives used to have to accompany their men down to the harbour and would often have to beat their husbands about their heads to ensure they fought their way onto the boat. This method of giving someone a good hiding became known as the Portrush Kiss.'

'As far as I can see our victim is not really a victim,' Aynesworth continued, looking totally annoyed his bubble had been burst before he'd a chance to show it off.

'Sorry?' DI Lily O'Carroll gasped, now most likely preoccupied by her broken holiday, 'you mean…'

'I can't say for sure until I've had a chance to open him up, but I'd bet either of you a dinner tonight our friend here died of natural causes. I will admit he was cheated out of at least 10 years, or put another way, caught out between stumps or bases.'

'Really?' DS Johnson asked.

'Well on my first quick examination I didn't discover any visible wounds, trauma, bruises, ahmm…Portrush Kisses, nor even any injection marks visible to the naked eye.'

In his reply all he did was shake his head to the negative.

'What about drowning?' DS Johnson continued.

'Yes, well I agree his clothes were very wet, however I understand he was found on the rocks by the Pilgrims Steps and not actually in the water, so in a seaside town don't you think drowning would have to be considered a natural cause if not a self-induced one?'

'Well I'm just surprised,' O'Carroll admitted, wondering if she could be back to Belfast in the morning in time to catch a later flight. 'I thought it had already been ascertained the circumstances were at the very least suspicious, hence the reason why McCusker and myself were conscripted up here.'

'McCusker, did I hear you say?' Aynesworth asked, his smile disappearing from his face as gracelessly as a baby elephant on an ice rink. The disturbing thing was how sinister a being, he'd just transformed into. 'Not the retired D.I. Brendan McCusker? Surely the PSNI aren't so desperate for recruits they've let him enlist again?'

'Yes, it's the same McCusker,' O'Carroll replied, 'he's no longer a DI but attached to the Custom's House, Belfast, branch of the PSNI as a freelance officer by way of the Grafton Agency.'

Aynesworth looked like he was trying to head an imaginary football, a football he was having great difficulty in locating. He pulled these shapes for a few seconds as he considered O'Carroll from head to toe before he continued with, 'well I only agreed to a quick examination because Superintendent Ivan Valley called in a favour. He thought Thomas Barry's death was suspicious, but I don't buy into that.'

Johnston, appearing as stunned as O'Carroll, was looking to say something but she was cut off by the pathologist continuing, 'but look science is not about speculation, it's about meticulous examination, so let's delay further conversation until then, okay? Now how about dinner? My offer is still on the table, come on, either one of you.'

'I think we're done here,' O'Carroll offered, rising from her seat, 'when do you feel you'll have concluded your autopsy of Mr Barry's remains?'

'I'll get to it as soon as I can,' Aynesworth replied, dramatically closing the file and slapping it down on what looked like the "parked" stack. 'So, who's it to be for dinner then?'

'Sorry, Doctor, we only come as a pair, and I'd bet we'd be too much for you,' O'Carroll said sweetly, as she and Johnson departed the office. As they entered the hospital corridor she continued, just loud enough for Aynesworth to hear, 'besides which I would never date anyone I couldn't lift and throw out of bed.'

Chapter Six

McCusker felt that even though the sun was shining, and the sky was blue, rain wasn't too far away. He never knew how he knew, maybe just the years of pounding the beat in Portrush had made the instinct part of his fibre, but it had never let him down.

He figured Superintendent Valley and his crew were all still busy (enjoying themselves) over at The Royal Golf Club, so he resisted his returning to the PSNI nick at 21 Lansdowne Crescent and popped up to The Estate Agents who'd been on Main Street for as long as McCusker could remember. The Estate Agents was the name of the company as well as their job description.

The agent responsible for McCusker's former home introduced herself as Sandie Pebbles and just when McCusker was guessing she'd a made up name, she handed him her business card which bore the legend: "Mrs Sandie Pebbles—I specialise in homes…not houses."

McCusker's idea had been to just pop in and collect the keys to the house. Really, he didn't need to view the property, and he knew he'd be a fool if he didn't take up the offer to buy it back. The bossy estate agent was pissed and didn't mind giving McCusker chapter and verse of why she was pissed. Mrs Pebbles reckoned if the sellers had been a bit more patient she could have got them the asking price of £240k the very same figure she'd already achieved when she brokered the deal to sell the house on behalf of McCusker's soon to be ex-wife, Anna Stringer, who oversaw their property investments. It was one thing to have the property on the market for a steal "must sell to a cash buyer in a hurry deal" of £160 K. Yes, that was one thing. The other even bigger thing was the new owners would not permit the agent to rent the property to an American golfing family for £50,000 for the week of the UK Open at Royal, and their refusal was, in her view, was nothing short of criminal.

'In fact, if you were still a member of the PSNI, I would have you arrest them,' she offered, rather pleased with herself.

What the agent couldn't accept was the fact the new owner, who wanted to become the old owner as quickly as humanly possible to ensure he avoided tax complications, didn't want to risk having the house trashed by a US golfing family and thereby scuppering the potential deal with the new owner (McCusker) who in fact was an even older, old owner. The agent also admitted she had pleaded with the current owner to allow her to approach McCusker direct and offer to share with him the £50,000 the week would have earned. The seller refused. He'd made the offer to McCusker not even aware there was a golf tournament taking place, let alone aware the UK Open was a historic, town-changing event. The current owner just didn't want to have anything to do with it at all. He figured McCusker, having been the original owner of the house would have been happy to reclaim his house which he had lost in a well gossiped dubious deal conducted by his future ex-wife.

McCusker imagined the estate agent had given the new owner chapter and verse of the sorry proceedings.

McCusker offered by way of condolence, 'perhaps the seller, as someone capable of mistaking Ulster for Ireland, also mistook golf for football?'

He knew the estate agent was way off in her valuation of the property. It was certainly worth the £240,000 when Anna Stringer sold it, but the current market price would have been much closer to £204,000 and maybe even as low as the late £19OK. The seller wouldn't have been aware of this, but the deal was even sweeter than she had thought for McCusker because, in the end, he'd already received 50% of the £240,000 his wife had received for it. So, what with half the income from the sale of their other rental properties, he was quids in. In fact, so quids in he still stood in the property market with enough money left in the kitty to buy a home with Grace O'Carroll in Belfast. They'd agreed she was going to sell her flat and they'd pool their money to buy a home together. To still be able to retain, for next to nothing, the house he loved in Portrush, made him feel happier than he'd ever dreamed he could be. Particularly when just over twelve months previously his wife had disappeared to the USA; she'd absconded with 100% of the proceeds of all their properties. Her recent change of heart had only occurred when she'd met someone else stateside. They wanted to get married, she needed a divorce and the by-product of her new romance was McCusker becoming a richer man.

None of which was enough to stop the estate agent spitting blood. 'I missed the biggest bonanza since the Coloma, California, Gold Rush of 1948,' she claimed.

As she stood talking to McCusker, continuously jingle-jangling the keys without physically passing them over to McCusker, she continued, 'you think I'm joking but I'm not. One American family of golf fanatics found a Portrush house they loved, and they kept on badgering the owners until the owners eventually agreed to rent it to them for a week. Guess how much they got for the week?

McCusker took a wild guess at £50,000.

'Try £120,000 and just for one fecking week.'

McCusker found it disconcerting to discover a well-dressed, blue-rinsed, mid-aged-plus, mumsy type, who went by the name of Sandie Pebbles, was swearing like a sailor on the high street of Portrush. It seemed as alien to him as hearing his mum swearing, which he never had.

On top of which it had started to rain.

Encouraged by the swearing, he did a very ungentlemanly thing by attempting to snatch the keys out of the estate agent's hand.

She flipped them into her other hand at the very last moment.

He tried another tact.

'Of course, I will need to talk to you about the Strandmore property when we are ready to rent it out.'

'Really...of course we'd love to help,' she replied, melting to all sweet and light.

'Well I'm happy to commit to you that when we're ready to rent you'll be the first person we'll speak to?'

The keys and an offer of a cup of coffee were his. If it hadn't been for her swearing McCusker would have felt guilty for not admitting he'd never ever rent out his house.

Chapter Seven

Instead of using his keys McCusker felt an instant need to visit the first Mrs Barry.

Apart from the obvious professional reasons, he felt he owed it to at least pass on his condolences to Thomas Barry's ex-wife. If he needed to persuade himself more, and he didn't, he could also mitigate his concern as it was now lashing down *and* DI O'Carroll and DS Melodee Johnson still hadn't returned from their meeting with pathologist Dr Aynesworth.

Mrs Thomas Barry was formally Miss Isabella Scott, aka The Green-Eyed Girl, aka the Hi Love, You Just Dropped Your Glove, girl. She had also divorced her second husband, Ryan Shannon, who was a former star of the Irish showband scene and whose real name was Lenny McGuire. To avoid all of the above confusions and complications, Isabella had reverted to using the name Miss Isabella Scott again. This was the name on the apartment bell McCusker buzzed on the recently converted former grand Northern Bank building, which was located on the usually hyper busy corner of Main Street and Church Pass.

A disjointed female voice answered the intercom immediately, buzzed McCusker into the building and instructed him to come up to no less than the penthouse.

The apartment which took up the entire top floor, aka the penthouse, was set in the eaves of the old listed refurbished bank. McCusker was just beginning to surmise the building conversion had been accomplished to the highest possible grade when the door opened and, try as though he did, he couldn't find a way to operate his vocal cords and offer a single word.

He found himself speechless at the vision before him. He blinked his eyes furiously in disbelief and shook his head as through trying desperately to refocus because he couldn't possibly be seeing who his brain told him he was seeing.

Then, in a split second, he blinked again and thought he sussed it, he'd suspended the image from what he thought it couldn't be, or more correctly from who he thought it couldn't be, and eventually his brain managed to activate his vocal cords again.

'I've come to see your mother.'

'Ah shit McCusker, spare me one of your crap BLT chat up lines, they didn't work then and they certainly don't work now,' the woman said as she wrapped her strong arms around him and pulled him into a warm and tender hug, 'come in you daft apeth.'

Isabella Scott, to McCusker's eyes looked like she hadn't aged a day since the night Thomas Barry had met her on the streets of Portrush all those years and three marriages ago.

Yes her jet black hair was much shorter and had started to show hints of greying, which she wasn't bothering to try and hide, and yes if you looked very closely there were a few age-lines around her eyes, but she was as slim and as wiry as ever and still looked like the tall ball of energy who had truly thunder-bolted one of McCusker's main teenage friends.

Isabella was dressed in figure hugging black yoga pants with a very expensive looking cream blouse, which if you looked at closely, as McCusker would have to admit to himself, he did, you could make out the outline of her white bra and the contours of her perfectly shaped breasts.

McCusker immediately felt a powerful charge through her hug. It wasn't sexual in nature, more, merely, a barometer of her sensual energy level. Her grip had been so strong she'd expelled the air from his lungs.

She disengaged, let him go and then immediately hooked her arm into his, closing the door with the heel of her foot as she pulled him into her million-dollar apartment. The accommodation and furniture most certainly looked to McCusker to be in the million-dollar range. It was stunning and then, as if that wasn't enough, didn't she only have a view of both the Mill Strand to the west and the Curran Strand to the east from either end of her lounge.

As McCusker's eyes flicked backwards and forwards a hundred and eighty degrees from east to west he remembered the tale of a Sir Thomas Phillips, an English Knight and soldier of fortune who took out a 21-year lease on the townlands of Port-Rush in 1595. Sir Thomas wanted to create a waterway from where the Arcadia now sits on the east strand through to Barry's Amusement Arcade on the west strand. His idea was to make Portrush an easier to defend island where he suggested they could garrison 6000 of King James the First's troops. McCusker figured if Rory McIlroy won the Open, he'd probably be granted the same townlands and if he managed to carry out Phillips' plans he could declare Portrush independent, as seems to be the modern thing, and the world class golfer could become the uncontested King of the small island of Portrush.

'There's even better views from up on the Widow's Landing…' she started, in her sing-song Ulster voice but seemed to have tripped up and her eyes started to well up, as she was mouthing the word "Widow."

She slapped herself abruptly on the face a few times. She used the forefinger of each hand to arc under her eyelashes, either to protect her perfect make-up or to prevent the tears from spilling.

'But that's for another day, when the weather is better,' she said. McCusker wasn't sure if she meant the views or grieving over her husband.

He let the quietness grow between them as a mark of respect for the faithful departed.

She ended the silence by exhaling loudly and pensively. 'We've a lot to talk about Brendy, shall I make us some coff…sorry you're a tea man, aren't you? I'll make us some tea.'

'Just the job, Isabella, just the job,' McCusker replied, as he remembered Isabella's two central top teeth protruded a little, not exactly as in buck teeth but more where he worried every time she exposed them, she might not be able to cover them up again with her top lip.

'Let's go through to the kitchen, you can sit with me as I prepare and then we can come back in here. I suppose you've heard Rory is having a disastrous start over at The Royal?'

'No?' McCusker started and then felt very awkward because he found himself pitying Rory at a time he should have been considering the demise of his former friend and her former husband.

Then McCusker remembered in Ulster, from an early age you are taught, when you attend a wake, to always start off talking about something safe, something neutral like the weather, the house, the farm, the country, the county, the car, Daniel O'Donnell, the tractor, politics (carefully), sport, music or any combination from several of the above. Next, you've be offered tea, sandwiches and buns (all on the same plate) and you'd have to accept. Next, you would let the relatives of the deceased, when they were ready, lead the conversation around to the reason for the visit. They would usually start with something like, "He woke up yesterday morning and he was his usual self. My wife, (husband, father, brother, sister, mother) never had a problem getting up early. (S)he was a great worker." And you'd chip in with, "Oh aye, none better." And then they would pick up again with something like, "But as (s)he put on their coat I noticed the hand go to the arm as if they'd caught a stitch…" or maybe they'd offer an edited version of "Their heart just stopped." After the relative had described the demise in detail you'd offer, "They'd a great innings," or, "Sure they were robbed, they were in their prime with their whole life ahead of them."

The Ulster wakes are a great, supportive, necessary tradition. The familiarity of continued talking about their loss and the details of the departure is vital for the dependents. The talking through of the process is as important for the host as it is for the visitor. The talk is repeated so often the grieving unconsciously start to process the magnitude of the loss by reducing it, bit by bit, to acceptable and bearable levels of grief.

Miss Isabella Scott had an alternate approach to dealing with her grief.

'Tom's biggest problem was that he thought life should be full of those "Hi love, you've just dropped your glove" moments,' she started, as she directed McCusker to a low backed, high stool, in her ultra-modern black and metallic kitchen.

The problem for McCusker was with all the cupboard doors being opened and closed, kettle lids being removed, water running, kettle lids being replaced, wetting teapot, placing cups, saucers, plates (he was happy with the plates because they meant there was going to be something more than tea) on a tray, he was having to strain to hear her talk. It became a bit like moving from beautiful, perfectly formed handwriting to a doctor's scribble, mid-line and the stop start approach meant he wasn't allowed to get comfortable with either.

'But he was okay, wasn't he? Youse were okay for the times you were together, weren't you?' McCusker said, because he felt he should.

'Brendy, you're a romantic and spare me the romantics of the world. Romantics deal in fantasy. Fantasy doesn't put food on the table. I think your big problem is you didn't know the man Tom became; you really only knew the lad you hung out with in the BLT days.'

'Well, Isabella, they say you can see in the boy of seven what the man will become.'

'If you really can then I should have run a mile in the opposite direction the night he picked up my glove. I could have saved the both of us so much grief, not to mention shame. I could have saved both our families so much stress.'

'Augh, Isabella, the poor man's dead…'

'Aye, he is,' she admitted, sounding somewhat regretful. McCusker couldn't be sure what she said next, because she said it close to a whisper, but her words sounded like, 'perhaps we've drawn the line now.'

Tea prepared and plates packed with freshly baked fruit scones, they made their way back into the lounge. He had smelt the scones the second she'd opened the door but his initial sight of her had been so powerful it had removed the scone smells from his memory banks.

'How's Anna doing?' she asked as they sat down.

McCusker thought she was trying to lead the conversation away from where she felt he wanted it to go. Was she just punishing him for being a romantic and now she had successfully done so, had she decided to rub his nose in it by raising the subject of his own failed marriage?

'Oh, you know, we split up.'

'Of course, I know,' she started, and then stared directly into his eyes as though she was in the process of making a decision. 'I mean, we all could see you'd never last. The only mystery really was how or why you managed to stay together for so long?'

'You know all I can tell you is, I thought that's the way it worked. I thought marriage was what I had. I don't think my wife was ever young. I mean, I accept the mistake was entirely mine. I do remember when I told people I was going to marry Anna, the general reaction was: "Why, is she pregnant?"'

'You never did have any kids, did youse?'

'No,' McCusker admitted without regret.

'The worst favour I ever did for Tom was to stop resisting his sexual advances. Once we eventually did the wild thing, he seemed to be very disappointed in discovering me to be a willing and participating partner. I swear to you, everything changed from that moment onwards. Yes, yes, I know we got married, but I figured Tom was just doing the gentlemanly thing. But afterwards I came to realise the more he was pushing me to consent to his amorous' advances, the more he wanted me to reject them.'

'So, you think it would have been better if you'd consummated your physical or carnal relationship after you were married?'

Her lips were forming the first word of her reply to his question when she stopped. She looked like she was considering the question for the first time in her life.

'Nagh, I don't think so,' she sighed, 'I believe Tom wanted me to remain a virgin forever. I think I ruined it for him when I let him ride me for the first time. From then on, I always had the impression I was damaged goods. I know that sounds a little weird. But he was always pestering me to playact like it was our first time.'

Her honesty shocked McCusker into silence. Encouraged by him appearing not to be obliged to talk her down, contradict her, or subtly try to change the subject, she continued with:

'Look, Brendy, I enjoy sex—that's what I want. I don't want to know about a man's mum, his childhood. I don't want to know about his socks, his yellow teeth. I don't want to pity and I don't want to be pitied. I find the sixth, seventh, or eighth times are never ever anywhere near as good as the second time. Fact is for me the second time is always the best. Let's not mess with the facts. Let's just stop there and call it quits. I have my friends for all my other needs. Both male and female friends, so what do I need anyone else for? Feck companionship in your later life, there's just much too high a price to pay for all the compromising involved if you choose such a route. Kids? Feck kids they are much too selfish for my liking. Look, here's the big thing. Say we manage to get seventy years on this earth, it's not really a lot of time, you know. Before you know it, you are fifty years old and you have to accept, you're on your last lap. I certainly don't want to be sharing body fluids with anyone when I pass sixty and especially not with someone who is also over sixty themselves. Oh, Jeez, please spare me from those images. I certainly don't what to be embarrassing myself by showing off my pathetic bag of skin and bones to a younger man. Oh no, no, no. I don't want to be in bed with someone if I feel I need to hide my body. Nor any of the old, "over a bit, no, up a bit, out a bit, in a lot. You're too quick, you're too slow, you…you're too Sting."'

'Sorry? Too Sting?' McCusker felt obliged to ask through their laughter.

'Code for, you're taking too fecking long,' she offered, when she had regained her composure.

'Look, you don't have sex from you're born until you're about twenty,' she continued, before McCusker had a chance to say anything. 'Yes, there's a bit of fumbling about in your later teenage years, but let's, for the sake of our discussion say, we become sexually active at twenty. So, I believe we should accept the years from twenty, to say, fifty-four are our vintage years'

'But you don't seriously—'

'Look, here's the thing, you'd never take four desserts with a meal. Okay, okay, some clearly do, but you shouldn't. So why not just agree with yourself sex is for those precious thirty-four years, plan accordingly and move on?

'I'm not being rude. I just don't want to direct, neither do I want to be directed. I just want things like sex to happen naturally and I don't want to risk it not being great every single time.

'I don't want to be taken advantage of, and I don't want to take advantage of someone, anyone.

'I want to be frisky. I want to know a man is attracted to me. I never take his open attraction as an insult to my gender. It's flattering and with the right bloke it can be a complete turn on. Equally I will admit to feeling like a million dollars when I see the effect my look has on men.

'I'm not saving it up for later.'

She paused for the first time in minutes. McCusker felt she was an ex-wife dealing with her pain in the best way she knew how. She was prioritising the living, herself, over the dead, her ex-husband.

'Were you still in contact with Tom?'

'I couldn't stand the sight of him,' she blurted out.

'Augh, c'mon, Isabella.'

'Look, Brendy, if you're working on this… Are you working on this? Do you know yet what exactly happened to him?'

'We don't know what happened to him…'

'Your use of the word "we" confirms you are working on this case. Please continue.'

'Look…am…'

'Brendy, don't feel you need to spare me. Believe you me, I'm a big girl now and I can deal with this, I have to deal with this.'

'What I was about to say is Tom's body is currently with the pathologist and we'll have a better idea what happened to him when the autopsy has been concluded.'

'Okay, fine,' she said, a little relief evident, 'I can deal with that, what I can't deal with is all the town gossips nattering away. One says he committed suicide; another said he drowned; another claimed Tom was drunk and fell over the wall and bashed his head on the Pilgrim's Steps; yet another stated he was mugged and thrown over the wall; while a few others claim it was a drugs deal gone wrong…'

'Did he do drugs?' McCusker asked, trying to get her off the trail while thinking O'Carroll and Johnson were probably back in the Port with the autopsy results.

'Not that I'm aware of, Brendy. He was scared of them, to be honest.

He even hated taking medication when he needed to. He wasn't really a drinker Brendy, maybe a little wine with dinner. He didn't mind a pint, a single pint, of Guinness every now and then, but mostly, his poison, as he used to say, was Bushmills. Equally he'd only take a drop of his whiskey, and on very rare occasions.'

'What was his health like, you mentioned him not taking medication?'

'Really apart from his annual winter flu he was quite healthy. He was convinced one year the flu was going to kill him, yet…' she paused again, '…well he was too vain for his own good. On the positive side, he looked after himself, ate well, kept fit. He used to run with me but then gave up jogging, said he could burn the same fat while stationary in a gym and save his strenuous activity for other endeavours. So, what I was about the say was he was health conscious, very much so, yet, at the same time, he didn't want people thinking he needed to take a flu jab.'

'So, when was the last time you saw him?'

'Well, first let me ask you this, Brendy, when was the last time *you* saw him?'

'Must be a few years ago…' McCusker offered and when she was showing no signs of contentment at his answer he continued. 'When my wife left me, I needed to find a job again and eventually I found one down in Belfast, working for the PSNI but not as a member. Anyway, I was settling up, dumping stuff I didn't need for the flit down to the city and I needed to sell my car. The first person I thought of was Tom, on the grounds he knew everyone here in town and seemed, if the bush telegraph was anything to go by, to be part of every deal going down. I gave him a shout, we met up in the Harbour Bar for a Guinness, he made a few calls, fixed me up with a buyer in a garage just outside of Portstewart. Tom pretty much agreed the deal for me on the phone. I took the car over the next morning, I was paid most of the money in cash, but the garage owner owed me a grand, which I picked up when I was back in town a few months later, settling up my affairs.'

'Sure you never had an affair in your life, Brendy,' she said, through a smile. A smile McCusker feared was a smile of pity. 'How much did he take off the top?'

'Not a penny,' McCusker confessed, 'I mean I offered him a luck penny, he'd got me top dollar, but he wouldn't hear a word about it.'

'Eighteen months ago,' Isabella said more to herself, 'yeah, he wouldn't have needed a luck penny then, we were back together again, our tears had stopped flowing and we were living happily ever after.'

'Yeah, he told me. He knew all about my woes with Anna Stringer and he said I was much better off without her. At the same time, he confessed he just couldn't live without you and was sad because it had taken him so long to figure it all out. He said he never dreamed you would get back together again. But he seemed happy.'

'Yeah,' she sighed, 'I'm always playing my best hands too quickly, first off, he had me at "Hi love, you just dropped your glove," then I made the fatal mistake of sleeping with him, and the second time with Tom, my third marriage, I said yes too quickly. I should have learnt my lesson and just kept him chasing after the carrot on a string—slowing down every now and then to allow him an occasional taste. On reflection, I should have kept him chasing for a few years; maybe even forever might have been better. Once he thought the carrot was his, then, just like Bugs Bunny, he was off again, chasing a new carrot.'

She appeared to be living in this cartoon imagery for a few seconds before she continued with, 'Well, truth be told, the new carrot was also on a string and this one being yanked by his other ex-wife, aka my sister Colette, aka the wee shite.' Isabella paused, seeming to regret what she'd just said. McCusker couldn't be sure though if it was genuine regret or if she hadn't wanted him to see how much she hated her sister. Eventually Isabella continued, 'How was Tom with you, how did he seem?'

'He acted like I always expected an older brother might, you know, not so outwardly friendly, while, at the same time, being protective,' McCusker replied.

'You're an only child, Brendy, aren't you?'

'Yes indeed,' McCusker confirmed, 'when was the last time you saw him?'

'The last time he broke my heart…again.'

'And this would have been?'

'Three weeks ago,' she admitted, 'listen, can I make you some dinner? I've got something ready to put in the oven, it'll be enough for two.'

McCusker checked his watch. It was coming up to 5.30 pm, 'oh Isabella, would you look at the time? Look I need to run now and meet my colleague, we're meant to meet up with the Super at 18.00. Can I take a rain check?'

They both knew their interview, chat, catch-up, call it what you will was far from over.

'No need to be polite,' she offered, appearing a little bit taken back at his refusal.

'No…really…I'd love to…I'm famished,' he admitted. 'I really have to meet Superintendent Valley at 18.00.'

'Okay, I'll cut you some slack on this occasion, but only on one condition?'

McCusker's imagination started to run wild, but still, he nodded to the positive.

'I'll agree if you promise you will personally accompany me to visit Tom's remains when they're ready for presentation.'

McCusker didn't really understand the complexities of the request but saw no harm in agreeing.

'Thanks, Bendy, I really do need to be there and pay my respects and if I'm seen not to go, all the town chatter-boxes jaws will be jigging like fiddler's elbows.'

McCusker promised he would accompany her to the wake.

As she walked him back to her apartment door, she broke into a gentle smile and then started to laugh.

'What?' McCusker felt obliged to ask.

'You, you daft apeth, when you knocked on my door with your, "Can I speak to your mum, please?" line. Jez, Brendy, once a member of the BLT gang, always a member. Get outta here.'

Chapter Eight

DS Melodee Johnston and DI Lily O'Carroll were waiting, as agreed, for McCusker on the steps of the entrance of the temporary pavilion hall, to The Royal Golf Club, Portrush.

The first thing to hit McCusker right smack between the eyes as he walked past the massive merchandising shop, up towards the first tee to the right and the 18th green towards the left, was how everyone seemed to be walking around in a zombie-like state. McCusker risked Valley's wrath by stopping at the giant scoreboard on the right. Rory McIlroy had quadruple boogied the 1st hole and from there onwards it had all been downhill. McCusker had most definitely felt from the vibe of the crowd how bad a day Rory had, no-one knew a way to hide their disappointment.

When they'd made their VIP way through the official clubhouse, Valley and his team were comfortably ensconced in a private corner with their own table and a non-stop supply of tea, coffee, mineral water, sandwiches and very dainty pastry. Even the usual happy-go-lucky Superintendent Ivan Valley looked like he was having trouble getting wind in his sail.

DS Johnson told them how they had gotten on with Dr Aynesworth.

'Oh, don't worry about him,' Valley replied, 'Bartholomew's first response on cases is natural causes, his second is suicide. Remember the wee man who was found beaten to death during the North West 200 and Dr Bartholomew Nevercide claimed the poor crater's injuries were self-inflicted?'

'Aye,' Johnson replied, for it was she who found the body, 'his logic seems to be, the absence of foul play equals the absence of paperwork.'

'He won't be happy to see McCusker back on his patch then,' Valley suggested with new found gusto, 'even if there is nothing to this, the trouble we'll go to will be well worth it because he knows McCusker won't let him get away with anything.'

McCusker was still distracted, so much so in fact, Valley turned to him and quietly said, 'Don't worry man, you know Rory, he'll go out tomorrow morning and shoot a round to put Tiger and everyone else in the shade.'

'Aye, if anyone is capable of it,' McCusker agreed, 'it'll be Rory, my only worry is that he is now 13 shots behind the leader, which means he's going to have to go out and shoot about 7 holes-in-one to get back in contention.'

Valley seemed to ignore the negative part of McCusker's positive response, and he continued, 'How did you get on this afternoon?'

McCusker explained his progress or lack of it.

'So, you've breakfast in with Lefty and lunch with Isabella,' Valley offered, 'sure that's stickin' out big fella. At the very worst my catering budget for you and the DI is safe as houses. Work away the both of youse.'

'Where's Rory now?' O'Carroll said as she sidled up to the other side of McCusker.

'I imagine he'll be doing his PR duties somewhere,' McCusker replied.

'What, you mean here in the plush clubhouse?'

'I doubt it, most likely in one of the TV trucks.'

'Oh.'

'Don't worry, the Super knows Rory's dad, I'll mention it at the appropriate time. He and I also know the Club Captain very well.'

O'Carroll made no bones about her intentions; she walked straight over to the Superintendent and said, 'What are you having?'

'I'll have a kit,' the Super replied, somewhat distracted.

'A kit?'

'Yeah, a kit; a half of lager and a short.'

When she returned with half a kit in each hand for Valley and fresh air for McCusker, the Superintendent announced to the table, 'Look I have a feeling about this Thomas Barry death. No matter what Dr Nevercide says, DS Johnson here spoke to Thomas's doctor this morning at the time he was called to confirm the death at The Pilgrims Steps. Thomas's doctor also advised the D.S, Thomas was in good health. He had regular check-ups, took care of himself and the doctor was in complete shock over his death.'

'How well did you know Thomas, Sir?' McCusker asked.

'I knew of him more than I knew him. I would bump into him at various functions. He seemed to be a mover and shaker on the charity scene.'

'Did he have political ambitions?' O'Carroll asked.

'I used to think he did, and I asked a few friends in those circles and one of them thought because Thomas was a wheeler-dealer, plus there was something about the VAT man chasing him back quite a while, he was content to keep his nose below the parapet.'

'Also, he'd have avoided public office because he'd wanted to avoid any attention being drawn to the fact he married his wife's sister. Any idea who he was in business with?' McCusker asked.

'He still had his own company, Ramore Investments, I believe it does very well,' Johnson offered.

'He was also quite heavily involved in buying and selling properties and land,' Valley added,

'Did he have any partners in Ramore Investments or the property investment side?' McCusker pushed.

'A question you'll need to ask his accountants, DS Johnson is already on them,' Valley replied, but the word around town is Thomas did very well over the last couple of years, thanks to the facelift the wee town received due to the hysteria, not to mention government grants, caused by the anticipation of the Open.'

Valley sighed loudly, waving his hand expansively around the interior of the clubhouse, before adding, 'My only worry is now The Open is here and this time Sunday night we'll be as far away from it as we ever were, so what will we do for an encore?'

'Declare independence would be my best recommendation to you,' McCusker offered, as he rose from his seat.

'Where are you off to now?' Valley asked.

'We'll go and visit the scene where the body was found,' he said. nodding at O'Carroll. 'Maybe visit the Harbour Bar and see who we might bump into. Do you know where Colette Scott lives?' he asked DS Johnson, 'and Ryan Shannon? We need to speak to them both as soon as possible.'

'I think I can find a recent address for Ryan for you,' the detective sergeant offered. 'I don't know a Colette Scott, though?'

'He means Colette Barry, she kept her married name when they divorced,' the Super offered. 'Right, I'm off to see the Captain again so we can do our rounds together. See youse tomorrow, I'll be here all day, based here. The Captain is expecting a riot if Rory doesn't make the cut, so all hands on deck. DS Johnson will be with you all day.'

Chapter Nine

'Jez McCusker,' O'Carroll gushed, as they crossed over the walkway and avoided the exiting traffic, 'so this mate of yours, Thomas Barry, married his childhood sweetheart, Isabella Scott, then he cheated on her with her sister Colette, then Isabella dumped him, married a singer in a pop group and then Thomas and Colette marry as well. But it doesn't end there as it would have done if it was a movie, but no, not in Portrush. Thomas also then only goes and cheats on Colette and so Colette dumps him. Am I getting this right?'

'Pretty much, yep, just one big mistake?'

'Oh really, I thought I'd been paying attention.'

'Yeah, the bit about Isabella marrying the singer in a pop group after she and Thomas were divorced?'

'Yeah?' O'Carroll prompted.

'You were wrong there. Ryan Shannon was not the singer in a pop group.'

'No? Are you sure?'

'Yes, one hundred percent sure, Ryan wasn't a singer in a pop group. He was the singer in a showband.'

'A showband?' O'Carroll asked.

'Yes, he was the singer in one of the legendary Irish showbands,' McCusker responded.

'And what's the difference between a pop group and a showband?'

'Are you sure you want to ask that particular question?'

'I'm sure, but I've a feeling I'm going to regret it.'

* * *

As the rain had just broken, McCusker then proceeded to take O'Carroll and Johnson on a walking trip around Portrush while he gave an audio commentary on the history of the legendary Irish showbands.

However when he took O'Carroll and Johnson down past the Arcadia Ballroom—well more accurately what remained of the Arcadia Ballroom, namely the entrance hall which now served as a café downstairs and a space upstairs for both yoga and as an exhibition centre for paintings and photographs – O'Carroll froze in her tracks, speechless and pointed in awe out over the beach and towards the rolling waves.

'She's from Belfast, you'll have to forgive her,' McCusker announced, addressing Johnson, 'I don't think she's ever been out of the city before, she's never seen the seaside.'

'No, you fool, I'm talking about the rainbow,' she gushed, her eyes glued to the vision before them on the East Strand, 'you've been going on, and on, about the ginormous rainbows in Portrush for over a year. I didn't even know what the word ginormous meant. Even when you explained to me the rainbows in Portrush were so big, words like gigantic and enormous couldn't accurately describe them, so you had to put both the words together to do the rainbows credit. To be honest, that confused me even more, but now I'm here, I get you, I really do. I never imagined they'd be this spectacular, this vivid, this real. It's like for the first time in my life I realise rainbows are not an illusion, they are really there. I feel as if I could walk through the bottom of it, just over there in the sand-hills.'

O'Carroll looked and sounded as though she was drinking the rainbow.

Then right before their very eyes, and if conscious of all this attention, didn't the first rainbow only start to show off by calling out its equally beautiful smaller sister. Staged against the contrast of the approaching threatening dark clouds closing out the pure blue sky and sunshine, the overall effect was more Hollywood than anything McCusker had ever seen Hollywood produce.

All three seemed happy to just stand on the beach and be part of the picture rather than observe it.

Eventually McCusker, not aware if they'd been standing there for seconds or minutes said, 'Right let's dander over to the Pilgrim's Steps before we're hit with another downpour. I fear with the drop in temperatures of the sun starting to go down, it'll probably rain all night.'

So off they headed in the direction of the Arcadia again. As they passed the Arcadia, McCusker said, 'You know the Stranglers and The Undertones played there on the same night, 8th September 1978.'

'If you remember the date it must have been a great show,' Johnson offered.

'Well, the music from both bands was definitely amazing but I remember the night mainly because, Fergal Sharkey, the original lead singer of The Undertones, was very annoyed when his new Parka-jacket was absolutely drenched from the peak of his hood to the bottom of the back vent and all places in between.'

'Was the roof leaking or something?' Johnson asked.

'Not at all,' McCusker happily recalled, 'this new craze had just come over from England. They called it gobbing and it was directed, quite literally, at all punk acts.'

'Gobbing?' O'Carroll asked, slowly coming out of her post rainbow bliss.

'You know, where the audience would spit at the musicians on stage,' McCusker continued.

'Spitting?' Johnson repeated in disbelief.

'Disgusting, sharing all those germs, do you mind if we talk about something else?' O'Carroll said, her rainbow moment now very clearly over.

'I find it interesting,' Johnson said as O'Carroll shot her daggers.

'So, just so I make sure I've got all of this straight,' O'Carroll started, innocently, appearing to totally ignore the Portrush PSNI detective sergeant, 'what exactly happened to the Irish showbands, after the Clipper Carlton threw away their music stands?'

McCusker was thinking the Arcadia building, perched on the rocks on the water's edge, looked like a weird gigantic slab of unsymmetrical ice cream topped with grey vermicelli.

Somewhere in the distance, church bells rang out six o'clock.

Six o'clock in Portrush and the streets felt like post doomsday. It felt like a ghost town or a town after the gold-diggers left due to the gold seams running dry. McCusker wouldn't have been in the slightest bit surprised if the only thing they met rolling down the once busy streets was tumbleweed. Either they were in a ghost town or everyone had rushed indoors to their homes; caravans; campervans; mobile homes; bed and breakfast establishments; guesthouses or hotels, to put the kids to bed and catch up on their mobile activity. The mood around the empty streets seemed more devastating than any post gold-rush blues.

Six o'clock is a very definite demarcating time of the day in a seaside town.

It's the borderline time when families retreat to their accommodation with their road-weary kids, who were, one and all, overdosed on: Barry's; ice-cream; candyfloss; chips; sand and sea; donkey-rides; Cantrell & Cochrane Pineappleaide; more ice-cream; sweets and more sweets. The problem with all this intake of sugar was it made the kids super-hyper but, no matter how much they wanted to keep going, they no longer had the legs for it.

"There, there, turn out the lights, surrender to your sleep and we'll do it all again tomorrow," the parents would gently offer in hope and self-interest.

Then with a babysitter, or one of the older children in charge, the parents would venture out around eight o'clock-ish for a meal as they sought out their own action. Yes, maybe even their own late-night hit of Barry's.

Chapter Ten

The Pilgrims Steps are in the shadows of the Mermaid Wine Bar, which is facing up Main Street. It is either the beginning, or the end of Main Street. McCusker figured it was most likely the end of Main Street if only because the pilgrims would travel down it, in the 1830s to descend the Pilgrims Steps and board the small boats, which would ferry them out to the ships waiting in the deeper waters of the Skerries, to set sail for America, the land of the free and the home of a brave and somewhere you could lose your hair, if not your entire head, if you happened upon the wrong prairie.

At first, O'Carroll couldn't figure out where the actual steps were. McCusker kept pointing to them.

'Just remember you're not looking for a carpeted staircase with a polished wooden banister,' McCusker cautioned them both.

'I've lived here for a few years now,' DS Melodee Johnson admitted, 'and I've never seen them before.'

'Oh, are those the steps?' O'Carroll shouted, 'Down there about fifteen feet. They're just one, two, three, four large stones coming out from the harbour wall at right angles and descending from the harbour end, towards the town. Just four measly steps, McCusker? I thought you said they were legendary?'

Multiple enjoined strands of seaweed appeared to be a living creature trying to rise up and out of the lapping harbour water and creep over the soaked stones towards the historic Pilgrim's Steps.

'So how did our victim get here?' Johnson asked. 'It's too far to climb down safely?'

All their eyes scoured the nearby harbour walls looking for an easier way down.

'Maybe he was dropped over the edge?' McCusker offered.

'Not possible,' Johnson replied immediately, 'Dr Aynesworth reported no marks at all about the body.'

'Maybe he was dead when he was placed here?' O'Carroll chipped in.

'He'd still have abrasions or bruises of some sort even if that was what happened,' McCusker offered, as he started looking at all the small boats peppered about the harbour.

'Do you think one of these wee boats were used to ferry him over here?' O'Carroll asked, clocking McCusker's eye movement.

'Even if he was lowered down from here,' Johnson stated, as she examined the two-foot six inch stone wall, which separated the road (and them) from a twenty-foot drop into the harbour, for recent marks, 'there would be tell-tale rope burns under his oxters.'

'And even someone as blinkered as Aynesworth would have spotted those,' McCusker offered. 'Let's see if we can find someone to take us down there and approach the steps from waterside.'

Johnson knew the Harbour Master, Melvil Edwards, a friend of hers was dating his son, and he was happy to take them over in a wee rowing boat.

'Sorry auld do about Thomas Barry, wasn't it?' Edwards offered. As befitting his occupation, he was weather-beaten with a newish looking dark blue corduroy trousers and a thick black crew neck jumper. His strawberry coloured hair was nicely unkempt and hat free.

'Aye, it was,' McCusker replied. 'Did you know him?'

'Augh, aye sure didn't he drink over yonder,' Edwards replied, in a hoarse voice and nodding in the direction of the Harbour Bar. 'Sure, I know you as well, knew your dad better.'

'How well did you know Thomas?' McCusker continued as they neared their destination.

'Now I knew him well enough,' Edwards replied, 'but as the man said, not well enough to know his secrets. He'd always give you the time of day, wasn't loud with his money but would discreetly set you up with a pint and wink at you. I know he had troubles, sure everyone knew he had troubles, but fewer knew what was fretting him. Wasn't there some problem between him and the Scott girl? I hear they broke each other's heart. Couldn't live with each other and couldn't live without each other. None of my business mind you, but as the man said, if they'd only had a couple of kids the family life would have soon taught them how to live with each other. As I say, none of my business you understand, just saying. Well, here we are...'

Melvil Edwards gently nudged the boat towards the rocks. From down on this level McCusker thought the rocks looked like a mini visage of what was depicted on Led Zeppelin's *Houses of the Holy* album sleeve. The band had chosen hand-tinted photographs of one of the local Wonders of the World, at The Giant's Causeway. The Giant's Causeway consisted of about 40,000 interlocking basalt hexagonal columns formed either by the giant, Finn Mc Cool's acidic teardrops for a lost love, falling on the rocks and crystallising them, or by the lava from an earthquake. The rocks were not as symmetrical by the Pilgrim's Steps but generally a tight, miniature, hexagonal grid, similar to The Giant's Causeway. The top surface was flat and smooth as though this grid had been fused together.

'Careful there, the surface will be very slippery,' Melvil cautioned them. 'High tide is not due for another hour or so, but the stones will already be drenched, what with the rain and all.'

The Harbour Master kept the boat pressed against the rocks by gently continuing to stroke the water with the oars, while, one by one, O'Carroll, Johnson and, finally, McCusker gingerly stepped off the wobbling boat onto the rocks.

McCusker searched in vain for recent marks on the rocks. He realised any evidence would have been well washed away in the intervening fourteen hours. But more than anything he wanted to try and get a sense of how, whatever might have happened, had in fact happened. If he could figure this out, then hopefully the rest would follow. Johnson and O'Carroll both seemed to feel the need to touch each and every one of the four Pilgrim's

Steps.

McCusker was impressed by Melvil Edwards' respecting their work by remaining silent. The only sounds were the lapping of the water on the rocks and the infrequent squawking of seagulls.

McCusker and co searched around the bottom of the steps for ages unable to come up with anything worth consideration.

They, even more precariously, re-boarded the boat, and Melvil used one of the oars to push them off the rocks.

'Have you any idea what happened to Thomas?' Melvil asked, after they'd returned to dry land and were making their way towards the safety of the Harbour Bar.

'Not so far,' McCusker admitted, 'you'll have a pint?' he offered the Harbour Master. McCusker ordered drinks for the four of them and stayed to pay for them as O'Carroll, Johnson, and Melvil Edwards went to find a cosy corner.

The bistro was busy, and McCusker guessed most of the buzz was about Rory's sad start.

When McCusker joined them at the table, O'Carroll was scouring the menu with her, "I could eat a horse" look written all over her face.

'I don't think Arkle is on the menu tonight,' McCusker whispered to O'Carroll

'I didn't think I had said that out loud,' she replied equally discreetly.

'You didn't but I still heard you.' McCusker said.

'Be careful when you're ordering in here,' Melvil cautioned, as he sipped his Guinness, 'the portions are massive, plan on one order being more than sufficient for two people.'

'Should we order some food?' McCusker asked the table in general and O'Carroll in particular.

'I'm off to have my dinner with my family in half an hour, so I'll need to protect my appetite, but youse could do worse than ordering a Harbour Fish Pie between you,' the Harbour Master suggested.

Johnson shied off as well, so McCusker and O'Carroll took Melvil's tip and ordered a Harbour Fish Pie between them. McCusker waited until

Edwards was down to the final third of his pint. Chatting about this, that and the other and about McCusker's long departed father.

'If I wanted to get a body to the bottom of the Pilgrim's Steps how would I get it down there?' McCusker asked, eventually reaching the question he'd been longing to ask.

'Aye, as the man said, you'd need two men and a wee boy for something as heavy as a dead body,' Melvil replied.

He took another generous sip of his Guinness before continuing, 'but seriously though, I've been pondering on solutions to your puzzle, when I was sitting in my wee boat in the harbour waiting for you. And the best I can come up with would be two men tumbling him over the wall? It would be difficult but not impossible with one man.'

'Could he have just washed up there?' McCusker offered, as an off the wall guess.

'Nagh, with the tides he'd have been taken out to sea, he would have ended up out at The Skerries, maybe never discovered,' Melvil guessed.

'Could he had been brought into the harbour in a wee boat like the one you took us over to the Pilgrims Steps in?' McCusker asked.

'Again, it would boil down to manpower. You would need someone to steady the boat while another two lifted Thomas in and out of the boat. As you witnessed with our manoeuvres it would be a very shaky operation with no guarantee of success. Anyway, look at the time, I need to be off.'

'I might need to pick your brains a bit more. Is it okay if I come and see you tomorrow?' McCusker asked.

'You'd be very welcome. I'm on duty from 08.00 to 20.00 tomorrow. I'll always be around the harbour and never far from the Harbour Master's Office, the wee whitewashed building a few doors down from here and just before the viewing platform.' Melvil Edwards said, as he scribbled a number down on a page out of a notebook and passed it on to McCusker.

After he'd gone and as they finished up their delicious Harbour Fish Pie, O'Carroll offered, 'I can't believe it here. You already have a girlfriend and you're only in town a few hours and men are positively throwing pieces of paper with their telephone numbers, at you. No one has even asked me my name yet, let alone requested—discreetly or otherwise—my digits.'

'There's a lough full of men in here,' McCusker offered as he looked around the Harbour Bar Bristo, while draining his pint, 'don't let me cramp your style, don't forget you got your own room and I'll only charge you by the bed and not by the bodies.'

'Aye, but look at the place, would you, thanks to Rory, it's more like a wake than a party. Come on, I'll walk you home and you can tell me why the mere mention of your name sent the Dr Aynesworth into a fit of the heebee geebees.'

Chapter Eleven

As O'Carroll and McCusker walked back down Kerr Street towards the town, they kept stopping to look out to sea. Just as they passed the Lifeboat House cum cosy and informative museum, he declared: 'You know I had a weird dream last night.'

'Not about my sister, I hope.'

'No,' McCusker chastised, 'I actually dreamt I'd died and gone to heaven.'

'I knew your Blue Peter Badge would come in handy one day,' she said.

'Funny you should mention Peter,' McCusker laughed, as they passed the steps bridging Kerr Street up to Causeway View, 'because I actually got to meet him at the gate.'

'Okay, I'm biting McCusker, what did St. Peter say to you?'

'Actually, he was a really decent bloke,' McCusker claimed. 'He's very sociable by the way. St. Peter asked me where I'd travelled from today. He asked me who I fancied to win the Open. He claimed to me to be a big golfing fan, but I'm not so sure he is really.'

'And why?' O'Carroll asked.

'You know, playing golf up in there in the clouds, well those golf balls may be small but they're heavy wee buggers, aren't they, so they're going to sink through the clouds, aren't they? Stands to reason, doesn't it? So, I'm imagining there's not a lot of golf played up in heaven. But Peter, he did tell me to drop the Saint bit, you know, from the front of his name, he feels it leaves the modern-day youth market cold. He does have a lot of time for Rory, though. Anyway, at the end of our conversation, he asked me what I thought about heaven. Apparently, business is dropping off for them and they're trying to find ways of making it more attractive again.

'And what did you say?' O'Carroll asked, giving a faultless performance of Ernie Wise.'

'Well, I have to tell you I looked around for a bit and eventually I said, "Yeah…it's okay…but…it's not Portrush, is it?"'

O'Carroll tried unsuccessfully to stifle a laugh.

'No, no, McCusker,' she declared, 'I'm not laughing at your joke, I'm laughing in pity as to what my sister has to put up with. Tell me this will you, what does Grace do when you come out with things like that?'

'She laughs her socks off,' he replied immediately.

'Oh, is that all?' O'Carroll said.

'Well, at least it's a start.'

They walked on in silence for a few minutes until they passed the big temporary Ferris wheel. Then she started to giggle, which in turn set off the giggles in McCusker.

'OMG I just realised what you meant there,' she gushed, with tears streaming down her cheeks, 'can I just remind you we're talking about my sister, so you're in danger of sharing just too much information McCusker.'

They laughed for a minute or so, like two carefree kids up at the Port for their annual holiday.

'Heaven is okay, but it's not Portrush, is it?' she conceded a few minutes later, 'now that is one of your better lines.'

They collected O'Carroll's car, which they had parked near the railway station end of Kerr Street. They drove across to Causeway Street and passed Craig Vara, Lefty Kelly's street on the first left and then pulled up further on the left in a house at the mid terrace.

McCusker carried his overnight bag and O'Carroll's two (full suitcases) into what appeared to be a very nondescript, dirty-pebble-dashed, house. From the outside, the Edwardian house was very forgettable. When he opened the dirty yellow front door, the hallway appeared dark and dingy.

It was coming up to 22.00, so the reality was, everywhere looked a bit dark.

McCusker showed her straight up to her room, hoping O'Carroll would be impressed with the en-suite bathroom and power-shower. He stifled a yawn before retiring to his room, announcing he was going to call Grace before he turned in for the day.

McCusker and Grace O'Carroll chatted on the phone for about half an hour. She broke the brilliant news about her plan to come up to the Port on Saturday morning and stay through until Sunday evening. She didn't quiz him about the case. Very early in their relationship, Grace had explained she never asked her sister about any of the cases she was working on, but equally, she was always very happy to discuss them when Lily wanted to. Grace proposed she and McCusker worked under the same agreement. He spun her his meeting St Peter at heaven's gate joke, this time greatly embellished of course, and he could hear her laughing her socks off, which in turn set him off into another fit of laughter. Grace O'Carroll had a very sensual laugh, which always got to McCusker. When he explained the laughing her socks bit to Grace, she absolutely screeched with laughter down the line, then teased him with, 'Well they're lying on the floor now.'

They said their goodnights and a few seconds later, he heard Lily O'Carroll's mobile phone ring in the next room. Grace was ringing her sister, he assumed, and they chatted on for another twenty minutes. Every now and then, McCusker could hear similar screeching of laughter, only this time not from his girlfriend but from his partner.

Chapter Twelve

Friday 19th July

Early the next morning McCusker woke up in the middle of a dream. He dreamt he was hearing DI Lily O'Carroll screeching somewhere away in the distance. Eventually as he finally woke, he came to realise the screeching wasn't part of a dream. No, it was real, and it was happening somewhere in his house. He threw on his trousers and a t-shirt, although he'd never really fully worked out how one threw on a pair of trousers, but for some reason or other, unknown to himself, or any other human he knew, he accepted this was exactly what he'd just done. He rushed to her room, her door was open, but her bed was empty. His brain then translated her noise was coming from downstairs. She was directly under him in the living room. He scarpered down the stairs four at a time, rushed into the living room only to find his partner, not in agony or in any kind of trouble but totally blissed out.

She was staring at the view of the Atlantic Ocean in sheer disbelief.

Although they've entered technically through the front door of his house in Causeway Street, the house had been biased towards the back, which had become the front, located on Strandmore and enjoying uninterrupted spectacular views of the East Strand and the Atlantic Ocean.

'McCusker, I don't understand how you couldn't have been happily married in this beautiful house with these life defining views?'

'Sadly, I was never around enough to enjoy them.'

'Well at least you didn't say, "My wife didn't understand me,"' O'Carroll continued, in her rarely used, compassionate voice, she went on without taking her eyes away from the sea, the sky and the sand, appearing concerned should she look away even for but a second, the life-enriching scenes might disappear, 'But surely you must have been in love with her at one point or other?'

'I love Grace; she continuously takes my breath away. When I'm not with her I can't wait to see her again. I feel my life force depends on her love. I think she is the most beautiful person I have ever seen. I thought her looks would wear off the longer I knew her. If anything, I think she's even more beautiful today than she was when I first spotted her in McHugh's. I accept this is because I have now grown to know she is also a wonderful human being. I never felt anything remotely similar for my wife, Anna Stringer,' he admitted, sadly.

'You forgot a bit there about my sister, didn't you?'

'Sorry,' McCusker replied as if waking quickly, too quickly perhaps, from a dream. 'I forgot something?'

'You forgot to mention were you ever to let my Grace down, I'll have your guts for garters and wear them proudly as I stroll down Royal Avenue.'

McCusker did his utmost to repel the scenes fast-forwarding through his mind's eye.

'So, what did you feel for your wife?' O'Carroll asked.

McCusker laughed.

'What, sorry, did I miss something?' O'Carroll asked.

'No, just there, as you asked the question, I realised for the first time in my life, the overriding feeling I had of my wife was one of fear.'

'You feared her?' O'Carroll spat in pure disbelief.

'Well, I feared her the same way you fear schoolteachers when you first go to school.'

'McCusker, if you think you're going to get my sister to dress up in a school uniform for you, you've got another thing coming.'

'Well, I suppose it all depends what the—'

'Shut it, McCusker! Now!' she ordered. 'It's my sister we're talking about.

When I arrived here last night, I was convinced this place was a dive and I started to wonder what you'd being going on and on about. But now…well, on the inside, everything is finished off perfectly. It's a beautiful wee house, McCusker.'

'I take no credit for it; Anna Stringer did it all by herself.'

'At least you didn't take some credit by saying, "but I paid for it."'

'I can't even claim I paid for it. She paid for it out of our rental funds.'

'All I can say is the woman has the eye.'

'Well, she did pick…'

'She must have had the good eye closed when she met you,' O'Carroll interrupted, cutting him off at the pass.

'Yes, as I was about to say, before I was so rudely interrupted, "Well, she did pick…the curtains."'

Shortly thereafter, DS Melodee Johnson arrived as arranged the previous evening to pick up DI Lily O'Carroll. She advised McCusker & O'Carroll on Ryan Shannon's address and telephone number, ditto for Colette Scott, nee Barry. Valley had instructed her to also pass on details of Thomas Barry's accountant, Donnie McCartney, and Barry's builders for his property projects, The Buckley Brothers, Sean and Seamus.

O'Carroll, Johnson and McCusker arranged for O'Carroll and Johnson to head off to interview Ryan Shannon and agreed they would all, minus the showband singer, of course, meet up at the PSNI station on Lansdowne Crescent at 10.30. At this meeting, they would compare notes and organise the rest of their day. In the meantime, McCusker had a breakfast date with Lefty Kelly, the former wing man of the BLT gang.

Chapter Thirteen

McCusker stopped off at Tom Tom's Bakery, which was on the corner of their (his and Lefty's) adjoining streets, Craig Vara, which ran behind, the 55 Degrees North Restaurant, and Causeway Street which appeared very suburban and unloved on the front and with O'Carroll's life-affirming views on the back. She felt Causeway Street should be renamed Schizoid Street. McCusker bought a generous supply of Paris Buns, pancakes, wheaten farls and fadge before he went knocking on Lefty's door. Lefty wore the same uniform as yesterday with slight colour variations, namely his white shirt, red tie, dark blue trousers, and green V-necked, sleeveless pullover. His one main noticeable change from yesterday: he'd swapped his tan cord jacket for a very light blue full-size apron.

'Goodness, Barbara, is a bit of a looker, isn't she?' McCusker started, by way of a greeting. He was immediately distracted when his nostril-radar-system homed in on the smells coming from the kitchen in general and the rasher wagon in particular, 'she must be every inch of six foot?' he added without continuing his original intended thread.

Lefty basked in this glory for a good few seconds before saying, 'she's six foot and half an inch, and she claims to be a direct descendant of Mary Murphy.'

'Not the Portrush-born, seven-foot, giantess who toured the European music halls in the early 1700s?'

'The very same,' Lefty boasted, as if he was now, by association, part of the celebrated family. 'Mary was very honest though about her stature. Her official height was seven foot two inches and *her* measurement were taken when she was in her stocking feet and *without* a hat!'

'Now seven foot two is tall, Lefty,' McCusker said in awe.

'The first time I saw Barbara, though, I thought she was alternate, not really for me. The second time I saw her I realised it was only her dress sense which was alternate. The rest of her wasn't alternate at all. She was just traditional.'

'Tell me this, Lefty, do you know a man by the name of Donnie McCartney?'

'A giant?'

'No, an accountant.'

'Connected to Mister Barry?' Lefty continued as he piled an Ulster Fry— bacon, sausages, fried eggs, fried bread, fadge and baked beans—on to two separate plates and poured two Sgt Peppers' mugs full of tea which he milked and sugared up without even asking McCusker.

'Yes, apparently he worked with Tom.'

'So, he'll know all the secrets, then?'

'Remains to be seen,' McCusker replied between bites, 'top breakfast, Lefty, just what I needed. I was absolutely famished.'

'Any suspicions so far?'

'Well, we don't know much yet, but it is early days,' McCusker replied, trying his best to put a positive spin on a negative situation.

'I'd bet you find some jealous husband behind all the mystery,' Lefty offered.

'Would there have been a lot of jealous husbands?'

'Well, you remember Mister Barry; he fell in love with every girl he ever met on a day of the week, which finished off with the letter "Y".'

'Tell me, Lefty, did you ever date Isabella?'

'I couldn't possibly say,' Lefty replied, when McCusker felt the correct answer should have been, "No! Most definitely not!"

If McCusker included Annie Hull, Barbara Murphy and the first Mrs Barry, then Lefty was clearly more successful in his later years than he'd been in his teenage years, in fact, three times more successful.

'Come on, Lefty?' McCusker prompted.

'Have you talked to Isabella yet?'

'Ye-as,' McCusker replied immediately, deliberately stretching it into two syllables and trying desperately hard to pull off a knowing look.

'Look, Brendy, the only two rules I have about dating married women are: 1) Don't ever date married women, and rule 2) If you date a married woman never ever talk to anyone about it. The reason for my golden rule number two is: with no corroborating evidence from a third party, a strong enough doubt can be cast with, "It's my word against her word." If the husband was asking the question, he's probably already well on the way to believing his wife is unfaithful. If he is already of such an opinion, then there is also a good chance he's not going to believe you over her.'

'Yeah, sounds logical to me. I remember you'd all this female stuff really well figured out, the only problem I can think of is you never ever dated a girl during the BLT days.' McCusker said, because this was exactly what he'd been thinking.

'Oh, Brendy, what you fail to grasp is,' Lefty offered, 'sadly, we can never control who we are attracted to. Neither can we control the feelings of those who may be attracted to us.'

'What attracts a woman to a man or a man to a woman?' McCusker asked.

'Could it be as simple as availability?'

'Do we not need to have to create a stronger bond?' McCusker asked, thinking we did.

'We're programmed to be attracted to the package.'

'So, Lefty, you're saying we're powerless to resist the control of attraction?'

'Well, I'd like to hope not.'

'It can't just be looks, though, can it?' McCusker suggested.

'Perhaps,' Lefty offered, 'Although I'm not really sure, looks could be the big attraction from both sides. I really would love to see a man through a woman's eyes, because to me, apart from the Paul Newmans of the world, most men are generally not good-looking creatures, really, as the man says, we aren't exactly pretty pictures.'

'Speak for yourself, Lefty.'

'I am, and I do,' he admitted, sticking his hand up as if he wanted to get the teacher's attention. 'I often wonder if the power of attraction is something separate from love or is love part of the same magic potion? The reason why love may not be part of the original attraction bug is because most people refrain from using the L word until the last possible moment. The declaration of love is either a watershed moment or, sadly, a negotiation tactic to get to the ultimate base. I have found when you remove love from carnal relations, the situation becomes much simpler. You thereby avoid the "if we do this, then you must make this commitment, spiritually, financially, maybe even matrimonially" type of negotiation. This approach allows you to proceed to a relationship based on mutual enjoyment of the pleasures afforded humans through the joys of sex.'

'I still wonder how much of the initial attraction is connected to the other person voicing or showing they are attracted to you?' McCusker mused.

'It certainly must be a big part of the dance, Brendy.'

'Can a person see a fine-figured woman and just feel the need to connect?' McCusker said. 'Or is it more important to get to know someone first. Is becoming friends really a big part of the process?' he asked, realising he just wanted to hear Lefty, the most unsuccessful wingman in the history of the universe, discussing his specialist subject.

'Well, it most certainly has to be if they are to mate together for life?' Lefty suggested. 'But don't you see that something being forbidden until basic requirements are met, simply makes the forbidden a turn on...?'

'A challenge?' McCusker offered.

'Maybe so. I think perhaps this was the problem Mister Barry and Miss Scott suffered from. They felt they truly loved each other but...but because each were the other's first love and lover they were thrown into a complete turmoil when both were tempted by the availability of others. If they at least had some experiences before they had met, they would have realised the other man's weed wasn't always Columbian Gold. My point to you, Brendy, and I feel this is very important, is when they both betrayed each other, behind each other's backs, as it were, they were more disappointed in themselves than they were in each other.

'I don't know if this will help you or not, but I hope it does. I would suggest to you what they both felt for each other all those years ago, when you and he and I bumped into Isabella, Gilly and Jane, on the streets of Portrush, was genuine 100 karat love. But the integrity of the foundation was compromised by the conflict caused over humans needing to procreate against their need to love and feel love.'

'So, you think a man looks at a woman to see if he thinks it is physically possible, they could make love together?' McCusker asked.

'I will say, I certainly do,' Lefty Kelly admitted instantly.

'Is that really your key attraction? Is this how two strangers interact, more to the laws of the jungle than a romantic calling?'

'It's not unpleasant, Brendy, if you take the time to do your research.'

'Well, it sounds like you certainly have, Lefty.'

'I have, and I'll also admit I enjoy it,' Lefty replied firmly. 'Yes, people, although appearing to generally lack in self-esteem and self-confidence, never feel they'll be the last one picked for the team. They'll have a multitude of excuses for themselves for what they feel are their own shortcomings, but really at the end of the day, nine times out of ten, they will always back themselves. Girls might even admit to themselves, "yeah, he's not George Clooney, nor even Charles Laughton, as Quasimodo, for that matter, but he's clean, washes his teeth, polishes his shoes, so he'll do for now."'

'But then no one else does come along,' McCusker continued, picking up the theme, 'and so they fall even deeper into their convenience rut. When they realise this is the state they were at, to start with, they try to make more of it. They both try to put more into the relationship until they eventually reach the stage where they have to accept, they—their partners— aren't the people they want, stroke need, stroke think, them to be. This revelation coincides with their anger. The next stage is when they realise why they've been angry all along. This is usually the stage where the PSNI are introduced into the equation.'

Chapter Fourteen

As O'Carroll and DI Melodee Johnson were driving to Ryan Shannon's ivy covered house in Kerr Street, O'Carroll was trying, as politely as she knew how, to explain how some people, a PSNI Detective Inspector for instance, although academically sufficient, incapable of carrying a lot of common sense. She was referring to a colleague of hers, DI Jarvis Cage from the Customs House who was just too gullible for his own good, and particularly while in the company of McCusker for instance.

'One morning I needed to pop out of the Customs House and Cage, he innocently enough asked me where I was rushing off to, he wanted, in his own words to know "my whereabouts,"' O'Carroll recalled. '"Oh, I just need to go off and find something urgently." I said out of the blue, as I grabbed my jacket and ran out of the office without another word.'

'"What's she looking for?' Jarvis asked McCusker when I'd left the office.

'"Oh, she's off searching for her virginity.' McCusker said, tapping away on a computer keyboard while trying his hardest to look busy.

'"But I thought once you lose it…' Cage spluttered

'"Have you never heard of the morning after pill?' McCusker continued.

'"Yes…yes, of course," Cage bluffed. "Oh I see…well, yes, yes of course."'

'No!' Johnson roared, 'he didn't fall for it? He couldn't be so gullible?'

'He did, and he is,' O'Carroll confirmed, 'but you must have your own station house…id…we can't use the word idiot anymore, can we?'

'No need to, I know exactly what you mean, we've a DS Basil Healey,' Johnson said.

'There you go, the name says it all,' O'Carroll replied.

'Yeah, Basil's main claim to fame is that he's the best dummy piper in Portrush.'

'What? He doesn't even play the pipes?' O'Carroll posed.

'No, of course not, but he's got a great swagger though and he doesn't half wear a kilt well.'

'Just one quick question,' O'Carroll said, sounding innocent enough.

'Go on?' Johnson offered, in encouragement.

'Can you tell me what exactly it is a piper actually does?' O'Carroll asked, 'Is it another name for a plumber?'

'Away with you, you big eejit...I nearly fell for it...'

'Aye, but you did use a forbidden word?'

'It's not forbidden if you're accusing an actual eejit of being an eejit.' Johnson laughed, 'Anyway, here we are.'

By which point they pulled up just outside Ryan Shannon's house, not a million miles, it had to be said, from the Pilgrim's Steps.

If Cliff Richard wasclaimed to be the English answer to Elvis Presley and Daniel O'Donnell is Ireland's answer to Cliff Richard, then surely Ryan Shannon could equally claim to be Ulster's answer to Daniel O'Donnell. O'Carroll only thought this because she figured this would be McCusker's take on the aging Peter Pan of the showband world who greeted her and DS Johnson barefooted on the steps of his four-story accommodation. She also imagined McCusker wouldthink it was much more telling Shannon would be happy, very happy, with the comparison. The singer appeared to enjoy a natural tan, maybe had a wee bit of work done around the eyes (any crow's feet were still attached to the crow and probably, currently, anchoring it to a chimney stack somewhere in the neighbourhood) and his bouffant hair looked like a hairdresser had gone to great lengths to ensure each and every single hair (brown with white highlights) on his head was in the absolute correct place and would remain in its assigned position until sundown.

O'Carroll reckoned he was sixty-plus but was going for the not-quite-turned forty look, the latter being the kind of man she also seemed attracted to. Her personal preference was a man in his thirties who had the maturity of a fifty-year-old. She wasn't having much luck in the romantic stakes at the moment. In fact, she currently wasn't having any luck at all, full stop. Her worry about going straight for the fifty-year-old man was based on the fact he'd be decrepit sooner than she wanted. Ryan Shannon, most likely (hopefully) looked much better the other side of the stage lights as he did in plain daylight on his doorstep at 9.00 in the morning. He was wearing frayed blue designer denim jeans and a brand new, expensive looking, brilliant-white, logo-less t-shirt. It was so new the manufacturer's sharp shipping folds were still clearly visible.

The singer, O'Carroll, assumed at this point he was a singer, for all of his grooming was genuinely friendly and greeted them as if they were long-lost fans.

His blue-doored, ivy-covered house, benefited from off-street parking by having a one-story entry, just to the right of the front door, wide enough to accommodate an SUV, quite literally straight through the house. The house was four windows wide and four storys high, so he would never miss the front and back rooms sacrificed to accommodate modern-day traffic.

His opening words were, 'Hi, I'm Ryan Shannon, please call me Ryan.'

DS Melodee Johnson introduced herself and DI Lily O'Carroll, and they both produced IDs.

'Com'on through,' Ryan said, 'I hope you don't mind but as it's early I had my chef do his special magic on a bit of brekkie for us.'

'Sound,' Johnson offered in acceptance and thanks. 'Very generous of you Mr Shann...'

'Now, what did we agree on the steps, please call me Ryan?'

'Thank you, Ryan,' O'Carroll said, as he led them through to the cosy breakfast area, just off the kitchen and built out as a conservatory into the back garden. The overall effect was very Farrow and Ball, busy, personal and extremely tasteful.

There was no chef in sight, but all the food had already been laid out around the table. There were four settings.

'So here we are, Luggai has worked wonders again,' Ryan gushed, 'he had to nip off to The Royal Golf Club. I believe he's doing a sit down for Rory and some friends this morning. I think we all hope it might just be the missing factor. So, we have an egg white herb omelette, sugar-free OJ, glutton free croissants and some of the latest Bullet Proof coffee from California. The secret to this one is we blend quite a large chunk of Kerrygold butter into the mix, it's very healthy-long-life-a-rama. Please… help yourselves.'

'Sounds perfect,' O'Carroll replied on behalf of both, but whispered at a volume only Johnson would hear, 'he must be a real head the ball if he puts butter in his coffee. Lucky McCusker is not in on this interview; he'd be fit to be tied if he saw an Ulsterman sit down to a breakfast like this.'

'Coolio,' Ryan said in reply to O'Carroll's, "sounds perfect." 'So, very sad about Thomas Barry, wasn't it? Have you any idea yet what happened to the head?'

McCusker had explained to O'Carroll in his showband lecture how showband musicians call each other "head" or "heads." In fact, he had said he didn't know where the exact delineation line was as some showband heads also seem to call all other humans, heads.

'We're still at the early stages in the investigation,' Johnson offered.

'I heard the head had a heart attack,' Ryan Shannon posed.

'We should have a bit better of an idea whenever the autopsy results are in,' O'Carroll replied, offering something without actually saying anything.

'Did you know Mr Barry very well?' Johnson asked.

'Well, there's a bit of in-law-a-rama,' Ryan started.

'Sorry?' O'Carroll asked, thinking how strange it could be when two people from the same country and while conversing in the same language still had trouble understanding each other.

'So, we were brothers-in-law…and twice in fact,' Ryan offered, 'or put another way we both suffered from Scott-Sisters-a-rama.'

'Okay, I think I get ye,' O'Carroll said, 'So you were married to Colette and Isabella was married to Thomas.'

'Coolio,' Shannon jived. Coming from a NYC cat was one thing, coming from an aging Northern Irishman, although very well spoken generally and with a voice perfect for local radio, it was very sham.

The thing which got O'Carroll the most, though, was how confidently he dropped his "Coolio" or "Head" or infrequent hyphenating "a-rama" on to the end of certain words. The secret, she felt, was not to throw him off his mark by drawing attention to it or by asking him to repeat himself in good olde Ulster English. She feared doing so might make him, self-conscious and lose his natural flow. All she needed to do was to figure out all of Ryan's idioms and have her brain automatically translate them as she went along.

'Tell me, did you and Colette, or Isabella and Thomas, marry first?'

'Okay, here's the thing, I'm going to be honest with you in all of this stuff. I know it's difficult because Thomas is not here to contradict me, but I'm sure you can get confirmation-a-rama, from relevant third parties.'

'Coolio,' O'Carroll replied, which brought large smiles from both Johnson and Shannon.

'Fair play to you head, fair play,' Ryan said.

The three of them had a chuckle.

'So, when I met Colette Scott,' Ryan continued and then stopped talking and stared off into the distance. He refocused on the two members of the PSNI, looked a bit embarrassed, appeared to be mentally pulling himself together and continued, 'It was the year after Thomas and Isabella married. I believe they married in 1982. Yes, it was October 1982 they married. I met Colette the following June. June the 14th, her birthday. I remember the date because of her birthday. She was twenty-one in 1982.'

'Is Colette or Isabella the oldest?' O'Carroll asked, taking out her notebook.

'Isabella is two years and a month older than Colette,' Ryan replied, 'I'd be very interested to see which one of the sisters you feel is the oldest when you've met them both. Anyway, we were playing…'

'We?' O'Carroll asked, pen hovering at the ready.

'My band, Ryan and the Causeways, we were playing at The Arcadia. I'm the chanter, lead singer in other words,' he added swiftly when it appeared neither O'Carroll nor Johnson knew what he meant by chanter. 'We were part of the showband-a-rama which means we had to learn most of the top ten singles in the UK charts each week and play our versions for the dancers. All that June, The Police were number one with *Every Breath You Take*. Believe it or not the Police weren't a group of PSNI heads singing about breathalysers,' he laughed loudly at his own joke, when neither current members of the PSNI joined in, he qualified it by saying, 'I suppose I really should have said the RUC there, to be historically accurate. Right, so, anyway. Colette and a few of her mates,' Ryan continued, in a moving swiftly along manner, but when he saw O'Carroll about to ask another question, he invoked another tactic swiftly, by interrupting himself with, 'and no…Isabella wasn't with her sister on the night I met her. Colette wasn't in the slightest bit interested in me or the heads in the band, but her mates dragged her along to meet us. One of her friends was a big fan of the band and we'd always chat to the fans afterwards. Not a chore, just vital to do. The fan, Doris Derby, introduced Colette to me. Colette was so totally coolio. Oh, my goodness, she was gorgeous! And all the more attractive because she didn't even know she was so beautiful.'

'But not interested?' O'Carroll offered.

'But cold-shoulder-a-rama, as you say. I asked her if I could walk her home. She said most certainly not, she was going home with her mates. The next time we played the Arcadia the girls were there again. I saw them after the gig and asked Colette if I could walk her home. She said no, but she continued talking to me and eventually her friends walked away leaving Colette and I alone. She apologised, said she wasn't being rude, but I shouldn't ask to walk her home again. I asked her why, she said, "I never want to be part of this." And she paused and stretched her hand out across all the girls talking to the heads in the band who were starting to pair off. Colette continued, "I don't want someone trying to cop a feel of me against the outside back wall of the Arcadia ballroom."'

Ryan stopped talking. He looked as though he'd been transported back to the ballroom on the night they'd met.

'What did you say?' O'Carroll asked as Johnson simultaneously offered her own question, 'What did you do?'

'I said, okay, fair comment, I won't bother you in the ballroom anymore.'

Ryan said.

'But you'd didn't give up, though, did you?' O'Carroll said.

'Did I hell as like. The following Sunday afternoon, I walked up to her front door and knocked on it. Her dad answered the door and I asked him if I could speak to his daughter, and he said, it's not me you've got to convince it's Colette. So anyway, *eventually* Colette came out and she said, "I thought we'd agreed you weren't going to bother me again?" I reminded her I had in fact agreed not to ask her out *in the ballroom* anymore. I told her I was genuinely interested in her and I would follow whatever rules she wished to lay down. I told her I really needed to show her how serious I was about her. I wanted her to allow me to try and convince her about how serious I was. She lightened up a bit. I think she took pity on me and said we could go for a walk on the East Strand. I suggested we give the Arcadia a wide berth and we should walk the West Strand, down past Barry's instead.

'Wise move-a-rama,' O'Carroll offered.

'Well, she clearly thought so, she laughed for me for the first time. I reminded her anyone trying to cop a feel of her up against the back wall of the Arcadia, would be up to his eyebrows in troubled waters in more ways than one. She got my joke and laughed quite a bit, maybe more from relief. I did not dare admit to her how beautiful I thought she was or how much her principles impressed me, attracted me. She was friendly but still reserved, still a bit stand-offish. She said it was nothing personal, but she just couldn't date a singer in a showband. I told her she *was* being personal; she was judging me as if I was like every other showband head in the country. She said she knew they, me, all of us, had a different girlfriend at each dance and would only chase you until you did the wild thing-a-rama and then they'd be off chasing another girl. She did take the trouble to say she loved me singing *Every Breath That You Take*.'

'Please don't tell me you got down on one knee outside Barry's and sang the Police song to her?' Johnson said, looking like she was preparing herself for Ryan to make such an admission.

'Ah, that would be a no to that one. I didn't even consider it,' he said, paused and then admitted he had considered it by saying, 'I knew she'd run the whole way to Portstewart to get away from me if I did.'

'Then what happened?' O'Carroll said, admitting to only herself she was secretly waiting for the "ahhh" moment.

'I walked her home, she said goodbye.'

'Did you try to kiss her?' DS Melodee Johnson asked.

'Most definitely not. I knocked on her front door the following week. Her dad came out and shouted, "Colette, it's for you, the same boy as last week." As Colette came out and passed her dad on the doorstep, her dad said, "At least our Colette has a smile for you this week. *I* haven't seen her smiling since she passed her A Levels."'

'He's not meant to be on your side this early,' O'Carroll protested, 'the dad is supposed to protect the daughter.'

'We met each other every Sunday afternoon and went for a walk,' Ryan said. 'We had great chats-a-rama.'

'No kissing?'

'No kissing during the early weeks,' Ryan admitted, 'and it was eventually Colette who broke the no kissing embargo-a-rama.'

'Really?' O'Carroll and Johnson sang out in unison.

'Yes, she said to me, she said, "Look Ryan, I'm not going to break if you kiss me..."'

* * *

'So, did you and Thomas Barry and the two sisters get on well together? Did youse get on well as two couples?'

'Ah...a difficult question head,' Ryan started and stopped as if to consider, 'I'm not being bitchy here, I'm just trying to be honest in order to help you. Generally speaking, I'd have to say, the girls got on okay; even very well some of the times, but there was always this undercurrent thing where Isabella felt Colette acted, inappropriately, would be the best way to describe it, as the younger sister. She felt Colette pushed her way too far forward in family matters. I kept out of it but speaking about it today, I felt she, Isabella, might have had a point.'

'So, you felt your wife might have been too pushy?' O'Carroll suggested.

'No, no, you're most definitely taking my words out of context-a-rama. So, what I was saying was that yes, Isabella might have felt her sister was too pushy in family matters and might have behaved…well might have been out of order. But by putting it in such a way, don't you see, we are suggesting Colette was the one at fault. Really the question we should be asking ourselves is: Did Colette feel she needed to behave so, just because there was something lacking from Isabella's side?'

'Very fancy footwork,' O'Carroll suggested while, thinking she was totally blessed by having Grace for a sister.

Ryan's sheepish smile didn't contradict O'Carroll.

'What about you and Thomas?' O'Carroll asked.

'Well, let's put it this way, at the start, if we hadn't been brothers-in-law, we really wouldn't have made any other connection.'

'But for the sake of the family you both put on your best party mask?'

'Correct-a-rama.'

'Do you have any other brothers or sisters? O'Carroll asked.

'No brothers, no sisters, my parents passed when I was young. My mother's sister brought me up. We didn't discuss it much, she'd no family or husband of her own, so I always felt like she was protecting herself from any possible hurt by the way she lived her life. It turned out my father had passed first and then my mother, eighteen months later. I was ten years old at the time my mum passed and so I moved in with my aunt. I moved in here to this house, in fact. This was my mother's parents' house and my mother had moved out when she married and my aunt stayed on and eventually, she inherited the house when her parents, my grandparents, died. My aunt left it to me. At the time of her passing, when I was advised the house was mine, I felt I'd never be able to afford the upkeep of such a large house. Then didn't The Causeways only start to take off big time. I felt confident enough to take on the house as a labour of love project. I took the ground floor and the first floor for myself and converted the top two floors into four flats. All my tenants have their own entrance via the back yard. I plough the rent back into the upkeep of the house. On a property this size there is always something to do, something needing fixing. Sorry I've been waffling away, and I've most definitely gone off-piste-a-rama. Where was I? I know I was trying to make some point.'

'You were telling us about your Aunt talking to you about your parents' passing,' O'Carroll replied.

'Yes, I was…oh yes, so anyway when my Aunt was telling me about my mum dying of cancer eighteen months after my father had died of the same . I protested it just wasn't fair. I remember exactly what she said to me. She said to me, "The big C shows no favouritism, when he comes calling. He won't pass over a house just because he's visited there before." She wasn't wrong, but she'd a good few years before he came calling on the family again.'

'So…' O'Carroll started expansively.

'I'm guessing you've probably heard all the gossip about me and Colette and Isabella and Thomas.'

'Well…now you come to mention it…' O'Carroll replied.

'So anyway, Colette and I planned to marry. She was worried about me being on the road right from the start. I tried to tell her I had no need or desire to have affairs on or off the road. Yes, I would chat to the girls after the dance and sign autographs but signing autographs would be the full extent of it. We definitely wanted to marry, but I think she was starting to feel vulnerable because she was pregnant…'

'I didn't know you'd children,' Johnson offered. O'Carroll assumed what she really wanted to say was, "but you don't have any kids."

'Well, sadly, we didn't, but at the time she thought she was pregnant she completely changed. Feeling we really should be more of a couple and she said she was silly for being paranoid. She said she knew I loved her, she loved me, so we should just put all this silly stuff behind us and become husband and wife and, without mentioning the pregnancy, we announced our plans for the wedding. Even though we knew people could do the maths afterwards we felt it would be close enough to cast some doubt. Then there were complications and…' Ryan sounded like he was struggling for words, but he looked more like he was trying to look like he was struggling for words.

'Can we get you anything? Do you want to take a break?' Johnson asked, while looking like she was sorry she had raised the subject.

'Thanks, head, very kind of you,' Ryan offered while Johnson looked like she was happier to be addressed as head rather than "dear" or "love" or something similar, 'so…ah…well anyway, the pregnancy had to be terminated.'

'I'm sorry,' Johnson whispered, when "we're sorry" could have come across as insincere, so O'Carroll offered a quiet 'Sorry, Ryan,' as well.

'Colette seemed okay about it at the time, but I worried what it would do to us and if she would cancel the wedding. But no, she said no one but us knew, or needed to know about it and it would be very embarrassing if we cancelled or even postponed the wedding. She felt as we'd both agreed we were going to get married, so, she said, let's just get married.

'So, we did, we married, and all was good for some years. Very good in fact. She never came to dances. I never gave her any reason to doubt me. Then Isabella told Colette I'd been having a scene with a couple of groupies. She had a friend, might have been the same friend who dragged the birthday girl, Colette, to our booking at the Arcadia, the night Colette and I first met. Anyway, apparently this friend, according to Isabella, claimed to have been best mates with one of our groupies and she had told her mate, and her mate told Isabella, I'd been involved in an orgy-a-rama after a gig over in Greencastle. Long story short she believed Isabella. This was when physical relations ceased. The next time I met up with Isabella I had a go at her. I told her she had ruined my marriage to her sister. She said it wasn't her who told Colette. It was their mutual friend who had told both Scott girls the same shocking story. I calmed down a bit. She said, "Look I hate to see you this way, let's go and get a drink and chill out." We had a drink, then another drink, we ended up in my house…'

'What, with your wife in the house as well?' O'Carroll asked, fearing she knew exactly where this was heading.

'No…no…not in our part of the house, we went to one of the unrented flats in my house. It had recently been redecorated and re-furnished and it was just about to be put back on the market again. To be honest, I was quite proud of the way I'd done it up and I'd wanted Colette to see it because she always considered herself to be a taste maker. Well, she loved what I'd done with it. I remember her muttering something about having trouble with Thomas as well and before I knew it, she'd seduced me, and we christened the bed.'

D.I. Lily O'Carroll was visibly shocked. She couldn't hide it and didn't try to hide it. The interview concluded a few minutes later.

* * *

'I accept we should have continued the interview and, at the very least, asked him what he was doing at the time of Thomas's death. I feel it is totally unforgivable. To me the only thing worse than cheating on your partner, was, either cheating on your partner with your sister's husband, or, cheating on your partner with your wife's sister.'

'I know what you mean…' Johnson offered cautiously.

'I just didn't want to compromise the interview. I thought it was best to leave it for another day. I mean from the second he admitted, "we christened the bed," I was going to have trouble taking him seriously. Poor Thomas Barry, his wife cheated on him with her sister's husband.'

Chapter Fifteen

By the time O'Carroll and Johnson returned to 21 Lansdowne Crescent, the home of the Ramore Head branch of the Police Service of Northern Ireland, McCusker had already been in and left a message for O'Carroll, saying he would be waiting for her next door in Clair's Diner, the unofficial PSNI Staff Canteen. The big windowed, friendly eatery was buzzing, but once again O'Carroll was stopped in her tracks by the stunning ocean scenes all the diners were presiding over.

Johnson peeled off to check up on some emails she was waiting to come in on the case. She was still having trouble with her number one chore: locating Thomas Barry's mobile phone.

They agreed after McCusker and O'Carroll had finished their interview with Donnie McCartney, Thomas Barry's accountant at the time of his demise, they would all meet up at The Royal to catch up with Rory's progress and for a debrief with Superintendent Ivan Valley.

Donnie McCartney's company, Donald McCartney Financial Consultants (MCCFC), was based at number 20 Main Street between a noisy pinball and games arcade and a fast-food takeaway specialising in Chicken & Chips and Fish & Chips. McCusker had to admit he would have taken some comfort there if it hadn't been for the fact O'Carroll point-blank refused to allow him access to said premises. MCCFC was directly above Nash Photographers and both McCusker and O'Carroll were really impressed by the photographer's work on display in the shop windows.

'We've come to see Mr Donnie McCartney,' O'Carroll announced at the reception on the first floor.

'You may have come here to see Mr McCartney, but I can assure you Mr McCartney is not here to see you,' a middle-aged woman in an off pink, twin set, and grey skirt announced sing song style.

'I believe DS Melodee Johnson of Ramore Head PSNI booked an appointment for us to see Mr McCartney this morning.'

'Well she might have endeavoured to do just so, but Mr McCartney is at The Royal Golf Club and will be for the rest of the day and the rest of the weekend in fact. He did leave you a message, though. He said if you happen to be at The Royal, he'll see you there. And he said that even if you get into The Royal you'll still have trouble seeing him because he'll be in the Captain's Club lounge and you'll never ever get in there,' she concluded, sing-song style again and really laying it on with a trowel.

'And tell me this,' McCusker asked, leaning across her domain, the reception counter, like he was a farmer, 'was Donnie drunk when he said this to you?'

'How did you know he was a du...' which was as far as the shocked receptionist reached on automatic before she caught herself on. 'I could see if his P.A. could fix you up an appointment for the week after next, I know for a fact he's in Lanzarote next week.'

Donnie McCartney's pink twin-set-attired receptionist wasn't to know of Superintendent Valley's relationship with Captain Mannering. A fact proven when, a mere five minutes later, McCusker and O'Carroll were standing in the very same plush Captain's Club House at Portrush's Royal Golf Club and viewing the good and great of both Portrush and the golfing world. McCusker saw Detective Inspector Christy Kennedy, who was also a native of Portrush, now residing in Camden Town but back in the Port, for the big event. O'Carroll took great pleasure in informing McCusker the stunning (make-up free) woman holding Kennedy's hand was none other than up-and-coming actress Nealey Dean. Kennedy and McCusker had met up once before on a case. Both mouthed a "see you later," across the crowded lounge. McCusker thought he even spotted Steve Sands walking past. He thought Tiger Woods must be close by but then he noticed on one of the numerous TV monitors Tiger was out on the course playing his do-or-die round. Rain was never far away and McCusker hoped the links would get the rain out of its system before Rory was due to play his round at 15.10 in the afternoon. Every single person in Portrush knew exactly how big a mountain Rory had to climb to get back in contention. He was 13 strokes behind the leaders. Yes, that would be one, two, three, four, five, six, seven, eight, nine, ten, eleven, twelve and thirteen strokes he had to make up. However, those monumental 13 strokes wouldn't win the competition for him. No, not at all, those thirteen strokes would only put him in a position where he would be able to fight with the leaders for a prize, which would be—speaking in terms of pride instead of in terms of (quite literally) millions of dollars, or $1,560,000 to be exact. The pride aspect, and not the dollars, would be the biggest prize of Rory's career.

McCusker realised the investigation he was currently on (and he had a niggling feeling in the pit of his stomach, that just wouldn't go away) was, for the same reason as Rory's need to win, equally important to him. He didn't really know why the thought hit him just then. But he did know, with equal conviction, the character waddling across the wooden floor in the Club House was none other than Mr Donnie McCartney, Thomas Barry's accountant. The subject was walking in the same direction as McCusker and O'Carroll, towards the table where the Ramore Head branch of the PSNI had decamped. No, it wasn't really their table, but Superintendent Ivan Valley and his team had spread themselves selfishly around the ten-seater corner table, just as effectively as if they had thrown a German Beach towel over it.

'McCusker,' Superintendent Valley shouted, just as McCusker noticed his person of interest did a very deceptive last-minute body swerve. 'I thought you were out questioning witnesses this morning.'

'Yes, we're here to interview Donnie McCartney,' O'Carroll replied on McCusker's behalf.

'I saw him around a few minutes ago,' Valley replied, scouring the room, 'shall I introduce you?'

'Was he wearing an expensive looking blue suit, very badly?' McCusker asked.

'Yes, he was in fact,' Valley laughed, 'of course you want to chat to him because he was Thomas Barry's accountant. Let's go and find him?'

'Actually, I'd like to observe him for a few minutes before I speak to him if you don't mind.'

'Okay,' Valley replied, sounding unconcerned.

'Mind if I leave DI O'Carroll with you?'

'No problem…and before you mention it, yes of course I'll introduce her to Rory if he wanders through the clubhouse although he's sure to have other things on his mind this morning…'

McCusker got another quick flash of Donnie McCartney at the other side of the room, and he headed after him before Valley had a chance to finish his sentence.

To ask if Donnie McCartney stood out in a crowd would be like asking if George Best was a good football player. The former had blue spaniel eyes, which were highlighted by thick, heavy black-framed glasses, which were more Eric Morecambe than Buddy Holly. He was clean-shaven, flush-faced, absent of any facial or head hair, and was a big man, not a fat man but a big man in the way a schoolteacher or a village doctor were big men and carried themselves accordingly.

McCartney unknowingly led McCusker out to the first tee in time to see Tiger tee off. The former number one golf player in the world's compatriots for today's play were the UK's Mathew Wallace and Patrick Reed from the USA. McCusker was self-amused by the fact they're all wee men, not the giants they appear to be on TV. Equally noticeable was the fact they were all very solidly built, which also doesn't come across on the TV.

McCartney seemed to be joining in with the crowd who looked like they were going to follow, accompany might be a better word, these three players from tee to tee. McCusker in his black suit, fresh white shirt and black leather sensible shoes had more in common with McCartney than he had with the majority of the crowd in their heavily logoed, sports and golf wear.

'Welcome, Tiger,' someone in front of McCusker called out.

'Thank you,' Tiger replied, without breaking his stride or his concentration.

The crowd quietened down.

Then McCusker heard a loud: Wallop!

'Great strike,' a fan cried out and the rest burst into applause.

As play continued it became transparent Woods and Co were all having trouble concluding their work on the green.

'Must have been a cling-film over the 2nd hole,' an Ulster fan muttered to McCartney as he headed after the players to the 3rd tee.

'The 2nd hole just needs to open up a bit,' another armchair expert had offered.

'Aye, about to the size of a dust bin, might be handier,' McCusker added without even being aware he did.

Tiger enjoyed better luck teeing off at the third but for the first time McCusker noticed from the American's eyes he was actually in agony. He looked like his back was giving him serious jip and from the look on his face he was genuinely disappointed he wasn't fit enough to be enjoying the moment as much as he wished.

McCartney seemed to be enjoying himself though, drinking the atmosphere in and joining in himself.

When Tiger enjoyed a particularly magnificent second shot on the 194-yard, par 3, 6th hole, which was right beside the ocean with spectacular inspirational jaw-dropping, views. McCartney said, 'It's like he's got a magic wand rather than a golf club,'

A few shots later someone close by in the galley shouted after yet another missed putt, 'If I was him, I'd return the Magic Wand to the Harry Potter gift shop and consider using a golf club again.'

The crowd's confidence was now growing, and they all felt comfortable to chip in.

'He's on great form, he's dropping everything in,' a golfing fan in a Motorhead hoodie offered, 'I bet you he got a ride last night.'

'He better take care the next time he crosses the road,' his mate cautioned, 'his luck is sure to run out any time soon.'

'Is the rain just getting a wee bit heavier?' someone else said, and McCusker noticed McCartney had reacted immediately to this news by heading back in the direction of the club house by way of the first tee.

'He,' meaning Tiger, 'just needs to get on the range and bang a few in.' McCusker heard from behind him as he headed off after McCartney.

On the way back to the clubhouse McCartney melted into the crowd.

As McCusker wandered around he noticed people seemed to be in their own groups, gangs even. There would be boy gangs, as well as girl gangs. Not gangs in a negative context, but more like groups of people who hung out and did things together. He was shocked at the number of people in these gangs and other couples and singles, such as McCartney and himself, wandering around literally just yards away from where the real action was taking place. Yet, they'd still be glued to their mobile, where they were all focused on checking out the action, on a four-inch screen while, literally over their shoulders, the objects of their interest were playing out the game in real life size.

As McCusker passed the hospitality stand on the first fairway, he thought he caught sight of Donnie again in the middle of the mingling dense crowds up ahead of himself. Donnie looked like he was having the same trouble as McCusker, as they both were struggling against the tide of the crowds. Eventually, just when he thought he'd caught up with him, the accountant disappeared again. A few seconds later, McCusker felt a tap on his shoulder and turned to see the accountant, large as life, confronting him.

'Do you know me?' McCartney asked, a wee bit of aggression apparent in his heart-warming, baritone voice. 'It's just every time I see you, you seem to be staring at me.'

'Funny I was thinking exactly the same thing,' McCusker replied, which brought a large smile from McCartney. Something else caught his attention and he disappeared just as quickly as he had appeared.

McCusker checked the course scoreboard to see how the morning play was progressing. It looked like it was being manned and womaned by volunteer students who kept getting in McCusker's sightline. No one was turning in good scores, which McCusker took as both a positive and a negative for Rory. It meant no one was pulling further away from him, so far, but equally, with the rain due to start up again mid-afternoon when

Rory was due to start his second round, his play was going to be much more difficult. Tommy Fleetwood seemed to be playing well and moving up the leaderboard, which currently showed JB Holmes at the top.

Before checking the dramatic skies for the umpteenth time that morning, McCusker returned to the clubhouse. The first thing he noticed was DI Lily O'Carroll deep in conversation with a man at Valley's table. She totally ignored McCusker.

'Did you find your man?' Superintendent Ivan Valley asked.

'Actually, he found me,' McCusker admitted, 'then I lost him in the crowd before I could introduce myself.'

'How's the wee man from Holywood getting on?' Valley asked.

'He doesn't tee-off until 15.10.'

'Yeah, I knew his tee-off is at 15.10, I was just checking to see if you were following the golf or your case,' Valley offered, but delivered not as a reprimand. 'So, let's you and I go for a wee dander and find Donnie McCartney and I'll introduce the pair of you so you can get back on your course again.'

'Sounds good,' McCusker replied, 'let me just get O'Carroll.'

'Ah, leave her be as she is. I think she might think she's chatting to Rory. I haven't had the heart to tell her different,' he said, leading McCusker off through the milling chattering crowd.

Eventually, fifteen minutes later, they cornered Donnie himself holding court with a few mates. McCusker slowed Valley down, he was happy to enjoy a bit of observation time before interviewing the accountant. McCusker maneuvered himself and his old boss until McCartney had his back to them.

McCusker stood the round and knew Valley, although still wearing his Pioneer Pin, would go for a Kit again, but Valley seem equally impressed McCusker was going for a tea.

'So, a Kit plus an OJ and tea with milk and two sugars for the two ladies,' the barman cheekily chipped in.

'Do you know him well?' McCusker asked Valley.

'I know *of* him, rather than knowing him,' Valley admitted, 'what's your take on him, big man?' the Super continued, 'Do you think he's a fool?'

'Anyone who mistakes Donnie McCartney for the fool in the room is the real fool in the room,' McCusker declared, as their drinks arrived, 'he's got two drinks. One looks like it could be gin and tonic, but as he only repeats the bottles of tonic water, the gin has long since dried up and the other is sparkling mineral water. Every now and then his eyes work the room, he's clocking absolutely everything.'

'You think?'

'I bet he even told Mrs Off-Pink Twin Set to feed us the drunk line. When people start to discuss any business matter, you can see his ears perk up quicker than a bunny who has just sniffed a juicy carrot. He knows his shirt is sticking out, it's a look he's cultivates to ensure people dismiss him and let their guards down and freely discuss their business in his company. I followed him around part of the course, and his shirt wasn't out then.'

'Most of the people in here, including quite a few of my team, would file him as a fool by the look of him and the way he goes on,' Valley admitted, raising his half of lager to McCusker in a toast gesture, before downing the remains of it and then sending the whiskey down immediately after it. 'Tell you what, big man, you've not lost it, you know what you're doing, you work away there, and I'll leave you to it.'

McCusker knew if O'Carroll had heard what the Portrush Superintendent had just said, she would immediately have offered, "Be careful, remember pride always comes before a fall."

Of course, he knew she'd have been 100% correct and knew he needed to heed the warning she hadn't even needed to utter on this occasion.

He watched as Valley wandered off through the buzzing crowd, greeting and being greeted by dozens of people. McCusker was always amused by the fact his former boss, who was a good three inches taller than McCusker, frequently referred to him, or addressed him as, "big man."

Chapter Sixteen

McCusker caught Donnie McCartney's eye and nodded him in the direction of a quieter part of the room.

'So, you're the man from the PSNI who visited my office this morning,' he said as they finally shook hands. 'You mustn't pay any attention to my mum. She's never forgiven me for leaving my dad. I think it had something to do with the fact I took her with me. Mind you, I was only five at the time so I can't guarantee that was the exact sequence of events.'

'I figured one of youse had a sense of humour,' McCusker replied as McCartney led them up what appeared to be a private stairway, out through a door and onto a landing overlooking the historic event proceeding beneath them. Surprisingly, there was no one else visible, but as they took a seat at a table, a young waitress dashed out of another door leading to the balcony.

'You can't sit there you'll have to…' she said as she rushed over towards them. 'Oh, sorry Mr McCartney I didn't realise it was you,' she continued as she slowed down and redeemed herself by adding, 'Is there anything I can get you?'

'Yes, now as you come to mention it, as a matter of a fact, could I have a tea, some milk, no sugar and some of those brilliant egg sandwiches on brown bread please and Mr McCusker here will have…'

'The exact same will do me nicely as well, thanks, but maybe some sugar with my tea, please.'

'Are you sure you wouldn't prefer a BLT, Inspector?' McCartney said, breaking into a knowing smile. 'I'm just kidding, Charlene, tea and eggs will do us just fine.' He paused to address McCusker, 'Have you ever had the hot egg sandwiches in here, they're nothing short of perfection.'

'I'm looking forward to them,' McCusker admitted quickly, absentmindedly running the fingers of his right hand through his straw-like, copper-coloured, dishevelled hair. 'In the meantime, and on the record, I must state I am not an inspector, not even an official member of the PSNI. I am attached to the PSNI as a freelance officer.'

'Don't worry, I won't burst your chops over this, and I won't insist we're in the presence of a PSNI officer before we can continue our conversation. Apart from anything else, we don't want to share those precious egg sandwiches with another. Those sandwiches are so close I can already taste them. So, you're Thomas's former best buddy and founder member of the BLT gang. May the Sauce be With You, indeed.'

'Ah, you have me at an advantage then,' McCusker admitted.

'And sadly this is not my preference as to how we would meet,' McCartney continued, as he took off his glasses, removed a scarlet-coloured, cleaning cloth from his top right-hand pocket, put each lens in succession in his mouth and haughted on them, leaving a little moisture thereon. He quickly proceeded to clean the lens before returning the spectacles to his head. He carefully folded the cloth back into four and put it back in the breast pocket of his jacket. The removal of the glasses totally transformed Donnie McCartney's features and not in a good way. Without his glasses, he looked a lot older and less benign.

'You know,' McCartney started, when McCusker was considering the accountant's look, sans glasses, 'I often pity people who don't wear glasses. They will never ever experience the sheer bliss spectacles-wearers enjoy when we clean our glasses, or even better still when we put on a new pair of glasses. The first time you put them on, oh it's liquid bliss. It feels like God has gifted you a fresh set of eyeballs.'

McCusker had watched his little ritual without comment and even when, what looked like a perfected routine was completed and spectacles had been returned, rebalancing the accountant's head once more, the detective didn't speak, feeling McCartney had more to say. In fact, McCusker hoped McCartney still had a lot to say, and words would soon be tumbling from his tongue.

'You and Thomas had fallen out of touch? McCartney eventually asked.

'Sadly yes,' McCusker confessed, 'and as much my fault as his.'

'Have you any suspicions yet as to what happened to Thomas?'

'We're currently just collecting information,' McCusker replied, thinking he needed to get a few questions off the mark, 'when was the last time you saw him?'

'Well, Thomas and I would speak on the phone every day. And we'd meet up for lunch most Fridays. Let's see now, I saw him last Sunday, down here in fact, quite a few of the overseas players were already in town, so Thomas and I popped down to see several of them hit a few balls.'

Charlene arrived with trays bearing all they needed and a few sandwiches extra.

To McCusker, it looked like McCartney was eating two at a time, either this was the case, or he was devouring them a lot quicker than McCusker.

'And what kind of form was he in?' McCusker asked.

'The very best,' McCartney replied. 'Look, I know he had his worries. Don't we all, don't we? Look, I can tell you this: Thomas Barry did not die by his own hand.'

'And why are you so convinced he didn't?'

'He was a wealthy man,' McCartney said, 'he was about to get a lot wealthier.'

'Oh?'

'Yes,' the accountant said, sounding very confident, 'Thomas had bought up a lot of land about the town. The more he bought the more he'd say, "It's going to get better." And I'd ask him how he knew things were going to get any better and he'd always say, well actually he'd sing the words, "it can't get much worse." Now this was way before The Royal Golf Club here announced it had been successful in its attempts to bring the UK Open here for the first time in 68 years. The local government pretty much chipped in £17 million to assist rebuilding the town and, consequently, everything

Thomas had touched turned to sterling.'

McCusker was subconsciously racking up question after question, but kept them to himself

'When Thomas felt the developers were either too ambitious or too slow, he started to develop himself and, during this process, he teamed up with The Buckley Brothers, Sean and Seamus, the local builders,' Donnie McCartney continued. 'They specialised in apartment blocks.

'Portrush, as well as being a magnet for holiday makers in search of the seaside, also started to become a retirement location for people with their own romantic memories of visiting here for their annual summer holidays. I will admit the magnet may not have been as strong as it was back in your, Lefty and Thomas, aka BLT's, day. While the nostalgia magnet might have been on the wane, the student population was increasing proportionately.

'Thomas was a great man for the research. When he was interested in a property to either knock or refurbish. He would always walk the premises repeatedly. He'd hang around and quiz bin-men, sorry…sorry, of course I mean refuse collectors; gas men; Electric Board men; telephone men; men at road works; men down the drains; men up telegraph poles; local businesses; taxi drivers; ambulance drivers who covered the district in question; local door men at pubs and clubs; the owner before the owner who was in the process of selling the property. You name the man and he'd have spoken to him. He knew chapter and verse on the district before he'd even have entered negotiations. He'd work out what he felt the building plot was worth to him and his golden, unbreakable rule, was he'd never ever offer a penny more. He was always happy to walk from a deal. He knew there would always be more properties for sale. He would never allow himself to love a building until his deal was done.

'I'm very happy to admit to you I, for one, learned so much from Thomas's approach.'

'Thomas was driven. I don't know where his drive came from. He could have lifted his foot off the pedal and coasted for the rest of his life on his fortune. Yes, he made mistakes, he suffered losses and he made bad calls. For instance, he lost a lot of money investing in properties in Poland, an area which became very popular with Northern Irish investors about a decade ago. But I'll tell you this for nothing, he never made the same mistake twice. He learned from his mistakes and, more importantly, he never ever invested an amount more than he could afford to write off altogether. I believe in a way, he was happy to invest the money if he could learn something from it. Maybe not with Poland. I would have thought he could have bought the whole of Poland for the money he poured into that deal.'

'Was it not a big gamble for him?' McCusker asked, innocently.

'His logic was it was only a gamble if you couldn't afford to lose the money.'

'Were you in partnership with him?' McCusker asked, as more tea and egg sandwiches arrived. He hadn't even noticed McCartney nod the order to the ever-attentive Charlene.

'No, never,' McCartney replied immediately, 'I made a promise with myself I would always avoid any potential conflicts of interest. I would act 100% as an accountant and invoice accordingly. I'd be happy to get advice from Thomas, and he was happy to offer it on projects I was considering for myself.'

'So, the million-dollar question,' McCusker started, 'were there any deals Thomas was involved in where he was okay about taking the losses on the chin, but his deal-buddies weren't?'

'No, he didn't work with partners,' McCartney replied. 'The building trade has its reputation, you know, cutting corners, never finishing on schedule; going over budget; "cash deals" and the likes. Thomas couldn't abide having to worry about someone crossing the boundaries of the law in his name and him being liable. He was in control at all time. Consequently, he put absolutely everything through the books. "Thomas Barry doesnay carry cash," he'd say. No VAT fiddles. He paid every penny of tax. I don't know if this was due to some trouble his family were in when he was young.'

'No, I wouldn't have thought so,' McCusker offered, 'his father was the same, straight as a die. He took great pride walking around town with his head held high, owing neither man nor government a penny.'

'I figured as much. When I'd show Thomas a way of legitimately saving on income tax he'd always come back to me and ask two questions; One: could this loop hole be interpreted another way and, two: if there was a possibility of the same, could I ask the tax office for a ruling on it in advance. If there was any doubt, and I do mean *any* doubt, he would always err on the side of caution.'

'Who's the main benefactor in his Will?'

'You need to ask his solicitor,' McCartney replied quickly, perhaps too quickly, suggesting he didn't know, didn't want to know, or wouldn't speculate.

'These projects with the Buckley Bros?'

'Just walk around the Port, you'll see them all over the place. His buildings are never loud, they'll never win any awards, they'll gently blend into their surroundings, and I can guarantee you, they'll never fall. Blimey, I've just realised...' McCartney started, and then faded to a halt.

'What Donnie?' McCusker asked, trying to shake the accountant out of his trance.

'His current building...'

'And...'

'I was just wondering what would happen to it.'

'Is it in the town?' McCusker asked, just before he bit into another sandwich. McCartney had been correct, they were amazing. The eggs were scrambled in butter and hot, and not diluted by mayonnaise or anything similar, the bread was fresh and soft, and they were extremely more-able.

'Yes, it's just up on Kerr Street with perfect views of the harbour. It's a new classy building, called Colabella House. It's a seven-story apartment block, with twenty units plus a top floor penthouse. They're just about to start the second fix. I better make a few calls on this as soon as poss.'

Donnie McCartney seemed to get over his stress moment very quickly, so quickly in fact McCusker didn't have time to finish eating his sandwich properly before he had to point to his mouth with moving jaw and excuse himself before continuing, 'so can we talk a wee bit about his personal life?'

'I'm not so sure I can be of much help there, but I will assist in every way

I can,' Donnie replied.

'There are obviously stories,' McCusker started in hope, 'but now he's passed there will be a lot more stories.'

'I don't know McCusker,' McCartney started, 'I speak as I find and I found from my conversations with Thomas he felt he and Isabella were in love but thought they might have been too young when they met and too young when they were married. He said their lack of experience meant that around the same time they both began to question their love for each other—not because they were no longer in love with each other, but due to their lack of knowledge over the feelings of love—they both felt a need to see what it could be like to be with someone else. He said he felt very sorry Colette got caught up in the middle of it all. He never shared any more words on the subject with me.'

'And Ryan?'

'I tell you this because I want to help you. Thomas was good to me. I can tell you there was no love lost between them,' McCartney said, choosing this exact moment to repeat his spectacle cleaning ritual.

'Was there any hatred there?'

'Agh, there was the auld niggle there somewhere back in the—'

'Yeah, and?'

'Well, look here…in my opinion, Ryan needed for everyone to like him, maybe even love him, Thomas was more interested in doing good work.'

'How did Thomas get on with the Buckley Brothers?' McCusker asked, accepting the fact McCartney wasn't going to slip into gossip.

'Well, initially, before they got to know the way Thomas worked, there was a bit of static, particularly with Seamus.'

'Static as in?'

'Well, as I mentioned, Thomas wasn't interested in cutting corners, in dealing in cash, or employing workers who'd only work for cash, and well, Seamus…you have to realise Seamus is a bit of a wild one, a bit of a bandit. Seamus…well let's put it this way, if there was some crane work needing to be done, like unloading a load off a flatback, or transferring a load to an upper floor and there was no one around to officially operate the tower crane, then Seamus Buckley would take great pleasureclimbing up the rig himself, nipping in to the cab and standing in for the absent operator. He was totally fearless.'

'But you said the static was in the early days.'

'Yeah, they'd a few run-ins. Sean you could talk to, but Seamus harked after their independence when he and his brother could do as they wanted to without anyone "supervising" them. I cautioned Thomas to be careful. I warned him Seamus…'

McCusker thought McCartney was going to clam up on him.

'Look, what can I say? Seamus Buckley is fearless. He's a bit of a ladies' man, and this has gotten him into trouble over the years, particularly with farmers whose wives also fancied a bit of excitement. He's come out of the wrong end of a few scraps. Aye, as I said, he's fearless but he's not scared of paying the price.'

'But Sean…

'Yeah, Sean saw which side his bread was buttered on, and he was cute enough to realise the Buckley Bros in partnership with Thomas Barry were in another league to the league they were in without him. Sean was the diplomat and he and Thomas, between the both of them, succeeded in keeping Seamus under rein.'

'And recently? McCusker asked.

'They seemed to be getting on well.'

'Any other men or women I should be checking out?' McCusker asked.

'What I'd like to do,' McCartney started, 'what I'd really like to do, would be spend some time going through my files for you rather than sitting here speculating. On top of which I'd really like to have another quick scamper around the course before the rain comes again.'

Okay,' McCusker said, checking his watch and noting he'd fifteen minutes to get to Isabella Scott for their 2.00 o'clock lunch date, 'one quick question before you head off though…'

'Sure,' Donnie McCartney agreed, 'shoot?'

'Can you tell me what you were doing between eleven o'clock on Wednesday night and three o'clock Thursday morning?' McCusker asked.

'Yes, an easy question at last,' McCartney said, 'and I do know why you need to ask it. I went down to Belfast, to the George Best Airport Wednesday afternoon. I'd a meeting at the airport coffee shop with a UK Client. She flew straight back again to the Midlands early evening and I couldn't be arsed driving back up here again, so I checked into the Fitzwilliam Hotel in Belfast and checked out of there after breakfast, they do a great breakfast at the Fitzwilliam. The big secret is to avoid the buffet breakfast and have them cook it fresh for you. I was back in my office around one o'clock yesterday lunchtime.'

As McCusker departed The Royal and headed off in the direction of Isabella Scott's penthouse apartment, he wondered if McCartney could have gone to great lengths to make the point he wasn't involved with any of his clients as a partner because he wanted to avoid potential conflicts of interest. Then, later in his conversation, he said Thomas Barry was happy to share his knowledge with his accountant for his own projects. So, McCusker pondered, what if McCartney and Barry had been after the same project?

Chapter Seventeen

hen McCusker swung past Valley's table downstairs on the way out, O'Carroll and DS Melodee Johnson had already departed for their second appointment with Dr Aynesworth.

* * *

'Come on up, you know the way,' Isabella Scott instructed McCusker through the intercom.

When McCusker hit the top floor, he found the door to the apartment already open. His right-hand fingers surfed his hair again. He wondered why exactly he had to do so at any particular moment. He immediately thought of Grace O'Carroll, who was coming to visit him the following morning.

Then the smell of the food led him straight to the kitchen.

Isabella Scott had clearly decided not to adorn herself in sackcloth and mark herself with ashes in order to play the part of the grieving widow.

In fact, Ms Scott, formerly Mrs Thomas Barry, had scrubbed up well and McCusker remembered how Thomas's brief glimpse of this green-eyed girl (as she was then) had caught him hook line and sinker. The woman didn't look much different than the girl had. She was quite bubbly, maybe bubblier than a widow, admittedly an ex-wife widow, should be. She was wearing a blue off the shoulder polka dot dress McCusker referred to as a Nicole dress. McCusker called it after the dress a girl called Nicole wore in a famous, often screened, series of adverts promoting Renault Clio cars in

1995. Nicole was played by a French actress, Estelle Stornik. The dress was off the shoulder with shoelace ties holding it up and it was designed so as it flowed with the movement of the body. McCusker didn't know for sure but he guessed the adverts most likely spiked the sales of the dress more than it did for the car. The design of the dress meant any moving or leaning could be revealing but, it must be said, never naughty. Our Nicole was most definitely a vision of innocence and all the more desirable because of it.

Isabella Scott had the perfect figure to pull off wearing a Nicole dress. McCusker couldn't take his eyes off her. He suspected she knew exactly the effect she was having on him. He also noticed she was halfway through her glass of wine, whether or not it was her first glass of wine, or even her second, or third, might have been a more relevant question.

Isabella had made a cottage pie. She said she remembered it was McCusker's favourite from their BLT days. McCusker wasn't complaining. Drooling, maybe, but complaining, no.

When Isabella leaned across the counter to add peas to McCusker's plate, she didn't bother to protect her modesty by using the palm of her hand to push the top or her dress to her chest.

McCusker thought of Grace and averted his eyes.

'So, we were going to discuss Thomas some more?' he started, after he had his first taste of her delicious cottage pie.

'I actually knew Thomas was a mistake the moment we met…'

'No,' McCusker protested.

'But equally I realised and accepted it was a mistake I couldn't avoid,' she offered, in conclusion to the sentence McCusker had interrupted.

'But I was there the first night you met, Isabella, and the sparks were most definitely flying?'

'I often think about our big Sunday night, Brendy, when it was real, pure, true and just lovely. Sure, he was a lovely wee man and I was… I was hot. Hot is what they call it now, hot, I was fecking hot. I'm not boasting, I'm really not, I knew it because I was getting the same reaction all the time those days and my sister Colette wasn't. I say in those days, I still have my moments these days,' she offered coyly. She stood away from the counter and gave McCusker a twirl. Her Nicole dress obligingly umbrellaed up revealing her underwear.

McCusker couldn't work out if he was having more difficultly catching his breath or she—seeing the effect her display had on the detective—had. In McCusker's defence he was in the presence of the Hi Love You've Just Dropped You Glove, girl and he and all of his mates, particularly Thomas Barry, had ogled over her, as the goddess they all felt she was. And here the Hi Love You've Just Dropped You Glove, girl was, now a beautiful grown woman who'd just put on a mind-blowing sensual twirl for him.

In her defence, McCusker felt, she was now blushing red as a Ferrari and perhaps was enjoying just a wee bit too liquid a lunch.

'You know if both of us, me and Tom,' she resumed as she climbed back on her high stool, 'would only have had the sense to accept the first night really was as good as it was ever going to get. If we'd only had the cop-on to say goodbye to each other, then, don't you see, we'd have had those wonderful untainted memories to live with for the rest of our lives.'

'But come on, Isabella,' McCusker said, 'I was there, I saw youse. Youse were good together, you and Tom were great together.'

'But we were together every waking moment from then on. Don't you see, what we really needed was experience with other people; experiences in the work place; sexual experiences; chalking up hearts being broken moments; everything we needed, in fact, to armour ourselves to survive in the real world. I mean, you really need to have those experiences if only so you would realise you don't needthem.'

'So, you're saying you needed to have those experiences just so you would come to realise you din't really need them?' McCusker asked, thinking this was a great one for O'Carroll's cannon.

'Exactly, Brendy, you get it,' she gushed.

'But then would it not be better to have realised what you had and bypass all those other experiences with other people?'

'Exactly my point, and why it's all so fecked up. The only way it could have worked would have been if I hadn't dropped my glove on the night and lived my life for a few years and *then* met up with Tom. Then and only then, he and I would have been better equipped to deal with each other. Did I ever tell you Tom has…sorry, Tom still *had* that glove, the one he'd picked up, and he framed it? It's still in his house.'

'I didn't know, but knowing Tom, it makes perfect sense to me,' McCusker said, sounding regretful.

'I think I told you yesterday when you called around the biggest mistake I ever made was allowing Tom to ride me. I mean, what was I meant to think. You know, he was always copping a feel, he was always sticking his hand up my skirt. He was always sucking my face, and me his, I have to admit. We were always experimenting. How was I meant to know, no matter what he was doing, no matter what he was saying, no matter how many of my clothes he'd removed, no matter how much he'd turned me on, no matter I hadn't realised exactly what he was doing as he did it, until I felt the hot and sticky results and I realised he'd just been inside me for the first time, that really I was meant to be a pure girl and say no and not allow him to do it?

'How was I to know he wanted me to remain pure. From then on, we had to pretend I was still a virgin so he could seduce me. The problem was once Tom and I made love for the first time, I went from knowing this was something I was *meant* to do for my man, to thinking it was the most wonderful experience in the world and literally not being able to get enough of it. Which was a bit of a problem for Tom. Don't you see, my need for physical love and his need for pure love created an insurmountable barrier.

'I mean, I found ways, by playacting mostly and wearing one of the outfits Tom favoured, but we both had to suspend belief in order to awaken the hibernating serpent. Even our horizontal recreation got to be difficult.

'And we'd other problems as well, of course,' she admitted, without the slightest signs of guilt, 'the main thing was, we never had to struggle. Struggling brings you closer together, my mum would always say as she was encouraging my dad to write another cheque for us. She'd say, "Well, it'll either bring you closer together, or it'll break you up." But we both went into great jobs. We both were making good money. Our parents bought us our first house. I mean, it was all there on a plate for us.'

Isabella Scott cleared away the food plates and then removed a freshly baked apple pie from the oven. She served it with ice cream, which immediately melted all over the pie. Perfection. McCusker realised in all the time he'd been married to Anna Stringer, aka his ex-wife, she had never ever baked an apple pie for him. Nor had she playacted or dressed up for him, for that matter. But equally now he started to come to think about it, neither had he ever baked an apple pie for his wife, nor had he play-acted nor dressed up for her either. He wondered if wearing his RUC uniform would have counted. He realised he was encouraging all these thoughts in order not to reflect on Isabella Scott giving him the twirl.

'So, Isabella,' McCusker started, as he finished off his apple pie, barely able to resist licking his lips, 'can you tell me what happened between you and Tom to result in you breaking up, please?'

'Well,' she started through a large sigh, 'all was good for a few years, I mean, appearing good as in all of our bad stuff was being swept under the carpet. Our Colette married a singer, Ryan Shannon; he was at best a minor celebrity. Portrush's answer to Rod Stewart, he claimed. But he was doing okay for himself, making a bit of money. The fact Ryan was making good money was important for Colette. She was always competitive with me. I put it down to the fact she was the younger sister and our parents always held me up as a benchmark to her. She saw Tom and I were doing okay with our lives; the other man's grass is always greener and the other woman's glass is always cleaner, kind of thing. On the surface the four of us got on good. Tom really like Colette and he wanted to make sure Ryan wasn't taking advantage of her, so he started to be quite friendly to him, just so he could keep tabs on him. There was really nothing going on between Tom and Colette, they were close but, in a brother-in-law, and sister-in-law kind of way. For instance, Colette hated to go and see Ryan at the dances but if Ryan desperately wanted her to be there, sometimes just so she could take home some cash, she would only go if Tom and I went with her. And going to see the show with her was fine. We'd say a quick hello afterwards and then take Colette home just so she didn't have to deal with all the fecking groupie shit. I tell you some of them are so brazen, if they know you are the wife, *particularly* if they know you are the wife, they will walk over you, literally physically walk over you, to get to your husband.'

'Did Colette think Ryan was cheating on her?'

'Do Barry's Bumping Cars crash into each other; does a bear shit in the woods?'

'I've seen the bumping cars in Barry's, and I can confirm they do crash into each other,' McCusker offered, 'but so far in my life I've never spotted any bear droppings in the woods.'

Isabella started to laugh; her laugh was disproportionate to the quality of the joke, if in fact it was a joke. For instance, McCusker knew when he cracked the joke, if he had been in a car with DI Lily O'Carroll at the time he told it, she would have stopped the vehicle and deposited him on the pavement. But it appeared the joke was a watershed moment for Isabella and it was an outlet in a way, McCusker thought, for all her grief and having to relive parts of the life she and the deceased had lived together. Her laugh started off throaty and sensual and eventually it melted into sobbing. McCusker walked around to her chair and took her in his arms and tried as best he could to comfort her. She too got down from her chair and hugged him even tighter than she had yesterday. She was a lot more charged than yesterday as well, McCusker felt.

'Please don't ever tell my senior DI Lily O'Carroll one of my jokes had you intears,' McCusker said quietly, after her sobbing had faded out altogether.

She made a bad attempt at a faux laugh.

She excused herself and went to freshen up and returned a few minutes later looking very freshened up but with heavier eyes.

'Can we talk about you and Thomas breaking up?' McCusker asked, as she served them both a cup of coffee in the lounge. McCusker left his untouched. He really couldn't abide the stuff, but he didn't want to slow the interview process down any more by her having to go off and prepare tea. He did sample several of her colourful French Macarons. They didn't taste anywhere near as good as they looked, and he tried one of every colour just in case.

'Must we,' she sighed, but then proved it hadn't been a question. 'Okay, as I mentioned, Colette and Tom were very tight. My theory is Tom always secretly fancied Colette. He used friendship as a way of keeping close to her. I think the reality was Tom was seriously looking for a good excuse to cheat. He kinda didn't but he did really if you know what I mean.

'I know Colette and Ryan had a problem…'

'With the showband groupies?' McCusker asked.

'No, Colette wanted children; she made no bones about it. Either Ryan didn't want kids, or he was firing blanks, but either way, Colette admitted to Tom she was so desperate she was going to doll herself up, go out, have a few drinks, pull the first eligible male and get pregnant.'

'Did Colette really put it so frankly?' McCusker asked.

'Well, never to me,' Isabella admitted, 'but she told Tom.'

'Did Tom tell you?'

'No, I don't think Colette knew I knew, but it's all a bit hazy as to who knew what and when,' Isabella replied.

'Tom's a bit of a prude and he was aghast when Colette admitted her plan to him,' Isabella continued, 'he said it was too dangerous, apart from anything else, she could get hurt or catch a disease.'

'Well, in fairness, Isabella, Tom wasn't wrong,' McCusker offered.

'"I don't care, I want a baby, maybe even two, before it's too late,"' Isabella reported as being Colette's alleged response.

'Then Tom said he would be prepared to donate his body…'

'His body or his sperm?' McCusker asked.

'Oh, he's an Ulsterman, he definitely meant his body, you know what you're all like, you'd do anything in the name of science, especially if there's a fecking quick ride involved,' Isabella said. 'Colette was happy with this but instructed Tom to discuss it with me first. Tom said he would.'

'Did you and Tom have such a conversation?'

'No, of course not,' Isabella admitted, 'but our Colette being the goody two-shoes she is, only went and discussed it with Ryan.'

'Oh-kay.'

'I was out at a function somewhere; I don't remember where. I bumped into Ryan,' Isabella claimed, 'Ryan had a few and had a go at me about my husband wanting to service his wife, my sister.'

McCusker thought he could see where this was going and didn't particularly want to go there.

'Two things. First off, Tom always had the hots for Colette and two, he never forgave me for not remaining a virgin. It was not so much *if* he was going to have an affair, but more: *who* he was going to have an affair with. The way Ryan described it to me, Colette and Tom had all but already done the evil deed. At the same time as all this was going on, if I'm being honest, I was also considering testing my wings a bit as it were, just to see what it was like, you understand. Ryan wouldn't have been top of my list, but he was there, I was vulnerable, he wasn't as drunk as I was, but we went back to his house…'

'What? With Colette already in the house?' McCusker asked, fearing he knew exactly where this was going.

'No, no,' she barked, 'we went to one of his vacant flats with their own entrance. He really wanted me to go back and see the job he'd done on the apartments he was renting out. He was really proud of how he'd transformed them and felt confident his work was going to increase the rent. I thought we were only going back for some sobering up coffee, honest to goodness, but he seduced me, the cad, he seduced me.'

'And did this happen before or after Tom and Colette had…?' McCusker asked.

'You'd have to ask Colette, at this stage she'd be the only one who knows for sure,' Isabella suggested.

'How did Tom find out?'

'Ryan went straight back home and told Colette and Colette told Tom the following morning.'

McCusker thought the interview was all but over, but Isabella had more to say.

'Needless to say, Ryan did not turn out to be the love of my life, or even of that particular afternoon. I think it was a case of re-arranging into a well-known phrase or saying, the following words: Pencil Fecking No The Lead In.'

McCusker mused with her riddle for a while until the penny dropped.

'But at least I'd started if you see what I mean…'

'But if am…well you know…'

'I was so keen for am… some interaction, I think I would have enjoyed it even if Ryan hadn't been there at the time. On second thoughts, I might even have enjoyed it more if he hadn't been there,' she said, sounding like she was relieved her confession was nearing an end. 'As I said, I'd started and then for a time embarked on a voyage of discovery.'

'Did Tom know…am…'

'About my fellow travellers?' she asked helpfully.

'Well, yes, actually.'

'Some of them but not all of them,' Isabella Scott admitted, before looking at her watch and gushed. 'Oh, look at the time. I've an appointment shortly, sorry I really would have loved to hang out with you some more.'

'What were you doing on Wednesday night between 11.00 and 3.00 in the morning?' McCusker asked as he stood up.

She looked genuinely shocked, and her look of shock visibly changed gradually to one of hurt.

'Feck Brendy!' she hissed, 'how could you?'

'Sorry, Isabella, it's really just PSNI procedure, we have to ask all people connected with the victim just so we can rule them out and reduce the number of people we have to speak with.'

'And then when there's only one left,' she offered, 'you have your man.'

'You've discovered Sherlock Holmes's biggest secret,' McCusker admitted.

'Okay, in that case, I can tell you this. I was with a friend, a gentleman friend, all night and if I need to, I will give you his name, but for obvious reasons, I'd prefer not to have to disclose his name at this time.'

'Is he married?'

'Happily, with a family.'

'Gotcha,' McCusker replied as he thought, "Yes," under the circumstances, might have been enough. 'Ryan Shannon?' he asked, thinking in for a penny, in for a pound.

'I can 100% confirm for the record I was not in the company of the showband singer,' Isabella offered, baring her perfect protruding teeth as she continued, 'additionally, I can confirm I have only lain with my sister's husband on the one occasion outside wedlock.'

* * *

She kept looking at her watch and getting a bit twitchy and McCusker wondered if her appointment was with her mystery man from Wednesday night. Looking on the positive side, which McCusker always liked to do, if the mystery man was a player in this particular mystery, then he was making progress on the case at last, because one alibi was going to clear two people.

'Brendy, please don't forget you promised me you are going to take me to Tom's wake?'

The detective nodded his agreement as he leaned over to accept her hug and peck on the cheek at her front door.

'Thanks for not making a pass earlier,' she said, barely above a whisper, 'I wouldn't have been able to refuse, but you always were a gentleman, weren't you?'

Chapter Eighteen

McCusker checked his watch when he hit the pavement on the corner of Main Street and Church Pass. It was 2.50, so he imagined Isabella Scott's appointment would arrive at 3.00. Nothing ventured, nothing gained, he thought as he wandered to the opposite side of Main Street and entered Bob & Berts Café. The staff were very friendly and McCusker ordered a tea. He needed to get rid of the taste of the French Macarons some way, and what better way than with another alleged French delicacy, a Paris Bun.

'I thought you'd have been packed out today?' McCusker asked the very attentive assistant as he looked around for a chair.

'The numbers about the town were down drastically yesterday,' Bob (or maybe it was Bert) offered.

'But I would have thought with the open…'

'Well, there are a lot of people up there, alright, something like 200,000 I hear, but TThe Royal are not issuing pass outs so we're all suffering. Once you're in, you're in for the day, and equally, once you come out you can't get back in again until the following morning. All the traders are up in arms, this was meant to be our Gold Rush week.'

McCusker offered his condolences, took his tea and Paris Bun and found a seat in the corner window of the café. He checked his watch, 2.57. He enjoyed an uninterrupted view of the front door to the old Northern Bank building, which now housed Isabella's flat on the top floor.

By three o'clock, there was no action. Same at 3.02. McCusker braced himself for a quick departure. Rory McIlroy was due to start his round at

3.10. McCusker was in the process of persuading himself his hunch was wrong. Then he accepted he might have instigated this process, so he could nip down to The Royal and see Rory Tee off.

At 3.03 a man walked up to the grand old front door of the bank and pressed one of the buzzers. McCusker figured it was the same button he'd pressed, the top one, the one to Isabella's apartment. The man had his back to McCusker; he couldn't see the face because of his full head of black curly hair. He was wearing denim jeans, an American styled, red-checked, flannel shirt and a pair of Timberland fawn work boots. Within 30 seconds he'd disappeared in through the door and McCusker swallowed down the remainder of his tea, grabbed the remnants of his Paris Bun and scooted off down Main Street.

He veered left down the slope, immediately before the 55 Degrees Restaurant, down past the Arcadia, along the boardwalk, well, more like a cement (board) walk but McCusker and his fellow members of BLT had, back in the day, taken to using American words instead of the local ones. Even though the closest coast of American was 3,140 miles west of Portrush, the concrete walkways along the side of the beach became boardwalks; pounds became dollars or bucks; Eastwood's the bookies became Clint's; every white horse was called Silver; all female elders became mam; every Teddy boy with a metal comb to flick through their Brylcreem drenched hair became Kookie; every best mate, in other words, Lefty Kelly, became your wingman; every goodbye became adios amigo; every teenager called Charles became Chuck; your friend became your compadre and his cute sister became doll; single records became 45s; LPs became albums; a football trainer became a coach; a Vauxhall VX4-90 became a Cadillac and you'd say, "saddle up," rather than, "hit the road." Portrush even had its own grand White House, a massive department store, opened in 1891 by its *own* president, Henry Hamilton. These were the memories McCusker recalled as he walked on past the TV compound, backing into the sand dunes. He speeded up as he walked into TThe Royal Golf Club, but by the much quicker back entrance, where the temporary PSNI I.D. and lanyard Valley had given him, came in very handy.

By the time he'd reached the crowded first tee, even McCusker was shocked, as in totally shocked, by the mighty roar which greeted Rory.

McCusker figured any human would have had a problem living up to this anticipation, but then Rory was constantly showing he wasn't human. McCusker was convinced every single person on the golf course, probably every single person in Portrush, had witnessed, if not participated in, the Rory roar.

McCusker was also shocked to see O'Carroll and Johnson back in the clubhouse and sitting at Valley's table again.

'I thought you went to see Dr Aynesworth,' McCusker offered, by way of greeting.

'We did,' O'Carroll and Johnson said in harmony.

'But?'

'But he wasn't there,' O'Carroll replied.

'Where was he? McCusker asked.

'We don't know,' Johnson answered. 'He'd taken the day off?'

'He's taken the day off?' McCusker repeated.

'He'd taken the day off,' O'Carroll confirmed.

'Does Superintendent Valley know Aynesworth has taken the day off?' McCusker asked.

'He does,' Johnson said.

'What did the Superintendent say?' McCusker asked.

'He said we should, "tell McCusker and see what the big man wants to do." Those were his exact words,' O'Carroll reported.

'Can I borrow your mobile?' McCusker asked O'Carroll.

She handed it to him.

McCusker punched in some numbers, the phone rang. They could hear a voice answer at the other end.

'Anthony?' McCusker asked.

'Are you busy at the moment?

'So, you're not at the Forster Green Hospital at the moment. You're watching the golf, are you?' McCusker said, into the phone, narrating both sides of the conversation to keep Johnson and O'Carroll in the conversation.

'Funny you should mention it, but if I could fix you up with a pass would you be interested in coming up to watch it live?' McCusker asked, crossing the fingers of his free hand for the benefit of Johnson and O'Carroll.

'Yes, I'm up at the Port, already. Can you nip up?

'You can, great. When could you leave?

'Excellent, just one other wee thing…' McCusker paused for a second to listen to the other end of the conversation.

'Yes, I suppose you could say it was in return for the ticket.

'Yes. Anthony, am…here's the thing, it's a quick wee job.

'What kind of job,' McCusker repeated Anthony Robertson's reply for the benefit of his colleagues, and hesitated, 'Well, it's like this, Anthony, I was wondering if you could do a quick autopsy for me.

'Ha, funny Anthony, but no, it's not an autopsy DI O'Carroll wants carried out on me, to check if I still have a brain, it's *for* me.

'Yes, DI O'Carroll is up here with me.

'Sorry, yes, *of course* we're working on a case.

'Yes, Anthony, you're absolutely correct I wouldn't ask if I didn't need you to do it.

'Brilliant, you'll be here at 5.00.

'Yes, you *will* be in time to see some of Rory's round.

'Yes, I'll have Superintendent Valley clear everything at this end and set it up for you.'

McCusker handed O'Carroll back her phone.

'Way to go, McCusker,' she said in return. 'How are you going to break this to Dr Aynesworth?'

'I was figuring on getting the Super to deal with Aynesworth,' McCusker replied, 'I mean, I'd offer the Super a suggestion as to how he should break the news to the doctor.'

'Oh, and what would your suggestion be then?' O'Carroll asked, as Johnson, who was clearly getting to know their routine, was already betraying the lines of an oncoming smile.

'Well, I was thinking something along the lines of, "Aynesworth, I've got some very good news for you,"' McCusker said, in a very accurate take on

Valley's broader Ulster accent, "'You won't have a single report to write on this particular case." I would imagine Aynesworth, a.k.a Dr Nevercide, would then say something like: "Oh, and why, Sir?" and the Super could reply something like: "Well, because someone who actually knows what he's doing is going to do this autopsy for us." How does that sound to you, Detective Inspector O'Carroll?'

Chapter Nineteen

'I'd a postcard from my brother last night,' McCusker said from nowhere.

'I didn't even know you had a brother. Is everything okay?' O'Carroll asked, visibly concerned.

'Yeah, he's on holiday, and he just wrote home to say his hotel room was nothing to write home about.'

'Jeez McCusker,' she chastised, and then a few moments later, she started to giggle and couldn't stop.

'You know, Tom, Thomas Barry, when we were younger, when we were lads, he always looked like he'd be the last boy to be picked from the pool of players for a football team,' McCusker said, betraying his thought pattern.

O'Carroll at first looked bemused, then surprised, then sad.

McCusker tried to say something but either he just couldn't get his vocal cords to work, or if he did manage to get it out, he feared he would just lose it and embarrass himself.

'Such a sad image of him,' O'Carroll offered, sounding like she was trying to fill the silence and not risk losing him.

'Oh, it was okay because neither Tom or Lefty or I were interested in football,' McCusker said, who also seemed to be having trouble shaking the image from his mind. 'You know Lefty was always saying such and such was a pretentious thing to say. It became one of his key things to say. Eventually, whenever Lefty would repeat this saying, Tom took to announcing, "saying something is pretentious is a very pretentious thing to say." Well Lefty dropped his line post haste.'

'But we, the three of us…'

'The BLT Gang?'

'Yes, the BLT Gang,' McCusker agreed, 'Well, we used to walk around these streets blethering away, or we'd say…I think this one was Tom's…he'd say, "Even a hypochondriac gets ill some of the times." Or another one was, "never take your Grannie off the stove; you know how much she loves to ride the range."'

'Definitely wasn't one of yours, McCusker,' O'Carroll smiled.

'I used to have a sweet tooth or two,' McCusker said.

'Is this you today or a BLT routine?' O'Carroll asked.

'No, this is me today,' McCusker confessed.

'Okay, McCusker, I'll bite, you used to have a sweet tooth or two.'

'Aye, I used to.'

'Used to, how did you get rid of your affliction?' O'Carroll asked.

'Well, they're all implants now.'

'All the time you were sat there I thought you were thinking about our case, when in fact you were thinking up these silly lines of yours.'

'But don't you see you have to think about it to connect the dots. If you insert in a bit about sugar rotting your teeth, it becomes too unsubtle and doesn't work, however you do end up making the connection you were after, only because by having the second thought simultaneously, you allowed yourself not to be too preoccupied by the first thought.'

'I'll take your word for it, McCusker,' O'Carroll started, as he veered sharply left, 'where on earth are you off to now?'

'Nowhere on earth,' he replied, pointing to Portrush's famous Lifeboat House, 'as this building is technically built out over the sea.'

They found the door to the wee, funky and informative museum on the side of the Lifeboat House was open and McCusker and O'Carroll received a very warm welcome.

'We wanted to see if we could get a bit of information from you?' McCusker started, after they'd both flashed their IDs.

'Well Portrush have had a lifeboat here since 1860, the first one was called Zelinda and the current one, our tenth, sails under the name of Katie

Hannan,' their silvered haired host, with a gravelly voice, offered, 'but I imagine the information you are after would be on the untimely death of Mr Thomas Barry over at the Pilgrim's Steps.'

'Yes,' O'Carroll replied, 'and we apologise if you've already been asked these questions.'

'Well, funny you should mention it, I was thinking you're not locals, well actually *you* are,' he said nodding at McCusker, 'I knew your daddy. But you're not stationed here anymore, are you?'

'We're not,' O'Carroll replied, 'but we've been brought in by the locals, they're a bit stretched due to the golf.'

During the interview, she appeared distracted and let McCusker take the lead.

'As you're so close to where the remains were found, we're surprised no one has been to see you,' McCusker said.

'And so am I,' he said, and then proceeded to officially introduce himself and told the pair of police officers he was, in fact, a direct descendant of, and named after, *the* John Whitaker, the name Portrush's second Lifeboat sailed under when it was launched in 1876. He informed them he was Captain John Whitaker. 'Have you any idea yet what happened to Mr Barry?'

'We're still collecting information, Captain,' McCusker replied, 'I notice you have a camera above your front door?'

'And waterside as well,' the good Captain confirmed, 'but I'm afraid they wouldn't be much good to you, they're focused on the pavement on one side and on the water side, the harbour wall separates us from the Pilgrim's Steps.'

'Well, we really don't know if the remains were washed up on the Pilgrim's Steps, or if they were brought in waterside in a wee boat, or were discarded over the street wall above the steps…'

'You don't really know a lot, do you?' Captain Whitaker offered, but without making it sound like a criticism. At least this was McCusker's liberal interpretation of the sentence.

'Correct, but we're just in the process of collecting information, so we'd still really like to view your tapes for back and front, you just never know what they may show.'

'I think we could put money on the fact we won't have recorded Lord Lucan riding up Kerr Street on Shergar.'

'Well, if we discover such a particular pair of phantoms, we'll let you announce it to the world's media,' McCusker joked, 'so can we review your tapes?'

'Of course you can,' Captain Whitaker replied immediately, 'however as you can see they've taken me out of retirement to man the museum today, everyone else is down at The Royal supporting Rory and I haven't a clue with computers, could I get one of the boffins to come in in the morning at nine and meet up with you then?'

'Of course,' McCusker agreed realising all resistance is futile, 'we'll have someone come around in the morning.'

'Excellent then, if we're done, I'd better get back to our patrons?' he nodded in the direction of two shell-suited, blue rinse American ladies who had just entered the museum.

As he marched over proudly to his audience, the Captain glanced back over his shoulder at O'Carroll and McCusker and ordered (yes, it was definitely more of an order than a request), 'and don't ignore our donation box on the way out.'

Later, as they continued walking towards the harbour, she started to laugh.

'What?' he said.

'I've thought about it and I realise earlier before our Lifeboat House detour, you were trying to pull yourself out of thinking back to three lads, wandering around Portrush wisecracking their days away…'

'And looking for a love to drop her glove,' McCusker added.

'Aye, but I also have to admit your sweet tooth gag…it's…well, it's better than your normal lines,'

He beamed as he knocked on the Harbour Master's door in the two-story Harbour Master's Office, right next door to the Portrush Yacht Club building, one of the few more modern buildings guarding the harbour.

'However,' O'Carroll reminded McCusker as they heard footsteps from the other side of the door, 'we do need to remember you hadn't set the bar very high.'

'Ah, it's yourselves, come on in,' Melvil Edwards, the Harbour Master, offered by way of greeting and then rushed in past them into a back office, waving them to follow. There was a small TV with about six people glued to it in silence. The cramped room erupted in cheers as Rory chipped the ball squarely into the hole on the green of the 431-yard Par 4, 9th hole. The last time McCusker had played a round at The Royal this hole had been the 7th, but for the UK Open, they had a new number 7, and new number 8, holes and so this one, also known as the Tavern, was now the number 9 hole.

Following a massive cheer for Rory as he walked off the green, Edwards brought them to a quieter, nicer front room up on the first floor.

'Take a look out there,' he instructed them, pointing out to a spectacular view of the harbour, 'what do you see?'

'Nothing?' O'Carroll said.

'Seagulls? Cranes?' McCusker offered, to try and be constructive.

'Aye, you're both right, but maybe what I should have asked, what don't you see?'

They both looked out for a few seconds before O'Carroll chipped in with, 'Rain?'

'Rooks?' McCusker replied, while keeping safely with his aves theme.

'You're both right, but maybe what I should have asked was, who don't you see?'

'People,' they both replied in unison,

'Amazing,' O'Carroll continued solo, 'not one single person as far as the eye can see.'

McCusker was thinking of quoting Dylan's "Everyone is making love or else expecting rain." Especially in Portrush, it appeared. He was working on the principle Dylan was quite a few steps up for the detective from his usual beer mat philosophy. Nonetheless, he feared he'd still get nothing but an elbow in the ribs from O'Carroll for his trouble.

'Correct!' Edwards countered, like a schoolteacher who had just managed to coach their class to a successful conclusion. 'Everyone is either up at The Royal and can't get out until sundown or they're all in their houses stuck in front of the telly willing the wee County Down lad to make the cut. At least now he's only 7 over, mind you Lowry is 9 *under*. But all Rory needs to do is to make the cut today, which means he's going to have to pick up another 6 shots on the remainder of this round and then at least he'll be in with a chance of pulling it back tomorrow and Sunday. But I've never ever seen the streets so empty.'

'Tell me this,' McCusker said, 'did you have any further ideas on how Thomas Barry ended up by the Pilgrim's Steps but without a mark on him?'

'Still beats me,' Edwards admitted. 'At first, I thought a canoe would probably be more manoeuvrable in the water, than the wee boat we were in. But getting a comatose body into a canoe would be one thing and then getting it out, aye, would have been nothing short of impossible. Then I thought that a rubber dinghy could actually get you up onto the rocks without leaving any marks on the rocks and then you could just roll the body out, but…'

'Hang on, Melvil,' McCusker said, closing his eyes to try and visualise the procedure, 'I think you just might have something there,'

O'Carroll appeared to be considering this option as well.

'Why did you rule a rubber dinghy out, Mr Edwards?' she asked.

'Melvil is good for me, thanks, Detective Inspector.'

'And the dinghies would have a flat front rather than a pointed one?' McCusker continued, appearing not to be interested in hearing the Harbour Master's reservation.

'I actually think it's a good idea, I was just intentionally trying not to oversell it,' Melvil confessed.

They all continued staring out over the harbour.

The expected rain came in very quickly. It had been mizzling when O'Carroll and McCusker had arrived, now it was lashing down.

'Ah, the rain'll fairly dampen Rory's efforts,' Melvil said, as all three continued to glare at the rain as if staring out at the rain would stop it. If this was the case, then there'd surely never be a drop of rain in Northern

Ireland.

'If only he'd been out this morning with Tiger, Rory would be flying by now.'

'So where would you find a dinghy around here?'

'Well, people who have a bigger boat, which would have to be anchored out at the Skerries would have one to ferry themselves in and out ?'

'Would they have a power engine or row?' McCusker asked.

'Well, usually the rule of thumb would be: the bigger their main boat, the more horsepower they'd want in their service launch.'

'Could you rent one?'

'Generally, no,' Edwards offered, 'It would be more of a paddling pool plaything version. Mind you, now I come to think about it, these days where everything is disposable you can hire anything you need?'

Another roar went up from the TV viewers downstairs.

Someone at the bottom of the stairs roared up, 'He's clawed another one back.'

McCusker could tell they were outstaying their welcome. He'd a bit more info to work with now. He promised Edwards he'd stand him a drink later. If he'd given the Harbour Master £1,000 in cash, he wouldn't have looked any happier.

Chapter Twenty

'I thought you'd have wanted to stay there and watch Rory's round,' O'Carroll said, 'or do you want to get back there quickly and watch him live?'

'I'm happy to be distracted to be honest,' McCusker admitted, 'it's like I'm playing every ball with him. I want each and every shot he takes to be perfect. It's quite painful sometimes. I'm always okay afterwards when he's won, and I can watch a repeat of his round.'

'If that's how you're feeling, can you imagine the pressure he must be under?' O'Carroll said, surprising McCusker with her sympathetic approach.

'He has the weight of this entire island on his shoulders. You seem quite keen to get back yourself?' McCusker said, as the thought hit him.

'Well, now you come to mention it, I was chatting to a man earlier,' O'Carroll confessed.

'Who, not one of the PSNI crew?' McCusker said, sounding semi-protective and semi-dismissive at the same time.

'I like your big brother approach, McCusker. I'll put it down to you wanting to look out for your girlfriend's sister, but no, he's not PSNI, *please*, spare me. We didn't chat for long, but I did get his digits.'

O'Carroll took out one of her famous five-by three-inch, lined, green cue cards from her inside pocket and read out loud:

'Albert McQuilkery, from Portballintrae. Age: 34. In films, own business, clean shirt, jacket not creased, nice shoes, but dirty, so only a 6 marks out of a possible 10. Doesn't try and talk to you while on mobile. Car is a green

VW. Nice smile. Own teeth. Clean fingernails. Blue eyes. Clean-shaven. Not married. Confident but not full of himself, but maybe is more self-confident than he's letting on. Didn't use chat-up lines. Overall 7 out of 10 but might be nice enough to rise to 8???'

'Potential, I'd say.' McCusker offered, nodding his head back and forth, tilting his head slightly, and raising his eyebrows.

'You'd be saying right.'

'I have to say, Lily, I'm very impressed with your system, you've just met him, yet you've recorded all his bio information on your wee card.'

She laughed and passed him her small file card.

He read the entire contents aloud: 'Albert McThingy, tasty rear.'

McCusker flipped it over, searching in vain for more.

Chapter Twenty-One

O'Carroll briefed McCusker on her interview with the showband singer as they made their way back down Kerr Street, approaching Ryan Shannon's ivy clad house on the left

'That's all he told you?' McCusker asked.

'Pretty much, yes, why?'

'He didn't tell you about his songwriting and about his trophy room?'

'What trophy room? What are you on about now McCusker?'

He led her over to Shannon's side of the street, thinking the seaside really needs the sun. Today though, the Port looked like a place the sun had gone to die. McCusker knocked loudly on the door, rather than ringing the doorbell.

'So how come you hadn't told DI Lily O'Carroll here about your song-writing success and your trophy room?'

'My trophy room-a-rama, who told you about my awards?'

'The legendary DJ and musicologist, Ivan Martin,' McCusker admitted immediately. 'He said you've been a dark, although phenomenally successful, mover and shaker in the songwriting stakes for ages now.'

Shannon attempted one of those modest, "Who, me? But you're certainly on the right track," moments.

'You're not known as a songwriter, though, are you?' McCusker guessed.

'Well, not really, well not at all in fact,' Ryan started, 'c'mon in, you'll have a wee cup of tea in your hand and I'll tell you all about my other career.'

Once again, the showband singer was in his bare feet. McCusker had always felt bare ankles and bare necks are always the biggest betrayer of people's ages.

'Okay, I've always wanted to be in show business,' Ryan Shannon started off grandly. 'When I was a kid, an uncle of mine wired up a microphone into the back of a valve radio and I'd take the microphone on a long lead and disappear into the wee cubby hole under the stairs, close the door and do my own radio show. I would write up a wee script. I'd tell a few stories, tell a few jokes, talk about the weather, talk about news items. I would use different voices. I was great at voices. I did a great mimic of my granny. I seem to remember I had this recurring part in my *programme* called *Grannie's Words of Wisdom*. I delivered it perfectly; everyone would be in stitches. The Grannie routine was so popular, I expanded it into a wee routine I'll remember to my dying day. It was me doing both the voices of my granny talking to her son, my father, and I swear to you with the crackle of the ancient speakers in the radio it actually sounded like the pair of them.'

When it didn't appear, McCusker or O'Carroll was going to request a repeat performance, Ryan continued, 'Anyway, I finished off each radio show singing a song. Singing those songs at the end of my radio show is how I first became a singer and eventually joined a wee group, The Port Boys, which, a few years later, we expanded into The Causeways Showband to the current version, Ryan Shannon and The Causeways.

'The songwriting-a-rama really was just a continuation of my career in show business. Don't you see it was my way of being allowed to continue to do what I'd been doing all those years ago in the wee cubby hole under the stairs: remain in Showbusiness and I do mean Showbusiness with a capital S.

'I'll tell you how the song-writing came about.

'When we, The Causeways, would be working out how a song is put together, we would have to break it down into its very basic parts, so we could re-construct it again for our band. That was how, eventually, I got the hang of it, the structure of songs. I thought I could write one myself, if I would only set my mind to it. It turned out my first attempts were all crap-olla and I worried that I couldn't write a song. I couldn't crack the code of writing a song without it sounding unnatural or twee. Then about ten years ago, I had some surgery done on my right arm…'

'Are you right-handed?' McCusker asked.

'Yes, as it happens, I am,' Shannon replied, 'why?'

'Nothing really, you were saying you had some surgery done on your right arm?'

'Yes, yes indeed, medical-a-rama. I don't know what happened exactly but when I returned home after the surgery there was all this music floating around in my head. Stranger still, it was there all the time. I tell you what it was like, it was like the way I used to pick to pieces a song so I could work out how The Causeways could cover it without being laughed at. The only difference was this time I hadn't heard any of the melodies before and yet they were all there, and real to me. I could hear them all clearly in my head,' he continued, sounding like he was still having trouble believing it himself.

'Go on?' McCusker encouraged, fearing this conversation might turn out to be as long as one of his own rounds of golf.

'So, I thought to myself, no one will know so I'll give the auld songwriting-a-rama a go. That night I wrote three songs. They sounded great to me to be honest. I went to sleep, woke up the next morning and listened to my voice and guitar demos again and guess what?'

'You liked them?' O'Carroll offered, refusing to kick a man when he was down, while still going for the obvious option and realising she had a 50/50 chance of being right.

'Yes, well really,' Ryan spluttered, seemingly taken aback by O'Carroll's apparent positive response, 'in fact even better than I remembered. You know what, I was scared. I will admit my first thought was: these songs are just too good for The Causeways to be doing. I mean, I realise I wasn't being very charitable, I know, and no disrespect meant to the heads in the band, but well, the big truth was the showband scene was in fast decline. A lot of the ballrooms were shutting down and the emerging cabaret cum lounge circuit was taking over and whereas in the ballroom days, dancing was the priority, next came meeting potential partners and then came the showband and the music. However, in the lounges the top priority was drink, then the shouting and screaming and laughing so loudly you'd think each table had their very own Ken Dodd or Kevin Hart entertaining them. Followed by boys meeting girls and then, girls meeting boys, then the bingo and then the quizzes and then just outside the top ten priorities would have been the showband and the music. And please don't get me talking about the DJs and their rigs moving into the lounges.'

'But you had your new songs,' McCusker prompted when Ryan seemed to have hit a brick wall on his current theme.

'Yes, I did. Yes, I did. Yes, I did,' Ryan Shannon repeated with all the fervour of a TV evangelist.

McCusker refrained, only just, from shouting "hallelujah" at the top of his lungs.

'Well, I was still scared, as in worried about the quality of my songs. I played one to Colette. It was called, *Postcards From the Port...*'

'*Postcards From the Port?*' McCusker gushed, 'Sure even I know that one. 'Wasn't it a big hit for yer man? You know yer man in the rocking chair on TV...' McCusker started well and then faltered unable to recall "yer man's" name.

'Val! *Postcards From the Port* was Val's final chart entry,' Shannon announced, with immense pride, 'it didn't quite make the top-ten, but it reached as high as number fourteen, so it did. It even managed to hang around in the top twenty for fourteen weeks. I was told the record company just couldn't keep up with the demand for the song and if they had managed to keep it in stock, it would have made the top spot in the charts for sure. I was okay about it. I really wanted the No. 1 for Val, though. He really deserved it. He was such a great ambassador for this island. He'd such a wonderful career and he hadn't been in the charts for a few years when he'd released *Postcards From The Port*. He'd never been number one in the charts, he got close though. He had two hits which got as high as number three and one which reached number two. We were all hoping this would be his first number-one single. But you know what they say, "We all make plans, and God laughs." It eventually sold over a quarter of a million copies, though.'

'Wow!' McCusker gushed and meant it but also in the hope of drawing a line under the subject.

'It was written from the point of view of someone up here on holiday but he was regretting he'd not declared his love to a girl back home,' Shannon continued, in full flow and proving no one, including a DI of the PSNI and a Grafton Agency cop, was going to stop him now. 'The main character in the song was trying to let his true feeling be known via a series of postcards from Portrush, claiming how much better his holiday would have been if he'd only invited her, the subject of his undeclared love, to accompany him.'

McCusker was aware of and concerned over O'Carroll's efforts to stifle a yawn. He needn't have worried; Shannon was so lost in his moment he was oblivious to everything.

'I didn't tell Colette I'd written the song,' Shannon continued. 'She loved it. But you'll never guess what she said to me?'

He paused if only to show it wasn't a rhetorical question.

'She asked you which artist's song it was?' O'Carroll guessed.

'She asked you to play it again,' McCusker suggested.

'She asked me to play it again,' Ryan replied, and looking like he was about to fall off his chair in shock at McCusker's spot on guess. 'I played it again and at the end of the second performance, you'll never guess what she said.'

'She asked you to play it again?' O'Carroll said flatly, clearly bored with this game now.

Ryan wagged his right forefinger frantically in a "no" gesture and then gushed, 'She said she knew it was my song. I asked her how she knew, and she said she knew because she had never witnessed me being so nervous performing a song before. She also said she recognised some of the phrases in the song as being the way I would say things.'

'Wow,' was all McCusker could think of to say.

'I was very chuffed because right from the get-go, I'd always thought when we were considering covers if there was some of the writer invested in the song it was always an easier song for me to sing. So, I decided I wouldn't ever write anything where the words didn't mean anything to me. I figured if they didn't mean anything to me, then how on earth was the head who was going to sing it, be able to successfully convey some meaning.'

'So, what did you do with your songs? O'Carroll asked.

'There was a man in London, Arlon Dean, he was an ex-showband head who was doing well in the song publishing world over in London Town. I knew him because over the years he had pitched songs to me for The Causways. I rang him up and asked if I could come and see him and he said it was a long way for me to come when we could just as easily discuss it on the phone. I could tell he really didn't want to take the meeting, but I pushed, and he agreed. So, I nipped over the following morning with my guitar, took a taxi straight in to see him, didn't bother him with a preamble just took out my guitar and played him my three songs. He was shocked. Said he never knew I even wrote songs, let alone how brilliant they were. But he did say there was a problem.'

'A problem?' O'Carroll repeated.

'Yes, a problem. A big problem. The publisher said I was the problem. I was quite well known as a showband head and so if he, and he said he wished me no disrespect here, but if he sent the songs to some of his contacts then because of my name and the fact I was a showband head, they most likely wouldn't even listen to my songs. I prepared to pack up my guitar and make my way back to Kerr Street with my tail between my legs. As I was thanking him for taking the meeting and rose to go, he said, "Where are you going? Sit back down there. I have an idea to put to you."'

McCusker felt O'Carroll was going to punch the air.

'He said, "Here's what we'll do. We'll give you a new name, a new back story and I'll send out these songs as songs from my new discovery, but you must make a pact with me agreeing you will never ever tell anyone you have written these songs." He asked me if anyone else had heard them. I told him the only person I have played one of them to was my wife, Colette. I added it had been her response which had given me the confidence to contact him. He asked me if I had any suggestions for my pen name. I told him my original name was Lenny McGuire.'

'Lenny McGuire?' O'Carroll repeated in slight disdain. McCusker did not believe she knew she was doing so, 'You mean Ryan Shannon is not your real name?'

'Stage name-a-rama, I'm afraid. I'll trouble you to never tell a living soul. Anyway, the publisher thought we should change McGuire to Davies. He didn't like Lenny either, but he had a friend whose daughter had a King Edward terrier she was crazy about and she was allowed to choose her dog's name and for some reason or other, she picked Digby.'

'Digby Davies,' O'Carroll said, 'yes, I have to admit Digby Davies does have a certain ring to it.'

'Let me show you through to the trophy room,' Ryan Shannon a.k.a. Lenny McGuire a.k.a. Digby Davies, said as he stood up and led them out of his plush lounge into his wood panelled study, complete with rows of books and pictures and numerous gold, silver, platinum and multi-platinum discs for artists as varied as Cliff, Rod, Val, Ellie, Adele, Cher, Daniel and more stars of the American Country scene. The common denominator of all of the award discs, no matter who received star billing, was the name Digby Davies in the sacred space reserved only for the writer and composer of the song.'

'Goodness I bet the original publisher Colette persuaded you to take your songs to, must be the happiest man in London now?' McCusker said, as he moved from disc to disc. He'd managed to count to over 20 million sales before he gave up counting. He reckoned there was at least the same again.

'Well, not really,' Ryan replied, somewhat sheepishly.

'Define not really?' McCusker asked, if only to seek full clarification.

'Here's the thing, I put it all down to lawyer-a-rama?'

'As in it wasn't one hundred percent coolio?' O'Carroll suggested, quoting one of Shannon's frequently used words, back at him.

'Ah, no, you wouldn't, you couldn't say it was coolio,' the singer–song-writer continued.

'As in…' O'Carroll pushed.

'Here's what happened: the lawyers were making a meal out of the contracts, dragging it out for ages while their invoice metre was still expensively ticking away. The publisher in good faith had sent out the first three songs, plus another three tunes I had written in the meantime. Thanks to the roll I was now on due to the confidence I had gained by having an outlet for my work, the songs really started to flow through me. It was like they were all just up there waiting,' Shannon said, as he paused to point to the heavens, 'and I was the one being allowed to catch them. I still, have music running through my head all the time. The publisher felt the second batch were better than the first.'

'But?' McCusker asked, because he knew there was a big but coming.

'The first cover was about to be released,' Ryan offered, as he pointed to a Rod Golden disc.

McCusker had to move in closely to read out loud, 'published by Digby Music. Is this your own music publishing company?'

'Ah, yes,' Ryan admitted sheepishly.

'What happened to the original publisher?' O'Carroll asked.

'Well, their lawyers and my lawyer, one recommended by your old friend, the recently departed Thomas Barry, couldn't agree on some of the small print on the contract. My lawyer felt I was being taken advantage of. The Royalty percentage was low and there was no advance because I was a new writer. My lawyer's main point, and I believed it was a very fair one, was, as the first cover was already in the bag, as it were, added to which the cover was by an established artist, so the publisher's earnings were already guaranteed, therefore no investment was needed…'

'But it was by the publisher's endeavours you'd already secured the first cover?' McCusker suggested.

'Yes, very valid point of course,' Ryan conceded, 'but my lawyer's take on it, was that it was the song gained the cover and not the publisher.'

McCusker and O'Carroll in sync with each other mouthed a silent "O" with their lips.

'Yes, I hear you…disgrace-a-rama, but Thomas's point was you don't pay for a dog and do the barking yourself.'

'So, Thomas was fully in the picture at this point?' McCusker asked.

'Oh yes, sorry I forgot to mention an important part. During the negotiations which were taking so long, the invoices were mounting and needed paying. I put forward the notion I should just sign the best deal they'd offer and get on with it. The lawyer suggested I set up my own company. I realised, of course, setting up my own company was going to initially cost me a lot of money. Thomas said for a small stake, he would finance the deal.'

'Oh-kay,' McCusker said, sounding a lot happier than he had been a few minutes ago. He accepted his mood elevation might have had something to do with a hint of a motive appearing in the Thomas Barry case.

'So the deal we all agreed on was,' Ryan continued, sounding like, now he'd broached this stage he wanted to get beyond it as soon as humanly possible, if only so they could all get back to viewing all the vanity items in his trophy room, 'Thomas Barry would become a minority stakeholder in Digby Music. He would finance the project, oversee it and be an advisor and consultant and receive 10% of the income for his trouble. The original publisher, Arlon Dean, for his efforts and energy would now become a no-risk collector of all Digby Music's publishing royalties worldwide. For providing this service Arlon would keep 10% of the income he collected. This all left me with 80% of my publishing royalties rather than the 60% offered in the original deal. So, everyone was happy.'

'And Thomas Barry, thanks to the efforts of a lawyer he had recommended, became your business partner.' McCusker said.

Just as they were leaving, Ryan was in the process of closing the front door after them when he opened it again. McCusker and O'Carroll turned back towards him.

After a few moments of silence, McCusker asked, 'Did you just remember something else you wanted to tell us?'

'Agh, no, not really,' Ryan started, still sounding unsure if he wanted to say anything or not. 'It's just about Isabella...'

'Yes?' McCusker offered in what he hoped would be a prompt.

'Well, I just wanted to ask, how is she doing?'

'Are youse not still in touch?' O'Carroll asked, sounding somewhat surprised.

'Ah, sadly no, head, we kinda fell out of touch,' he admitted in a whisper, 'but I imagine she'll be in a bad state over this. I know they'd been through a lot and all, but I always felt she never really got over Thomas. I always remember…'

McCusker could see the showband singer was on the verge of losing his nerve. He offered, 'It could be important.'

'Well, I hope I'm not being insensitive,' Ryan started back up again, appearing to look to O'Carroll for approval.

She offered him a quick smile and a wee nod of her head.

'Well, what I'm trying to work up the courage to say is the night Isabella and I first got together, in this very house, in fact, she you know…God, why is this so hard to admit? But she, ah, she, well when we made love for the first time, it felt like not so much she was getting to know me, but more she was exercising the demons of her previous lover.'

'Who happened to be Thomas?' O'Carroll offered in a quiet voice.

'Who happened to be Thomas' Ryan agreed. 'Yeah, it was like she was saying goodbye to her first love more than she was saying hello to me. Although she was willing, and as I said earlier, instigated the proceedings, at the same time, she was totally devastated. So, I still worry for her…about her.'

'And youse are no longer in touch?' McCusker repeated.

'Heck no, cold shoulder-a-rama,' he admitted.

'Well, all things considered,' McCusker offered, in an attempt to say something, but admit nothing, 'she seems to be doing okay.'

'My main worry is Isabella,' Shannon offered, 'Well she always gave me the impression no matter the strife between them, deep down she felt someday, somehow, they'd get back together again. I know we all have those regrets over losing our first pure love, but now, for the first time since the night Thomas picked up her glove, she is going to go to sleep tonight knowing they, she, will most definitely, will never be able to re-capture what she coveted most.'

Chapter Twenty-Two

The rest of the day was a wash-out for McCusker, O'Carroll, and, consequently, Superintendent Ivan Valley.

They tried, unsuccessfully, it must be said, to make contact with Michael McKnight, Thomas Barry's solicitor; The Buckley Bros; both together and separately, and Colette Scott.

Anthony Robertson had been unsuccessful in his attempts to reach Coleraine Student Hospital. He was caught in the golf traffic and was running two hours late. Valley had ensured the Hospital was going to give him comfortable accommodation for the night so he could start the autopsy first thing in the morning.

Rory McIlroy, sadly it has to be said, failed to make the cut at the 148th British Open, and although he played a magnificent round, nay even a round of pure genius golfing, in adverse weather conditions, he failed to make the cut, with what turned out to be the second best round of the weekend. He was just three strokes off the course record of 61, which he had set as a sixteen-year-old in 2005. But in the end, the reality was he had failed to make the cut for the Saturday and Sunday's play by a single stroke. He'd certainly come out of the weekend, although personally scarred, as a hero who had resisted the easy way out after Thursday's national disaster round by rising to the challenge and fighting tooth and nail the whole way around the course.

Usually on the golf course, the golfers get a decent round of applause when they are introduced on the first tee, and then to varying degrees again when they hit a great shot, or hole a lengthy putt, or when they reach the final green of the final hole. But Rory McIlroy was applauded and cheered and worshiped every single step of the 7,357-yard course. Then, at 7.00 with McCusker and O'Carroll on the 18th green, his campaign finally and gallantly came to an end when he missed the cut by a measly single shot. When it would have been much easier to run away with his tail between his legs, he honoured all his media duties and owned up and took it, whatever was dished out at him, smack bang on the middle of his chin.

For all of his pain he departed The Royal Golf Club, Portrush and Northern Ireland a far better, humbler man, knowing how much the Irish fans loved him but more importantly, how much he loved the Irish fans.

There was a serene still which fell over the golf club, the town and even Northern Ireland on the Friday evening. Everyone was in shock, total shock and hadn't a clue as to how they should react.

Even DI Lily O'Carroll, while not feeling part of the sombre mood, was aware it existed in others, and she didn't do her usual ribbing of her partner.

It didn't stop her carrying on her dating auditions for Mr Right as per usual.

A little later, she and McCusker were sipping their pints of Guinness at Superintendent Ivan Valley's table in the clubhouse when this Brad Pitt lookalike walked towards them.

'Oh My God it's only Albert Thingamabob,' O'Carroll gushed, 'I know he's not Rory McIlroy…but he'll do me. Mind you behave yourself now, McCusker.'

After introductions, McCusker headed off to get a drink for Albert McQuilkery for McQuilkery was his name and he was from Portballintrae. As McCusker was waiting at the bar, and there was quite a wait, he looked over at the table to O'Carroll. He'd never ever witnessed her on an actual date before, although he had heard chapter and verse about quite a few of them. For all her gusto and energy in finding a romantic partner, when it came down to it, she was very ladylike, gentle even. She was warm, naturally beautiful, funny, she held up her own side of the table and Albert McQuilkery, for McQuilkery was his name and he was from Portballintrae, seemed to be really enjoying her company. McCusker mentally chastised himself for the "McQuilkery is his name and he was from Portballintrae," mental tangent, for fear if they worked out then it might become a habitual nickname, which could only serve to get him in trouble with her.

'So, Albert has just told me he works as a filmmaker,' O'Carroll started when they'd all settled back in again.

'How's work in the film world going for you?' McCusker asked.

'Great, we're very busy,' Albert replied, in a strong country drawl, in contrast to Valley's town tones.

'Would we know any of your work?' O'Carroll asked, genuinely enthused.

'Well, yes, or at least I hope so. We make the short clips featuring the big film companies' logos, you know, usually some kind of animation, or footage into animation. They always appear on the screen just before the credits at the start of a film.'

'Like the boy jumping off the end of the pier and then he freezes mid-jump into a drawing of the frozen frame?' McCusker asked, because it was one he thought was first class. He noted and admired Albert's Ulster pronunciation of the word "film." He personally had taken to use the word "movie" to negate all the "pardons" he'd been hit with when he'd unconsciously offered "filum."

'Yes, yes, just like the one you describe but sadly the Lakeshore Entertainment clip is not one of ours?' Albert admitted.

'Oh sorry,' O'Carroll said on both their behalf.

'No, perfectly okay,' Albert smiled, revealing his perfect teeth, the same perfect teeth O'Carroll had already boasted about, 'but the Lakeshore Entertainment one really does happen to be a perfect example. Your colleague here has just proven film fans do pay attention.'

'But would there be a lot of people wanting you to make these vanity clips for them?' McCusker asked, sounding more and more like a worried father checking out his daughter's chosen one's prospects. Right on cue, O'Carroll squirmed in her seat.

'Well, the greatest number of companies we've ever had involved in one film would have been nine.'

'Nine!' McCusker spat in disbelief.

'Yes, he did say nine,' O'Carroll chipped in, proudly.

'Yes, nine,' Albert confirmed.

'Ok-ay, so I see how you'd be kept busy,' McCusker said sheepishly.

After a bit more bantering and chatting on a safer topic, food, Albert excused himself and nipped outside for a ciggy.

After he was out of earshot, O'Carroll said, 'Don't you just love it, Albert is so fit, so health conscious, so handsome, exercises daily, so well groomed, yet wild enough not to be scared of contaminating his body with nicotine.'

McCusker raised his eyebrows, knowing if the situation was reversed, she would do the same. On second thoughts, if he, McCusker, had any such thoughts on any woman who wasn't her sister, O'Carroll would have his guts for a suspender belt she'd wear for Albert Thingamabobby, for this was his name, and he *was* from Portballintrae. This was as far as he got with his thought.

'You know, he reminds me a lot of my first husband,' she said, as she spied Albert walking back over to their table.

'Shit, Lily, you never told me you'd even been married!' McCusker barked, and then hoped Valley on the other side of the table hadn't heard him. He needn't have worried, as the idle chatter in the room was now so loud McCusker was convinced it was turning his Guinness sour.

'Only because I'm not…well, at least not yet…' she confessed, sidling up close to Albert as he sat down. She offered McCusker a quick wink.

Well, it was more a quick wink of her eye and then subtly nodding her head in a "time for you to get lost" direction.

McCusker was subtle. He had the good manners to wait all of nine seconds before he excused himself to go and have a word with Superintendent Valley.

About twenty minutes later, O'Carroll left Albert and walked over to McCusker. She apologised to Valley for the interruption and then asked McCusker could she check something with him.

'When someone says Ay-ie, or it might even have been Ayie as in an "I" with an "e" on the end,' she asked, when they were out of everyone's earshot, 'what exactly does Ay-ie mean?'

'It's the Ulster way of saying yes,' McCusker replied, having to lean close to her ear so he was not actually shouting at her, to be heard.

'Oh, brilliant,' she gushed equally close to his ear, 'it also means I'm going out on a date tonight. Don't wait up for me,' she said as a goodbye and she skipped back over to Albert.

When McCusker caught Albert's eye, he had a suspicion he was the kind of chap who might say, "Ayie," but he would then add a "get your coat, you've pulled," onto the end of it.

McCusker tried to project a "you mess with my friend, you'll have me to answer to" glare to Albert McQuilkery, for McQuilkery was his name and he was from Portballintrae. McCusker wasn't one hundred percent sure he carried the look off successfully, just as sure as he knew he'd broken his promise to himself to stop taking the piss out of Albert McThingamabobby's name.

Chapter Twenty-Three

Valley was talking on his mobile. McCusker heard him say, 'You can tell him yourself, he's here, I'll put you straight on to him,' Valley said, as he passed the phone over to McCusker, 'It's DS Melodee Johnson, working away.'

'Sorry, Mr…' she paused, 'I don't really know how to address you as you're not officially PSNI…'

'Just call me McCusker, as you probably heard from DI O'Carroll, everyone else does.'

'Okay, right, sound, let me just get my head around calling you by your family name,' she started and stopped and continued, 'so, McCusker, I was just ringing in to the Super to tell him I've spent a few hours reviewing the CCTV footage of the streets around the Pilgrim's Steps. My eyes are going square, so I'm on a break. I just rang in to let the Super know what I was doing, and he said tell him yourself…'

'Right, thanks, Detective Sergeant…'

'Melodee will do, or Johnson if you think Melodee is too personal.'

'Okay, DS Melodee Johnson,' McCusker started, fearing her first name was too personal but just calling her by her last name, even though it was his preference, seemed a bit too laddish to him, 'good work. Tell me, do you have any footage of over the wall above the Pilgrim's Steps?'

'Sorry, no,' she admitted, 'I got quite excited though. I found a camera on top of the restaurant complex which looks straight down there but there were Seagull dropping all over the camera lens.'

He told her the Lifeboat House camera footage would be available in the morning as well.

'Are you not joining the Super and the gang here? They seem to be in full swing.'

'Agh nagh, there's nothing to celebrate. I find it all so sad, such a let-down. I feel so empty,' she said, before saying her goodbyes.

McCusker gave the phone back to the Super and bid him goodnight and left the Clubhouse and headed towards the other strand, the one on Barry's side.

By the time McCusker reached the beach, quite a few were gathering to view the sundown. The scene was very dramatic, a combination of blue and black. A few dozen people appeared frozen lifeless, just like a draper's shop supply of mannequins had been plonked down on the water's edge of the beach. They were all looking out to sea in the hope of catching the last rites of the sunset. They all looked like they'd been frozen to the spot, in order to witness the end of the earth. And then just as the fading rays of the sun melted away, they all sprang into life again in order to speed from the beach before the cold of dusk set in. As the humans departed the beach, the seagulls, taking off from amongst the driftwood, seaweed and rubbish, all flew off into the west.

McCusker outwaited them all while listening to the sound of Barry's various amusements in the background.

To be honest, McCusker had quite expected the town to be heaving. This was not the case. The streets were relatively empty. All the people who were visiting for the golf were all still up at The Royal Gold Club trapped by the no-pass out rule, the local businesspeople were up in arms about. "How can we make money if none of these people are allowed to come out and do a wee bit of shopping?"

Anyway, McCusker did a wee bit of window shopping himself and made his way to Barry's.

Barry's Amusements Arcade is the most exciting place in Northern Ireland.

Or so McCusker had once thought.

It was empty!

It wasn't actually empty, as in absolutely devoid of people. There were (literally) a few people. McCusker had been visiting Barry's since the mid-60s, and he had never seen so few people in there in his life. He couldn't believe it.

Barry's might have been nearly empty but McCusker could still catch the sniffs of their trademark, hypnotic melange of smells. This unique blend of aromas was so intoxicating and seemed directly in proportion to kids' feel-good factor, leading McCusker to wonder if Barry's had found a way of piping the effective scents into the hallowed arcade of amusements.

'Where is everyone?' McCusker asked the man in the information booth. Well, McCusker thought to himself, "That's what information booths are for, aren't they?"

'I've worked here for over eleven years, and I've never seen it this empty,' he replied.

'But what about the golf influx?'

'They're all stuck up at The Royal and the ones coming out are used to Disney World and the likes of Barry's isn't really high on their bucket list.'

McCusker offered his condolences and said hopefully it would be better over the weekend. The man in the information booth said he hoped so but doubted it.

The detective walked further along the beach in the direction of the harbour, all the time shocked by the lack of people, while at the same time checking out all the stuff, which hadn't been there before the Open face-lift. He came across the town's new super-duper Ferris wheel. It was merrily spinning away. On closer examination, McCusker realised it was devoid of people, aka…empty.

There were absolutely no people in the big wheel's buckets—or whatever it was they called those pods humans sat in. McCusker wondered if a person would have a good view of the Pilgrim's Steps from the peak of the big wheel. He was about to try it out until he noticed the wheel was circulating in the wrong direction to afford a view of the harbour area.

A man eating a 99-infused ice-cream cone saw McCusker staring up at the wheel in amazement.

'Why do you think they have it spinning with no people in it?' he asked.

'As an advertisement to potential customers,' McCusker offered hopefully.

'Nope,' he replied, 'if you go further down to the green there, you'll see the BBC TV One Show are broadcasting on location tonight and so if they have the wheel spinning in the background then people out there in TV land will think Portrush is thriving and want to visit here. It's all part of a cover-up.'

Oh, McCusker did love a good conspiracy theory. He wandered on, chatting to people as he made his way over to the crowd gathered for the BBC TV One Show recording. People are so friendly and easy to talk to in Portrush. McCusker eavesdropped on one of the judges from Strictly Come Dancing going on about Ballroom Dancing in Ulster in the 1960s. It was very big, he suggested. McCusker wondered if Ryan Shannon was watching the broadcast live on TV. In fact, if the showband singer and secret songwriter had wanted to, he could have leaned out his window and really experienced the same scene, but live. McCusker felt the Strictly geezer might just have got the wrong end of the stick. From the detective's local knowledge, what had happened was people used to dance in ballrooms in Ulster in the 1960s, but he knew it was not Ballroom Dancing they were attempting. Well, at least not Ballroom Dancing as it has come to be known today. The main step was not the quickstep, nor even the foxtrot, but more like the shimmy step, where males would try to get closer to the girl and risk all by asking, "Do you come here often?" If you did manage to get beyond the first stage, there were several even more difficult stages to succeed at before you reached the final level and question: "Will you save the last dance for me?" Of course, if your first-choice lady answered, 'yes' or any variation thereof, it meant you had won not only the last dance of the evening but also an unspoken promise of walking her home and maybe even scoring a kiss. If she replied to the negative, and you'd been clever enough to plan for such an eventuality, then you've have enough time to invite your *other* favourite girl for the last dance, and maybe even another one after her if you were in dire straits.

McCusker figured this was what Ryan Shannon would have told them, if only they'd bothered to interview him, and he would have known because, unlike the Strictly cheeky chappie, he had been there and would have had *trophies* of his own to prove it. Of course, McCusker accepted he was thinking of different kinds of trophies if the legends were correct. He wondered if maybe Ryan Shannon, directly or indirectly, connected Thomas Barry to some of these legends. Could the AGA (After Gig Activity) have been what had ended up, either directly or indirectly, being responsible for landing McCusker's former friend in trouble, trouble of the worst possible kind?

The TV show had managed some way or other to drum up a bit of a live audience, maybe as many as 30 or so people. But, McCusker figured, thirty, forty at the very max, was the sum total of the people out on the streets of Portrush on this evening.

McCusker walked back towards his own house. He detoured back down towards the Arcadia and wandered around the back of the TV compound and back into Portrush, coming in by Causeway Street. He stopped at a mobile Chippie.

'How's business?' McCusker asked after he placed his order.

'You're my first customer in over two hours,' the keen young man said as he continuously rubbed his hands and hopped from foot to foot to get some heat back in them. 'Since Rory finished, it's like all life, as we know it, on the planet has ended. Everyone has gone indoors. There is just such an air of sadness around Portrush tonight. Everyone is so depressed about the situation they've all taken to their beds early. I bet you any money you like during March in 2020, we will see an almighty explosion in the local birth-rate.'

Chapter Twenty-Four

Saturday 20th July 2019

As on the previous morning, O'Carroll was already up and preparing breakfast when McCusker sauntered downstairs. As on the previous day, she was mesmerised by the view out of McCusker's front window, which was at the back of the house.

'Grace is going to want to move here when she sees this?' O'Carroll offered by way of a good morning.

'How did last night go?' McCusker asked.

'He didn't say he loved me,' O'Carroll replied, but upbeat.

'Realistically speaking,' McCusker started off slowly, scared his partner might still be upset, 'wasn't it just a wee bit too early to be talking about love?'

'No, not too early…it wasn't, at all, particularly when you consider the bleedin' things he explained he wanted to do to me,' she replied, and burst into a genuine fit of laughter.

McCusker had learnt something else about his partner. No matter how keen she was to find a romantic mate, she was just not prepared to break her principles in order to land the deal.

'Do you mind if we invite my old mate, Lefty Kelly, around for breakfast? McCusker asked, quickly changing subjects.

'Lefty as in the L of BLT in the BLT gang?'

'The very same.'

'Why of course,' she replied.

'No…I mean yes, as in good,' McCusker started, seemingly unsure, 'it's just…well, he stood me breakfast yesterday, and it's my turn if you see what I mean.'

'No problem,' she said, 'I made us loads.'

Just then, there was a knock on McCusker's front door.

'Aye, there's Lefty now,' McCusker said, crunching his lips to the left and raising his eyebrows.

'McCusker!' she hissed as he rushed for the door, just about avoiding the firing line of her dishcloth.

'So, you'll be Grace then,' Lefty offered, leading with his right hand, 'you're exactly as he described you.'

Lefty was in his usual uniform. On this occasion, his corduroy trousers were brown, his shirt was blue, his tie was a loud red, and his sleeveless jumper was bottle green

'No, I'm Lily, Grace's sister,'

'Jez…McCusker. Sisters, and beautiful ones as well, you auld dog, what's going on here, man?'

'No, no, Lefty, as usual, you've got the wrong end of the stick,' McCusker said, as he noticed Lefty was showing no signs of giving O'Carroll her hand back anytime soon. 'This is Detective Inspector Lily O'Carroll, my senior and Grace's sister.'

'Are you now?' Lefty letched, but in a harmless Terry Thomas kind of way, 'so you'd be the single one then?'

'Well, yes,' O'Carroll replied, looking like she was trying to reclaim her hand.

'Well now, Lily, maybe when your sister does arrive, you could nip around and see me, I'm only around the corner,' Lefty offered, upping the stakes somewhat. 'I could show you my BLT scrapbook?'

'So, you're Lefty Kelly, the BLT's wing man?'

'The very same, Lily. Happy to see my reputation precedes me,' he said, turning and offering McCusker a quick wink, and now grabbing her hand already trapped in his vice like grip, with both his hands.

'I'm sorry, Sir, I've always made a point of not dating wingmen,' O'Carroll replied equally sweetly, as she tugged her hand to freedom, 'I've always preferred the man who flies the plane as opposed to the navigator.'

'Put her down, man,' McCusker laughed. But Lefty had no need as O'Carroll speedily brushed pastboth of them, promising their breakfast would be ready in fifteen minutes.

'Bewitching McCusker,' Lefty started back up again in a whisper, 'of course you realise that's only round one.'

'Lefty, my old mate, I think you'll find what you've just encountered there was a first-round knock-out.'

They both spent a few moments in quietness, looking out over the dramatic, ever-changing landscape in front of them. Both seemed lost in their thoughts.

'Brendy, I always meant to ask you, did you get on well with your father?' Before McCusker had a chance to answer, Lefty continued, 'I never hung out with my dad, you know, hung out with him as an equal. We would never do things together as friends might. I wanted to be his friend and hang out with him, but he always needed to retain the "I'm the father, so we do as I say" type of approach. It was like he was stating the upper ground was his, and he was going to continue to hold on to it. I felt we both missed out a lot by not hanging together. I wanted him to take me to see his movies. I wanted to take him to see my movies. I wanted to suggest books and music to him, and I wanted him to suggest books and music to me. I think I got on better with your dad. I remember talking to him a lot about music and about Man United. I think those memories are where this line of thought came from, you know, when I knew I was coming around here to see you and I started to think of your father and how nice he was to me.'

McCusker smiled warmly at the memory.

'My dad was great with his hands,' McCusker said, repeating a memory which for some reason or other had just flashed into his mind. 'I remember when I was a kid, he worked out how to put a boat with full sails in a bottle.'

'I mean, don't get me wrong,' Lefty continued, appearing to have realised where he had taken McCusker, 'my dad was also a good man, a great man even. I just wanted to show him I was also a good man. Really, when it gets down to it, I suppose, when you really got down to it, we just had nothing in common. All of this came to me this morning for the first time in my life when I thought of your dad. I think my dad was always disappointed I wasn't in his image, whereas my take on it would have been we could have been better friends because of our very diverse interests.'

'What makes you think he was disappointed?'

Lefty thought about it for nearly a minute, a minute of pure silence, well pure silence apart from the sound of the sea when the sound of the sea only enhanced the sound of silence.

'I suppose my father and I were always going to be different because he had served in the army and fought in WWII and I hadn't.'

O'Carroll did them proud on a breakfast, veering sharply away towards the healthy, while focusing on porridge, fruit and breakfast breads she'd purchased at the late-night supermarket, which she'd come across after her disastrous date the previous evening. The supermarket was directly opposite the Town Hall and created a triangle with Barry's amusements arcade; Kerr Street—literally by the seaside- and Eglington Street—the link to the town centre. It had been the Town Hall which had first attracted her attention. What, with its witch's hat turrets, the magnificent building was Scottish Baronial by way of Disney World. She had detoured slightly to view it closely, although its grandness was better viewed from afar. She noted from the plaque, it was built in 1870, restored in 2005, and originally designed by Sir Charles Lanyon who had also designed The Customs House in Belfast, the current home of the O'Carroll's PSNI. O'Carroll would have only made this connection due to McCusker's love and knowledge of buildings and their history

'So, have you talked to Isabella Scott yet?' Lefty asked.

'Yep, I've met her twice.'

'What did you think of her?' Lefty said through a smile.

'You mean her look?'

Lefty nodded to the positive.

'Well I have to say, at first I didn't recognise her.'

'Don't pull my leg.'

'Really, I mean, more from the standpoint of how I was expecting her to have aged, but I was shocked by how little she had actually changed, if at all. I mean really, she took me right back to the night we all met.'

'Do you see her often, *Mr* Kelly?' O'Carroll asked, as McCusker chalked O'Carroll 2 to nil up.

Lefty admitted he saw Isabella now and again. He thought she was driven, strong-spirited, very strong-spirited, ambitious and self-confident.

'I'm not so sure she's handling Mister Barry's passing as well as she's letting on,' McCusker suggested.

'I mean, from what McCusker tells me about the early days, if ever there was a fairy tale romance going to work, it should have been the one between Thomas and Isabella?' O'Carroll offered.

'I always say no matter what dust may be being kicked up by others on the outside, there are always only two people in a marriage,' Lefty offered. 'If you are not one of these two people, then whenever you look in and observe these two people, well, you just never know. I mean it's very easy to assume. You think the wife looks stunning, as was always the case with Isabella. Mister Barry was no slouch himself. They looked good together. They acted as though they were good together. So, judging from their individual score cards, they should have clicked together in the bedroom. But we make all these assumptions only because we don't really know them. Brendy here can tell you we all felt, after the day they first met briefly on the street here in the Port, Mister Barry was convinced if he couldn't find Isabella again, his life would well and truly be over.'

McCusker nodded to confirm he was of the same opinion.

'So yes, Isabella looked like she was the most perfect physical specimen any of the three of us had seen who wasn't on the cinema screen at the time. Mister Barry, for his part, was always clean and smelt good. I've found from my female company this is always a big plus from their side.'

O'Carroll nodded to confirm she was of the same opinion.

'So, on paper, we all thought they were both keepers for each other. But, and it's a big but, we don't really know what goes on between two people. We don't know how unresponsive she might be, or maybe, just maybe, might not have been. We don't know if Mister Barry was someone who scored all his kicks from chasing and winning, and maybe, having won, wasn't as interested anymore. Maybe he'd hurt her or let her down or…well any one of a thousand other things preventing them from being happy together. So, it's no use for an outsider, even a family member, saying things like, "I don't know why they can't work it out." Or maybe even something like, "All the rest of us just had to learn to get on with it," or words to the same effect. Or, "No one ever said it was going to be a bed of roses." There are two things I would like to say to such people. The first one is: it's very easy to make such statements, when in fact it's not their lives. And the second thing is: I've always thought, who really wants to get their arses scratched on a bed of roses anyway.'

'I think you'll find we only have one,' O'Carroll politely interjected.

'Sorry?' Lefty said, responding as if it was O'Carroll who'd interjected a rude word.

'I think you'll find we each only have one?' O'Carroll replied. 'It should be singular, not plural.'

'Not if there are two of you in bed at the same time,' Lefty replied, with all the enthusiasm of someone who was about to punch the air.

McCusker seemed to give Lefty Kelly a wee nod of encouragement with this one as he mentally chalked it as 2 to 1 to O'Carroll.

'But the thing about this love lark most men don't realise is,' Lefty started back up again. If anything, McCusker knew once Lefty started off on his Mastermind specialist subject he wouldn't stop until he'd said his piece, 'it's not so much about the package as it is about the mystery. Looks really aren't what it's all about.'

'Amen,' O'Carroll chipped in. McCusker didn't know if she was joking or serious, but she seemed to have served to encourage Lefty onwards. Kennedy wondered if Love had really been Lefty's specialist Mastermind subject, how far would he have reached.

'On top of which, if a woman is "beautiful" in the perfect model sense, it's all out there as in leaving nothing to the imagination—as in lacking in mystery. A woman needs to realise when she puts it all out there, when they start to chase the butterfly, to lie on the bed of roses as it were, then the man is already up to step five of a seven-step dance. This, of course, can also mean it's (sometimes) very unrewarding for the women, if you get my drift.'

'We get you, Lefty, we got you,' McCusker said, hoping he was drawing a line under another of Lefty's lectures.

'Lefty, tell me this,' McCusker started back up again, 'what were you doing on Wednesday evening, say from eleven o'clock until three o'clock on Thursday morning?'

'So, you saved your most important question for our third meeting,' Lefty said as McCusker wondered for the first time if Isabella Scott and Lefty Kelly were going to be each other's alibi. 'Well, here's the thing, I was in the Adelphi Hotel for dinner.'

'With anyone I know?' McCusker asked.

'Solo,' Lefty offered. 'Always solo on Wednesdays.'

'Credit card receipts?'

'Cash.'

'Do you go in there regularly, Lefty?'

'No, hadn't been there in ages, but, this time of the year, the Harbour Bar is always packed. On top of which, their portions are too big.'

'Tell me this, Lefty, what time did you leave the Adelphi?'

'About 9.30.'

'And then where did you go?'

'I'd a wee walk around the town to walk my supper off.'

'Okay, then what happened?

'Well, I kept on walking until I reached Portstewart, I'd an ice-cream in Morelli's and then walked back.'

'Okay, Lefty, I've started to feel like I'm becoming a dentist. Then what did you do?'

'I walked back, reached my house about 11.00. I played Crosby, Stills & Nash; *Suite: Judy Blue Eyes*, on repeat play, washed my teeth. Do you want to know what brand of toothpaste I use?'

'No, won't be necessary, I'll assume you're still on the strawberry flavoured one.'

'Then I went to bed. It would have been around midnight. I read for an hour and fell asleep. I can tell you what I was reading if you want.'

'Not necessary, Lefty,' McCusker said through a smile, 'so in other words, no one saw you from teatime Wednesday until breakfast time on Thursday morning.'

'Aye, that would be the height of it,' Lefty confirmed.

'Any phone calls. In or out?' McCusker pushed, grasping at straws.

'Nope, sorry, can't oblige with any telephonic confirmations.'

'So, you don't really have an alibi?'

'I don't have one, Brendy, and nor do I need one.'

* * *

'Your friend didn't look like a communist to me,' O'Carroll said, after all remaining of Lefty was his Corpus Natural scent and his empty dishes.

'Sorry?' McCusker asked, not understanding his partner.

'Is his nickname Lefty because he's inclined to the left politically?'

'No, he's not,' McCusker replied, but didn't elaborate.

'Yeah, he didn't seem to be biased to the left, so why the nickname?'

McCusker laughed but busied himself helping her to clear and put the dishes in the dishwasher.

'Mind your eyebrows,' he said as they started to trip over each other in their endeavours. He was still chuckling away (he thought) to himself.

'Come on, McCusker, what is it? Why are you laughing?'

'Well, he, Lefty, is not even left-handed naturally, he's totally right-handed except for one sole, self-gratifying chore, where he's a self-confessed, left-hander, and so the name stuck.'

McCusker could see the wheels within wheels working in O'Carroll's mind, until, eventually, right on cue, the penny dropped.

'Augh, McCusker, how could you? How could you? I'll never ever be able to get that view of him out of my mind now. Augh, I want to go and be sick!'

'Oh, don't you dare be sick in my house today,' McCusker pleaded, 'Grace will be here mid-morning.'

'I respect your priorities, McCusker,' she offered warmly, signalling her moment had passed. 'I really do.'

They both finished their work in silence, he laughing to himself now and then, and then she had to turn to face the magic view of the beach to hide the fact she was giggling as well.

* * *

'Your friend looks unhappy,' O'Carroll offered, as they got in her car while watching Lefty saunter slowly up the road towards them. He was on his way back from the nostril-enticing Tom Tom's Bakery.

'He always looks unhappy,' McCusker replied, as he fastened his seatbelt.

'Is he genuinely always unhappy?'

'The only time he's happy is when he's found something else to be unhappy about.'

'So conveniently, every day for him is a good one, one way or the other.

'Yep, every day for Lefty Kelly is a Golden Day.'

Chapter Twenty-Five

O'Carroll suggested they split up to try and make some progress. She suggested McCusker go and interview Colette Barry, nee Scott, while she would nip back down to The Lifeboat House to review their CCTV footage. In the meantime, DS Melodee Johnson was continuing to review the Harbour CCTV footage or, at least, the Harbour footage which hadn't been vandalised by seagulls.

'Did you ever notice that although there are always flocks of seagulls flying all over the town,' McCusker offered, ' you never ever see a dead one lying about the streets or on the beach. The UK Seagull population is just over a quarter of a million, Black Bill Gulls, and they're massive, the biggest in the world, yet you never see a dead one lying around on the streets, do you? What I want to know is where do all these fecking seagulls go to die?'

'You really do live in your own wee world, McCusker,' she replied, 'seagulls surely go out to sea to die?'

'Apparently not, they fly to Spain or Morocco in the colder months, so they may die there, or they just drop where they are, and other birds eat them.'

'Charming,' O'Carroll offered.

'No, just nature working away efficiently in the background.'

'Anyway, getting back to our morning's work,' she offered, 'Melodee and I thought Colette would most likely be more open with you if there isn't another strange woman with you. Just be careful and record your interview. When I'm done at the Lifeboat House, I'll meet you back at Ramore Head Station House.'

'And then we'll head over to Coleraine and see if we can get our clock back from them.'

'Sorry?'

'Maybe not,' McCusker agreed, 'At least not this time.'

'Okay,' she replied, sounding bemused, 'and just so I know for future reference, why exactly not this time?'

'I've been thinking about it and realised we couldn't get it on the top of your car, it would be just too big.'

'Aye, as I said, you're always happy in your own wee world, McCusker. My poor sister, this is all I have to say on the matter, my poor sister.'

* * *

McCusker smiled away to himself as he walked down past The Royal Golf Club again and out the Bushmills Road. He took comfort from the fact O'Carroll knew him well enough now to realise, and accept, all his wee tangents were necessary for him to be able to put his mind to the case properly. It was one of the things he'd missed when he'd been "promoted" to desk work in Ramore Head PSNI station in the year and a half before he'd retired. All his tangents had deserted him, and he'd missed them. Since he'd started to work with DI O'Carroll, there were always dozens of things running around in his head again. He wondered if it was a similar feeling to the one Ryan Shannon had enjoyed after he'd the procedure, or operation in old money, on his arm. Ryan had claimed he discovered all these songs, melodies, running around in his head afterwards. McCusker wondered if medication had been the gear change in Shannon's life. If that was in fact the case, he wondered where his own inspiration had come from. He certainly hadn't needed any medication. Then he realised probably what had happened was that he had enjoyed a spike of the best medication known to man and womankind: fresh air. The fresh air he'd been deprived of while being desk-bound in the PSNI headquarters on Ramore Head.

By this point McCusker had reached the town land in which contained Colette Barry's house, up on Ballymacrea Road in the rural part of Portrush.

As McCusker headed in the direction of Colette's address, he passed house after house. He could hear a few lawnmowers buzzing away in the distance like wasps trying to deal with the concept of glass windows. He breathed in the agreeable smell of freshly cut grass. All the houses looked so idyllic, so perfect, and on previous walks, he would have been tempted to wonder what kind of person and/or family would live in such a house. The difference was this time McCusker was going to find out.

Colette lived in a very comfortable, cosy, detached, period half-timbered, Normandy-style farmhouse, with a beautiful natural well-maintained garden. The property enjoyed stunning and dramatic views over The Royal Golf Course and onward to the Atlantic Ocean, the perfect setting for the finest painting Charles McAuley never painted. Colette's house was all very neat and tidy, so well attended to, you would have the impression the grass was manicured uniformly by someone using a pair of scissors. What with the sun shining, the light fluffy white clouds, the blue sky and the aqua ocean, to McCusker, it was more like a house and garden you would find in New England. The only thing missing was the white picket fence.

Colette was working away in her garden as McCusker walked down her drive. She was wearing blue baggy dungarees over a Glastonbury 1996 festival, long sleeve, t-shirt, with her blonde hair bunched up into an aged and battered, working man's tweed cap, possibly even her father's. Her outfit was completed with a pair of dirty trainers. She wore not a single spec of make-up and yet this woman's natural beauty shone through loud and clear.

She dropped a trowel from one hand, and a handful of weeds from the other and ran straight into McCusker's arms. Her predominant scents were a strong mint toothpaste and a heather-infused shampoo.

Her action took McCusker somewhat by surprise. Before her visible display of emotion, he wouldn't have claimed to have been in Colette's inner circle, nor she in his. If anything, back when Thomas Barry had started to date Isabella, , her younger sister, Colette would really have been too young to have come on the BLT's radar. Yet here she was still hugging away at him and clinging onto him as though he was some solid driftwood she'd happened upon while caught by treacherous currents out at the Skerries.

She started to sob, and suddenly McCusker got it. She wasn't pretending to welcome him as a long-lost friend. She was mourning the death of her ex-husband. McCusker felt her refusing to drop her ex-husband's name was a massive sign he should have picked up on before. Colette was suffering from the loss of Thomas Barry and perhaps felt their shared grief was the bond she now had in common with McCusker.

She and McCusker remained standing in her colourful garden in each other's arms, rocking backwards and forwards as time stood still.

And then the rain came.

McCusker could see it coming in over her shoulder, but he felt it would have been wrong to cease this moment before she was ready. They'd barely spoken a word since she'd run towards him. As he looked out over her shoulder to the sea and the moving horizon he remembered when he was younger, and the rain would be making its way across the ocean and inland to the Port, it was so vivid, frightening really. Sometimes it looked like they were being physically invaded by another country.

'Oh, here it comes,' she sang to the melody of the famous Them song, and she grabbed his hand, and they both ran in via her back door.

She kicked off her trainers on the backdoor mat and threw her cap skilfully onto a hook on the back of the door, thereby releasing her uniform, brilliant, straight, natural blonde hair.

'Oh, the poor golfers, the rain looks like it is down for the morning,' she continued, leading him into her delightful natural country cottage kitchen.

'Yeah, I see JB Holmes and Shane are top of the leader board,' McCusker replied, feeling comfortable on the safer once-removed ground. His nostrils were completely overwhelmed by the varying scents circling from numerous vases packed with multi-coloured flowers, but in a very pleasant way.

'And poor Rory,' she volunteered, when no other words were needed, or offered.

'And poor Rory,' McCusker repeated the words every native in Ireland was most likely repeating at that very moment.

McCusker grew distracted by a few wasps busy about their morning chores.

'Oh, leave them alone, and they will leave you alone,' she advised him.

'Have you had any breakfast yet?' she asked, 'Tom used to go on about how much you loved your breakfast.'

McCusker thought back to O'Carroll's healthier option less than an hour ago, 'Augh, you know, I've had a nibble, but I could do with a bite.'

'Okay, come and talk with me in the kitchen and we will see what I can rustle up for you.'

'This was your parents' house?' McCusker started.

'Yes, it was,' she replied, as she very methodically took out all the pots and pans she would need and lined up all the food she needed, 'I lived here all my life until I married Ryan and then I moved into the Kerr Street house. It was okay there, but to be honest, I never really felt at home. I will admit my discomfort had more to do with the house than with Ryan.'

'When Ryan and I split up I was figuring out what to do. At first, I was thinking of moving down to Belfast. I even toyed with London for a couple of weeks. I felt it would be good for me to just get the town out of my hair, get the sand away from between my toes for a while, if not forever.'

'Been there, bought the T-shirt,' McCusker offered.

'Of course, you have been through all of this yourself,' Colette said. For someone who'd spent all their life in Portrush, she had a very BBC Radio 4 voice, not so much posh as educated and totally in contrast to her sister's more Ulster sing-song style.

'Well, I still don't really know what happened to you and Ryan and your sister and Tom,' McCusker started, working on the theory one had to give in order to receive, continued to tell his whole story.

'Yeah, I knew most of your sorry tale,' Colette admitted as McCusker completed telling the Ode of Anna Stringer and Brendan McCusker. 'Even *I* could not believe you had taken up with Anna Stringer. We all thought she was a spinster, even when she was in kindergarten.'

'Oh-kay,' McCusker said, as he hoped she would be as forthright when she came to tell her own story.

'Did you know Isabella's friend Gilly Hutchinson, she was out with Isabella and Jane Murray the night Tom bumped into our Isabella…'

McCusker nodded he knew who she was talking about.

'Well, Gilly's older sister, Adele, had an eye out for you. She told us she once hinted to you that you should take her out.'

McCusker was taken aback at Colette's revelation. Adele was older than them all, maybe the same age as Lefty, but definitely older than the rest. On paper, he should have been interested in Adele Hutchinson, but he had no memory of them ever talking about dating.

'Adele said she thought you were nice, quiet, thoughtful, maybe thinking a wee bit too much for someone your age,' Colette said, 'she said she felt you had been scared off because people around town used to say about Emmy Mai and the older sister, "Yeah, Emmy Mai, but Adele (most definitely) will."'

This hit some chord in McCusker's memory banks and seemed to have at least a pinch of truth in it. He'd always worshipped Adele from afar, apart from one incident, but he would never have had the courage to ask her out.

'But surely enough about me,' McCusker said, as his full plate of food arrived.

'I suppose it's only fair,' Colette offered, 'we would not want the food to go cold when you were telling me all about Anna Stringer. But tell me this before I start, what's this I hear about the new woman in your life?'

'Ah, we'll get to Grace later,' McCusker said.

'I'll hold you to your promise, particularly if I am going to have to spill all my guts out to you.'

'Sounds fair.'

'Okay, Brendy,' she agreed, 'I will tell you all I can because I need you to find out what happened to Tom. I know some people are saying he was drinking and fell over the wall and drowned, or he intentionally drowned himself. One, Tom had been off the drink, apart from a little wine at dinner, since we were married. After we split, we were still friends, and he stayed off the drink. Because of what happened to his father, he was very careful about his health. He had check-ups regularly. He had his most recent one a month ago, and he was in perfect health. He was very ambitious, as you probably remember. He was being incredibly successful at his work. He really enjoyed his life. He had plans. Believe you me, he was not going to take his own life.'

Chapter Twenty-Six

Colette paused, grew very thoughtful, and when he asked if she was okay, she waved her hand furiously by her eyes trying to stem the tide of tears. She seemed to get a grip on it. She excused herself, claiming she wanted to make them both a fresh pot of tea but McCusker knew she was taking the time to compose herself again.

In the intervening period, McCusker finished off his delicious, hearty breakfast, cleaned his dishes and put them away.

She gave him a "I'm impressed nod" as she returned, and said, 'You can come back again. Now, where were we?'

'You were about to tell me about you and Ryan and Colette and Isabella and Thomas and—'

'And me and Thomas and Ryan and Isabella…' she started, 'Jez, we will be here all night. So…you were there, legend has it, the night my sister and her two friends Gilly Hutchinson and Jane Murray bumped into Lefty Kelly and Tom on the streets of Portrush.'

'Right,' McCusker replied, strapping himself in for a bumpy and (hopefully) revealing ride.

'When I met Ryan or when Ryan started chasing me, I forget which it was, I felt he was as attractive as a dust bin on a hot summer's day,' she started. McCusker felt it was inappropriate to laugh, no matter how difficult he found it not to. 'But Ryan respected me, he paid me attention. More importantly, he was paying me attention when no one else was. Up until Ryan came calling, I think our house, my mother in particular, only had time for Isabella. I thought my mother always wanted, maybe even *felt* might be a better word, yes, she definitely felt she'd missed out by having to spend her life looking after her two daughters rather than having her own career. I felt my mother was very jealous Isabella had a public achiever fall for her and I had bagged a minor celebrity. I remember coming into the house one night and my mum and dad were sitting watching a TV programme about Ryan and The Causeways, and I was in the show from time to time as either his wife or, as he used to call me, his muse. Whereas my dad was beaming with pride, I could tell my mother was thinking, "I should be up there, certainly not either of my daughters." There were other instances where she would get really annoyed at us because she knew we were going to such and such a big public do, or other, and she wanted to come along but our spouses would always only have a plus 1.'

Colette stopped talking and started to laugh. 'Oh yes, I had forgotten all about this, but she suggested, "Okay, well then, I should go as Ryan's plus one, or Tom's plus one, if it was our Isabella she was talking to." But you know what was really funny?'

And she left it hanging there.

And so did McCusker.

'What was really funny,' she continued as she smiled at him for not rushing her, 'she was one hundred per cent serious. I mean it would be funny if it was not so flippin' sad. She really begrudged us our lives because she genuinely felt she had had to sacrifice her own life, just so we could have these wonderful lives. I bet you she would have sat home sipping her sherry, seething as she witnessed Isabella or I on the TV or social media. I think she always saw herself as coming third in a three-filly race.'

McCusker felt Colette might have been a wee bit harsh on her mother but he didn't say as much.

'Anyway, Isabella, now she and I were no longer competitors with each other, as wives whose husbands seemed to get on okay together, started, possibly for the first time in our lives, to enjoy a relationship together. Seriously! From where I was sitting here is what happened next. I became quite friendly with Tom. Nothing sexual with everything above board, just I now had a friend who was my brother-in-law. We had never ever seen each other when it was not as part of a foursome. But invariably, whenever we all got together Tom and I would rabbit away about everything under the sun and sometimes Ryan and Isabella would join in our conversation. Other times, they would have their own. Sometimes, wine weary, they'd just fall asleep beside us.'

McCusker nodded he was with her so far, and if he didn't remember it all, O'Carroll's handy tip of recording it all on her spare mobile was his backup. She was aware she was being recorded and was okay with it initially and then eventually was so relaxed about the recording device, she forgot all about it.

'The big mistake I made was thinkingeverything was fine between the four of us. I eventually realised our Isabella had started to get incredibly jealous over how well Tom and I were getting on. She would say something like "Goodness, Tom talks to you more in one night than he does to me in a whole week," and laugh, but then I realised she was very serious. So, I tried to back-pedal a wee bit. Tom was also aware of it and agreed…'

'What, you discussed this in front of each other?'

'No, he rang me up once and said he had noticed what was going down, and also mentioned he missed our chats, and he suggested we should meet for coffee, maybe once a week…'

'But without Ryan and Isabella?'

'Well, yes, you know, socially as friends, so we could still enjoy our chats without annoying our spouses,' she confirmed. 'The arrangement seemed harmless enough to me. But then one of her friends, Jane Murray, only went and told our Isabella she had seen Tom and myself out by ourselves. Isabella put two and two together and got sex, concluding we were having an affair.'

McCusker could see where this was going.

'Isabella, as far as I can tell, reported this friend, Jane Murray, knew a girl, a groupie in fact, who claimed to have had a three-way with Ryan in one of the dressing rooms at a Causeway show. Isabella met up with Ryan somewhere by accident, had a few drinks and told him a) I was getting very close to Tom and b) well…the shortened version of the story is, Isabella claimed Ryan seduced her and Ryan claimed Isabella seduced him (both citing revenge sex.) So…'

'So, you and Tom get together,' McCusker offered, trying to save Colette some embarrassment.

'Actually, no,' she claimed, 'neither of us wanted to get involved in anything as sordid as sleeping with our in-laws. We tried to support each other, be there for each other. Tom instigated divorce proceedings against Isabella. I was desperate not to become another of our generation to end up splitting up a marriage and so I innocently thought, I know what I will do, I will get pregnant.'

'Then Ryan could see how much you wanted your marriage to work and…'

'Yes, and I really believed he would make a great father. Tom and Isabella would see they had nothing to worry about and stop their divorce.'

'Okay,' McCusker said, for the record, because he thought he should.

'Not okay,' Colette said in contradiction, 'we could not get pregnant.'

'Oh!'

'Oh indeed,' she replied and raised him one, 'after tests I discovered our legendary showband singer was firing blanks. I did not tell him the result of the test. I was still convinced I could find a way to save our marriage. At one of my coffee mornings with Tom…'

'You were still seeing Tom for coffee?'

'It was the only part of the week keeping me sane,' she confessed, 'and Tom was the same. He was still going through with the divorce and was having a torrid time. Anyway, I told Tom I was now so desperate to get pregnant I had decided to get dolled up one night, go out and get drunk and pull someone, ride them and get pregnant.'

'Bad idea,' McCusker offered as politely as he could.

'Funny you should say so,' she said and offered him a big smile. 'It is exactly what Tom thought as well. He said it was dangerous on lots of different levels. I know you can see where this is all going, but I need you to believe at the time I was in the middle of it, and it was all perfectly innocent.'

McCusker couldn't find a way of shaking his head to signify both yes and no at the same time, so he didn't even bother to make an attempt at doing so.

'The next time Tom and I met, Tom said he had been thinking about my dilemma and he had come up with the perfect solution.'

McCusker bit his lip and refrained from an "Oh yeah."

'Gosh, Brendy, you should charge for counselling,' she said, and patted him on the arm. She patted him the way someone would pat a puppy.

'Anyway, we are nearly there, so I will plough on,' she continued, starting to blush. 'Tom said…Tom said, rather than me endangering myself, and these were his exact words, "and in the name of medical science, I will donate my body to the cause." He asked me to think about it. 'I said I had no need to think about it. I thought he was a good man. I knew he would keep his gob shut and most importantly I knew he would be the perfect man to father a child for Ryan and me.'

'So, you and Tom…'

'Yes, me and Tom,' she admitted, 'but I am not at the end of our story. Well, we quite enjoyed our time together, if you see what I mean. Enjoyed it a lot if truth be known. So, we decided to schedule a few more sessions, just to make sure we got it right. What I mean is I had never known anything like it in my life. You have to remember at this juncture Tom was divorcing Isabella. Well then, we only went and fell in lust, which lasted for about a month or so. And then…and then we fell in love.'

'Then what happened?' McCusker asked, only because she seemed to have hit a full stop.

'Then we agreed three things,' Colette announced proudly. 'One, I would divorce Ryan. Two, after a decent amount of time had passed, we would get married. And Three, in the meantime, we would start using protection.'

Chapter Twenty-Seven

'The decent amount of time I was referring to turned out to be two and a half years,' Colette announced, as they resumed the interview after a break Colette called so she could have a shower due to her sweaty morning in the garden. In the meantime, McCusker brewed them up a fresh pot of tea.

Colette returned after ten minutes, looking like a new woman and glowing from her shower. Her hair was damp, but she was letting it dry naturally, and she'd substituted her dungarees for a long, flowing red, sleeveless number. She led them through to her living room, as McCusker carried two dainty cups full of steaming tea after them, while ensuring he had his mobile in his back pocket, primed and ready to start the recording process up again.

'It turned out my marriage to Ryan was a lot easier to dissolve than Isabella's and Tom's wasand even when you take into account Tom was being very generous while Ryan was being his usual tight self. Ryan was fine with everything apart from the money and he would not budge on the Kerr Street house. As I mentioned, I was not in love with the house; it was so much noisier down there in the thick of it. More importantly, I just wanted it over, done. I did not hate him. I think he probably hated me for publicly humiliating him by not wanting to remain married to the great Ryan Shannon. In fairness to Ryan, no matter how much I tried to convince him otherwise he would never accept Tom and myself had not got it together until after we all went our separate ways. Isabella the wee skitter was right there in the middle of it, stirring it up and convincing

Ryan that Tom and I had been at it like rabbits for ages.'

'Why did Tom's divorce take longer?' McCusker asked.

'Well,' she sighed, 'it was like this, they had a few false starts. It was on, it was off, it was on again…'

'Really?' McCusker asked, a wee bit shocked, 'but I thought you and Tom…'

'Yes, so did I, but she was not giving up,' Colette said, equally exasperated, 'she tried to blackmail him…'

'Blackmail him?'

'Well, maybe not exactly blackmail. I will tell you what she did. They had pretty much worked out all the details of the divorce, and then she would say, "Okay, I agreed to all of your terms and conditions if you add one of my conditions to the agreement." The long and the short of it was her additional condition was that she would agree to the divorce if he would agree to give them both one final two-month trial period. They would move back in together and she would convince him they were meant to be together. Tom explained to me it was worth it for two months because at the end of the two months, the divorce would be finalised, and we could be together. He claimed he did not sleep with her during this period. Nonetheless I did not sleep with him either, during those two months.'

'So, you thought they may have been sleeping together?'

'Jez Brendy, I hardly know you and here I am telling you all my secrets,' she said, starting to blush again, 'but I know I will be sorry if I do not tell you everything and as a result of which you do not manage to catch the killer. You are probably not aware of this, but Tom had his weak spots.'

'Right,' McCusker said to mark the space.

'Tom was a bit of a sucker for play acting. Isabella would dress up and play all innocent and reluctant and Isabella would know which buttons needed pressing and in what order. Even if Tom was not into it, she knew how to get him into it. She would play the virgin and it would drive Tom wild; he just could not resist.

'Isabella would then shoot herself in the foot by sleeping with Ryan occasionally during this period and Ryan, to rub my face in it, would tell me and so I would tell Tom, and eventually it was over. Isabella's solicitor used the situation to up the ante a bit more; Tom accepted it all and Isabella and Tom were separated.

'Tom and I were married,' Colette said and claimed, 'and that, as they say, was that.'

McCusker was happy he wasn't writing all this down in his notebook; he felt he'd be up to volume three by now.

'Isabella played one more card. She felt if she married Ryan then Tom, who had called out Hi Love, You Just Dropped Your Glove, to her in their teenage years—and I always felt Tom was more in love with the idea of teenage love and it lasting forever, than love itself—he would get all soppy over his wife marrying a showband singer and at the final moment Tom would play the part of Benjamin (or Dustin Hoffman) and bang his way through a glass wall in order to win Elaine (or Katharine Ross) back at the last moment.'

'But it didn't work,' McCusker suggested.

'It worked for Benjamin and Elaine,' Colette claimed, 'but yes, you're right, it did not work for Isabella and Tom. Tom did not even show up. Isabella had egg on her face and Ryan permanently (or so he thought) in her bed. Meanwhile, Tom and I were ecstatic because we could finally be together and marry and live happily ever after.'

'Except for you and Tom were not together when he passed?'

'Correct, in fact.'

'What happened?' McCusker asked.

'Now that one is a lot more difficult to understand,' Colette replied, looking away from McCusker.

McCusker feared this was the point Colette was going to break down, and the interview would have to be terminated. He felt he was so close to the end he really wanted to try and find a way to encourage her to complete this chapter. She surprised him by summing it up very quickly.

'I, for my part, think perhaps we had met each other with much too much of our own personal baggage, some of it in fact interrelated because we were in-laws.'

Okay, McCusker thought to himself, I didn't see her explanation as the final frame before the end credits.

'You know, Brendy,' she began, appearing to pick up with his disappointment with her ending, 'I will share a secret with you now, and this is something I have never told anyone.'

He thought she was about to ask him if he would promise to keep the secret.

She didn't, no, instead Colette said, 'I always had this dream where somewhere down the line, maybe ten years or so after all the Tom and Isabella and Colette and Ryan and Tom and Colette and Ryan and Isabella gossip had long been forgotten about, Tom and I would meet up again and take up where we left off. I hoped we could manage it this time without any attention.'

McCusker knew they were both thinking to themselves, but not saying to each other, "Her happy ending scenario was most certainly never going to happen now."

McCusker respected her silence.

'I was totally devastated when Tom and I had to split up. I do not mean to speak ill of Ryan and my marriage to him here, but I will admit when he and I did split up, well yes, I was sorry because we were both acknowledging a failed marriage. You have to understand here, during all of my teens and twenties, I had promised myself not to allow a divorce to be part of my life. So, I was sorry, sad even when it came to pass, but I did not feel hurt, I did not feel any pain. But when Tom and I split up, it felt like someone had cut off my right arm. It felt like there was a massive hole in the pit of my stomach, and try as I did, I could not find anything, anything at all, to ease the grief.'

McCusker guessed what Colette was experiencing right now was a major relapse into her pain. He couldn't find a way to introduce his next question

Colette herself came to his rescue when she whispered, 'you look like you want to ask me something, Brendy?'

'Yes, I do,' he admitted, 'but first I need to explain to you why I need to ask this question.'

'Go ahead.

'At this stage in the proceedings, it is more important for us to rule people out than it is to suspect the wrong people.'

'Makes perfect sense to me.'

'Can you tell me what you were doing between 23.00 on Wednesday night and 03.00 on Thursday morning?'

'Oh, an easy question at last, Brendy,' Colette said quickly, 'I was here all evening. I watched a bit of telly. I went to bed about 11.00. I read for a bit and turned out the lights around about midnight.'

'Was there anyone here with you?' McCusker asked.

'Oh, on Wednesdays we usually have a book club meeting, but because of all the who-ha down at The Royal we took a rain-check on it this week. I can remember our current book if you want…it is…'

'There's no need, I just—'

'It's *The First of the True Believers*,' she said in interruption, sounding like she needed to prove all of this to McCusker, and she might be doing so by supplying additional back-up information, 'by Theodore Hennessy, it is a beautiful love story set to the backdrop of the Beatles story.'

'Sounds very interesting,' McCusker said, picking his words as carefully as he would if his boss, Superintendent Niall Larkin, was looking over his shoulder, 'I'm just trying to ascertain if there is anyone who could vouch for you being here during those hours?'

'If it had been the previous Wednesday, I would have seven names to give you.'

'Okay, let's talk about the TV,' McCusker said, 'Do you remember what you watched?'

'Ah, let me think, now I watched a bit of the local news, it was all about the invasion of fans coming to the Port for Rory. There was a quick chat with Rory.'

'Anything else?' McCusker asked, thinking Rory McIlroy not on the local TV this last week would have been equivalent to Lee Harvey Oswald not appearing on the USA small screens on the 23.11.63.

'Em I watched a wee bit of a rerun of *My Brilliant Friend*, it is a TV series based on a book we read for our book club by Elena Ferrante.'

'Was this series on cable?'

'On recall via Amazon.'

'So, you didn't watch *Coronation Street* or *East Enders*, where you could tell me a bit of the plot?'

'Can I phone a friend?'

McCusker thought she was serious and immediately, hopefully, said, 'Why yes of course.'

'Sorry, Brendy, I was joking, you know…*Who Wants to be…*'

'…*a Millionaire*…okay, yes, I get it, sorry,' McCusker cut in, happy to laugh at himself.

'You looked so hopeful there when I said, "Can I phone a friend," like you were really willing me to present a water-tight alibi to you, I immediately regretted saying it.'

'It's okay, Colette.'

'But I love you being so…supportive.'

'Did you phone anyone on Wednesday evening, by the way?' McCusker continued.

'Sorry, I never did,' she admitted, 'I just love to have those evenings to myself. Tom kept saying to me, these are the best days of our lives. We have to learn to love them.'

Chapter Twenty-Eight

As McCusker walked back into Portrush from Colette's house, he totally immersed himself in the wonderful sound of the seaside. The un-orchestrated sound of massive seagulls squawking away overhead—McCusker wondered if it was just the Portrush seagulls who could be so deafening and so threatening; the sound, growing louder, the closer he got to town, of teenagers screaming with the excitement of being in, or watching, some of the rides in Barry's Amusements arcade; the sound of weenagers whining lots of "can-Is"—can I have this, can I have that and can I have the other, particularly if the other is another ice-cream; the sound of preteens pleading for money to do their own bidding; the sound of laughing; the sound of babies crying with their non-stop, "oh please mammy, bla ,bla, bla…"; the sound of crying; the sounds of even more laughing; the sounds of tills ringing—all of those sounds joining together to create a soulful sweet refrain, never too far away from the streets of Portrush.

By the time he reached Ramore PS DS Melodee Johnson and DI O'Carroll, were back and reporting neither had picked up anything interesting on the CCTV footage. They had received a call from Anthony Robertson requesting they delay their visit to Coleraine. His results so far were "interesting" and most definitely suggesting foul play, but he'd a few more things he needed to do before he was ready to brief them.

'In the meantime,' DS Johnson started, 'I organised Mr Michael McKnight to come here to visit us.'

'Good plan,' McCusker said, tipping a cap he didn't have on with his forefinger.

'So Melodee can chat with him,' O'Carroll said.

'Okay, and you and I can track down one of the Buckley Brothers, either will do,' McCusker offered.

'I've already checked their office, and it's closed according to the answer phone,' Johnson replied, 'but there was an emergency number which I rang and got Sean. He didn't sound very happy. I'm not sure whether it was due to the fact it was the PSNI calling, or he was annoyed at being left on baby-sitting duties because his wife had joined up with her mates for a girl's day at The Royal. He said he'd be at the office—a two story Portacabin, encampment, the brothers have on a car park site they are developing— down on the harbour forecourt close to the Harbour Master's office—and could meet us there on Monday.'

'What's the number and I'll ring him and tell him DI O'Carroll and myself will be heading down there immediately,' McCusker said, acknowledging to himself at least, his dwindling patience was due more to the apparent lack of progress on the case.

He felt he was letting Thomas Barry down, and letting his former BLT friend down was what was hurting him.

McCusker and O'Carroll passed Michael McKnight on the steps of Ramore House. He recognised McCusker. He'd seen him speaking to Donnie McCartney. He still seemed somewhat shook up over having to officially identify his client's body on Thursday morning. He said he was very keen to help and happy to chat with DS Johnson. He did the Nashville Handshake, depositing his business card (rather than the CD or cassette the US brothers used) in McCusker's hand, claiming he would make himself available day or night if he could be of any assistance.

* * *

Michael McKnight turned out to be very old-school. He was dressed in a white linen suit, and a smart light blue shirt, with what looked like some regimental striped tie. He looked like he wouldn't have been out of place sitting on a white wooden, decked veranda, on some colonial island, sipping Pimms. His face , buffed, reddish and shiny, looked like he'd come straight from a wet shave with his favourite barber. He wore a battered straw fedora, which he removed, in the manner gentlemen do in the presence of ladies, as DS Melodee Johnson and he concluded introductions. His uncovered hair was sparse and weak and was soon covered again by his straw hat.

'I am delighted to make your acquaintance,' McKnight said and looked like he meant it.

For Melodee Johnson, the funny thing about McKnight she discovered was he did not look a bit like he sounded, or, put another way, he didn't sound a bit like he looked. Melodee thought of all the people she'd ever met, Michael McKnight might just be the only one who would get away with wearing white spats over his shoes. In fact, he wore the next best thing: a pair of spotlessly clean Dunlop Green Flash white gutties.

From his overall look, and it was most definitely a look, a dapper, posh, frail and aging look, Johnson expected McKnight to have a raspy voice, like one you'd expect someone important to use when announcing the last days of the Empire. However, his delivery was more befitting a virile, cheeky chappie, type character.

'I'm delighted to hear you've got the big guns in from Belfast to help on this one,' McKnight announced, officially commencing proceedings. He'd suggested they meet in the lounge of the Adelphi Hotel, 'not for its luxury, you understand, but for its convenience.'

For her part, to celebrate the start of the interview, she removed her notebook and pen from the inside pocket of her red Harrington jacket. She noted McKnight was clocking the Adelphi logo on her pen, and she seemed somewhat embarrassed by his observation.

'Well, McCusker used to be stationed here,' Johnson started, fearing she was sounding defensive.

'Of course he was, and if my memory serves me well, he was a rather splendid detective. In fact, some, including myself, would go so far as describing him as the North Antrim Coast's answer to Hercule Poirot.'

'Ha,' she said, 'I'm not sure what he'd say to that, but he'd probably prefer it to being compared to Jacques Clouseau.'

Solicitor Michael McKnight looked like he'd enjoyed her response and approach and he nodded his approval. Well, at least she interpreted his nod as one of approval. She also thought the process of "interpreting" things was a wonderful human invention in that she could always interpret things to her own advantage, something she would admit to doing regularly.

'How long had you worked with Mr Barry?' she asked.

'Must be coming up to twenty years now,' he offered, 'I was the family solicitor. I remember when I was the office junior, I was awarded this client David Barry, Thomas's father. Lookit, I was rather pleased with my first real client because I wrongfully assumed David Barry was part of the Barry's Amusements family, not realising Barry wasn't, in fact, even the amusement arcade's family name. It was a daughter from the Chipperfield's Circus family who, along with her husband, started up Barry's Amusements. She had decided she wasn't going to name her new venture, after the Chipperfield's because she didn't want any direct association between the legendary circus's family name and her new project. One of their first acquisitions was a second⁻ hand flat back lorry. The previous owner had started to repaint the lorry to ensure a sale. On one of the doors the only thing remaining from the previous livery was the word "Barry," obviously the Christian name of the former owner. They kept the name, and it became Barry's Amusement Arcade.'

By which point, as if by magic, a waitress appeared with tea and shortbread for them both.

'Once I picked myself up and dusted myself off realising and accepting my Barry's billing invoices were going to be a lot less than the lucky blighter invoicing David Barry's noisy neighbours. I started to enjoy working with *my* Barry, David, Thomas's father. In those less litigious days, my work was mostly property, drawing up Wills and resolving Wills and family squabbles. Lucky for me, although not mentioned directly in David's Will, apart from as executor, he did, in fact, bless me by leaving me his biggest asset, his son Thomas. At first, I figured Thomas would dump me and pick one of his contemporaries. But no, he seemed to prefer what I was bringing to the table.

'Thomas was very cute in that he can…sorry…he could…he could read situations and he could read them very quickly. Lookit, I once read a biography on LBJ and his biographer claimed one of Johnson's biggest assets, while accepting his numerous faults, was his approach to everything he did. He believed if you did every single thing to the very best of your ability, this approach was always going to be enough for you. He recommended you make lists, you set targets, you learned everything it was possible to learn about your chosen field. What you couldn't master directly, you went out and found someone who could teach you and you picked their brains until you knew just as much as your mentor. Now JFK enjoyed much better press than LBJ and maybe this was because of what happened. No one would argue JFK aspired to great things. Things, for instance, like leaving a better planet for his fellow men and women But here's a very important point, LBJ pushed more bills through the Senate than Kennedy, or any other president, for that matter. The end result being , no matter his morals, LBJ ended up doing a lot better in a practical sense than JFK did. Historians will argue if Kennedy had managed to win a second term, which was a definite, and complete his presidency, then his second term would have been the time JFK and his brother Bobby's vision for America would have reached fruition.

'But my point is this: just like LBJ, Thomas Barry's goals were to do the best possible work he could. To discover what he didn't know, others did, and even go beyond this and to push to find acceptable ways to do what had never been done before.'

'Goodness, I'd have voted for him,' Johnson, Melodee Johnson, gushed.

'Funny you should say that,' McKnight started off grandly, as a stick of dunked shortbread disappeared behind his yellowing molars, 'but Thomas would have made a great politician and he was considering it for quite a while. Again, typical for Thomas, he was doing his due diligence and research and getting ready to announce his campaign and then he pulled out.'

'Why did he pull out?'

'Because he wanted to spend more time with his family.'

'Which is shorthand for?' Johnson asked.

'That's all he would tell me,' McKnight admitted.

'Was this when he was with Isabella or Colette?'

'Colette, towards the end of his marriage with Colette.'

'I know you said he wouldn't tell you any more on the subject, but did you have any idea what *might* have been behind him pulling out?'

'Lookit, he didn't tell me, honestly, he didn't,' McKnight claimed.

'And you didn't ask?'

'Ah, the secret of good councel,' he offered, 'is listening when you're meant to and not asking questions you know you are not meant to ask. When you ask a question your client, or even friend for that matter, doesn't want you to ask, or can't, answer, well the potential conflict can in some way, maybe even in just a tiny way, fracture your relationship.'

'Okay, I understand. Over the years, has there been anything, any skeletons in the closet, enemies waiting to take revenge or something responsible for Thomas having to pull out of a political career? Can you suggest a reason why someone might have wanted to do Thomas some harm?' Johnson asked.

'All I can tell you is he did spend quite a bit of time and money setting all his projects up, getting all his ducks in a row,' McKnight said earnestly, 'Beyond that I don't think it would be wise for me to speculate on anything I don't know to be true and perhaps send you in the wrong direction.'

'Which kind of implies you might know where the right direction might be?'

'Speculation will be no good for you in this investigation; you'll need facts to solve it,' the older man offered sternly.

'Any clues?'

'I've already given you two clues,' he offered, through a knowing smile, 'why don't you speak to both of them?'

Michael McKnight glared at Johnson as though he was willing her on to do something, something perhaps vital.

'Sound,' she replied.

'And now I'm afraid I have another important appointment to keep,' he said, as he made to rise to exercise himself.

'Can I ask you about Thomas Barry's Will?'

'Lookit, you can ask,' the solicitor replied, 'but I can't divulge any information contained therein, due to the legal professional privilege law, which protects the client and not the solicitor. I can't disclose privileged information without approval from the client. Sadly, the client is deceased. I will of course advise you when the Will has been read.'

'Okay,' Johnson replied, graceful in defeat. In fact, she interpreted this as the old man managing to send her in the right direction. The only problem was she might not have noticed where the right direction he'd been pointing to, was in the first place.

She started to look for a waitress to pay for the tea and delicious shortbread. The taste of shortbread had been purely a deduction on her part. She hadn't managed to try one herself, but her assessment was due entirely on how enthusiastic the solicitor had been over their consumption.

'It's okay DS Johnson, I have a tab here.'

'Thank you, Mr McKnight, just one final question, can you tell me what you were doing from Wednesday evening at 11.00 o'clock until 3.00 o'clock Thursday morning, please?'

'I spent a very pleasant evening on the balcony of the Yacht Club, enjoying a light supper as the sun went down. We, my wife and I, arrived home about eleven o'clock, watched a bit of telly and were in bed just after midnight. I was up on Thursday morning at 06.00.'

Michael McKnight was having trouble rising out of his seat. Johnson immediately dashed over to help him. As she helped him up, she realised beneath his natty suit he was only skin and bone. She held securely on to him until he was steady on his feet.

'Are you okay?' she asked. 'Can I drop you anywhere?'

'My, my, that's delightfully, refreshingly, kind and generous of you, young lady, but I'll be okay. This stage of aging is a bit like trying to avoid the traffic but with less agility to call on.' He started, his confidence back, 'it's the next step I fear.'

'Oh, and what's that?' she said, as she walked him to the door, noticing with each step, he grew more confident.

'Aye, sure that's where life is a bit like playing a game of musical chairs where the only thing guaranteed, with this particular version, is there is never ever a final winner.

Chapter Twenty-Nine

'I went to a car boot sale once,' McCusker offered, as they piled into O'Carroll's battered and bruised metallic-blue Renault Megane. She was driving, and he, as usual, was riding shotgun.

'How did you get on?' O'Carroll asked on automatic.

'Well, I realised it was a false economy, and I should just fork out and buy the whole car at the same time,' McCusker replied.

'Makes sense,' she said, her mind still elsewhere, 'Sorry…what the heck, what did you just say there? Did you just crack another of your jokes?'

'I suppose, it's just a matter of opinion,' McCusker replied, 'but I suppose I just wanted to check we were still on the same wavelength.'

'It was actually quite funny,' O'Carroll replied to the positive for once.

'Okay, what's up? Are you feeling poorly today or something?'

'But it was quite good, for you, it's just it was very short,' she offered, in some kind of encouragement.

'Well, it was only a short journey, look, we're here already,' he suggested in justification.

McCusker and O'Carroll arrived at Sean Buckley's house in Glentage Park, a cul-de-sac. It looked like one of the Buckley Brothers, the builders, had bought two plots of land and used one of them as more of a builder's yard and used the other one to build at hotchpotch house for personal accommodation. The entrance hall looked like it was from a mansion, the left-hand wing looked like it was a shop front, while the right-hand wing looked like it started off as a bungalow, but then someone had decided to build another room on top of the slates.

The front door was open and a male voice from within grunted, 'What kinda of fresh hell is this?'

'The PSNI,' O'Carroll replied.

'Oh,' the grunter offered, 'oh well, you better come on in then.'

McCusker had never seen such an untidy house, both inside and out. He didn't think it was particularly dirty, he just thought it was so untidy. A sign of laziness, he wondered. He also wondered how humans could live and function in such chaos. He knew if he lived in this house, he would be permanently dizzy.

The grunter was wearing fake tan, (in the summer!). The fake tan was patchy and very badly applied to his neck, fingers and arms. To McCusker, he looked more like someone who had been rusting than someone who had been enjoying a few sessions of sunbathing. The grunter was wearing expensive-looking, well-pressed cream chinos, tan moccasins and a pink Ralph Lauren shirt, with button-down collar and sleeves rolled up to his elbows. His hair was brown, well-groomed in a traditional style, with a very sharp parting and he was clean-shaven. McCusker pegged him as being in his mid- forties. The grunter was clearly pissed off about something. McCusker figured DS Melodee Johnson had been correct with her assessment and Sean Buckley's bad mood was probably due to the fact he felt he'd been left holding the baby, and her sister, while the mum was out gallivanting. The grunter, while he was on the phone and as he prepared and served the food for the kids, acknowledged to the police officers he was, in fact, Sean Buckley. He slopped his children's food out the way one does with food for a dog, sometimes missing the plate altogether where some of the unappetising food ended up on the table, while he remained talking on the phone to someone else. He broke off the phone for a second.

'Eat it up anyway, the table is clean,' he ordered the kids before returning his attention to his call. 'I think you're wrong there, Rowdy. There was only one day when they didn't show up at your house and their non-appearance was entirely due to the fact they were back at the yard preparing material for the rest of your second fit.'

O'Carroll moved up very close to Sean Buckley and whispered, 'Can you finish your call immediately?'

He didn't.

He completely ignored her.

'Tell you what, Rowdy, first thing on Monday, Seamus and me will come down and spend a couple of days with the lads on your site and get you back up to your schedule.'

McCusker did not know whether he or O'Carroll was getting more frustrated with him, the Buckley Brother. O'Carroll nodded to McCusker to show she was intentionally remaining calm and refusing to rise to the bait and get rattled.

McCusker could see her silently counting.

She reached, by McCusker's reckoning, one hundred and twenty-three before he cupped his free hand over his mobile, said something they couldn't hear, and ended the call.

O'Carroll remained calm.

'Okay,' she started, trying to keep it friendly, 'do you just have the two children?'

'Three.'

'Three wee girls?' she asks.

'No, one gold and two silver,' he replied, looking like he was feeling very pleased with his answer.

'One gold and two silver?' O'Carroll quizzed.

'Yes.'

'One gold and two silver,' she continued as she glared at his neck, arms and fingers, 'well I'd have to admit to you, that's not bad…really…for a bronze.'

If dirty looks could kill, McCusker was convinced Sean Buckley would be in danger of competing with Harold Shipman or Gary Ridgeway in the high number stakes.

McCusker tried not to laugh. Then he caught himself on and had a great chuckle.

'Here's what we should do,' O'Carroll started up again, 'your two precious wee girls and I are going to see if we can rustle up something more appetising while their daddy and Mr McCusker here go into another room for a bit of a chat. What do you say, girls?'

The wee sister grabbed the bigger sister's hand and tugged it furiously.

'Melanie and I would like to,' she replied quickly, looking like she wanted to get her reply out before her father ordered otherwise.

* * *

'Do you know what happened to Tommy then?' Buckley asked as he brought McCusker through to the TV lounge, which had one of the biggest screens McCusker had ever seen even in a showroom. The picture was on with the sound off.

'Do you mind if we turn off the TV altogether, please?' McCusker asked. 'It's a class set, I just fear it'll be too distracting for me.'

'Yeah, no problem, there's no one to cheer for anymore, anyway,' he said as he sent the TV into sleep mode.

'Sorry, no, we don't know what happened to Tommy,' McCusker admitted, 'we're trying to find out. How long had youse been working together?'

'Whoa,' he blew through his lips for about five seconds, 'let's see now, the first job we, my brother Seamus and I, did for him would have been a hotel refurb here in town. This would have been in 2011. We came in under budget and we'd a brilliant team then and our work was second to none. In those days, it was easier to get good workers; there wasn't a lot of competition. Now, thanks to the new boom, everyone is stretched again.'

'But was the hotel the start of your working relationship?' McCusker asked, trying to steer him back on course.

'Yes, the hotel, and because of our work on the hotel, we became his go-to team. We'd look after him, he'd look after us. When he received a bonus, we received a bonus. He cut us in on a few projects, where we took part of the risk on staff and material, and he cut us in on a share of the profits?'

'Tell me this: Did you ever lose money on any of his projects?'

'Never did.'

'Never?' McCusker pushed.

'No, never,' Buckley admitted, grimacing, 'Tommy Barry knew his gig, he took pride in his work, no cutting corners, no messers on the job.'

'Did Seamus ever fall out with Tommy?'

'No, I mean me and Seamus work better together than when we're apart. I mean, now we're on a big project like the Colabella House project we keep getting offered everything going Seamus wants to do them all, everything we're offered. I say we can't do them all and even if we tried to, we'd end up doing some of them badly. Better to do a few great buildings and have them stand as a testament to our good work rather than lots of badly finished projects, which will only serve to blow our reputation. Tommy was quoting on a Belfast project recently. I'd love to do a project in the city. But that was the class of projects Tommy was pulling us into. I think we need to cherry-pick our projects carefully.'

'What'll happen to the Colabella project now?' McCusker asked, knowing it was a flagship project for both the Buckley Brothers and Thomas Barry.

'I think all work will be frozen for a while. I believe this will be until the insurance clicks in and the building can be finished. The banks know they won't have a chance to get their money back until the building is finished. But dealing with the likes was where Tommy was brilliant. He knew all of those minefields backwards. I used to walk some of our work sites with insurance agents who had come to quote and Tommy would say, "could you please give me a quote on what it would cost me to insure the site and if anything went wrong you'd pay me what you owe me, not a figure you want to negotiate me down to?" and they'd say, "we'd never do that," and he's say, "well you just did it on such and such a job of mine, so if you want to quote on this site you need to pay me what you under paid me on the last site, otherwise you can take a running jump from my top story." He had the measure of them, and he'd get his deal.'

'Did he ever fall out with anyone?' McCusker asked, while noticing Sean Buckley grimaced a lot. So much so, and what with his uneven fake tan, it got to be distracting. He would actually contort his face between words sometimes.

'I know he'd a Polish project go belly up on him,' Buckley started, 'he took it on the chin though.'

'Did he make any enemies on the Polish project?'

'The honest answer is I don't know. He wasn't a loudmouth or a bragger. He didn't like people knowing his business; he tried to keep low key… althou—'

'Although?' McCusker prompted.

'Although he'd a couple of wives who kept him in the spotlight,' Sean Buckley replied, through a knowing smile.

'What about your own projects, did you ever have any static on the projects you worked on together? You know, maybe someone who you didn't know, who'd been looking after themselves at the expense of the project and were now looking for someone to transfer the blame to and claim a pound of flesh from.'

'I think I get what you're after there, and no, we never had anyone turning up claiming their pound of flesh.'

'Do you and your brother fight?'

'The only thing my brother and I fight over is me trying to convince him he doesn't need to do all the manual work himself. I try to tell him we have people to do the heavy lifting, but he always wants to roll up his sleeves and get stuck in. I try and explain to him how much him not being able to supervise teams because he's stuck on a job doing manual labour is costing us in time.'

'Does…did Tommy…did Tommy ever get involved in any of these discussions with your brother?'

'Here's the thing Seamus and I both realise, is when you really get down to it, my brother has got my back like no one else in the world has my back, and he realises there is no one else in the world who has his back as much as I have it. And unlike a lot of brothers, neither of us feel this is a bad thing.'

'Okay, I get what you're saying,' McCusker said, feeling Sean hadn't really answered the question, 'but did Thomas and Seamus ever get into a fight?'

'Well, if I'm being very honest here, there were times when our Seamus would have been really pissed at Tommy. I tell you this because I know you'll hear it around the building sites. Seamus likes to walk through walls. Tommy liked to work out if there was an easier way to do the same thing. He likes to consider if we might destroy the integrity of a building if we just knock a wall down, without considering the consequences.'

'And were there ever any bad fallouts where either of them was upset at each other?'

'You mean the kind of fallout where one of them was ready to kill the other?'

'Well, yes?' McCusker replied, knowing this was not the time to be beating about the bush, and still slightly distracted by Sean's continual grimacing.

'That's what I was trying to explain to you,' Sean said, 'Seamus and I knew what each other's faults were, and we both covered each other's backs when necessary. We never allowed anything to get to the stage of it getting out of hand. So, in short, I was our politician, and he wasthe engine who kept us both on track. In other words, I never allowed anything between Tommy and Seamus to develop into anything serious.'

'On a social level, how did your wife get on with Seamus's wife, and how did the both of them get on with Thomas's wife?

'Which one?' Sean Buckley asked

'Well, Isabella?' McCusker offered.

'Definitely a question for our Seamus,' Sean grunted, with a poker face.

'And Colette?'

'Colette's okay, she's friendly to everyone,' he replied.

'And you and Seamus's wife?'

'I don't see the relevance?'

'There may be none, that's what I'm trying to discover.' McCusker admitted.

'Well, Seamus and I agreed ages ago we would never let girlfriends, wives or children get in the way of our relationship. It's made clear to everyone involved with us it's a no-go area. So, it's never become an issue.'

'Okay, Sean, thanks for being candid with me,' McCusker said, 'just one more question for now, can you please tell me what you were doing last Wednesday evening from 11.00 pm until 03.00 am on Thursday morning.

'Yes, my brother and I were going through all the iron-mongery for our building over by the harbour. It's a long, laborious job, but Seamus has always insisted we do it ourselves, our personal attention guarantees we never get ripped off. Obviously, it used to be an easy job which took an hour at most, but…with the Colabella building…well.'

'I see,' McCusker replied, thinking on, 'and would you do the stock-taking in the actual building?'

'No, we would do it over at our suite of four portacabins, a temporary base we have set up in the harbour. We use one of the units exclusively for storage. I think it was about 05.00 o'clock when we eventually finished, and we have a couple of bunks in one of the portacabins where we caught a few hours kip before starting our new day.'

'Would there be anyone else helping you with the overnight work?' McCusker asked at the exact same timehe figured out what Sean's incessant grimacing was all about. The man obviously suffered from chronic heartburn.

'Nope, just me and Seamus,' Sean grunted, 'as I mentioned, it's one of our traditions, or rituals, and I suppose it's too late to stop now.'

McCusker knew he had another question he should ask. A question he needed to ask, and he was trying to formulate it.

'What?' Buckley started, back up again, beating him to the punch, 'you mean brothers can't be each other's alibis. I mean, if we were with each other and no one else, then isn't that our truth? Surely you don't expect us to tell a lie just so we can give you an alibi acceptable to the PSNI?'

'No, Sean, of course not, I'm just trying to cover all my questions when I'm here with you. I think that will do us for now. Let's go through and see how the girls are getting on?'

* * *

'Noreen, would you do me a big favour, please?' O'Carroll started when McCusker and Sean Buckley entered the much tidier kitchen area. When both Noreen and Melanie nodded yes enthusiastically, she continued,

187

'Would you look after Melanie for a few minutes while your daddy and Mr McCusker and I say our goodbyes in the next room?'

'Is Daddy going away again?' she asked.

'No, no, it's just a quick chat.'

'Okay then,' Melanie replied.

'Can I just say, sir,' O'Carroll started, when she was confident they were out of the kid's earshot, 'I know it's none of my business but those two wee dotes in there deserve more of you. They worship the ground you walk on. They seem to me to be great kids and you know we see so many kids who grow up not being shown love by their parents and those stories usually have a very sad ending.'

'As you said, it's none of your business,' Sean grunted, and paused for another grimace, this one appeared milder than usual, 'now if you're done, you know where the door is.'

'Yes, it is none of my business, Sir,' O'Carroll started back up in her calmest voice, while avoiding a sickly-sweet patronising tone, 'but it *is* social services' business. So, I'm going to get them to call in twice a week at random for the next couple of months, and if you're not doing your duty as a parent…'

Sean Buckley looked like he was considering his options. He looked at McCusker with the look of a chess player working out the consequences two plays on from his considered move. He looked like he was happy to accept a stalemate…for now.

'Look, pay no attention to me,' Buckley started. 'I'm just still annoyed Shelia, my wife, their mother, has left me to look after the girls while she's off galivanting at the golf club. On top of which, Tommy Barry is dead and we have a pile of jobs on with him, and half my staff have been skiving off this week. All of a sudden everyone has gone from being Man United faithful to becoming Rory Fans. But you're 100% spot on, I shouldn't take it out on the girls, they're good as gold.'

Perhaps, McCusker thought as they walked back out to his colleague's car, I might have got my predictions of Buckley's chess moves wrong.

Chapter Thirty

What time is Grace getting here?' O'Carroll asked when they were back in her car, engine still silent.

'She had originally planned to get to the house around lunchtime, but all the morning trains were packed, so she decided she didn't want to arrive here frazzled. She is now going to delay her departure for a couple of hours. She thinks she'll arrive at about 18.00, now.'

'Good, we should be done by then.'

'We will be done by then,' McCusker replied.

'Who's next on our list?' O'Carroll asked, looking very pleased at McCusker's response.

'Well, as we're in the neighbourhood, let's stick with The Buckley Boys and drop in on Seamus,' McCusker offered, unbuckling his seatbelt, 'Sean thought he was at home.'

'He's probably on the phone to his brother at this moment,' O'Carroll replied.

At the far end of the opposite spur on Glentage Park, Mr Seamus Buckley resided in a stunning off-the-peg design, dormer-bungalow as made popular in the Dallas TV series. Before McCusker and O'Carroll had even a chance to ring the doorbell, the door was opened by a petite, mid-fifties, maybe even sixties, colourfully dressed woman who introduced herself as Mrs Elaine Buckley.

'My husband is expecting you. He's in the lounge, second door to the right. Can I get you tea, coffee, mineral water?'

McCusker nodded to O'Carroll, as in, "You go first." When she'd asked for coffee, McCusker opted for tea, crossing his forefinger and third finger of his right hand behind his back, as he wished for nibbles as well.

Instead of the roustabout McCusker was expecting, Seamus Buckley, on first impression, seemed quite dignified, aristocratic even. He scrubbed up well, even beneath his fingernails. He certainly didn't seem like the kind of man who would throw down his jacket and scramble up a tall crane just to get the job going. He looked older than his brother, maybe even fifty, but not anywhere near as old as Elaine. McCusker had mistakenly got the impression Sean, not Seamus, was the older of the brothers. So McCusker had been expecting him to be younger than Sean. He had longish, greying black, curly hair, with a middle parting and tucked behind his ears. He maintained a chin beard and so the overall effect was quite old-world gentlemanly. He wore two pieces of a three-piece, dark blue, pin-striped suit with a dazzling white shirt, a Queens University tie, a pair of carefully preserved, brown leather shoes, which McCusker guessed had served him well for at least the previous dozen years. The only item of clothing which connected him to his wife's more vibrant style was his pair of multi coloured hooped socks.

The sitting room looked like a showroom direct from the pages of *Country Life*, and McCusker could literally feel himself sink into the deep pile cream carpet.

Seamus rose to meet them, his pink, weekend FT, still in his left hand as he shook their hands and nodded acceptances of their IDs.

'McCusker, I've heard so much about you *over* the years. I'm amazed our paths haven't *crossed* before now. It's a small *town*,' he said, as he invited them to sit down on a Royal blue sofa which was so lush McCusker was convinced he'd never ever be able to rise up out of it again.

'We managed to get him down to Belfast nearly two years ago,' O'Carroll said as she sat down. McCusker wondered if she was actually suggesting a reason why he and this particular Buckley brother had never met before.

'Yes, I had *heard* about his relocation. Mind you, there were a good few years before then when he was in the *Port*,' Buckley continued. He had fallen into a habit—frequently incurred by Ulster Folk who spent some time stateside before returning to live at home—of picking a word in each sentence and over-emphasising it, maybe even trying to make it a question.

'Did you spend some time in America then?' McCusker asked.

'No, I *can't* say I did.'

His wife returned with a tray containing a cup of black tea, a cup of black coffee, milk, sugar cubes and, in answer to McCusker's prayers, some nibbles, some very appealing looking nibbles, it had to be said.

'Should I stay, dear?' Elaine Buckley asked sweetly.

'We will be *oh-kay*, darling,' Seamus replied, as he focused his attention on the PSNI members, one official, one freelance.

He dropped his copy of the FT to the floor next to his chair by the mothballed fireplace.

'Do you *know* what happened to yer man? Seamus asked.

'We're still working on our investigation,' McCusker admitted, because O'Carroll had left enough space for him to know she was only going to observe on this interview.

'No, I suppose I meant did he *jump* or was he pushed?'

'Too early to say,' McCusker replied, without admitting he would bet his Good Friday agreement early retirement bonus on the fact Thomas Barry did not die by his own hand.

'So how will this *work* then?'

'You mean our questioning?' O'Carroll jumped in.

'No, I didn't mean the *questions*. I meant will we and the insurers have to wait until the *outcome* of your investigation before we can start up work again on our Colabella House project?'

'I assume the insurers will appoint a loss adjustor and they'll start work immediately and will take a view on any penalties incurred due to work being suspended?' O'Carroll offered.

'Is the project currently on schedule?' McCusker asked.

'We are currently just under two weeks *ahead* of schedule.'

'So, no penalties?'

'I would *hope* not. But perhaps more a question for *Sean* and Tomm… sorry…Tommy's solicitor, Michael McKnight.'

'What kind of a relationship did you have with Tommy Barry?'

'My baby brother was the link *between* Buckley Brothers and Tommy Barry.'

'Did you socialise with him? McCusker asked, continuing with the questioning.

'*Never.*'

'Never?'

'*Never.*'

'You're kidding?'

'I am *not* kidding.'

'So, you just saw him on site?'

'On site, aye, on *site* of course.'

'*Only* on site?'

'Well, if we had any *business* meetings, there would be him and McKnight and Donnie McCartney and Sean and me.'

He grinned to himself.

'Have you *met* McCartney yet?'

'Yes, I have,' McCusker replied.

'He is known as *Bald* Buddy Holly around town,' Buckley offered, as a piece of useless information; a piece of useless information which, once it had one trip around the town, would probably stick to McCartney for the remainder of the accountant's life.

'Tell me this,' McCusker started off, 'would there be any word around town on Tommy?'

'They say his ex-wives are not *fans* of each other.'

'Wouldn't be unusual for ex-wives,' O'Carroll offered.

'Were the ex-wives upset due to the fact Tommy was having affairs around town?' McCusker asked.

'Well, they were probably more *preoccupied* by the fact he was cheating on each sister with the other sister?'

'But what about other women, maybe women with angry husbands?'

'I wouldn't *know.*'

'You must have heard stories about Tommy playing away from home?'

McCusker asked.

'Sean says we should never ever badmouth anyone we are doing *business* with.'

'Do you know of any bad deals he was involved with?' McCusker asked, trying desperately to salvage what was turning out to be a useless interview.

'I cannot *say* I do.'

'When was the last time you saw Tommy?'

'I saw Tommy on site *Wednesday* just before lunchtime,' Buckley admitted.

'Did he say where he came from?'

'I do not *believe* he did.'

'Did he say where he was going to?'

Buckley appeared to give this one some thought.

'He did not say to me where he was *going* to. Maybe *check* with Sean.'

'Mr Buckley can you tell me what you were doing between the hours of 11.00 on Wednesday evening and 03.00 on Thursday morning?'

'I believe my brother has already told you we spent those hours checking the ironmongery for Colabella House.'

Chapter Thirty-One

Whiskey Tango Foxtrot was that?' O'Carroll hissed when they were back in the car

'What did you think of Seamus Buckley?' McCusker asked, knowing he'd just heard his colleague get as close as she ever would at swearing.

'I think either it was the cleverest "no comment" interview I've ever witnessed or…or…'

'He answered every question, but he didn't tell us a single thing,' McCusker continued.

'Do you think he was being clever, and he gave short answers, so he didn't give anything away?'

'Well, you're implying he'd something to hide, but he seemed to have had little to do with Tommy. He had no motive. In fact, he had a big reason to want to see Tommy continue to live.'

'You mean their construction company being involved with Thomas Barry's company on mutually beneficial projects?'

'Yes, and definitely one big reason for him to wish to see Tommy alive,' McCusker continued. 'We need to check with McKnight and McCartney…'

'Ah, the one bit of information he gave us,' O'Carroll interrupted McCusker mid-flow, 'McCartney is known around town as Bald Buddy Holly.'

'Let's get our info up on our notice board and let's remember to ask McKnight and Bald Buddy Holly what exactly are the ramifications for the three principles, Tommy, Sean and Seamus, if one of them dies?

'I imagine the super-efficient DS Johnson will already have asked this question,' O'Carroll replied, as she started up the car, absentmindedly turning on the radio, only to find DJ Ivan Martin announcing Otis Redding's classic *Mr Pitiful.*

McCusker started to say something but O'Carroll put her hand on his arm and shouted, 'Whist man,' as she turned her radio up loud.

The hypnotic intro did exactly what intros are meant to do, jump right out of the radio and grab you by your heart and unmentionables and not loosen their vice-like grip until one of the most exciting journeys in recording history was concluded, and, along the way, bless you with a joyous, glorious, middle-eight horn riff.

'Every time I hear this track reminds me of Francie,' she started, at the end of the infectious track, just over two and a half minutes of recorded perfection

'Francie?'

'Yes, a boyfriend of sorts,' she said, in a wistful tone he'd never ever heard from her before and he knew all he needed to do was just keep his gob shut.

'Francie would say, "'Mr Pitiful,' he'd say, 'they call me Mr Pitiful because I'm so in love with you.'"'

'Did he really?' McCusker replied, not knowing whether to laugh or cry, breaking his promise to himself because he, too, was lost in this moment.

'Then he'd place one hand, palm open on his belt buckle, the other would be up in the air as if he was balancing on the highwire.'

'It sounds like he was high on something,' McCusker offered, and then immediately regretted it.

'Oh, he was,' O'Carroll admitted. 'I tell you what he was high on. He was high on fresh air. He didn't even drink on our dates, and I'd never smell any tobacco off him.'

'You got close then?'

'Anyway, he'd do his wee shimmy dance, and he would appear like he was sliding across the floor, heels and toes arcing backwards and forwards furiously. We're talking way, way before wee Jimmy Osmond did his Moonwalk.

'I think you'll find you're thinking of Michael Jackson?'

She seemed to consider this for a while before saying, 'I always thought wee Jimmy Osmond came up with the moonwalk.'

'What happened to him,' McCusker asked, fearing he was spoiling the moment but feeling it was vitally important to their continued relationship. She didn't think he meant Little Jimmy Osmond, 'I mean Francie, of course?'

'He just *loved* the first date. He loved the performance. He loved the game. He hated staying in. He always wanted to be out there. Out of his house was the only place he could be himself. Outside his house was his stage. When he was in his house, it was like he left his character on the coat hanger in the hallway and became a grey man until he'd go out again. He was no good at all indoors.'

'So, you split up?'

'I just wanted us to be happy together,' O'Carroll said quietly, mentally shaking herself up a bit. 'That's all I wanted. What do you want, McCusker?'

'I just want to reach the point where I'm happy. I'm desperate to be happy. At the same time, we're all led to be focused on striving for something all of the time. But I don't need or want to be rich and or famous. I just want to be happy. I want to be happy before I'm too old to enjoy it.'

'Define happy?' she asked, looking like she was trying to come up with her own definition.

'Happy is the state where you feel your life is more enjoyable than your dreams.'

'Wow!'

'Wow?'

'Sounds like something a character in a script would say,' she offered. When McCusker looked a bit too pleased with himself she continued, 'but they'd only say it because it was in the script.'

'What…you mean like West Wing?' McCusker asked, desperately seeking some more glory to bask in.

'No…not the West Wing…I was thinking more of Teletubbies, actually.'

They fell into silence. McCusker felt it better to leave it just so, she'd definitely won that round, but he could tell she was still preoccupied with

CHAPTER THIRTY-ONE

Mr Pitiful.

'Do you ever hear from Francie?

'No,' she eventually said, as she turned off the radio, started the car, and pulled away from the kerbside, 'but I often do wonder who came after me.'

Chapter Thirty-Two

Mrs Maude Hughes was as good as her word, and even though James Lamb had been on annual leave, she'd tracked him down and organised for James to pop around to the east side of Ramore Head, where the PSNI local headquarters were located. DS Johnson updated the case notice board before she and O'Carroll nipped out to meet up with James Lamb.

It turned out Mr Lamb did not want to risk embarrassing himself by being seen walking into the local nick, so he sent a message via Mrs Maude Hughes proposing he would meet them by the public benches on Lower Lansdowne Road. Lower Lansdowne Road ran parallel to Lansdowne Crescent, the home of the PSNI, it was very close to the sea and frequently used by campervan owners to park overnight so they could wake up the following morning to the sound of the waves either thrashing against the rocks or gently lapping there among. When McCusker had been stationed at Lansdowne Crescent, he'd frequently use these benches on concrete slabs for "clearing me head" time by the rocks. On the Saturday in question, the water was gently lapping against the rocks, and O'Carroll noted a few fishermen, suitably kitted out and trying their luck on the precarious rocks further down by the sea.

'Are youse Johnson and O'Carroll and here to see me?' a polite, well-spoken lad asked.

'Are you propositioning us?' O'Carroll replied.

'Jez no, you'd be much too old for me,' he replied quickly and added a smile.

O'Carroll acknowledged his banter for what it was worth.

'Just codding, I'm DS Melodee Robinson and this is my colleague, DI Lily O'Carroll.'

'Melodee Robinson, I know your girlfriend, Dawn Leng. Dawn is one of my sister's best friends,' James Lamb replied as he responded to their production of IDs by shaking both their hands.

'I am she,' Melodee replied with a genuine smile. 'So, you'd be Aoife's brother?'

'That would be me,' Lamb replied, looking really relieved he'd a direct connection with one of his inquisitors.

'It's a small world,' O'Carroll said, thinking she was happy James Lamb had just progressed from a potential reluctant witness to a family friend. The odds of him being helpful and indiscreet had just swung in their favour. Then, she regretted her, "he's dating my sister," scaring-off, line she'd used with Melodee in their first meeting.

'In a small town like this,' Johnson said, mostly to O'Carroll, 'they say we're all connected by two degrees of separation, instead of the five degrees you city folks enjoy.'

'I'm warming to it, but don't you dare tell McCusker.' O'Carroll smiled, then directed her attention to James Lamb.

He was in his late twenties. Very preppie in his choice of clothes: tan chinos, with turn-ups; black leather shoes; blue, button-down, Oxford shirt with collar open and a black, silver buttoned blazer which he carried over his shoulder, hooked in his left-hand forefinger. He looked like his first shave was several years away and his hair was blonde, short and ruffled in a designer way.

He passed O'Carroll's quick fab four test, with honours.

Clean hands and fingernails: Check

Clean, polished shoes: Check

Clean hair: Check

Smells good and masculine: Check

'How long had you worked with Thomas Barry?' she asked.

'Four years this September,' he replied immediately, 'I came straight from

UU.'

'Ulster University,' Melodee offered O'Carroll in explanation for the UU initials, and then asked Lamb, 'What did you study there?'

'T & T.'

'T & T?'

'Travel and Tourism,' he said, 'or, treading tonic-water, as we used to say—and there is a lot of it around—until you decide what you really want to do.'

'So why did you decide on Ramore Properties?' Johnson asked.

'Well, in two words, Thomas Barry,' James Lamb answered, 'he was inspiring, totally inspiring, offered a decent salary and although the company is called Ramore Properties, he encouraged me to interpret the word Properties liberally. He persuaded me he wanted to go beyond bricks and mortar. He wanted to develop his portfolio.'

'So, what exactly do you do at Ramore?' O'Carroll asked, thinking this was sounding more like a pre-dinner conversation than a line of inquiry.

'I suppose trouble shooter should be on my business card,' James offered.

'For example?' O'Carroll pushed.

'Well, let's see, currently I'm working on Thomas's Colabella House project, and it is my responsibility to ensure necessary materials arrive by the due date. It's not as easy as it seems because once one item is late, you can have teams of workmen hanging around with nothing to do, but they still have to be paid just for showing up. Then you must pay them for when they have to return to do their work. It all adds up, very expensive and I have to keep an eye to the budget. It can also cause a log jam, freezing up the entire job. The main advantage we have is Thomas has…sorry, Thomas had…so many projects on the go, and coming up, and so, no one wanted to let him down and pish him off.'

O'Carroll thought her eyes must have started to glaze over because Lamb suddenly changed direction.

'Curveball,' Lamb announced, 'Thomas also wanted me to develop some more youth market projects. He had a music publishing company of sorts which was in some sort of default with him and he was about to take it over totally, so he wanted me to scout out some new young talent for it. Handy enough for me, some mates of mine from UU had gone off into the entertainment business, meaning, by default, I've now a few connections in the music business. I'm currently chasing a few promising artists. Thomas was prepared to come up with some serious money for the publishing side. He kept telling me this was where the real money was. He claimed the big secret was you didn't have to do anything other than collect the money.'

'So, this company, who was in default with Thomas, did you know anything about the details of the company, or the people involved?' O'Carroll asked.

'Well, it's meant to be confidential,' he started, looking around him as if to check who might overhear him, 'but I suppose now Thomas is dead the secrets die with the owner. The writer is called Digby Davies…'

Johnson didn't strike any chord of recognition.

James Lamb smiled to himself. 'The company is called Digby Music.'

'Would we know any of their songs?' Johnson tried, while searching for another direction.

'Okay, full disclosure, Digby Davies is just a pen name, but you'll never guess the real name,' Lamb teased, 'we're talking about Ryan Shannon,

'I'd have never in a million years got that one,' Johnson confessed.

'I had heard the name for the first time recently,' O'Carroll admitted. 'Ryan Shannon?'

'The very same,' James Lamb boasted, 'and he's in some breach of contract. I don't know but I think it's over him not delivering the requisite number of songs so he will have to forfeit the copyright to all the songs under the agreement, which still turns over of a tidy sum each quarter. Thomas was prepared to invest all our publishing income in our search for new acts.'

'Have you had much dealing with Ryan Shannon?' O'Carroll asked, but he deemed to have not heard her.

'Have you had many dealings with Ryan Shannon?' Johnson repeated

'The self-confessed, The Dean of The Scene, yeah, I've sat in on a few meetings with them and he's by the office quite a bit, particularly around the time the quarterly royalty statements are due.'

'Have there been any arguments or fights at the meetings?' Johnston asked.

'They're usually quite civil, it's usually Ryan, Thomas and Michael McKnight and Donnie McCartney and myself and Mrs Hughes and because Mrs Hughes is there, people are usually on their best behaviour.'

'Did you see Thomas a lot socially?' O'Carroll inquired, curving the interview.

'No, we wouldn't hang out together, like we orbited differently. But he did keep encouraging me in my own networking.'

'Earlier this week, did you see much of him?' O'Carroll said, still in the driving seat.

'Yeah, I bumped into him a few times at The Royal during practice days, but he was based in the Club House, and I was in the Mastercard Hospitality Tent in the Secondary Village close to the 18th Green. It was extremely cosy, massive screens, very comfortable, great food and drink, not over-crowded and the perfect bolt hole between showers and all you needed to gain entrance was an up-to-date credit card. So, it was totally within my and my mates' budget.'

'How did he seem?' O'Carroll and Johnson asked at the same time.

'He was great,' James Lamb admitted, 'I don't know if you knew him or not?'

Both shook their heads to the negative. McCusker knew the boy he once was but not the man he'd become. McCusker hadn't revealed the former to his colleagues, so he could perhaps discover more about the latter through them.

'Well, he was very sociable, mixed well; don't get me wrong, I don't mean in an insincere way. He didn't ask questions in a diplomatic way, you know, just to pass some time until it was socially acceptable to move on to someone else. He only ever asked questions he wanted to know the answers to and so his conversations were always natural. I always thought he would have made a great politician.'

'Did he have the drink on him?' Johnson asked.

'He didn't drink,' Lamb said, shaking his head to the same negative, 'I've never seen him take a drink. I know a few people say they don't drink but while in the privacy of their homes they'll guzzle away, but not Thomas. He said he used to drink, and he stopped because he didn't like what it was doing to his body. I bet you he didn't do drugs either. I don't know about the drugs for a fact.'

'But he seemed happy?' Johnson asked.

'He *was* a happy go lucky person, and it wasn't an act. He could brighten up a room the minute he walked in, but not by being loud…'

James Lamb stopped mid-answer. He just pulled up as quickly as a sprinter occasionally does mid-stride when they realise something is drastically wrong, like they've pulled a muscle or something similar.

'I'm…I'm…'

'It's okay, James,' Johnson offered in comfort.

He remained tongue tied. Tears slowly started to fall from his right eye. He was very embarrassed. He tried to stop the tears, but he eventually had to submit to the inevitable.

O'Carroll noticed Johnson's eyes had also started to well up.

'Ah, for heaven's sake,' O'Carroll said, 'don't you start, Melodee, or I'll be at it was well. What are we like…balling our eyes out like wains on the streets of Portrush?'

'We can always say we've just heard Rory is out of the open,' Johnson added, fluttering her fingers furiously in front of her eyes.

This was when the tears changed to laughter.

'Take me home,' Lamb eventually gushed, 'Curveball, I'm sitting with two of the most beautiful women on Ramore Avenue, and here I am crying like a baby.'

'I note you no longer consider us too old for you,' O'Carroll offered, 'and thanks for the compliment, but could I also ask you to review your "two of the most beautiful women on Ramore Avenue," line, please. Take a look around you, there are *no* other women on Ramore Avenue!'

They enjoyed another quick spell of light relief.

'It's when I was talking about Thomas, just there,' Lamb continued, 'I remembered what a great man Thomas Barry was, how nice he was to me, and how much everyone loved him. Then I realised he was dead, and it just came to me exactly what it meant. And I found it unbearable…the sense of the pure loss. The complete emptiness I experienced was totally overwhelming. It was a feeling I'd never experienced before.'

'Are we okay to keep on talking?' O'Carroll asked, once their shared moment had passed.

'Sorry,' he replied, 'yes, please, let's continue. I just hope I can be of some help to you.'

'When you saw Thomas up at The Royal, was he with anyone or was he by himself?' O'Carroll continued, needing no further encouragement.

'He was with someone.'

'Do you know who he was with?' Johnson asked, when it became clear Lamb wasn't going to volunteer the information.

'Thomas was with the same woman on the two occasions I saw him up at The Royal. I'm not being awkward, but I didn't know her name. She was tall, blonde, very beautiful, in her mid to late thirties.'

'Did they seem…am…did they seem like they were…' Johnson couldn't find the correct words.

'Like they were on a date or friends?' O'Carroll suggested.

'Well, they were friendly alright, enjoying themselves and having a laugh. He wasn't trying to hide her. I can also tell you they weren't making out.'

'Okay,' Johnson continued, seeming happy to have passed any awkward-ness.

'Did you know Isabella Scott?' O'Carroll asked.

'Everybody knows Isabella and how her dropped glove brought her and Thomas together; sure, it should be a movie. They were childhood sweethearts, married too young, divorced, Thomas married Isabella's sister, Colette, Isabella married Ryan Shannon, Thomas and Isabella realised they'd made a mistake by splitting up and so they divorced their current partners, remarried and then split up again. I suppose with such a happy beginning they were doomed forever as a couple?'

'So, you know of Isabella, but did you know her as a person?' Johnson asked as O'Carroll replayed Lamb's Ballad of Thomas and Isabella through once more in her mind.

'No, I mean yes, I saw her around, bumped into her from time to time, she was always mostly chatty and friendly.'

'You said, "mostly," as in "mostly she was friendly and chatty,"' Johnson said, 'Do you mean *sometimes* she wasn't?'

'No, not really, but…'

'But?' O'Carroll nudged, feeling they might be on the threshold of something important.

'Well, I'm not being rude, but I always felt she appeared to like me and… curveball, for example: I met her at the launch of the Town Hall's summer season at the end of May. Thomas was there, they were there together but they seemed to be avoiding each other. She came up to me and hit me with the big networking cliché, she said something like, "In one quick sentence, can you tell me again what your course at UU was about?" It was clear she just wanted to paddle water for a few seconds in my company and make a connection with me, in order to continue—whatever it was—our relationship was, while, simultaneously, cherry-picking her next person to schmooze. Really, what I always thought she was doing was trying to keep in with me so she could keep tabs on Thomas.'

'And Colette?' O'Carroll asked, feeling he was opening up to them a bit more since their moment together.

'Yes, I like Colette,' Lamb admitted immediately, 'we get on well. She's always worrying about Thomas.'

'Worrying about something in particular?' Johnson asked.

'Well, I think I meant she seemed to genuinely care about his well-being.'

The three of them sat listening to the lapping water and watching the unsuccessful fishermen.

'I don't know,' Lamb eventually continued, 'Isabella was all about Isabella, but Colette genuinely cared about Thomas.'

'In the course of your work with Thomas, did you hear anyone threaten him or see or hear of any of his deals going so wrong someone would have it in for him?' O'Carroll asked, and realised immediately she was starting to sound desperate.

Lamb looked deep in thought for a while.

'Sorry, not to my knowledge, but maybe a better question for Michael McKnight or Donnie McCartney?'

'What can you tell us about Sean Buckley?'

'Well, the Buckley Brothers do deliver for us. They do good work. Thomas likes Sean and gets on well with him. Sean would be the main liaison between Ramore Properties and the Buckley Brothers.'

'And what about Seamus Buckley? Johnson asked

'Well, he's a bit like a stopped clock.'

What, he's not working? O'Carroll asked.

'No, but at least he can claim to be right twice a day.'

'So did Thomas and Seamus not get on with each other?'

'Well, it wouldn't exactly be right to say, they did not get on with each other. Might be safer to say Sean always ensured Seamus and Thomas avoided confrontation, if you see what I mean. I think the best way to put it would be if Seamus had his way, then the Buckley Brothers would be like quite a few other cowboy outfits in the building trade. Sean knew better and he knew how Thomas liked to work and so Sean ensured the Buckley Brothers delivered the kind of service preferred by Ramore Properties.'

'When did you last talk to Thomas?'

'It would have been late Wednesday afternoon at The Royal, the time I told you about, when I bumped into him at the practice green.'

'How did he seem?' Johnson was back in the questioner's chair again.

'He was in top form. Looked and sounded happy. That's how I knew when some of the talk around town started to suggest how he might have, you know…committed suicide, well, I knew for certain they were way off base with their opinions or suggestions.'

'Are you a Golf fan?' O'Carroll asked, trying to lighten things up a little.

'Not really, well, especially now Rory is out of it. I mean, I love the spectacle of it all. There's a gang of us, we all met up at UU, and we're working our way through our bucket list, where we're trying to tick off all the big events. So far we'd done Wimbledon, blimey those were expensive strawberries; Silverstone, Button's final year went flat when we knew he wasn't going to win, noisy and a heck of a lot of walking; Glastonbury, amazing like cramming three months entertainment into three days. But I'm also attending the Open for a bit of networking. Thomas got me the passes.'

'Okay, James,' O'Carroll offered, 'just one more question, for now. Can you tell us what you were doing from 11.00 pm on Wednesday night until 3.00 am on Thursday morning?'

'Oh, that was a major curveball,' James Lamb replied instantly, 'let's think now… We were out of The Royal at 8.00 pm, we went to Coleraine, nipped into the Riverside Table for a few drinks and a wind down. I was on mineral water for a break. We headed to Hukkabaloos about 9.30, we were thrown out of there about 11.30. Two of the gang who are now in London Town were crashing with me for the Open week. We got back to the Port… I imagine probably after midnight, went for a moonlit walk on the East Strand. We were back in my apartment on Mark Street just before 01.00 a.m., had a late-night tea, herbal of course, talked more rubbish, and went to bed probably just before 02.00. We were back in action again at 09.00 a.m., had a quick breakfast at Bob and Bert's, and walked across to The Royal.'

'Okay,' Johnson said, after she finalised writing this in her notebook, 'and your two mates from UU, could I have their names please?'

'Yes, of course. Derek McCelland, the best one of us at Uni, but now struggling a bit in the real world, and Big Martin, Martin McIvor. They're staying with me this week, but their digits are,' he paused to fish his mobile out of his canvas rucksack and pulled up their numbers.

'Good,' Johnson said, snapping shut her notebook to let him know they were finished.

'I can go?' James Lamb asked, as he put his mobile back in the rucksack.

'Why yes, of course,' O'Carroll replied, noting James wore the relief of someone who had just finished his final exam. At this point in the proceedings, he looked like completing them took priority over the results. She knew fretting over results would come later, maybe even before he reached the end of the campervan lined Ramore Avenue as he headed back into Portrush.

'Thanks, James,' Johnson offered, 'give my best to Aoife.'

As they watched him walk off into the distance O'Carroll asked, 'what did you think?'

'Oh, he's easy on the eye,' Johnson replied.

'No, woman, I meant what did you think about the interview?'

'I think he gave us a bankable alibi,' Johnson asked, now appearing distracted.

'I'm inclined to agree with you,' O'Carroll replied.

'Look, back then at the start of the interview, the thing about Dawn, you know about Dawn and me, I didn't *not* tell you, I...I mean, I think...'

'Ha...don't worry about it. Sure, I didn't tell you about any of my romantic adventures, or should I say the lack of them, either,' O'Carroll smiled, 'Look, I like you, Melodee, because you're cool; you're brilliant company; you're a great cop; and, maybe most importantly, you've got the measure of McCusker. I never look beyond those qualities.'

Chapter Thirty-Three

When O'Carroll and Johnson walked back up the medium incline to 21 Lansdowne Crescent, the PSNI HQ, McCusker was already waiting for them in the incident room.

'What's happened?' O'Carroll askedMcCusker the second she walked in and spotted him.

'What do you mean?'

'You've changed since I saw you a couple of hours ago?'

'Yes, I suppose this is real now. Tom is dead,' McCusker replied, nodding in the direction of the notice board, which Johnson had been meticulously updating.

'Wow,' DI Johnson said, more to herself than to McCusker or O'Carroll, 'you guys are, genuine partners.'

'Guilty,' McCusker admitted.

'I knew right from the start you guys were the real deal, like as in real partners.'

'Really?' O'Carroll said.

'Yeah, on the second day, when we came back from Dr Aynesworth and you saw him and you were both up to speed with each other without saying a word, and the same just now. You immediately noticed something had changed in him. I was thinking I've never really had a partner I had a built-in telepathy with, you know, like Watson and Holmes. I saw with you guys it was possible.'

'Can I be Holmes?' McCusker posed but not as a question. 'I quite fancy wearing a smoking jacket and playing the violin.'

'And can I just say,' O'Carroll started, appearing quite moved by DS Melodee Johnson's comments, 'Holmes here is spoken for, we have an O'Carroll exclusively on him, if you get me. He's my partner during the day, and my sister does the late-night shift.'

'But we could always get DI Jarvis Cage posted up here if you want in exchange,' McCusker suggested to DS Johnson, 'it would be a big loss for us but you—'

'Behave, McCusker, or you'll not be Holmes for much longer.' O'Carroll said, but instead of giving him the punch on the arm he was expecting she gave him a quick wee side-by-side hug while both made a great job over pretending to be preoccupied by the notice board.

'Sure, I'll behave if you get me the Smoking Jacket and violin you promised.'

From top to bottom, the notice board names, with pictures where possible, read:

- Thomas Barry—married three times, divorced twice,
- Lefty Kelly: alibi ??
- Ryan Shannon:—alibi
- Isabella Scott was with someone but would only disclose if she needed to.
- Colette Barry
- Donnie McCartney
- Michael McKnight
- Sean Buckley
- Seamus Buckley
- James Lamb—sound alibi
- The Mystery woman at Royal.
- Dr. Aynesworth
- Alibis
- Need copy of Robertson's autopsy report.

'So, what do you think the two clues were McKnight was suggesting?'

O'Carroll asked, more to the notice board than her two colleagues.

'I think he was suggesting Colette or Isabella might be of more help to us,' McCusker replied, 'and when you asked when this happened, you're sure he said between Isabella's second marriage…'

'To Thomas?' O'Carroll asked

'Yes, between Isabella's second marriage to Thomas, and Colette's separation from him, Thomas?' McCusker replied and then asked.

'Yes,' Johnson said without beating the drum or making a fuss. 'McKnight was most definitely, yet discreetly, suggesting either sister might have some important information for us.'

'Okay then, let's split up and talk to both Isabella and Colette?' O'Carroll suggested.

'I think I should chat with Colette. It might work more in our favour if I do. You know what, I'd really like to chat with Colette again and then assess her info before we decide who best to chat to next.'

'Okay, McCusker,' O'Carroll said, 'happy to follow your lead on this one. You've got a head start on character intel.'

McCusker rolled his eyes. Perhaps the smoking jacket and violin might not be a pipe dream after all, he thought.

'Let's you and I head down to Colette's now,' he said, 'the impression I got earlier was she's very much homebound these days.'

'Okay, and I can wait for Anthony Robertson, he's due here in half an hour,' DS Johnson said, volunteering to hold down the fort.

'Oh, I don't know…' McCusker said, perhaps as much to himself.

'What,' O'Carroll offered, looking concerned, 'what's troubling you?'

'Well, if Anthony has been decent enough to come and see us, perhaps we should wait for him with Melodee,' McCusker eventually suggested, 'hopefully he'll have some inside information which might help us in our questioning with Colette and then with Isabella?'

Chapter Thirty-Four

Anthony Robertson arrived twenty minutes later and was keen to talk them through his report immediately so he could get straight down to The Royal to see the rest ofSaturday's play. He seemed to be the only person in Ulster who wasn't suffering adversely from Rory's premature departure.

'I realise I am behind enemy lines, but I have to state for the record, my money,' he started in his beautiful soft Hebridean accent, 'and I do mean all one hundred sheets of it, has been on Lowry to take the wee Claret Jug.'

He calmly walked over to a table, which he carefully cleared. He opened his ancient, brown leather doctor's bag and meticulously laid out seven mania files in a row on the table. He had strategically placed the table so it was separating himself from DI Lily O'Carroll, DS Melodee Johnson and McCusker.

McCusker couldn't remember ever seeing Robertson without a snow-white lab coat before, but then he'd never seen him outside of the morgue at Forster Green before. The pathologist was dressed in a mustard waistcoat; blue denim jeans; white shirt and tie; expensive looking, multi-coloured trainers and a dark blue, hooded anorak, which he was carrying over his arm when he arrived. He now carefully placed it over the back of the chair he'd pulled up to his side of the table. He was small but muscular and always gave off the impression of being a wee ball of energy.

'Mr Thomas Barry, from his medical records, was 60 years old when he died on 19th July this week. He was in good health and had regular check-ups.

'The approximate time of death would have been somewhere between 1.30am and 2.00 am.

'He died as a result of drowning.

'Approximately 370,000 people in the world die from drowning each year.

'There are five main stages involved in the drowning process.

'1. Shock/Surprise.

'2. Involuntary holding of breath.

'3. Unconsciousness.

'4 Hypoxic Convulsions.

'5 Clinical Death.

'It takes approximately 6 minutes for the brain to die if its oxygen supply is cut off.

'Osmosis is the movement of water from a less concentrated solution to a more concentrated solution through a partially permeable membrane. The important thing to remember is that osmosis is the movement of water (or other solvent), not the particles dissolved in the water.

'Sea water contains salt. Salt does tend to slow down the osmosis process.

'Freshwater contains less salt than blood and therefore will be absorbed quicker into the bloodstream by osmosis, meaning we drown quicker in freshwater.

'As you are drowning, eventually your lungs will pack up. This is when you will crave the taken for granted pleasure of breathing by gasping for air in your desperate search for oxygen. But what in fact you experience is the water filling you up, this makes you feel heavier and you feel its unbelievable weight as it clogs up all your orifices.

'If you are at sea, you also suffer what is known as the Gasp Reflex. This is a torso reflex or a cold-water inspiratory gasp due to a sudden immersion in cold water. You can experience a version of it when you stick your head in a sink of cold water. You can feel your body automatically gasp to breathe in as much air as possible. You can hear your loud, involuntary gasp when you remove your head from the sink.

'In the drowning process, your brain proves once again what a miraculous organ it actually is. It is most certainly more advanced than any computer so far developed. Sensing the danger to your body, the brain moves into automatic and starts to close down work on the functions it deems not necessary to saving your life. This is to allow the brain to focus solely on its priority: saving its life support system, your body.

'The brain's objective will be to try to help you breathe and slow down your heart rate.

'When people are submerged in water one of two things will happen:

1. Water enters the lungs:—Water in the lungs in large amounts causes drowning immediately. Or;
2. Your vocal cords may go into a severe spasm—the spasm temporarily prevents water from reaching the lungs but, unfortunately, it also prevents you from being able to breathe.

'You will start to feel a little woozy. You possibly might start to view an out of body experience where you would actually watch yourself die. This sensation, I'm assured, is not as Stephen King as it sounds.

'There will be a sudden surge of brain activity just before you die. This is where that explosion of white light we have all been told about comes from. This is not a religious revelation as some have claimed. It is merely the brain aborting all existing activities as it tries to switch on again. The reason dying isn't instantaneous is because the body and the brain in partnership are really good at keeping things running as smoothly as possible.

'Once they eventually lose control, everything will shut down.

'We die because the lungs can no longer transfer oxygen to the blood. The decrease in the levels of oxygen in the blood leads to brain damage, if the brain is deprived of oxygen for more than six minutes

'I'm led to believe what you'll actually experience at this point is a massive wave of relief as a euphoric sensation engulfs your consciousness immediately before you die.

'So, we've addressed the bit about the process in general, but let's focus on Mr Barry's remains.

'I found alcohol in his blood; he certainly wouldn't have been stocious. There was a tad under 35 milligrammes of alcohol per 100 millilitres of blood. The legal level for driving is 80 milligrammes of alcohol per 100 millilitres of blood. What this means is, he would have been merry and consequently not in full control of his senses, which would have made his ending easier.

'A healthy adult can hold their breath for about two minutes, although the current record is held by a gentleman from Spain who can endure not breathing for about twenty-five minutes. We should bear in mind the fact athletes who attempt to beat the "holding their breath" record will spend months in training, practising, drawing very large breaths of pure oxygen before they submerge. What I'm saying is they know well in advance what they are about to attempt. Thomas Barry had no such time or advance warning to prepare himself.

'There were no bruises or abrasions about his body, apart from both his heels had bruises beneath the shoe level. Pretty much identical on both feet actually. I originally thought his shoes might have been too tight for him or his laces might have been tied too tightly. But his shoes were a comfortable fit, Converse slip-ons with no laces.

'Any tattoos?' McCusker asked.

'No, there were no visible blemishes to his skin,' Robertson replied. 'He did have both his ears pierced, but we only found one ear-stud, a diamond one to be exact. It looked quite expensive.

'We found traces of sand and cement in his hair. We've sent samples of both, plus his polo shirt and trousers, away to forensics for closer examination. There seemed to be some foreign objects in both items of clothing.'

'Foreign objects?' McCusker posed.

'Some fibres, which to my eye looked alien to the make-up of both the trousers and shirt.

'It is my opinion Mr Barry drowned in freshwater, not in the sea. This opinion is based entirely upon the water we found in his lungs. It was not saltwater.'

'But he could have been in a swimming pool?' McCusker proposed.

'Not enough chlorine for that,' Robertson reported, and continued. 'It is also my opinion Mr Barry wasn't in the water too long. His skin hadn't started to break up, nor had it started to wrinkle, the way it does when you overstay your welcome in the bath.'

'Any idea how long he would have been in the water?' McCusker again asked the question, not because he was the only nuisance in the room, but more because O'Carroll and Johnson seemed happy to leave all the questions to him.

'I could hazard a guess at about thirty minutes. I can do some research on the subject to get you a more accurate figure.'

'Thank you.' McCusker said, as Johnson made a note.

'The contents of his stomach were lentils, salad and salmon, consumed earlier in the evening and washed down with white wine, although there were also traces of red wine on his molars.'

As they were breaking up McCusker asked the pathologist when forensics would have the results. He was advised Monday late morning. McCusker was content with the promise because he knew the pathologist would stick to it.

Anthony Robertson's reports were why McCusker positively loved working with him. McCusker loved his performances, because that's what they were, performances of his reports. The end result, McCusker felt for him, and whomever else he was working on the case with, was, with each performance, Anthony Robertson managed to give the vital third dimension to the report. You came away from the theatrical delivery of the report not only with a better understanding on the facts of the victim's demise but also the feeling you'd been brought just a wee bit closer to the victim as a person, knowing exactly what he'd endured in his final moments.

Chapter Thirty-Five

'I have not seen you for a good twenty years and now twice in one day,' was Colette's greeting for McCusker, 'or is it one of thelunch time drop-ins for "anything in the pot will do," visits you are famous for?'

'Sorry? What? No,' McCusker spluttered, his mind still caught in Anthony Robertson's descriptions of Thomas Barry's final seconds, 'Sorry, I really didn't recognise the time, on this occasion,' he had the good grace to add, 'but a couple of more things came up on Tom.'

'You better come in then,' she said, opening the door wider in welcome. She had added an unbuttoned, cream coloured, cardigan to her long, shaped, sleeveless chaste, red dress of earlier. 'But as you are here at this time,' she started back up again through a very large smile, 'I have just made myself some soup. I do abhor cooking for one. There is usually such a waste, particularly with soup and pasta. I never get it right. I find it difficult guaging the balance of being careful of the wastage while at the same time having enough to let the flavours breathe through. I have made my soup and I realise I've made enough for a week.'

'Oh, go on then, as you're asking,' McCusker said, as he followed her into her calm country cottage kitchen.

'I really love your house, Colette,' McCusker said and meant it.

'Yes, I do too, I really do,' she said and smiled.

McCusker figured Colette was enjoying a memory rising to the surface moment. He wondered if she'd share it.

'You know my sister really did not like this house. She could not wait to get out of it,' Colette continued, sounding like she was happy at the chance to share her memory, 'when she started at Coleraine University, even though it was only seven miles away from Portrush along the Gateshead Road, she insisted on taking student accommodation in Coleraine. I do not know if you remember or not, Brendy, but on the night Isabella first met the BLT gang, she was staying at the Hutchinson mother's guest house, in Portrush and only a walk away from this house. She always had a troubled time with our mother, though.'

A few moments later, they were sitting at Colette's solid kitchen table, tucking into to her potato soup and her straight-from-the-oven wheaten bread. The bread was exactly the way McCusker liked it, hot enough for the Dromona to melt into. And the soup, he had never ever tasted soup like it in his life before. Colette had lots of different subtle hints of herbs and vegetables inoffensively infused, but the foremost flavour celebrated the magic of the potato. McCusker had come from a family where soup was considered either a stopgap between meals or a first course, but Colette's soup was a full, satisfying meal in itself. He would admit it might have had something to do with the three extra helpings she had ladled out for him. Colette, for her part, seemed delighted at his evident enthusiasm for her cooking. McCusker conceded to himself her joy might have had something to do with the distraction it had offered to her current dark thoughts. Towards the end of the meal, McCusker started to feel guilty about having to bring up the Thomas Barry topic again.

For the third time that same day, Colette Barry came to his rescue.

'So, something has come up on Tom?' she asked, draining the remains of her second glass of white wine. McCusker had gone for an "I'm on duty cup of tea" option.

'Oh yes, I got so engrossed in your soup…'

'Yes, I did notice,' she laughed.

'I understand Tom was considering going into politics?'

'Yes, he was very excited about the possibility,' Colette enthused.

'When would this have been?'

'It was 2012,' she replied, a little bit of anxiety creeping onto her impish face.

McCusker remained silent while trying to figure out if her anxiety had to do with her thinking about Thomas again after the distraction of their pleasant lunch, or if it could possibly be about their current topic, Thomas's political career.

'Yes, Tom was very serious about it, and everyone was getting very excited about his chances.'

'You and Tom were still married at this point?'

Colette grimaced.

'We were just in the process of splitting up, actually,' she admitted, her mood now totally transformed from five minutes previously.

'Okay,' McCusker said through a gentle breath, 'which party?'

'Tom was going to run as an independent. I think a change was what people were getting excited about, or the potential of change.'

'Did you and Tom breaking up have anything to do with him pulling out?'

'No,' she replied with a firmness which implied she wasn't going to expand.

'Did Tom pulling out have anything to do with him and you splitting up?'

'Such a sweet way to keep on the same topic, thank you for being so kind.'

'Well, I'm certainly not trying to be unkind,' McCusker offered, 'but although it is the same topic, they are two very different questions.'

'Of course they are, Brendy, and I am not trying to be obtuse. It is just so very difficult for me to talk about that period without getting tremendously upset. I have been trying to be all adult about this and not run around crying like a baby all the time. I cannot change things, and even if I could, it is too late to change them now.'

'I understand, Colette, I just…I just need to find out what happened, so all of this *is* so important.'

'I know Brendy,' she replied, visibly trying to pull herself together again but only half succeeding. 'All I can tell you is this. Tom had to pull out of the political race for personal reasons. Those personal reasons…those personal reasons…Well, let us just say…let us just say they also affected our relationship.'

'To the point you divorced?'

'Yes,' she said, very quietly.

'Did you file for divorce or did Tom?' McCusker asked, equally quietly.

McCusker could tell she was starting to lose control and pretty soon she'd lose it altogether at which point the questioning would have to stop.

'Okay, Colette, I'll leave the subject for now, but before I do, I'll ask you a question and you just nod me a yes or no answer, okay?'

She nodded yes.

'That wasn't the question by the way,' McCusker said, trying to distract her and appearing to succeed.

She smiled, reluctantly.

'Colette, my question is this: Did you divorce Tom?'

She grimaced. She tightened her lips. She glared at him.

After about a full minute of this, she, very slowly at first, started to move her head from side to side in a very definite no.

'Thank you,' he said, as she breathed a major sigh of relief.

He had so many other questions to ask her about this, if only because it was really the first main area he felt might lead somewhere on this case. Yes, he had Ryan Shannon and the publishing deal, and he had the mysterious tall lady who had accompanied Thomas to The Royal Golf Club, but he favoured the political angle, if only because politics had so many cloaks it liked to hide behind. The main question he would liked to ask her was, "Who else could I speak to who might know more revealing information about why Tom retired from politics before he'd even started?"

He feared his next question, particularly if it was on the same topic, would be his last.

Instead, he said, 'Tom was found with a diamond ear stud in his right ear.'

She nodded yes, implying she knew about this item.

'His left ear was also pierced,' McCusker started, 'would you know if he only wore the one stud or did he have two?'

'Tom was modest, he did not like to wear jewellery,' she started, sounding like she was going to circle his question. 'He thought it was too flash, too show-offey. For heaven's sake he still wore the same Timex watch he had for donkey's years. He said he loved it because it had such beautiful numbers, rather than the roman numerals or simple "I"s most modern time pieces have. But I wanted to get him something he would be as fond of as his watch. I thought of a neck chain, too Ryan Shannon for Tom; I thought of a simple cross on a chain, too standard religion for Tom; I thought of another ring, too Ringo for Tom and he thought they would take away from the power and commitment to his wedding ring; I thought about a bracelet, too David Beckham for Tom; I thought about wrap around shades, too Bono for Tom. I was only flippin' joking with that last one by the way,' she said.

McCusker smiled.

'Then I thought about ear-studs, small, subtle,' she continued, 'I figured he would not go for them either because they would mean he would have to get his ears pierced. But he surprised me, saying it was a brilliant idea. So, I bought him a nice pair, he had his ears pierced and now…but…now you have only found one of them.'

Chapter Thirty-Six

The streets of Portrush were so quiet O'Carroll and Johnson could hear the sound of the flapping wings of seagulls as they flew above and around them. Apart from the lack of humans, it was a typical summer's day in Portrush when the weather was great…between the showers.

When Ryan Shannon opened the door of his ivy-clad Kerr Street house the first thing O'Carroll noticed was the crease in his yellow trousers were up the sides and insides of his legs, instead of up the front (from toe to waist via and over the knees) and back (from heel to hip). The overall effect was not so much he'd been run over by a steamroller, but they looked like a pair of trousers a clown would wear.

'They're all I had dry,' Shannon offered in justification when it became clear O'Carroll couldn't take her eyes off them, 'the drying is terrible in the Port this week, but I certainly wouldn't have ventured out in public in them.'

Before they'd a chance to say another word, Shannon blurted out, 'OMG, just listen to me? Here I am standing on my effing doorstep sounding like Jimmy Young. Com'on in, before I embarrass myself further.'

'No need to worry,' DS Melodee Johnson reassured the showband singer, 'there's no one about the streets today.'

'Agh, they'll all be down at the Open.'

'Who's Jimmie Young?' O'Carroll asked.

'Oh, you mean you don't know?' Shannon offered, looking like he'd escaped an embarrassment. He then addressed the local, 'She doesn't know,

DS Johnson, can you promise me you won't tell her?'

'Ryan, the last time I was around here to talk to you, you told me and McCusker you had a side career as a songwriter under the name of Digby Davies.'

'Well, actually, head,' Ryan replied, 'it would be more accurate to say my singing career is a side career to my song-writing career.'

'Okay,' O'Carroll replied, 'however, I understand you were having some contractual problems with Thomas Barry over the Digby Music setup?'

'A bit of Perry Mason-a-rama,' Shannon offered, as Johnson was wondering where Luggai, the showband head's personal chef, was today, 'I made the mistake of using the same solicitor as Thomas Barry used to finalise the deal. The basic rule in the how to be a pop star rulebook is, you must have alternate legal advice from your manager or business associate. It's not coolio to sit on the same side of the table. It all makes a lot of sense to me now. You have to realise the better your associates do in a deal, the worse you do and vice versa.'

'I got the impression it was a messier situation?' Johnson offered, in support of O'Carroll.'

'Why, what did you hear?' Ryan asked.

'I heard there was a chance you would lose ownership of your songwriting?'

'Really?'

'It appears so.'

'Well, technically I suppose I could, but I have found in situations like this, solicitors always like to paint the worst picture. I think it's so they can prepare you for the worst outcome and the biggest invoice, as it were.'

'So technically, what could happen if you lost ownership of your songs?' O'Carroll asked.

'Disaster-a-rama?' he admitted.

'Can you explain the situation for me, please?'

'Okay,' Ryan sighed, 'Thomas and I had agreed to keep our personal lives out of our business lives. Which, as you can imagine, proved to be a bit difficult thanks to the Scott sisters.'

'Okay so far,' O'Carroll said.

'Colette wanted a divorce. She claimed she hadn't been with Thomas by then, but I'm not sure this was the truth. But anyway, I agreed to facilitate our divorce, mainly because Isabella and Thomas had already been divorced, and Isabella was keen she and I should marry as quickly as possible. Shotgun-a-rama wedding.'

'What? Was Isabella pregnant?' Johnson asked.

'No way, José.' Ryan claimed, 'although she was in a hurry for me to make an honest woman of her.'

'Okay,' Johnson nodded.

'I decided I would make it easy for Colette,' Ryan continued.

'Very decent of you.' O'Carroll said, hoping it didn't come across as a compliment.

Ryan grimaced painfully, 'I agreed to admit I had broken the sanctuary of my marriage by sleeping with another person.'

'By committing adultery?' Johnson pushed.

'By committing adultery,' Shannon conceded. 'All good so far? The only problem was Isabella, in order to protect her divorce package with Thomas, forbade me from citing her as the party in question. For the divorce papers, I had to name another person, and so I had to admit I'd been very naughty one night after a Causeways show and...'

'And?' O'Carroll pushed,

'Well, the girl in question would only agree to confirming my infidelity if I also named the third person in the episode. Apparently, she, the second girl in the ménage á trios-a-rama felt it was a badge of honour of some kind.'

'But I don't see how this has a connection with your publishing contract,' O'Carroll said, as she thought Ryan Shannon seemed to be getting his rocks off just a little too much telling his story to two females.

'I'm getting there, head,' Ryan continued. 'In the early days of the Port, quite a few Scottish people settled here. The Scottish flag is still one of the official flags to be flown around town. Some of the town fathers were Scottish, and they drew up some of the ancient laws, pretty prehistoric and archaic and well Michael McKnight, was of Scottish heritage, wrote some of the language of the contract binding myself and Thomas Barry together on the publishing. However, Michael had inserted an old-fashioned morality clause into the contract. Both Thomas and myself had laughed about it at the time. Thomas said, "I'm prepared to sign it, if you are," and so we both signed it.'

'But it came back to haunt you?' O'Carroll prompted, desperate to get to the end of this sorry episode.

But Ryan Shannon was determined to have his moment in the spotlight-a-rama.

'Fast forward to 2011, when Isabella and I are getting divorced, she cited this incident and labelled it as an orgy. And so, when I pissed off Thomas by being friendly to Colette again after he and Colette had separated. McKnight, who was also meant to be my solicitor, and I have the invoices to prove it, dug up the morality clause in our contract and put me on notice that I was in breach of my contract and as such they, as in Thomas Barry, would no longer honour the contract.'

'Cutting off your prime source of income?' Johnson posed.

'Not coolio at all,' Shannon grunted in agreement.

'Mr Shannon,' O'Carroll began, her notebook at the ready, 'what were you doing between the hours of 11.00 pm on Wednesday 17th July until Thursday 18th July at 03.00 am?'

'Surely you don't think I had anything to do with Thomas's death?' Shannon pleaded.

'At this stage in the proceedings, it's more a case of us trying to rule people out,' Johnson continued, offering the standard line of justification, as O'Carroll made it appear it was her pen, and not herself, who was agitated by the lack of response.

'Okay, I see,' Ryan started, 'well, let's think now, Wednesday evening. Phew. Oh, why yes, of course we, the Causeways, had a gig over at the Redcastle Hotel in Donegal. We would have finished playing at 01.30 and the hotel laid on a late supper-a-rama for us and we would have left at 02.30 and arrived in the Port about 4.00?'

'Would youse all have travelled in the band bus?' Johnson asked.

'Yes, of course,' he confirmed, very matter-of-fact, 'I mean, we would probably have made it back twenty to thirty minutes earlier if the Greencastle to Magillian Ferry was still running. I think the last sailing of the evening is around 20.25, so we have to go the long way down by Muff and then back up again towards Coleraine.'

Chapter Thirty-Seven

McCusker was waiting at the Kerr Street Train station when the NI Railways train pulled in ending Grace O'Carroll's two-hour and fifteen-minute journey from Belfast. As McCusker was standing on the deserted platform (no one was going to be leaving Portrush at this time of the day on a Saturday, particularly this Saturday, and it was too late in the day for a new influx) he thought either the train-station had been built to service the nearby Barry's Amusement Arcade or the Arcade had been built to take advantage of the convenience of the terminal at the end of the line. Then he remembered Portrush had only become a popular seaside town in the mid-1850s when the Ballymena to Portrush train line was opened.

Grace, being Grace, stepped off the train, carrying her trusted Rimowa silent wheelie, smiling and totally relaxed. McCusker had been wondering if she would be nervous visiting his hometown.

McCusker thought maybe he was biased; he acknowledged to himself that he was *completely* biased, but Grace immediately stood out from the crowd. He remembered the night he spotted her first in McHugh's in Belfast. She was so beautiful and perfect to his eye, he couldn't help but stare. He knew he was being rude, socially speaking, and try as he might to avert his gaze, his eyes always found their own way back to her.

Her signature French Bob styled, jet-black hair was the first thing which caught his attention as she stepped down from the train onto the Portrush station platform. She was dressed as though on her way to a three-cocktail lunch. The only thing missing really was smoke wafting up into the air from a cigarette on the end of a cigarette-holder. This was the first time they had spent two nights apart since they officially moved into each other's living space. His was a comfortable but small apartment in the University area and conveniently right around the corner from his favourite bookstore, No Alibis. Hers, a modern apartment in the perfectly refurbished St Anne's Square in the city centre. Door to door, by foot, they were sixteen minutes apart.

There was neither strangeness nor distance between them as they walked towards each other. To McCusker, it seemed being together with Grace was the most natural thing in the world. He felt neither of them fretted over the "what would have happened if we hadn't met each other" factor. In his book, they were meant to be together, and they were. The fact they were was enough, not *more* than enough, but enough, when enough was what humans deserved. He didn't regret his time with Anna Stringer, and Grace didn't regret "the many frogs she'd kissed to meet her prince." McCusker didn't think his and Grace O'Carroll's lives and situations were better or worse than his friends Thomas Barry and Isabella Scott's lives had been. This was their lives, not *just* their lives, but *their* lives.

'Gosh, it's empty,' Grace said, in shock as they walked up Kerr Street and turned right at the Craig Vara fork just before 55 Degrees North, past the enticing aromas of Tom Tom's Bakery, on to McCusker's humble back-to-front house, which was right next door to Strandmore House on Causeway Street. Strandmore House was renowned due to the fact it was visited by the young JFK and his father, Ambassador Joe Kennedy, in the summer of 1940.

'Yeah, there's a lock-in over at The Royal,' McCusker explained, as he opened his front door. 'Well, there was, but then when Rory didn't make the cut, no one seemed to give a…well, here we are.'

She rushed past him and in to the front room, which was at the back of the house, 'Oh my, oh my, Brendan,' she gasped, 'our Lily was correct, this is totally…this is much better than anything I've ever viewed on a cinema screen!' and she stood in silence, beckoning him to come over to the window and stand by her side.

* * *

'I don't want to see youse two come rushing in here, flush faced like you're teenagers straight from the hay shed,' O'Carroll offered McCusker and Grace in the Club House at The Royal Golf Club, an hour or so later, 'hang on a minute McCusker, she continued, 'that's not a piece of hay still sticking out of your hair, is it?' she asked, doing her best impression of an ape, daintily examining a mate's head, usually for food it had to be said. 'No…oops…sorry…it is your hair.'

Johnson and the two O'Carroll sisters enjoyed a raucous fit of laughter.

McCusker just broke into a sly grin and fixed it on O'Carroll (his colleague) while nodding his head ever so discreetly in the direction of O'Carroll (his lover).

'No McCusker, no,' O'Carroll gasped as the smile swiftly disappeared off her face, 'ah no man, I don't want to know.'

'Look, there, just there,' Johnson gushed, 'they've done it again. They keep doing this thing where they know what each other is thinking without actually saying a word to each other.'

'And you think this is a good thing, why?' DI O'Carroll pleaded.

Now it was Grace and McCusker, and, eventually, Johnson's turn to have a good chuckle, this time at Lily's expense, until they all joined in.

'The craic, as they say in these parts, was 90,' James Lamb said as he walked up and kissed Melodee Johnson on the cheek, 'particularly in your corner of the clubhouse.' He shook O'Carroll's hand. Johnson introduced him to McCusker and Grace.

She hesitated for a split second over Grace's status, but Grace saved her potential embarrassment by being brutally honest and nodding at McCusker and saying, 'He's my fella, and I'm his woman.'

'So, you worked with Thomas Barry then,' McCusker said, still proud as a peacock.

'Yes, I did,' Lamb replied nervously.

'Now don't be fretting, man.' McCusker smiled. 'We're not all going to gang up on you.'

James Lamb looked relieved, not from any guilt, McCusker assessed, more from the fact he was out with his mates for a night of fun.

'What I would like to talk to you about is crosswords.'

'What?' DI O'Carroll spluttered as her sister offered a, 'Pardon?' simultaneously.

'Crossword puzzles?'

'*You* want to talk about crossword puzzles?' DI O'Carroll said, shaking her head in wonderment.

'Yeah, I found a good one today,' McCusker continued, as Valley and a couple of his PSNI officers joined the group, 'it was on the back pages of the *Mid Ulster Mail*. Two words, first word seven letters and second word, six letters and the clue was: a flightless bird from Iceland.'

McCusker looked around the group, encouraging them to offer suggestions but finding nothing but several heads shaking to the negative.

'*Frozen Chicken*,' McCusker eventually announced.

Everyone, including DI O'Carroll, roared with laughter, not so much from the content of his line but more from a "I can't believe what he just said" stance.

'Oh my goodness,' James Lamb said, putting his hand on Johnson's shoulder, 'curveball, the woman I was telling you about, the woman I saw with Thomas in here on Wednesday night, look…she's over there, with the two other girls.'

'Are you sure?' Johnson asked.

'Oh, totally, I'm 100% sure?'

'So she's the woman you told DI O'Carroll and DS Johnson was with Thomas Barry in here on Wednesday?' McCusker asked.

McCusker looked at Grace, looked back at DI O'Carroll, looked over at the woman who was with Thomas Barry on the evening of his final day on the planet, looked back at O'Carroll again and gave her a discrete nod over in the direction of the lady in a beautiful oriental style, long tight green dress, as he took an equally subtle side step towards Grace.

O'Carroll nodded back to McCusker. She understood and was very happy with his choice. She took DS Johnson by the elbow and guided her over towards the beautiful, blonde-haired lady.

DS Johnson and DI O'Carroll very discreetly offered their IDs to the tall woman with blonde hair in the green oriental dress. She was totally unfazed at them approaching her.

'Could we have a quiet word, Miss?' Johnson asked.

'Yes, of course,' the lady in the green dress replied.

McCusker noticed the green dress had several embroidered dragons on the front of her dress, which was probably where James Lamb's oriental description had come from.

'How can I help you?' she offered as the two girls she had been chatting to wandered off.

'I believe you were also here on Wednesday?' O'Carroll started.

'Why yes, I was?'

'And you were in the company of Mr Thomas Barry?' Johnson asked,

For the first time since Lamb had pointed her out to them, she stopped smiling.

'Well, I was, yes,' she admitted, in a sadder, quieter tone, 'it's so terrible what happened to him. I'm still trying to take it all in. Is it Tommy you want to talk to me about?'

'Yes,' Johnson said, through a very large breath.' Can you tell us your name, please?'

'Yes, of course, my name is Ellen, Ellen DiVito.'

'And you were good friends with Thomas?' Johnson asked.

'His...ex-wife...Coco is my best friend,' Ellen admitted.

'Coco?' Johnson said, arching her eyebrows in a question mark.

'Sorry, Colette, I meant Colette,' Ellen replied, 'Coco is my pet name for Colette.'

'Just so I'm getting this clear,' O'Carroll started, 'you are best friends with Thomas's ex-wife, Colette, and you're still on good enough terms to go out with your best friend's ex-husband?'

'Look, the man laughing with the beautiful woman, is he Brendy McCusker?' Ellen asked, pointing over to Grace and then on to McCusker.

'Yes, he is,' O'Carroll replied and then added, proudly, 'and the beautiful woman is in fact my sister, Grace.'

'Colette told me about McCusker. She said she trusts him. Do you mind if we speak to him, please? Ellen asked. 'It won't take long.'

Now it was O'Carroll's turn to look at the tall blonde woman they now knew as Ellen DiVito, then she looked over at McCusker and next at her sister Grace, and then back at Ellen. She left Ellen speaking with Johnson and walked over to McCusker and returned with him.

'Ellen DiVito, I'm a good friend of Colette's,' she said to McCusker as she offered her hand to him.

'Any relation to Paul DiVito the singer?' McCusker asked, as he noticed how energetically she was shaking his hand.

'Funny you should ask, most people ask me if I'm related to the ice-cream family,' she replied, 'and the answer is yes, I'm related to both those sides of the family. I understand Paul sang in a beat group?'

'Oh, not just any beat group, Ellen, but *The* Interns,' McCusker enthused. 'I'm reliably informed they were by far the best beat group in Ireland back in the day. Some still say Paul could give Van the Man a run for his money any night of the week.'

'So very nice of you to say,' Ellen offered, appearing taken aback by McCusker's tangent.

McCusker knew O'Carroll was totally aware of where he was going.

'Oh, it's not false praise,' McCusker continued, 'Thomas and myself, and a friend of ours, Lefty Kelly, we had a wee gang, well just the three of us really…'

'The BLTs?' Ellen offered.

'Yes, as it happens,' now it was McCusker's turn to be taken aback. 'Anyway,' he continued, 'we used to dander around the streets of Portrush, sometimes in the pouring rain, debating the qualities of Paul DiVito from the Interns and how he and Billy Brown from the Freshmen, Paddy Shaw from the Blues by Five, and Van Morrison from Them, rated against each other as singers.'

'Yeah, Ryan would also lecture Colette and I on how absolutely amazing Billy Brown was,' Ellen remembered. 'The Freshmen was the only band he'd take her to see at the Arcadia.'

She looked at McCusker and smiled warmly, 'Look, Brendy, I know you are out on a date with your girlfriend,' she paused as they both looked over and admired Grace, 'but I just wanted to say to you I can't really tell you the truth of why I was out with Thomas on Wednesday evening. I know you've already chatted with Colette a few times. She said if this situation came up, I should advise you to talk to her direct and she could explain everything to you.'

'Okay, good enough for me,' McCusker said.

'I, ah, I can give your two colleagues the details about the rest of my couple of recent evenings with Thomas, but I needed them, and you, to know I wouldn't betray Colette's confidence. She said you would no doubt see her over the next few days if only when the hunger came on you again.'

McCusker returned to Valley's corner of the room just in time to hear Grace say to James Lamb.

'Are you currently dating anyone?'

'No, I'm not,' Lamb admitted, but didn't sound sad about it, 'you know what? I have discovered, my life is so much less complicated when I'm not getting intimate with anyone.'

'What I would be interested in, though,' McCusker said to Lamb when the excitement died down and people started to talk again in ones and twos, 'is you giving me a lowdown as to what happened out on the course today.'

'Shane had an amazing day, went around in 63, but it could have been a 62, which would have been a record for the new course. No one will ever beat Rory's 61. I think they had to change the course to give someone else a chance of beating his record. He shot it when he was only sixteen, you know.'

'He knows,' O'Carroll chipped it, 'believe me he knows, I only know he knows because he's told me often enough.'

Lamb smiled and continued. 'Anyways, JB Holmes was in with a shout, he'd a good round, a really good round but I think towards the end of the day, Lowry's play was taking the heart and soul out of the rest of the golfers. Fleetwood also gave a good account of himself, but I'd bet you no one is going to catch Shane Lowry now. I think he won the Jug today. It's his for the taking and you know what, he deserves it. He and his caddie have been having an absolute ball, playing great adventurous golf and enjoying themselves. Also, it's great for the competition, because everyone felt so flat after Rory's departure on Friday night. But now Shane has given them…well, he's giving the crowds something, and someone, to cheer for.'

'Goodness, James,' Johnson offered, 'for someone not into golf, you seem well versed in it.'

'Oh, I see what you're saying. The big thing about all the events on our bucket list is, they're all important to us and we treat them all very seriously. When we go to these various iconic gatherings, we just don't go on the razzle. We totally immerse ourselves in the event and the history of the event and the players. It makes our visits all the more enjoyable if we know all going on and what has gone on before.'

'I'm the same with crosswords,' McCusker admitted.

Chapter Thirty-Eight

The following morning for breakfast, Grace O'Carroll and McCusker were both up early. McCusker and Grace had planned walks along the West Strand and the East Strand, or as McCusker called them (in the same compass order) Barry's Beach and the Arcadia Beach. The same beaches he and his mates in the BLT gang had wandered along discussing the best singers in Ireland, (McCusker always opted for Billy Brown); the best recording artists in the world (Barry and McCusker always voted for the Beatles, while Lefty never faltered on Dylan's behalf); the most beautiful girl in Portrush (McCusker always chose Adele Hutchinson); the most beautiful girl in the world (McCusker always opted for Barbara Parkins); the best football player in the world (they all, always agreed on George Best); who baked the best apple pie (McCusker's mum always won this category); the best snooker player in the world (McCusker always picked Alex Higgins) and the best comedian in the world (Ken Dodd was consistently McCusker's choice.)

It was a very small step from there to McCusker deciding if he could ever find a girl who could sing like Billy Brown; made records like the Beatles; played football like George Best; baked apple pies like his mum; played snooker like Alex Higgins, told jokes like Ken Dodd and looked either like Barbara Parkins, or Adele Hutchinson, then he definitely would have to marry her.

Funny enough, Anna Stringer hadn't ticked any of the above boxes.

As McCusker and Grace were tempted (but resisted) the sand-dunes on the Arcadia Strand he turned to look at Grace in her blue, nautical, hooded windbreaker, her snow white jeans, her cute French Bob and Ferrari red lips, which had caught McCusker's attention in McHugh's, way before he knew Grace was Lily O'Carroll's sister, and before he even knew her, and he thought…he paused his thought. What did he think? The first thing he thought was he really hoped Anna Stringer and her new man were as happy as Grace and he were. He didn't want to tempt fate and so he parked the thought for good and returned to just enjoying being in Grace's company, when being in her company wasn't a "just" anything.

Grace was keen to sample as much of McCusker's Portrush as she could. So McCusker showed her everything including the corner of Mark Street Lane and Atlantic Avenue, where Thomas had literally bumped into Isabella for the second time. The first time was outside the Town Hall, and so he took Grace there as well, telling her the full story as they walked along.

When they returned to McCusker's house in Strandmore the second thing which caught McCusker's attention was two people talking in the kitchen. The *first* thing to hit McCusker the moment they walked through the front door was the mouth-watering smell of breakfast.

'Look who the wind blew in,' O'Carroll said, referring not to her sister and McCusker but to Lefty Kelly, who was proudly sitting at the head of the table with a mug of tea on the go.

'Hi Lefty,' McCusker smiled, 'this is…'

Which was as far as he got before Lefty was up out of his chair faster than a homesick angel on its way back to heaven, knocking his chair over behind him in the process.

'The delightful, Grace O'Carroll, I've heard all about you,' Lefty said, as he fawned over Grace, 'and I have to say none of what I've heard does you justice. Neither Solomon nor all of his…'

'Put my sister down, Lefty, or I'll get McCusker to tell us how your nickname came about.'

Lefty upended his chair immediately from the floor and returned to his seat.

'You're incorrigible, Lefty,' O'Carroll said, and then she turned to address McCusker and her sister and continued, 'just before you arrived, he was chatting up one of his gloves, "just to keep his hand in," you understand.'

'And was he doing any better than he does with humans?' McCusker asked, as the laughter subsided.

'Not a lot, it has to be said,' O'Carroll admitted, 'however, in his defence, I have to advise you he did come laden with gifts this morning, all fresh from Tom Tom's Bakery, so we've a feast ahead of us.'

'Thanks a million, Lefty, you'll stay for some yourself, will you?' Mc-Cusker said, noticing the four places already laid out at the table.

'Thanks, Brendy, I don't mind if I do, I've been trying to persuade your woman here…'

'Lefty, I'm actually still in the room,' O'Carroll interrupted, as she delivered the plates laden with savoury food to the table.

'I suppose you couldn't give me an extra egg?' Lefty asked, clearly taking comfort from the Ulster approach of letting yourself, and your host, down easy by presupposing a predicted negative answer to your request. On top of which, he'd obviously noticed the single egg still luxuriously reclining in the frying pan.

'Oh, go on, Lefty,' O'Carroll replied, as she delivered another egg to a plate already packed as the stands over on the 18th Green at The Royal Golf Club.

'I've been trying to persuade Lily here the way to a man's heart is through his stomach,' Lefty said.

'Tell that to Mary Ann Cotton's four husbands,' O'Carroll started, 'pass the arsenic, sister!'

Lefty looked like he wanted to check the frying pan. McCusker's legendary more-for-me tactical eating soon brought Lefty's appetite back again.

'I think Lily thinks I'm quite cute, really,' Lefty offered, as he tore into his eggs

'I'm *still* here Lefty.'

'You need to worry about your usage of the word cute, Lefty,' McCusker said, but very preoccupied with his breakfast.

'How so?' Lefty asked.

'Well, a baby human, a puppy, a goose, a calf, a lion cub, all of them have something in common.'

'Apart from being cute?' Lefty asked

'Yes. They will all unconditionally depend on you for love and for food and shelter, and in return, they will be affectionate with you and lick your face and purr.'

'Which *is* kinda cute, don't you think?' Lefty offered.

'Perhaps,' McCusker kind of agreed, 'but at one point something inside will click outta place and their love will change to varying degrees of hate. But only the lion club and the human will eventually be content, at the bat of an eye, to kill you stone dead in cold blood.'

'Blimey, I didn't see that coming,' Lefty says, and then he addressed Grace. 'Where did you take him on your walk? Surely it's too early for the hyperness of Barry's?'

'I hear it's never too early for Barry's,' Grace replied.

'Talking about Barry's,' Lefty said, and then looked at McCusker and the PSNI O'Carroll sister, 'how are youse two getting on with Mister Barry's case.'

'In a word, slowly, very slowly, Lefty,' McCusker admitted.

Lefty just tut-tutted.

'Well, we are making progress, but, you know,' O'Carroll added, 'and without giving anything away, I find the whole story very sad. Two sisters and two men and how with all the potential they all had, they couldn't find a way to live together.'

'You know,' Lefty started off expansively, as he had a habit of doing, 'I think it is incredible really how some men, Mister Barry for instance, when they meet the person they feel they are going to marry, they might not even let the girl of their dreams know what they are really thinking. They just feel they know: "This is the perfect one for me!" They expect the "chosen one" to just drop everything…'

'We're not talking literally everything, I hope,' O'Carroll cut in.

'Drop their own plans for life and follow the man as if he was the Pied Piper,' Lefty continued, either not having heard O'Carroll's line or choosing to ignore her, 'I had often wondered what happens to such a man when the girl in question would turn and say, "Sorry you're not the one for me." I fear with Isabella Scott and Mister Barry, this in fact could be one such sad story.'

'But my understanding of their story,' Grace offered, 'and McCusker just showed me the corner they met on, was, after that night, they had eyes for only each other and were with each other non-stop until they married?'

McCusker made to speak but Lefty beat him to it.

'But don't you see they both fell in love with the idea of how they met. Their big thing was the romance of their first meeting. You know, Mister Barry picked up her glove, being too tongue-tied to speak, literally running away because he thought she was too beautiful to talk to, then running around like a madman for the next twenty-four hours feeling he'd let her slip away, let his life slip away, and then quite literally bumping into her again. All their fairy-tale meeting really served to do was to distract them from what they were really feeling for each other. It seems to me when they both woke up from this spell several years later, they both began to ask, "What happened to my life?" I know for a fact Isabella really thought, "Is this it? Is this really all there is?"'

'So, you think they weren't really in love?' Lily O'Carroll asked, appearing intrigued with Lefty's theory.

'I suppose it all depends on whether or not you believe there is only really the one man for the one woman, and you have to struggle through your life to find the right woman in the hope she feels you are the right man?'

'Do you believe that Lefty,' O'Carroll continued.

'It's a long and perilous journey, I can assure you,' Lefty replied and then laughed, 'I mean, I'm quite happy to carry on my work in this field of research and donate my findings to science…'

'You have to understand he's kidding now,' McCusker said to Grace.

'No, but we'd need to monitor a man as he finds a woman,' Lefty continued.

'Or, a woman as she finds a man,' O'Carroll interrupted.

'Or, as Lily says, a woman who finds a man, and in her case she hasn't quite realised it yet, but she's found him, no need to worry though, I'm one of the rare breed of patient men.'

The four of them laughed.

'So was Methuselah, and look what happened to him,' O'Carroll replied.

'Anyway, say we find our man and he really thinks this special person,' Lefty Kelly continued, now looking directly at O'Carroll, 'is the perfect one for him and then she turns around and says no,' this time it was O'Carroll turn to glare directly at Lefty, who ploughed on, the terrain growing rougher and uninviting, 'or…they try and it…their relationship falls apart and she leaves him and they go on (each of them) and find someone who is even more perfect for each other.'

McCusker thought from his side with his first wife, Anna Stringer, he believed his marriage, his exclusive relationship with a woman, was what it was, all of what it was meant to be, but then when she left him, he realised exactly all it should have been, could have been.

'Look Lefty,' O'Carroll said, 'I think we're all mature enough to admit there is just one ideal partner for each of us in the world, and we don't really know what we're after or what we should be looking for, so we're designed to be receptive to little tingle moments, the ones which make us look at perspective partners in a different light, because a %age of each generation carries the responsibility for continuing society. Now all we have to do is surrender to the rhythm and go with the flow when we feel it's working.'

'And what happens when we feel what we have, what we thought we had, stops working? Lefty asked.

'We owe it to ourselves, no matter how painful it is, to move on,' O'Carroll replied.

'And what happens if one of the principals in the relationship doesn't want to split up, doesn't want to move on?' Lefty countered.

'Are you suggesting Tom, really behind it all, didn't want to break up with

Isabella?' McCusker asked, now intrigued by where Lefty had taken the conversation.

'No, I'm saying Isabella didn't want Mister Barry to leave,' Lefty replied, 'but wait, maybe it's not so simple. Maybe what I should be saying is that Isabella accepted it was over between her and Mister Barry, and she certainly has had other relationships she hasn't hidden, but maybe what was troubling her was the fact she just didn't want Mister Barry having a relationship with anyone else.'

'Even her sister?' O'Carroll asked.

'Particularly her sister?' Lefty suggested, looking like he felt he'd maybe said too much, 'but look at the time, would you, it's a quarter past dishwashing time; time for me to hit the road.'

They bid their goodbyes. As Lefty was walking out the door, McCusker called after him. Lefty waddled back into the kitchen.

'You called Brendy,' he said, from the kitchen door.

'Sorry, Lefty,' McCusker started, 'I forgot to say to you if you bump into Finn McCool this morning, could you please remind him he left the wheel of his bike down at the Kerr Street green just before the public toilets.'

When Grace started to laugh, her sister said, 'Please don't encourage him, I've got to listen to this all day.'

'Outta here,' Lefty chuckled as he headed down the hallway again

No more than thirty seconds later, there was a tap on the door. McCusker answered it only for Lefty to say, 'Sorry, I hoped it would be herself, but I'm here. I better say what I have to say now I've worked up the courage. Can I come in?'

'You're a braver man than I,' McCusker replied, as he stepped back, making way for Lefty.

'Oh, hello again,' Grace said warmly.

'Jez Lefty, we've only finished breakfast, the lunch sitting doesn't start for another four hours,' Lily offered, with a smile to equal her sister's.

McCusker noted they looked more like sisters whenever they smiled.

'No, no, of course not,' Lefty replied, looking like he was faking a smile in the hope it would show he was in on the joke. 'Look, Lily, I'm going to be down in Belfast week after next, on the Saturday night. I was wondering if I could invite you out to dinner?'

'That's very sweet of you, Lefty,' she replied, 'but sadly I'm out of the country then.'

'Oh really,' Lefty replied, looking like he was thinking her reply wasn't the very negative answer he'd been expecting. 'Oh really, where are you off to?' he continued, still in shock and not really thinking his reply through the whole way, 'anywhere nice?'

'Am, yes…possibly even Nice now you come to mention it,' she joked, looking like she was still having trouble collecting her thoughts, 'I don't actually know yet, but I'm sure I'll find somewhere to go.'

'Okay, that's three to one and game over, I'm out,' Lefty Kelly, the wingman of the BLT gang, conceded good-heartedly.

Chapter Thirty-Nine

'Don't you think him sad?' Grace asked, after they were convinced Lefty wasn't going to come back again and make another pitch to Lily or confess he was feeling guilty and offer to help with the dishes.

'Ach Lefty enjoys his life,' McCusker said.

'And he's not serious, he loves the wooing,' Lily offered, 'he was telling me the other day he needed to buy a new headboard for his bed.'

'Really?' Grace said, sounding semi-shocked.

'Yes,' Lily continued, 'he claimed he'd so many notches on it, the whole thing just disintegrated. Seriously, I think he's a very contented, happy man.'

'I think we all want to reach the point where we're happy,' McCusker offered. 'I'd like to be happy. But part of being happy is our ability to be unhappy occasionally. At the same time, we're all led to be focused on striving for something bigger, better, more. But I don't really feel the need or want to be rich and or famous. I'll settle for being happy.'

'Define happy?' Lily asked, looking like she was testing McCusker's memory, for the fun of it.

'Happy is the state where you feel your life is more enjoyable than your dreams.'

'At least you're always consistent!'

'Wow?' Grace said quietly.

'You sounded like something someone who had just returned from Glastonbury might say,' O'Carroll offered, appearing to give McCusker's line great consideration.

'What, do you mean, like, Michael Eavis's Glastonbury Festival?' Mc-Cusker asked hopefully.

'No, I was thinking something more like the Glastonbury Infirmary,' O'Carroll replied, with a mimed roll of the drums and crash of the cymbals.

Dishes finished, Grace was very courteous with both her sister and her lover. She wanted them to get on with their murder investigation. She felt like they all had a vested interest now. First, McCusker volunteered to stay for a while. When Grace wouldn't hear tell of it her sister offered to hang out with her for an hour or two. Lily's offer was also kicked into touch pretty quickly. Grace insisted she would luxuriate around the house, enjoy the amazing views for a while and maybe head back off to Belfast after lunchtime. She knew her way back to the NI Railways station; she knew where 55 Degrees North was and would dine there before heading off. She proudly produced the front door key McCusker had presented her with only a couple of hours ago, as he had said, "It's yours, you use the house as your own as and when you wish." She reminded him he hadn't concluded the deal yet, but accepted it was a technicality.

Grace stood on the doorstep as her sister and McCusker made their way to the car.

On her final wave to them, she said, 'I'm so happy you two work so well together.'

'Please don't tell him, he'll take it as a license to...' O'Carroll said, the rest of her reply was lost in the noise of her door closing.

* * *

'So, what's the plan for today?' O'Carroll started.

'I think I need to have another chat with Colette, a chat with Sean, a chat with Isabella, and another chat with Michael McKnight because we still need to find out why Tom pulled out of politics. I'm convinced the solicitor knows. Colette knows, but why are they both resisting, telling me? Surely, they must know it might help our investigation. I also need a visit to the

Pilgrims Steps again. See what another walk around there turns up. Now Anthony Robertson has confirmed the Tom didn't drown in salt water, I keep wondering did I miss something up there. I thought maybe I'll see Colette first,' McCusker suggested.

'Yep, I agree. It'll probably be more productive if you interview Colette solo. I'll head back to Ramore Head Station House and help Melodee check the alibis.'

'Okay, sounds good, drop me off here,' he said, as they hit the corner of Eglinton Street.

'I could drop you off at Colette's first, if you direct me,' she offered.

'Nagh, it's okay, you'd get lost in the one-way system on the way back,' he said as he started to unbuckle his seat belt. 'Besides, I've a wee message I want to get.'

As he watched her drive off, he nipped up Eglinton Street, took a sharp right where they had started at Craig Vara, and down Causeway Street to a shop on the left called Causeway Collectibles Portrush.

McCusker had been in twice before for a browse. The owner was friendly, proud of the new storefront the council had gifted him. He knew his stock. McCusker found an item he'd noticed on his previous visit. An Otis Redding album, *The Great Otis Redding Sings Soul Ballads*. McCusker checked the track listing and only recognised two cuts, the first, *That's How Strong My Love Is*, and the last, the song he'd been praying would be on the album, *Mr Pitiful*. The sleeve was in good nick. He carefully removed the vinyl from the sleeve and was amazed at how unblemished it was. He was happy with the condition of the album and hoped O'Carroll might like it.

'How much for this?' he asked the owner.

'Will you give me twenty quid?'

'I'll give you two quid,' McCusker countered because he felt he should.

'Two quid?' The owner laughed. 'Are you buying it or renting it?'

They eventually agreed on a compromise of £12.00 and the owner even threw in a brown paper bag for free.

***

Colette was waiting for McCusker, knowing after Ellen DiVito's appearance and introduction at The Royal Golf Club the previous evening, his appearance was pretty much guaranteed.

'So, Ellen DiVito?' McCusker asked, as a fully-fledged question as they sat down to Colette's delicious home-made fruit scones and strawberry jam.

'My best friend.'

'Yes, so I've heard,' McCusker admitted, 'but what's this thing about her been seen out with Thomas on the night he died, what was that all about?'

'Look Brendy, the point of it all was Isabella. As you most probably remember, is a very jealous woman. Tom and I, even though we were divorced, were still *good* friends. Now if my sister had known Tom and I were even in the same town at the same time she would have gone apoplectic, so I persuaded my good friend, Ellen, to go out with Tom as his plus one on a few high-profile social engagements as a ruse to stop Isabella thinking there was anything still going on between me and Tom.'

'Are you suggesting Isabella didn't mind Tom dating other beautiful women, just as long as it wasn't you, she didn't mind.'

'Well, yes, Isabela's priority would have been to keep Tom away from me. Once she had accomplished this, then she would deal with anyone, including the likes of Ellen DiVito, who came along to crowd her scene.'

'Okay,' McCusker said, 'makes sense to me. So, you and Tom were quite close recently?'

'We had always been great friends. Throughout all of this, our friendship had never changed.'

"But you weren't…you weren't…' McCusker left it hanging there in the hopes she wasn't going to make him spell it out.

She remained quiet. She was going to make him spell it out.

'Were you lovers?'

'Oh, Brendy, you have become so cultured.'

McCusker thought if any of them had become cultured, it was her, as she'd proven with her answer where she admitted her relationship with Thomas Barry without sullying it.

CHAPTER THIRTY-NINE

'Now what about Tom giving up on his political ambitions?'

'Not something I'm at liberty to discuss with you, and especially on a beautiful sunny Sunday morning like today.'

'But Colette?'

'Sorry, Brendy, this is just not something I can help you with.'

'But it might offer us up a lead which could then solve this.'

'It would not be worth it if all we do is help tarnish Tom's name in the town,' was to be her last words on the subject.

McCusker only accepted it on the proviso this was only for now. He didn't dare ask her for confirmation on his unspoken condition.

Chapter Forty

As O'Carroll was driving McCusker to interview Sean Buckley at his Glentage Park, hotch-potch residence she updated McCusker on their morning.' progress.

'James Lamb's alibi checked out.

'Michael McKnight's alibi checked out.

'Ryan Shannon's alibi didn't check out.'

'Sorry!' McCusker gasped as he realised what she'd just said, 'Ryan's alibi *didn't* check out?'

'No, I mean DS Johnson tracked down the Red Castle Hotel in Moville and it turned out yes, The Causeways did play there, the times were correct, the hotel did lay on a meal for the band *but* it was on Tuesday night, not the Wednesday night.'

'Oh My, Oh My, Oh My,' McCusker tutted, 'so the publishing contract dispute between Thomas and Ryan moves to the top of our motive list.'

'Which is exactly where Melodee placed it, as a result of this morning's developments,' O'Carroll confirmed, 'but do you really think he would murder him over his song-writing. I mean, I could see why someone might murder the writer of certain songs…no…no, let's not go there, too obvious.'

'Well we're talking serious money over his catalogue, all those songs listed on all his gold discs they go on and on earning him money.'

'How much would we be talking about?'

'Well, Donnie McCartney, aka Bald Buddy Holly, claimed Ryan was getting £200K in a good year and £100K in a bad year,' McCusker said, 'and year in, and year out.'

'That's some serious change,' O'Carroll said through a whistle. 'I think we need to get him up to the station and get his statement on the record.'

'You're not wrong.'

'And one more bit of info for you,' O'Carroll claimed, 'there's a foolscap page on the back seat, it's a memo DS Johnson did for you. It's a summary of our chat with Ellen DiVito up at The Royal as to her rendezvous with Thomas Barry at the golf club on Wednesday last.'

McCusker went through a farce of trying to reach into the back seat to pick up the memo, but being unable to reach it due to his safety belt.

'I can't get to it, as a compromise, why don't you tell me what's in it and then I can read it later?'

'Well, the problem with a compromise,' O'Carroll started off as only she could, 'is all you create is a situation where both sides are left unhappy.'

'Fair point,' McCusker said, while making no further effort to retrieve the debated memo.

'My logic would have to be why have two people unhappy when a much easier, not to mention, pleasing situation is where only *one* of the two people are unhappy.'

'Also makes sense,' McCusker replied, still not admitting to himself where this was going.

'So, I'm delighted to tell you we can quite easily accommodate this by doing it my way and you getting the memo out of the back seat and reading it, thereby granting me a few moments of peace and quiet.'

He unclicked his seat belt and blindly stuck his right hand through the seats into the general direction of the back seat. He still couldn't reach it, so had to get up on his knees, on his seat and lean through the middle of the front two seats and eventually, with a lot of huffing and puffing, he rescued the memo, and his pride, and sank back into his seat and started to read.

'Seatbelt,' O'Carroll cautioned.

'Seatbelt,' he confirmed, as he clunked and clicked and continued reading.

Memo: Notes on conversation between Miss Ellen DiVito and DI Lily O'Carroll and DS Melodee Johnson on Saturday 20th July 2019 at The Royal Golf Club, Portrush.

Miss DiVito said she knew Mr Thomas Barry through his second wife, Mrs Colette Barry. Miss DiVito and Mr Barry were friends with no romantic intentions on either side.

Miss DiVito picked up Mr Barry at 16.30 at his office at 13A Ramore Avenue. They drove to The Royal Golf Club. Mr Barry had a car pass for the Golf Club. They wandered around, met someone from his office at the practice putting green around 17.00. They had a coffee. They met one of the golfers she didn't know, Graham somebody or other, he spoke with a funny Ulster-American accent. They met a few people he knew; none she knew. He held her hand when there were photographers around. They hung around until about 18.30

She dropped him off at a "friends."

Miss DiVito arrived home at 21.00 where she and her flatmate stayed in for the rest of the evening watching TV.

Miss DiVito suggested Mr McCusker speak to Colette Barry for further info.

And so endeth the memo and the journey.

* * *

By this time, they were outside one of the Buckley Brothers' two houses in the reclusive leafy Glentage Park. One of them looked quite elegant, while this one, Sean's residence, looked like it was designed by the same committee commissioned to design a horse and came up with a camel.

Sean seemed to be in a much better mood today, maybe this had something to do with the fact his wife and kids were missing. Well, at the very least, he seemed to start off in a better mood.

'This alibi of yours,' McCusker started, 'we're having great difficulty with it.'

'Really?'

'Yeah, I mean your alibi is your brother. He's also your business colleague and you tell us, you're the only ones who can vouch for each other.'

'But don't you see all I'm guilty of is informing you as to what we were doing, I mean if I had known someone was going to murder Thomas then I would have dragged Seamus out and around the town kicking and screaming and made sure we'd hundreds of witnesses, so when you came calling we'd already done all your work for you.'

'Surely in the course of the time under discussion, the four hours you were stock checking in your offices, somebody must have seen you, somebody must have called you, you must have called someone?' McCusker pushed.

'Sounds to me like you're grasping at straws Mr McCusker.'

'Did anyone in your office know you were going to pull the late shift? Would anyone in your office have witnessed you pulling a late shift in the past to carry out the same work?' McCusker asked.

Buckley slowly turned his head from side to side with a smirk on his face.

'You mean to tell me the joint managing directors of The Buckley Brothers, have to stock take their own fixtures and fitting in the middle of the night. I mean, come on, it must be a multi-million-pound company and you try to tell me two millionaires like yourselves keep your eyes open with matchsticks and burn the midnight oil, so you both could count bleedin' light-switches and door handles and bathroom taps. And then…and then you kip down on camp beds in your Portacabin, even though you both have beautiful homes with luxurious beds to come home and kip in. We now know your two houses are a two-minute drive or a 10-minute walk away from your offices. I mean, come on, Sean. At least help us out here?'

'Maybe the reason we are such a big and successful multi-million-pound company is because my brother and I pay attention to the small details,' Sean suggested, breaking into a full contorted face grimace.

'Hang on, Sean, just a minute.' McCusker stepped over to the window and looked up in the clouds before returning to his seat. 'Sorry, Sean, I can't see any pigs flying around today.'

'Do you not feel bad doing what you do?' Sean snapped.

'No, not at all'

'But surely—'

'You have to realise,' McCusker said, feeling a need to put an end to this line of discussion as soon as possible, 'we only come along into criminals' lives, after they commit a criminal act. Criminals do not commit criminal acts because of law enforcement officers.'

'But what about all the innocent people or suspects, you question along the way?'

'It's just a process. We interview people not because we think they are guilty (at least not to start off with), but mainly because we want to eliminate them from our enquiries. In my experience, the vast *majority* of people are very happy to talk to us and give us relevant information about the victim and the crime and give us a creditable account of their whereabouts at a crucial time or period, so they may be eliminated from our inquiries. '

'So, if they, these witnesses, say they didn't do it, should your next question not be to yourself, where you ask yourself: who did do it and why? And why am I letting the real killers escape justice by spending my time pursuing innocent people.'

'Well, what you have to accept is the perpetrator of the crime in question may not want to stick up his hand and say, "Fair cop, guv, you got me, I did it, lock me up and throw away the key."'

'And is this not how innocent people are hurt,' Sean continued, like a dog with a bone.

'We have found people who are guilty will do what they need to do to avoid incarceration. By and large, they are professionals. This is their chosen career. They will put as much thought, energy, research into their crime as a teacher, a designer, a doctor, or a policeman will put into their careers. We have to accept the path they have taken is their chosen career. They know exactly what they are doing. They know the flaws of the legal system, and with the assistance of their lawyers, they know how to evade the basic laws of the land. They and their lawyers are continuously refining their methods. They spend as much time perfecting the escape routes as the police and prosecutors spend trying to apprehend them.'

'But...'

'There are few things in this world as heartbreaking as listening to an interview tape, after the fact, where a murderer and his lawyer will sit in front of a couple of police officers and the murderer answers each and every question with a smug, "No comment." Then it later turns out, through the police work the original person of interest, with all their "no comments" caught on our interview camera, was in fact the murderer.'

'Yes, I get that, I really do, but I'm talking about innocent people.'

'And so am I,' McCusker replied quietly. 'And the important point for us in our inquiry is: As soon as we can rule out the innocent people, we can get on with our search for the murderer. In the early stages of an investigation, it is as much about who didn't do it (or in fact who couldn't have done it) as it is about who did it. Don't you see both are connected?'

'Yes, of course, but—'

'It is also very important for us we never allow the story to become *the* story. Our main worry over that route is the victim and their families are in great danger of being forgotten about.'

'I know, but—'

'We need to help the families, Sean,' McCusker said, 'meaning we're not interested in the Texas Verdict.'

'The Texas Verdict?' Sean offered through what looked like a very painful grimace. McCusker looked quickly behind himself to check if there were any mirrors or reflective surfaces behind him. There were none. This served to put an end to the theory which had just hit the detective: he thought Sean Buckley might be grimacing when he caught sight of his fake tan in a mirror. Mostly definitely it was a heartburn-related reaction.

'Yes…innocent but don't do it again,' McCusker said and continued quietly and patiently. 'So, with all that in mind, why don't we stop wasting precious time and get on with the important job in hand of trying to rule you out of our inquiries?'

'If only because, due to your continued delaying tactics, you'd have to forgive us if we were to grow just a wee bit suspicious,' O'Carroll added, drawing a line under the tangent.

'I can't help you.'

'Okay, let's change the topic for the moment,' McCusker said, as Sean Buckley looked very relieved. 'Mrs Barry, how well do you know Mrs Barry?'

'Which one?' Sean Buckley asked.

'Good question, Sean,' McCusker conceded, 'so let's take them one at a time. Let's start with the current Mrs Barry, Isabella.'

'Yes, I know Isabella, I mean I wouldn't say she was a friend, but we always pass ourselves when we meet in Thomas's company. The other Mrs Barry, Colette, I would hardly know at all. She took no interest whatsoever in her husband's business. I met her perhaps two or three times; I know what she looks like. If we met each other on the street we'd mostly likely just nod at each other and carry on with our journey.'

'But Isabella you'd know quite well?' McCusker asked.

'Better than Colette.'

McCusker wondered if Buckley was avoiding the question or just describing the situation as he saw it. McCusker felt it was time to fly one up the flagpole.

'Did you ever see Isabella when she wasn't with her husband?'

'What are you implying?'

'Nothing really, just asking a question, trying to pick up a wee bit of information,' McCusker replied, as innocently as he could muster, 'Well?'

'Well, what?'

McCusker pulled a notebook out of his inside pocket and flicked through to a page a third the way through and appeared to study it. It was an old trick, but then again, he wasn't a young detective.

'Did you and Isabella ever meet up when her husband wasn't about?'

Buckley looked at McCusker, then he looked at O'Carroll, then his eyes betrayed him and looked down at McCusker's notebook.

'Well, I'm quite sure moving in the circles we both move in, we surely must have been seen in each other's company at one time or another.'

'And these occasions would they have been rare or infrequent?' McCusker continued.

'Oh, definitely rare,' Buckley declared.

'And on these rare occasions, Mr Barry would have been absent?'

'Well, he might have been,' Buckley admitted, 'but maybe Mr Barry would have been in another part of the function room.'

* * *

'So…I see you're missing our Grace already?' O'Carroll offered patiently, as they returned to her car.

'What?' McCusker grunted, 'sorry, yes I guess I am. Sorry!'

'Oh, don't apologise,' O'Carroll said, 'I find it very refreshing to witness.'

'I thought I nearly had something there,' McCusker volunteered, 'I was on the right track, but I followed the wrong thread and lost the chance. But there's something happening, and I don't know what it is…yet!'

'Okay where to next?'

'Our number one suspect, of course,' McCusker sang out, 'the "head" aka Mr Ryan Shannon.'

Chapter Forty-One

'Ah, coolio, it's the PSNI-a-rama,' Ryan Shannon, offered by way of greetings to McCusker and O'Carroll when they came calling at his Kerr Street residence. 'Com'on in. You know your way to the kitchen by now.'

He followed them through the house, closing the door to the lounge on the left very carefully and very quietly, he hoped, but clearly not quietly enough though as it appeared McCusker's echolocation was tracking perfectly. He offered them coffee or tea and had both on the go, which made McCusker even more suspicious about the attempted discrete shutting of the lounge door.

'I'll have tea please and my colleague will have some coffee,' McCusker replied, attempting to take Shannon out of his comfort zone.

'What can I do for you today?' Ryan asked, as O'Carroll removed her notebook from her inside pocket.

'Nice cup of tea,' McCusker started, 'I do like a good cup of tea. But anyway, yesterday you told DI O'Carroll here and DS Johnson what you were doing on Wednesday evening through to Thursday morning...'

'Around the time Thomas Barry was killed?' Ryan offered, appearing to want to speed the proceedings up a bit.

'Yes, in fact, that's correct,' McCusker continued leisurely, 'No...DI O'Carroll here will correct me if I'm wrong, but you and your band, the Coastways—'

'Ah, The Causeways,' Shannon offered in correction.

'Sorry?'

'The band?' Shannon offered, nodding his head up and down, 'the heads are called The Causeways?'

'The Heads, now I'm confused,' McCusker stooged, 'is the band called the Heads or the Causeways or the Coastways?'

'Well *head* is a generic name for a member of a showband, but the actual band is called Causeways.'

'Okay, well tell me this,' McCusker continued with his Columbo moment, 'so the Heads are actually called the Coastways?'

'Ah no,' Shannon replied as O'Carroll, appearing to be writing down all these details which seemed to infuriate Shannon even more. 'Let's just forget all about the heads and let's just forget all about the *Coast*ways, let's just stick with the *Cause*ways—'

'But what happened to the Heads, did they split up?'

'Another time hea…' Ryan Shannon caught himself on, just in time. 'Let's just focus on The *Cause*ways.'

'Good, okay, the Causeways it is,' McCusker agreed, 'and it's a great name when you think about it, you know, ties in with Portrush, the causeway, Causeway Street, lots of local associations.'

'You're not wrong,' Shannon sighed.

'Any way you and your band the…' McCusker paused.

'The Causeways.'

'Your band The Causeways were appearing in the Redcastle Hotel in over in Donegal last Wednesday evening…'

'Yes.'

'Well so you say, but in fact by the time you finished singing on stage, 1.30 I believe?'

'Yes.'

'It would have been Thursday morning."

'I see what you're saying,' Shannon agreed, technically yes it would have been the very early hours of Thursday morning.'

'Then I believe you and your fellow musicians, I believe the word you used to describe them was heads?'

'Yes.'

'You and the heads from the band were treated to a meal by the hotel?'

'Yes, correct.'

'Do all hotels treat you to a meal after your performance?' McCusker asked.

'The performance is actually called a gig,' Shannon started. He saw the look on McCusker's face, thought better of it and continued, 'If the gig…the performance…takes place in a hotel, then yes, they usually will provide a hot meal for the hea… Sorry, of course I meant for the musicians.'

'Good to know, gigs, heads, hot meals, performances, band members,' McCusker said remembering how Tonto sometimes would trail a bush behind his horse in order to cover up his tracks. 'So, tell me this please, on Wednesday night you would have had a meal at the Redcastle Hotel in Donegal.'

'Well as you already mentioned,' Shannon started off very confidently, 'technically it would have been the early hours of Thursday morning.'

'Of course, Ryan, of course, sorry…Thursday morning in the early hours the hotel would have laid on a meal for you.'

'Yes indeed, they did.'

'Thanks for your patience Ryan, we're getting there, just a few more questions,' McCusker continued, 'then youse drove home and arrived back at the Port around 04.00?'

'Correct.'

'And that would have been because?'

'Sorry I don't follow?'

'Apparently the ferries had stopped running and you had to drive the long way around?'

'Sorry, yes I see, yes by the time of the night we were coming back the Magillian Ferry at Green Castle would have stopped running and we had to drive the two long sides of a triangle via Muff to get back.'

'And if you have caught the ferry then it would have saved you half an hour.'

'Yes, it would,' Shannon replied, looking a bit bemused.

'Which means you would have reached Portrush half an hour earlier on

CHAPTER FORTY-ONE

Thursday morning?'

'Well yes,' Shannon replied, starting to look concerned over where McCusker was taking this.

'Which in fact was last Thursday morning?'

'Yes.'

'The morning Mr Barry was found dead at the Pilgrims Steps in the harbour?'

'Well yes, but I was travelling back from Moville at the time he was…he was meeting his maker.'

'The Pilgrims Steps are in fact not very far from this house?'

'Yes of course,' Shannon agreed, 'but we've already ascertained at the time Mr Barry was dying I, in the company of my band members, was in Redcastle?'

'You see we have a problem with that,' McCusker replied, proving, no matter how big a circle might be, once you start walking around it, at some point you're going to reach the end of your journey.

'Oh?'

'Anything you want to tell us, Mr Shannon?'

'Sorry?' Shannon asked, looking in genuine shock. 'I don't understand?'

'Well, you know you told us you were at the Redcastle Hotel, last Wednesday night, Thursday morning?'

'Yes, I thought I'd just clarified this?' Shannon replied confidently.

'You see when we spoke to the Redcastle Hotel, they did in fact confirm you appeared at the hotel *last* week.'

'Yes,' Shannon said, now looking a bit relieved

'But, here's the thing…' McCusker said, stringing it out for what appeared from Shannon to be an unendurable amount of time, 'they told us you did *not* appear there last Wednesday night. They confirmed to us you and your band, The Causeways, appeared there last *Tuesday* night!'

Ryan Shannon looked like he was going into shock. He looked from McCusker to O'Carroll in disbelief. He looked like he'd just been shot, but he hadn't worked out yet where he'd been hit or how bad or lethal the wound was. He looked like he was going to go into meltdown.

He patted the left-hand side of his chest with his right hand and then when he realised, he wasn't wearing his jacket, he scoured around the room looking for it, couldn't locate it and raced straight out of the room.

O'Carroll mouthed, 'Should I go after him?' to McCusker, who nodded to the negative. He wanted this to play out for a wee bit longer. He figured even if Shannon's alibi had been shot, he was hardly going to try to escape to the street and run away? Where would he go where the PSNI couldn't find him? Twenty seconds later, Shannon returned to the lounge frantically searching through the pockets of his retrieved fawn cotton designer-creased jacket. First, he retrieved a large bar of Green and Black Butterscotch Chocolate, which he set down on the coffee table before continuing his search. When he found what he was looking for—an expensive-looking black leather pocket diary. He quickly flicked through pages—as swiftly as David Copperfield sans Dickens, shuffles through a card deck—until he found the pages he was after.

'Here we are,' he eventually announced, as he flopped down languidly on his sofa and started to read, 'Okay… Wednesday 17th July… Oh shit…you're right… I…we, the Causeways, were booked for Redcastle Hotel, Moville on *Tuesday* night. My confusion came from the fact we didn't get back until Wednesday, and so I'd mentally filed it as a Wednesday gig.'

'Tell me this *head*,' McCusker began slowly, 'so what were you doing from 11.00 o'clock on *Wednesday* evening through to 03.00 o'clock on *Thursday* morning?'

'Okay, I've just noticed in my diary an appointment for Wednesday 17th July,' Shannon admitted, as he turned the diary around, so the pages faced the detectives, without actually handing the black leather page-a-day diary over to McCusker and O'Carroll. 'You'll see there, for the Tue 16th it states: Redcastle Hotel, Redcastle, and our fee was £1500 plus 60% of every ticket sold over 500 tickets. However, for the 17th it says: Ballymoney.'

McCusker and O'Carroll glared at Shannon with a "Yeah, and?" look clear on their faces.

'That's code for a rendezvous with my wee Ballymoney woman,' Shannon said, as he tore open the distinctive orange wrapping on the Green & Black chocolate bar. He didn't offer them any. He started to devour it square by square as if he was satisfying a fix. There was no apparent pleasure in the process.

'Yes, a Ballymoney woman,' O'Carroll prompted, 'and?'

'And there you have it,' Shannon said, crunching away and with a tone suggesting he expected this to be the full and final explanation on the matter.

Sadly, this was not to be the case as far as the detectives were concerned.

'Yes, and her details are?' O'Carroll asked impatiently.

'Can I assume you'll be discreet about this?'

'You can assume we'll be very discreet if she turns out to be genuine...' O'Carroll began, but then at the last moment appeared to back off and didn't utter the veiled threat bit.

'When Isabella and I fell out, I met up with Maureen McCarthy, she was the daughter of a woman who used to come and see The Causeways at the Arcadia, she was in her mid-twenties then, and she made a point of introducing herself to me and to tell me her mother had passed and she had always spoke fondly of me and the band. Anyways, she came to see the band a few times and we'd always end up talking and then once, after I'd been having a real rotten time with Isabella, Maureen noticed I was looking stressed, looking like I'd lost weight and she...well she invited me to come over to her place in Ballymoney with the promise she'd cook me a proper dinner. This is not as sordid as it sounds it's going to be, but anyway, it started to be a regular thing and I go to see the wee Ballymoney woman maybe twice a month, she cooks me dinner and I stay the night. Well, I was with my wee Ballymoney woman on Wednesday night. I drove over there, left Kerr Street at 7.30, it's about a twenty-minute drive. I reached her house just before 20.00, and I left at 07.30 the following morning. She always heads off to work at 07.30, and she always chucks me out before she leaves for work.'

Shannon reluctantly passed over the wee Ballymoney woman's details to the detectives neither of whom looked convinced, especially as Shannon's diary clearly stated he'd played the Tuesday night and not, as he had originally claimed, the Wednesday night at the Redcastle Hotel in Donegal. So, if Shannon had been lying with the first version of his alibi, why would he not lie with the second version of his alibi?

O'Carroll was patting down her own pockets, looking like she was searching for a pair of bracelets; the ones you need a key for.

Chapter Forty-Two

O'Carroll and McCusker left Ryan Shannon's house with yet another alibi from the house owner to check out. McCusker wasn't sure. His logic had always been people lie for a reason. People lie because the truth will land them in trouble. Yes, Ryan made a major song and dance about mistaking the day he'd been in the Redcastle Hotel in Redcastle. McCusker had always figured singers tended to have to make a song and dance over a song when the basic song was not all it needed to be. Put another way, if the basic song was good enough, there would be no need for any additional sparkle, magic, call it what you will, the truth of the song would shine through. Equally, when the truth is the truth, it was all needed to sell your alibi and get you out of any potential trouble. It wasn't like they were discussing a time, say, years, months, even weeks ago in the past. McCusker and O'Carroll were talking about an evening less than five days ago. Did Shannon's suspicious behaviour prove he'd been lying? Not necessarily, but at the same time, even if he wasn't actually guilty of the murder, it did hint he knew more than he was letting on.

McCusker was distracted by the magical colourful big wheel, located across the road from Shannon's house in Kerr Street, and a wee bit closer to town, midway between Barry's Amusements Arcade and the Lifeboat House.

McCusker studied the customers up on the big wheel.

'When you go on the big wheel,' he said to O'Carroll as they walked towards the fairground attraction, 'as you get to the top of the cycle, you start to unconsciously prepare yourself for the dangerous bit; the peak of the journey, you know, just before you start to go down the other side. This is the point you fear things can, and maybe will, go wrong.'

'Yep and you'd be right to be nervous just before the wheel peaks,' O'Carroll confirmed, 'I mean, speaking from a personal perspective, I think you'd be crazy to subject your nervous system, to a ride on the big wheel in the first place but, you know, if you do go on the wheel, well then I could see the crest of the cycle being a potential problematic sector.'

'Right,' McCusker said as they arrived at the foot of the wheel, where the mixture of newly cut grass, which is quite pleasant; grass deprived of sun light under the foundation, which is not so pleasant; add to these distinct aromas a mixture of human sweat and dust being burnt by the numerous white permanently lit bulbs, surprisingly seems to add to the excitement, 'but I can't see why people subject themselves to this if they really feel so apprehensive. So, the big question must be: what exactly do they think they are going to be able to do when, or if, something goes wrong? I mean, just how long do they think they'd be able to cling on by their fingertips if they were tipped out of their bucket?'

'So, your point is?' O'Carroll said, as she moved from foot to foot to ensure she didn't get stuck in the rain-sodden (but not yet muddy) earth.

'My point is to just lie back and enjoy it.'

'Whatever the journey becomes?'

'Whatever it may become.' McCusker confirmed.

'Right,' she said, shaking her head in an "okay, I can see the logic, yes," then she asked, 'and why would that be?'

'Well…you can't change what's going to happen,' McCusker offered, 'so surely it's best to embrace it.'

'I suppose,' O'Carroll semi-agreed, 'equally you could just make a decision not to get on the big wheel in the first place!'

'Well, really where I was coming from, was, why bother, why subject yourself and your neighbours to the trauma and to your perspiration.'

'I'm not getting your tangent on this one, McCusker?' she said as they both, their neck severely creaked, looked up to the top of the big wheel.

'No, I mean yes,' McCusker started, trying to articulate what he was thinking, if in fact he was thinking anything at all. 'I was just wondering, why did Tom Barry go through all the trials and tribulations of his life, his loves, his dreams, his slog just to end up at the foot of the Pilgrim's Steps. Why did he bother?

'And yes, I accept, we just don't know when it will be our time to meet the grim reaper. Electing to never go outside the front door of your house is rarely a priority, if only because we're going to discover our life would already be over before it has a chance to start.'

'Good to know McCusker, good to know,' O'Carroll said, both of them still staring skywards as if awaiting a divine revelation

'Thanks, you're welcome.'

'No, not just for the tip, but for also sharing your philosophy on life with me.'

'As I said, you're welcome.'

'Can we go now and get on with our job?

'Ah… I have a wee bit of a problem,' he confessed.

'Sorry?'

'Actually, my neck has frozen in this position.'

'Really?' she said, turning swiftly in his direction.

He turned to face her, winked, and said, 'Just kidding.'

'You big eejit, you,' she laughed and punched him affectionately on the arm.

They walked down towards the Pilgrims Steps, McCusker kept getting distracted by the squawking of the seagulls as they sky dived around the harbour. Occasionally, he would turn back to look at the big wheel again.

'C'mon,' he said to O'Carroll as he caught her by the elbow and turned her back towards the big wheel again. He realised he'd been wrong about the direction the spectacular Ferris Wheel was turning. 'I've got a wee treat for you,' he continued, taking some money out of his pocket, 'we're going to be seagulls!'

He paid his money, bought their tickets, and a few minutes later, they were climbing on board the aforementioned big wheel.

Securely strapped in their "bucket" and as close together as a "D" and an "E" usually are, they gradually rose into the sky until a few minutes later, when they were momentarily able to enjoy a seagull's eye view of the harbour. It was a wondrous, breath-taking (quite literally) sight. The only things higher than them were the seagulls and the yellow tower crane keeping guard over the far end of the harbour behind the Neptune & Prawn Restaurant.

They could see the location of the Pilgrims Steps, but they couldn't make out the actual steps as the ancient stone, on ancient stone, from this distance, served to camouflage each other. As the wheel spun onwards, they descended to the street level. This was a major anti-climax for McCusker. O'Carroll, at first, seemed happier to have reached terra-firma level again, but then, when she realised the wheel wasn't going to stop but repeat its cycle, she gritted her teeth.

McCusker found himself freezing in a safe position and barely moved a muscle for fear it might upset their safety. He once again scanned the harbour area searching for inspiration. The only solution to their puzzle he could come up with was the remains of Thomas Barry must have been delivered from the direction of the sea rather than from land side.

'Right, what next?' a relieved O'Carroll asked once she felt comfortable with her land legs again.

'Let's just wander down to the Pilgrims Steps again and view it from ground level,' McCusker said as he headed up towards the harbour.

And then the wind came up, and the rain came down and they were getting wet. They nipped into O'Carroll's Mégane, which was still parked outside Shannon's house. They waited for the rain to stop. It didn't. He turned on the radio to discover Shane Lowry was currently seventeen under, six ahead of his current rival Tommy Fleetwood. The rain was hampering everyone's play but not their spirits. McCusker flicked the radio switch and found Ivan Martin playing Van Morrison's sublime "Into the Mystic." McCusker allowed himself to be transported on the journey, and as the saxophone faded out, just after Van sang, "It's too late to stop now," the rain ceased, and the sun came up just as quickly as the rain had started.

McCusker and O'Carroll walked over to the harbour wall to the smells the lashing rain had created. They walked around and around and eventually ended up on the viewing platform right beside the Harbour Master's office. There didn't seem to be anyone around the office. McCusker reckoned the Harbour Master, Melvil Edwards, was, like most other humans up at The Royal, watching the golf, hopefully mostly on sheltered TV screens.

'Okay,' McCusker declared, while checking his watch, 'I'm going to see Isabella Scott again.'

'Okay…don't forget your protection.'

'It's okay, we're only going to talk.'

'McCusker! Behave!'

'Just kidding,' he said, as he patted his pockets. 'All good,'

'I'll check Ryan Shannon's new alibi,' O'Carroll said.

'Could you maybe have DS Johnson dig out the log of the calls which came in to the station Wednesday, from say 10.00 p.m. to 04.00 a.m. on Thursday morning. Tell her we are just interested in any calls from the houses and apartments around the harbour end of Kerr Street and Main Street. Also, I keep meaning to ask her if she's had any joy with tracking down Tom's mobile phone.'

'Oh yes, I forgot to tell you,' O'Carroll admitted. 'it still hasn't been found and the company has been unable to locate a signal. Apparently, wherever it is, it's been turned off.'

McCusker had to pull himself away from comparing Thomas Barry's life to his friends' phone signal.

Chapter Forty-Three

The green-eyed girl who had turned Thomas Barry's head back in 1976 was now turning McCusker's head. When he arrived at her penthouse apartment in the former bank building, she looked like she was either on the way to playing tennis or had just returned from a game of tennis. The lack of perspiration suggested the former. In her all-white outfit, she was successfully pulling off a look more befitting for someone twenty years her junior. McCusker figured she'd noticed, he'd noticed, and didn't appear upset over the attention.

Isabella Barry showed McCusker through to the lounge and returned with two glasses of white wine.

'Thanks, Isabella,' he said, 'if I even have a whiff, I'll be bluttered for the afternoon. How does a cup of tea sound?'

'You know where everything is in the kitchen, please help yourself,' she replied with a very friendly smile, 'I'll just have a quick shower to freshen up.'

McCusker did as bid and even managed to ferret out a few munchies, namely a fresh packet of Jacob's Kimberley biscuits. As he was returning to the sitting room, she was just emerging from what he assumed was her bedroom, hair wet and in a chunky white bathrobe. He could smell a scented candle burning from inside the room. McCusker found the smell to be very pleasant and somewhat invigorating in contrast to the rain drenched streets he'd recently come in from. The rain had been so heavy, McCusker was able to see, in the pavements, the reflections of the seagulls flying above.

She hopped upon her sofa and curled her feet up under her as she finished the first glass of wine and then started into McCusker's untouched glass.

'So how is your investigation going, Brendy?' she started, and then, on noticing what he was munching, 'Don't you be eating my whole pack, they're my favourites.'

Even though she was reprimanding him, she still had this very friendly smile on show for him.

'Yeah, we're making progress,' McCusker started. 'Tell me this, Isabella, did you see Tom last Wednesday at all?'

'Who have you been talking to?'

'No, we're just trying to work out the timeline for Tom for the day—'

'It's okay Brendy, I'm not upset about it anymore, you can say, "for the day he died," or, "his last day,"' she started off confidently, 'I mean yes of course I'm upset over what happened to him but I've decided I have to deal with this properly, if I'm to have any life of my own.'

'Okay, I can appreciate your approach,' McCusker started. He noticed, as she reached over to the coffee table to lift her glass of wine, her bathrobe slipped a little bit from her shoulder, exposing quite a bit of bare skin. She didn't try to cover up as quickly as McCusker would have expected.

'So, what else do you need to ask, Brendy,' she continued, as the front of her robe fell open and she coyly opened it more in order to close it.

'Well, we've a few things left to discuss from our last chat where you had to rush off for an appointment,' McCusker offered. 'I wanted to talk about the last time you saw Tom?'

'Which reminds me, when will the wake be?'

'The body is currently being held by the Coroner,' McCusker started, 'I don't know how long it will be until the remains are released.'

'Oh.'

McCusker was just about to prompt Isabella on his question when she said, 'Just look at me. I've no cop on at all. It's the middle of the fecking afternoon, and I'm sitting here with not a stitch on under my bathrobe. If anyone came around, what would they think, Brendy? It would be okay for you, you're a man, you're divorced, but I've very recently become a widow.

Let me just pop into something more suitable for the occasion, I won't be a mo.'

The detective was a bit concerned about how long it was taking to get the interview started, but, at the same time, he also had started to worry a little about how much flesh she was flashing, so he welcomed this particular interruption.

A few minutes passed, and Isabella's singsong Ulster voice called out, 'Can you come in here a minute Brendy, please?'

McCusker was up out of his seat and heading in the direction of her voice without thinking the whole thing through properly.

'I'm in here,' Isabella said from inside the room he'd assumed earlier was her bedroom. 'C'mon in, Brendy, I won't bite, I promise,' she continued, 'I just need you to fix something for me.'

When he opened the door to the dark room, scented by a burning candle, he discovered a scene which would have been the number one fantasy of all the members of the BLT Gang. Miss Isabella Scott was sprawled over the wine-coloured satin sheets as though she was on a Victoria's Secret photo shoot.

McCusker strode into the room, more Clint Eastwood than George Clooney, turned on the full bright lights with, 'Jeepers I can't see a thing in here, oh my gosh, you'll catch your death of cold in that outfit,' and he grabbed her recently worn bathrobe from the back of a velvet chair and hurled it over her and blew out the candle with, 'and this is a fire hazard, Isabella.'

McCusker didn't know where to put himself. He noticed the bedroom and bathroom wereopen plan. The bath was one of the biggest he'd ever seen in a domestic residence, and it was sunk into the floor with steps down.

'It's big enough for two, Brendy, do you want to join me in there?' Isabella said, when she realised how much attention he was paying to her bath. She flung off the bathrobe again, jumped up from the bed and rushed over to him, 'No? Okay, let's just go to bed. I know you want to; you've always wanted to. It's okay, sweetie, I want to as well.'

'Isabella, you're truly a beautiful woman,' McCusker said, realising he still needed to find a way to finalise his interview.

'I know, sweetie,' she purred, 'it's okay, I'm ready for you.'

'No, Isabella, please make yourself decent, woman, and put on some clothes for heaven's sake.'

'Oh, why not, Brendy, I think it'll be beautiful.'

'I don't cheat, Isabella.'

'I don't want to fecking marry you. I just want to ride you,' she replied, turning down the sensual notch a few degrees. 'Oh, please, Brendy, I promise you…We won't regret it,' she continued, reverting to her purring tone.

'I don't cheat,' McCusker replied, this time a bit less friendly.

'It's better to cheat than to be cheated on,' she snapped, 'believe you me, I've played both roles, and there's no comparison.'

'I'll be in the lounge waiting for you when you get dressed,' McCusker offered, as he left her bedroom.

By the time she returned to the lounge, she was a changed woman. It was as though the bedroom interlude never took place. She was dressed in a large red Kinks sweatshirt and black loose-fitting trainer bottoms. She was barefoot and had removed her blood red lipstick.

McCusker marvelled how in her bare feet, she was nearly the same height as he was. He'd kept forgetting just how tall she was.

'So, you still have some questions for me,' she offered as she breezed past him and sat back on the sofa again.

'Well, yes, actually,' McCusker started, fearing his relief might be a bit too obvious. 'Two main points, though, you were going to tell me the name of the gentleman you were with on Wednesday night?'

'Yes, I said I would, if you needed me to,' she replied sweetly. McCusker was still having trouble understanding her transformation. To the extent he wondered if, with the make-up and the bright orange cum red lips and the lingerie, she had become a certain character, maybe even a cougar and now in her sweats she'd reverted to Mrs Barry again. Then he realised he was too old a potential conquest for her to qualify as a cougar.

'Yes, Isabella, I really need you to tell me who you were with on Wednesday night so we can rule you out from our inquiries.'

'Okay, now I know you need to know, I'll speak to the gentleman in question and get back to you,' she replied and added impishly, 'I suppose you won't need to know chapter and verse over what we got up to?'

'Behave, Isabella,' he chastised, 'just a name and times will do fine, thank you all the same.'

'Okay, I'll talk to him later and get back to you,' she confirmed, 'and your other question?'

'Yes, my other question we started on last time as well, when was the last time you saw Tom?'

'I believe it was about two or three weeks ago.'

'And what was the occasion?'

'We met to discuss our divorce,' she replied.

'And where was this?'

'In Michael McKnight's office,' she said quickly, 'the solicitor said something along the lines of, "Okay, here's the thing, you've both done this before. There is a prenuptial agreement in place. There are no kids. So, I suggest we just go the easy route and follow the original agreement. It's fair to both sides." We both agreed with him. We both signed off on it. We went for a few drinks, ended up in bed here in fact, and then started fighting because I wanted to get back together again. Did McKnight ever reveal to you the contents of the Will?'

'I didn't do his interview,' McCusker admitted, which was the truth, but not all the truth. 'Tell me this, did you and Tom speak on the phone since your meeting where you had your argument?'

'Yes, a few times. I tried, I really tried. He felt it was better if we were separated friends rather than married enemies. He said he just couldn't do it anymore. I think he had someone else waiting in the wings.'

'Do you have any idea who it was?'

'I thought it was my sister again, but apparently not.'

'Why did you marry a second time? Surely you both knew from your first marriage it was never going to work out.'

'I ask myself this same question many times and keep coming back to the same thing. We married too young; we didn't have enough experience to launch a successful relationship; there were third parties who took advantage of the both of us, but, despite all of that, we both genuinely loved each other and we could never escape this simple fact.'

'That's sad, Isabella.'

'Yeah, been there, bought the t-shirt,' she replied flippantly.

'But it still doesn't really explain why you married the second time?'

'Well, I thought it would have been obvious.'

'Oh?'

'Okay, I'll spell it out for you, Brendy. I feel the second time around we both felt, maybe I should say we both *hoped* we'd have more cop on. Yes, *hoped* is definitely more apt. By that point, we both hoped we had the intelligence to accept how much we really loved each other. Add to this, we also had gained the experience which we were clearly lacking first time around.'

'Yet still…' McCusker faltered, not really wanting to spell it out.

'Yet still, no matter how much we wanted it to work, to be together again, we had to accept we had both become completely different people to the young couple who met up on the streets of Portrush one Sunday in 1976.'

McCusker was about to say "But that's so sad." Because it was what he was thinking, but he pulled himself up, just in time.

'Okay, now if you've no more questions,' Isabella said sounding like she might be acknowledging her sadness, 'I've got to go back to my bedroom and finish what we never started,' she said hopping enthusiastically out of her sofa, which, with its numerous, multi-coloured, plump cushions, which McCusker had picked as being her favourite hanging space. 'You're welcome to join,' she added as if it was an afterthought.

McCusker gave as gracious a negative head-shaking signal as he knew how.

'There was a time, as I said, when I would have needed to fecking barricade myself in to keep you and Lefty and Tom away from my bedroom.'

McCusker smiled a smile of someone who'd also just tripped down the very same memory lane.

'What changed?' she said, standing up and putting herself on display by swiftly removing her sweats in a quick, but discreet routine. A well-rehearsed routine he imagined. She stood proud and looked physically charged and magnificent as she pointed both her hands towards herself, in a: "Look what's on offer, man?" gesture. 'I mean, come on, Brendy. No disrespect or anything, but you're not going to get an offer like this very often. What's changed?'

McCusker was going to mention Grace; he was also going to say someday Isabella would meet someone, and everything would fall into place for her. He could say this because this was what he believed. Instead, he just said, 'I never cheat, Isabella.'

She walked him to the door, in her VC outfit, and kissed him on the cheek and as she did she put her arms around his neck and whispered, 'Now you've turned me down, you realise you've made yourself so much more attractive. Now I most definitely have to ride you. Watch out, old man, I usually get what I want.'

McCusker chuckled and then said, 'Isabella, what ever happened to you?'

'I realise I used to be like Snow White, but then I kinda drifted.'

McCusker offered her a sad smile and conceded, at least to himself, she'd managed to do the impossible and successfully pull off one of Mae West's classic lines. She let him go and stood back from the door, her hand on the edge, ready to close it.

'Last chance McCusker,' she tried again, and when she saw her seeds of invitation were falling on stony ground, she offered, 'I will be thinking of you, you know, so you could come and watch if you like.'

McCusker turned and walked away. He never heard the door close.

Chapter Forty-Four

'Colette,' McCusker said after a brisk walk, with a quick stop off, from Isabella's apartment up to Colette Barry's house up on Ballymacrea Road.

'Brendy, it is yourself,' she said as she leaned over to accept his peck on the cheek. 'On my goodness, man, you reek of vinegar.'

McCusker felt like a kid snagged red handed with orchard apples in his pockets.

'Ah, caught out,' McCusker offered, only slightly embarrassed, 'I will admit to a slight detour to Dolphin's for one of their tasty fish suppers. Hard to resist. I'd been trying to nip in over the last three days, but never found the time, until now.'

'Yeah, I would also admit to sharing a similar guilty pleasure… occasionally,' she said through a generous smile, 'tell you what, you should nip into my bathroom and give your hands and face a good wash with my sweet mandarin and grapefruit soap and I will make you a cup of tea to wash your supper down.'

She looked at her watch as if to suggest, even for McCusker, it was frightfully early for supper. 'I will also see what else I can whip up for you for your dessert. I will not tell anyone if you promise the same.'

McCusker did as he was bid and returned to her cosy kitchen. On the way through her comfortable house, he thought some people, including himself he had to admit, merely occupy their living space, while others, such as Colette, and Grace O'Carroll, now he thought about it, create more of a home for themselves in their habitat. They do this by personalising their space with their "stuff", décor, furniture, scents and ambience to the extent it grows to become part of themselves. He, without any difficulty, could imagine Colette Barry contentedly rambling about her house and gardens for days on end without needing the company, or solace, of another soul. One of his biggest dreams was he and Grace creating such a space for themselves when they found a house they could make into such a home. He wondered was it easier for one person to accomplish this, than it was for a couple, where the word (and deeds) of compromise must have to come into play.

As if to further amplify the ideal cosy home dream to McCusker, tea and mouth-watering hot scones with cream and jam were awaiting him in the kitchen.

'So, I was not expecting you back so soon,' Colette said, after she sat watching him take so much enjoyment from his first half of a scone. It looked to McCusker as though she was taking as much joy from watching him as he was from eating.

'Really?'

'Pardon?' she said as her head darted back in mild shock reflex, more bemused than angry.

'Well,' McCusker continued, pausing to polish off another ½ a scone with a cup of tea. 'I'm not sure you were fully open about Ellen DiVito?'

'I did not tell you any lies.'

'Sometimes lies are less damaging than not hearing the full truth.'

'Okay, Brendy,' Colette said, 'I knew I would have to tell you this at some point, but I hoped it would be later when this is all over. I suppose I am still trying to deal with what happened. It has been such a…I still refuse to even set myself the task of thinking what this is. But I assure you, I meant you no disrespect.'

'I'm listening,' McCusker said, feeling he couldn't really get upset with her after how genuinely friendly she had sounded when she'd called him "Brendy."

'Tom and I were back together again, properly, if you see what I mean?'

'And he was here on Wednesday?'

'And he was here on Wednesday, stayed over on Tuesday night,' she agreed. 'With all the stuff which had been thrown at us over the years, we'd agreed to stop trying to deal with it and to just try to enjoy being together. We agreed to ignore divorce, marriage, ex-husbands, ex-wives, and just focus on ourselves for a change, but this time discreetly.

'We had agreed this last November and were dealing with it okay, but then we got a wee bit too careless in May this year. Tom took me to the North West 200. We were there on Sat 18th May. Tom wanted to go because it was the special 90th anniversary of the famous motor-cycle race. We based ourselves at The Metropole Corner, which was handy for us, we can walk there and you get a great sense of how exciting the race is as they have to slow way down and then get ready for speeding off down the straight. They have a big screen there were you can view the action around the remainder of the circuit. Anyway, as it was the 90th there were lots of minor celebrities in attendance. The TV cameras would pick up on some of them and flash them up on the big screen. One of the cameras picked up on Tom. The second I noticed they flashed him and me up there on the big screen, I knew there would be trouble. Would you not know it, but the last person in Ulster you would expect to be watching a motorcycle race, our Isabella, saw Tom and I together on the TV coverage. She went nuclear. And then the smelly stuff hit the fan! She said she did not really care what Tom and I were up to as long as we kept it private. Those might have been the words she was using, but I know, beneath it all, she was seething with jealously. You do not know what our Isabella is really like, Brendy.

'She had already told Tom she would not agree to divorce him because she knew he would come running back to me. Tom and I finally decided to take the easy route, to commit to being together, whatever way we needed to. We dedicated ourselves to enjoying the best days of our lives while we still had them.

'She said we both disrespected her on TV. She had hurt us badly before. We could not win, and we refused to even want to try.'

'So, you had your best friend, Ellen, be Tom's plus one in public to throw up a smoke screen?' McCusker offered.

'Exactly!'

'Tell me this, Colette,' McCusker started back up again, 'did Ellen collect Tom from here last Wednesday afternoon?'

'Yes.'

'Did she bring him back here afterwards?'

'Yes.'

'What time did she arrive?'

'About 18.45.'

'What happened then, did Ellen leave?' McCusker asked, feeling he was making progress on Thomas Barry's final day for the first time.

'No, she had supper with Tom and I here.'

'And what time did she leave?'

'She left at 20.45.

'So, Tom was…'

'Tom went with her.'

'Oh?' McCusker said.

'Yes, he had an appointment in town at 21.00.'

'Oh?' McCusker said, but really wanted to say, "Do you not think it might have helped us if you'd told me this earlier?" She hadn't, so what was the use? He couldn't change what had been. There was no point in potentially upsetting her more at this point. 'So, he had an appointment set up for 21.00 last Wednesday night, the night he died?'

'Yes.'

'And this appointment was with?'

'I do not know. I did not like to crowd Tom, the way Isabella did.'

'Did Ellen ever tell you where she dropped Tom off at?'

'I asked her, she said she dropped him off outside the 55 Degrees North.'

'But he'd just had supper?'

'Yes, exactly, so he must have been going somewhere near there.'

'Did Ellen see where Tom was going?'

'No, she said he stood on the pavement as he waved her off. She said she could see him in her rear-view mirror still standing there as she turned the corner and he dropped out of her sightline.'

CHAPTER FORTY-FOUR

'Did he have any projects near there?'

'I know he had toyed over buying what was left of the Arcadia Ballroom,' Colette said, 'as you know it would have been a labour of love but would not have made any commercial sense. But I do not think he had completely given up on the idea.'

'Hmm,' McCusker mused, 'and when he didn't return, what did you think?'

'I thought Tom had finished his appointment late, was being his usual considerate self and stayed in his house in Antrim Gardens as he did a few nights a week.'

'Okay,' McCusker said and felt he should say more, 'Colette, I'm happy you and Tom had made your decision to get on with your life and not waste any more time being preoccupied by all the stuff getting in the way of people being together...'

McCusker started to struggle.

She came to his rescue.

'Only last St. Valentine's day did Tom and I take our private vows out in my back garden. He swore on a bible he would love honour and obey me until death do us part. At the time neither of us thought that within five months, one week, three days and a few hours he'd have fulfilled all of *his* promises.'

Chapter Forty-Five

The second McCusker walked into the Ramore Head PSNI station, the receptionist gave him two message slips. The first one was from Mrs Hughes, Thomas Barry's P.A. who had rang in to advise she had discovered Thomas Barry's mobile phone on the top of the out tray in his office. The phone wasn't charged. Mrs Hughes said Thomas was forever letting it run out of power. The other message instructed McCusker to go and see Superintendent Ivan Valley immediately.

'Ah, Mr McCusker,' was his greeting from the Superintendent.

'Oops, sounds ominous,' McCusker said, as he took the seat he was shown to. Valley's office, apart from the contents of his notice board, was very much like the way McCusker remembered his local headmaster's office. Very tidy with lots of books, lots of photos from throughout the Super's career with the good and the great of Ulster. Comfy chairs and not so comfortable chairs and a TV in the corner, perfectly positioned for the Superintendent should he swivel his chair 90 degrees to his right, with the screen activated and the sound not. It was the continued coverage of the Open, currently coming to a climax on a wind and rain-swept course less than a mile from where they sat. Valley couldn't resist, no matter how hard he tried, to steal a glance at the screen every few seconds. He looked like he was angry at something. McCusker, knew he was being grossly immature, but he could feel the butterflies rising in his stomach. It wasn't a pleasant feeling. He knew he was in trouble.

He immediately thought of Grace O'Carroll.

'I have to advise you, Mr McCusker, a serious complaint has been made against you.'

McCusker went to speak.

Valley held his hand up with enough control to stop a fight, or even start one. Certainly, the leathery hand ensured McCusker's continued silence and obedience.

'A Miss Isabella Scott claims earlier this afternoon you entered her bedroom, when she was in a state of undress, and tried to sexually assault her.'

'I...'

The hand was raised again.

'Mr McCusker, I have to advise you, in this day and age, we have to handle each and every one of these charges seriously and investigate them thoroughly.'

'I...'

The hand was raised yet again.

'Mr McCusker, is there anything you can say to me to stop me from suspending you immediately?'

'I...' McCusker started and then subconsciously stopped as he had on the previous three occasions. Only this time the hand signal was not in a stop sign, but palm upward with fingers motioning for McCusker to speak.

With his other hand, the Super was writing something on a sheet of paper, which he held up so McCusker could read it:

Keep it clean!

Official!

Being recorded!

'Well, Sir,' McCusker began, trying to sound as official as he knew how, 'myself and DI O'Carroll discussed this very subject in advance. We both felt I could get more information from certain witnesses, mainly Miss Isabella Scott and Mrs Colette Barry, were I to interview them alone. DI O'Carroll supplied me with her spare mobile phone, showed me how it worked and instructed me to record all my solo interviews with Miss Scott and Mrs Barry as a precaution.'

'I see,' Valley said, stealing a glance at the TV screen where two golfers,

McCusker couldn't work out who they were, and their caddies were walking up the fairway leaning forward at a 60 degree angle in order to counter the power of the gusts of wind and rain, 'and do you have this device with you Mr McCusker?'

McCusker reached into his breast pocket and produced O'Carroll's spare mobile. He found the apt and played the interview from the first three knocks on Isabella's door to her inviting him to come and watch her entertain herself.

'I have to commend DI O'Carroll on her advice, and I have to commend you on your super-human powers of restraint, Mr McCusker. No further action called for. This interview is terminated at 16.27 on Sunday 21st July 2019.'

Valley looked like he was turning off a recording device; McCusker could not see a system. If there was one, in fact, he doubted it was legit, but McCusker assumed the room was wired for sound. The controls for some reason or other, seemed to be in his top left-hand drawer.

'Right, that's the official bollix out of the way,' Valley offered, enthusiastically, 'I just wanted, needed really, to have it on record that we discussed the matter. How did you ever manage to avoid the potential train wreck? I can't believe you actually turned on the light, blew out the friggin' candle, and covered her up. She must have been going crazy. I'm surprised she didn't totally blow her cool. Let me get a bit of the interview again. Yes, here it is,' and he hit play again.

'Jeepers, I can't see a thing in here, oh my gosh, you'd catch your death of cold in that outfit,' and then on to extinguish the candle, *'and this is a fire hazard, Isabella.'*

'Let's get some of Isabella's classic lines,' Valley said, and he started to futter with O'Carroll's spare mobile again.

'It's big enough for two, Brendy. Do you want to join me in there?'

'No? Okay, let's just go to bed. I know you want to; you've always wanted to. It's okay, sweetie, I want to as well.'

'Isabella, you're truly a beautiful woman.' McCusker's voice this time on the mobile phone.

'I know, sweetie,' Isabella lamented, *'it's okay, I'm ready for you.'*

'No, Isabella, please make yourself decent, woman and put on some clothes for heaven's sake.' McCusker again.

'Oh, why not, Brendy? I think it'll be beautiful.'

'I don't cheat, Isabella.' McCusker yet again and Valley commended him on his resolve.

'I don't want to marry you. I just want to ride you,' Isabella was heard pleading

'Oh, please, Brendy, I promise you...we won't regret it.' Isabella again.

'And then the classic one where she suggests if you don't want to join her, she'll pleasure herself but she's happy for you to stay and watch her as she does it,' Valley says concluding his summary. 'But I'm surprised she remained so cool with you. I mean, you turned her down every which way and more, and if she had any self-respect, she would have stopped after she dropped the first hint, and even at the end, where she warns you, it's not over yet, she's out to get you. I mean, why did she not lose it?'

'You know, in a way, it was like watching a junkie who'd already started to take their drug of choice. She seemed like she was already on her journey, her trip, whatever you want to call it, and she would have done anything, and I do mean anything, including humiliating herself in order to satisfy her craving.'

'I knew it wasn't true, of course,' Valley admitted, 'right from the start.'

'What convinced you?'

'Well, her language for a start,' Valley started, 'she said you sexually assaulted her. Like it was her key phrase. She said it like she'd heard it a lot in the media. It sounded like she hadn't thought it through any further. And when I asked her what you actually did to her, she just kept saying, "he assaulted me." And when I asked her what colour your underpants were, she said, "How would I know?" But you know what convinced me you didn't do as she suggested?'

'What, because I tried to be a decent cop and keep my trousers on?'

'No, because I saw over at The Royal, how good you and Grace are together,' Valley said and immediately changed tone with, 'now can you get the hell out of here. You are certainly not guilty as charged, but you still managed to dump a load more paperwork on my desk. The ironic thing is, if you'd been guilty, I'd have had a lot less paperwork to do.'

McCusker turned to go.

'Sorry about that, Sir.' McCusker said, knowing the wisecrack he'd initially thought of adding at the end of his sentence, "I'll remember next time," could have backfired drastically for him.

'McCusker,' Valley said, just as the innocent agency cop was about to close the door. 'Make sure you bring either DI O'Carroll or DS Johnson with you next time you visit either of the Scott sisters.'

'Okay,' McCusker said and started to close the door after him.

'McCusker!'

'Yes?' he said as he opened the door again.

'Aren't you forgetting something?'

'Am…thank you, Superintendent Valley?' McCusker guessed.

'No,' Valley said, glaring at O'Carroll's mobile phone still sitting on his desk.

'Oh yes, sorry,' McCusker smiled as he walked back in and collected said item.

He'd very nearly made it the whole way out and closed the door when Valley said, 'McCusker?'

'Yes?'

'Let's be careful out there,' Valley offered, through a growing grin.

* * *

McCusker made his way to the incident room, where Johnston and O'Carroll were busy working away. McCusker wandered over to the notice board.

'I notice Ryan's alibi checked out,'

'Yes, I spoke to Maureen,' Johnson said, 'Maureen McCarthy, and she confirmed she cooked for and slept with Ryan on Wednesday night. She was a very nice woman, and I was half-expecting her to be upset Ryan had betrayed their relationship by spilling the beans. In fact, if anything, she was really chuffed he'd admitted to someone else in the world they had something going on. She said she was happy to go into the PSNI station in Ballymoney and give an official statement.'

McCusker explained to O'Carroll and Johnson about his meeting with Valley and the claim Isabella Scott had made. He was happy it hadn't travelled around the PSNI station yet. Valley obviously hadn't made a fuss about it.

'Do you still have it on my spare phone?' O'Carroll asked.

'Yes, of course,' McCusker replied, 'thanks to you, it saved my bacon.'

'You should discuss it with Grace, and we'll play it to her when we get back to Belfast. Sod's law says if you don't, she'll hear about it from elsewhere and if you do, there is an equally good chance she'd never have heard about it.'

'I'd already phoned her,' McCusker admitted.

'Sound,' O'Carroll said.

'Sound?' McCusker repeated, 'I've never heard you use "Sound" in such a way before. You're starting to sound like a local already.'

'It's Melodee's fault, actually, she's to blame; she uses it all the time,' O'Carroll admitted.

'Guilty,' Johnson confirmed, 'I grew up hearing my dad and my older brothers say it about everything.'

'Sound!' McCusker said, in a very self-conscious way.

His audience of two laughed, and O'Carroll said, 'Yeah, you need a wee bit more work on the delivery before you try it in public.'

'Okay, alibis,' McCusker announced, drawing a line under the "sound" topic, 'let's see how we're progressing. Ryan now moves from the top of our suspects list and onto our cleared list. Which leaves us with…'

'Sean and Seamus Buckley being each other's alibi,' DS Melodee Johnson said, 'I'm still having trouble with this. What about Mrs Colette Barry?'

'She was doing a Macaulay Culkin,' McCusker said.

'Sorry, a Macaulay Culkin?' Johnson asked.

'Oh, he means she was home alone,' O'Carroll volunteered in clarification, 'which in effect means she doesn't really have an alibi.'

'Which sometimes we have to accept, humans don't always know when they're going to need to prove they were somewhere else,' McCusker said.

'So, you're happy with her claim?' O'Carroll said.

'Yeah…nearly…I'm not actually at one hundred percent yet,' McCusker replied, forcing himself to consider it. 'I mean, I think there is still something she is not telling us, but at the same time, she seems the one most upset over Thomas's death.'

'And then there's Portrush's answer to Mrs Robinson, Isabella Scott, herself,' O'Carroll added, 'who claims to have an alibi, but she needed to clear it with her gentleman-caller before she could betray the party in question.'

'Yeah, she promised me she would check with him and get back to me,' McCusker said.

'From what you were saying, she was promising you a lot more, Mc-Cusker,' O'Carroll offered, but not as a rebuke, 'let's you and I go and pay Miss Scott a wee visit.'

'And I'll continue to sift through these late-night-caller dockets,' Johnson said, contently.

McCusker and O'Carroll were standing in the reception of the station house debating whether to risk the teaming rain and wind or sit it out.

Before McCusker had even a chance to think about it, let alone answer O'Carroll, the receptionist called over to say she had a call for McCusker.

The side of the conversation O'Carroll could hear was:

'Oh, hello, Mr McKnight,' pause, 'sorry, Michael it is,' pause, 'Yes I'm good, thanks, and you?' pause, 'really? Is it not a bit early for the reading of a Will, I thought it had to be at least a week and a half, which is why most people go for ten days,' pause, 'can DI O'Carroll come along with me?' pause, 'really, okay, I see,' pause, 'who else will be there?' pause, 'okay, I understand,' pause 'okay I'll see you in your office at nine in the morning.'

The side of the conversation O'Carroll didn't overhear, McCusker recalled for her was:

'He introduced himself, said I should call him Michael. He asked me how

I was doing. He said he was inviting me to the reading of Thomas's Will tomorrow morning in his office. He agreed it was usually a minimum of a week and a half, but in this instance, he and the main beneficiary of the Will felt it would be in everyone's interest in solving this case if the Will was read sooner rather than later. When I asked him if you could come along, he said, "No." He explained only the people who are mentioned in the Will can come to the reading of the Will, and I was being invited, not as a member of the PSNI but as a former friend of the deceased.'

'Make sure you run it past the Superintendent,' O'Carroll ordered.

'Good point,' McCusker replied, as he walked back over to the reception door to check the skies again.

'What do you think?' O'Carroll asked.

'It's bound to pass, eventually,' McCusker claimed, 'look over there,' he continued as he nodded, rather than pointed, in a north-eastern direction, 'there's blue sky over there.'

'There's always a blue sky in your life, McCusker, isn't there?' she offered, sounding more envious than contemptuous.

By this point, McCusker's blue sky, and glorious it was too, had arrived, and they headed off to O'Carroll's jam jar and five minutes later she parked in a side street by the church buildings next to the former majestic bank building, the top floor of which was the residence of Miss Isabella Scott.

Two minutes later, McCusker was knocking on Miss Scott's principal residence.

Isabella opened the door all bright and breezy, back once again in her all-white tennis outfit, a freshly laundered version. The first words out of her mouth, in gushes were,' Oh Mi God…you've come back…you've changed your mind… you've accepted my invitation… Oh, Brendy, I've been sooooooo looking forward to this…' and immediately grabbed him by the arm and started to pull him into her hallway.

'It's great to hear the other version of the incident you reported,' O'Carroll announced, stepping out from behind the corner of the corridor where she'd been slyly hiding.

'Oh for heaven's sake, cop on, Detective Inspector, I think you must have misunderstood what I was saying to Brendy, Isabella eventually replied, 'I was just welcoming him back, he's an old friend of mine, you know.'

'Maybe I did misunderstand you,' O'Carroll said, 'but just so there is absolutely no misunderstanding, why don't I play the conversation back for us all to clear this up. And then when we've played your most recent greeting, we can also play the recording of Mr McCusker's earlier interview with you.'

Isabella went beetroot red, amplified spectacularly by her white outfit.

In her defence, she made a very reasonable attempt at a comeback.

'Oh, I'm so sorry you'll have to forgive me,' she started, as she ushered them into her apartment, 'I'm afraid since this Thomas incident, I'm all over the place. My nerves and hormones are completely out of kilter. I'm walking around in a daze. I don't know what I'm doing. I don't know what I'm saying. I can't be by myself. I needed to feel close to him.'

McCusker knew, as O'Carroll looked Isabella and her outfit up and down, his colleague was thinking, "hardly an outfit, you'd expect to see a grieving widow in."

'Yeah, we understand, but I still don't see why you would then go and try and get him in trouble with Superintendent Valley?' O'Carroll said.

'Yeah, I know, I was just lashing out because I wasn't thinking properly,' Isabella claimed, 'my mind is all over the place at the minute.'

'You need to be very careful, Isabella, sometimes one's mind can be a very bad person,' O'Carroll said, totally shocking McCusker in the process. He wondered where these words had come from and if, perhaps, she'd started to read the same beer mats he was reading. He sincerely hoped not.

'So how can I help you?' Isabella asked as she appeared to have to make an effort to cover her protruding teeth with her top lip.

'Did you speak to the gentleman you spent Wednesday night with, Isabella?' McCusker asked.

'I hate to use this tone with you, Brendy, but oh please, for heaven's sake, just give me a break, I mean…' Isabella snarled.

O'Carroll interrupted her with, 'I find when I find myself hating to use a tone, it's always best not to use the tone.'

'Of course, yes, sorry. No, what I really meant to say was, not yet, I mean I tried,' Isabella Scott explained, 'I've left him a few messages, but he hasn't returned my call yet.'

'I don't know what I can tell you, Isabella, pretty soon we're going to have to…'

'I promise you if he hasn't contacted me by first thing tomorrow morning, I'll give you his details then, either way. I can't be fairer, now can I?'

'Mr McCusker already has a previous appointment booked for tomorrow morning, but I'll come around at 09.00,' O'Carroll offered.

McCusker felt his colleague had pulled off a: this is not a negotiable offer, delivery, quite successfully.

Isabella looked like she was going to protest, then clearly thought better of it and said, 'Okay, it's a deal, I'll see you at 09.00.'

McCusker felt a little deflated. He couldn't work out if it was because Isabella hadn't yet revealed the name of her mystery man or if it was because she hadn't supplied tea and Kimberley Biscuits again. Either way, he also noted Isabella Scott didn't swear whenever she was in the company of two. Then he wondered if maybe she just didn't swear in the company of women.

Chapter Forty-Six

'Let's pick up DS Johnson, and I'll take you both for a wee treat,' McCusker said when they were back in her car.

Fifteen minutes later, the three of them were on the Promenade in Portstewart four miles along the coast to the west of Portrush.

'Okay, and now for a wee secret and a bit of a treat,' McCusker began, sounding as excited as if he was a kid on holiday with his parents. 'Don't move from here and I'll be back in three minutes.'

O'Carroll and Johnson observed McCusker's movements until he became part of the busy crowd on the pavement. The two car-bound members of the PSNI followed what they felt was his line of travel along the pavement, sometimes fellow pedestrians obscured their vision of him. Then, just outside Morelli's To Go, he disappeared from view completely.

Six long minutes later, McCusker returned to the car with two large 99 ice cream cones for his compatriots and a large 99 ice cream slider for himself.

'These three beauts and 25p change out of a tenner, ach sure you couldn't beat it,' he enthused, beaming from ear to ear.

'And the wee secret?' O'Carroll inquired as her eyes rolled in an impressed way after her first lick, 'Oh my goodness. Major treat McCusker, and what was the wee secret you promised to reveal?'

'Ach, the secret,' McCusker gushed, as his eyes disappeared in ecstasy behind his eyelids. 'the best-kept secret in Portrush is, in order to buy the best ice cream in Portrush you have to visit Morelli's in Portstewart.'

The three of them exited the car, walked over to the seafront, found an empty bench, and sat down together. The trio contentedly licked their ice cream in silence, while enjoying a similar sunset to the one which had once inspired a local prolific lyricist, Jimmy Kennedy, to write the words for *Red Sails in the Sunset* in the early 1930s. The song, with music by High Williams, celebrated the yacht, *Kitty of Coleraine,* sailing through this very scene. The celebrated song had been successfully recorded hundreds of times over the years most noticeably by Nat King Cole, Louis Armstrong and Fats Domino. There was even a live recording of the Beatles performing the song in the Star Club Hamburg.

McCusker knew all about this song because it was a song his father could always be relied on to have a stab at on family occasions. When McCusker senior had a few jars on him, he'd need no coaxing at all.

McCusker junior waited until he'd completed the challenging task of work on his slider for fear of losing any precious drops, or from spilling some of the same treasured melting ice cream over his clothes, before he broke their silence by saying, ' You know—'

'Hold your thought, McCusker,' O'Carroll said, as she answered her mobile. 'Hello…yes, it is… Oh hello… Yes, I'm with him now, Isabella, I can give him a message… Right… No, I'll still need to come visit you. I'll need to take your official statement, or you could drop into the police station… Okay, I'll see you in the morning, an hour later at ten o'clock… Thank you… Goodbye… Goodbye.'

'Wow,' O'Carroll gushed, 'that was Isabella Scott.'

'Okay, I think we guessed,' McCusker said.

'Yes, but what you didn't guess was… well, guess who Miss Scott was with the night her husband was murdered?' O'Carroll showboated.

'Lefty Kelly,' McCusker replied, before O'Carroll's words had withered on her lips.

'Nooooo, why would you mention Lefty?' O'Carroll said, sounding like she found the thought of that particular coupling to be offensive. He couldn't work out if O'Carroll has secretly grown fond of Lefty to the degree where she felt Lefty would never dream of favouring Isabella, cute and all as she was, or, if someone as cute as Isabella would ever be seen dead with Lefty.

'Ryan?' Johnson offered, looking like she was having trouble coming up with an alternate, 'but then Ryan was with Maureen McCarthy…unless… you know Maureen was ultra-co-operative, so maybe Maureen was in on the farse, thereby covering up for Ryan. She was so keen to offer a statement which cleared Ryan.'

'No,' O'Carroll said, dragging the short word out into several syllables, 'oh come on, it's not difficult really?'

'I don't know,' McCusker said, not wanting to offer up who he secretly thought it was, 'bald Buddy Holly?'

'Nao,' O'Carroll wined. 'I give you a clue. We're talking about one of the Buckley Brothers.'

'Wow, Sean Buckley,' McCusker said, admitting who he thought it was.

'Wrong again,' O'Carroll grandstanded.

'Not Seamus Buckley? Holy shit,' Johnson gasped.

'It probably exists, but I bet you anything you want it still smells,' McCusker offered, still in shock. 'Hang on a minute, this means Sean no longer has an alibi.'

'So it does,' O'Carroll said.

'Let's just consider this,' McCusker said, while trying to figure out if they'd just broken the case or if they were now further away from the truth than they'd ever been.

'What does this mean?' Johnson said. 'Llet's recap.'

'Talk us through it again, McCusker, please,' O'Carroll asked.

'Okay,' McCusker replied, closing his eyes and blocking out Jimmy Kennedy's sunset scene so he could recall the notice board in the incident room. 'Thomas met Isabella Scott…'

'Goodness, not so far back,' O'Carroll said, 'actually, on second thoughts, maybe you *should* start at the very beginning.'

'Thomas Barry meets Isabella Scott in 1976.

'They marry in 1982.

'Colette Scott met Ryan Shannon in 1983.

'Colette Scott marries Ryan Shannon in 1990.

'Isabella Barry cheats with Ryan Shannon probably late 1999 early 2000.

'Thomas Barry and Isabella Barry split up in the summer of 2000.

'Ryan Shannon and Colette Shannon split in 2001.

'Ryan and Colette divorce in 2002.

'Thomas and Isabella divorce in 2003.

'Isabella and Ryan marry in 2004.

'Tom and Colette marry in 2005.

'Ryan and Isabella split in 2010.

'2011 Ryan and Isabella divorce; she returns to her maiden name, Scott.

'2012 Tom and Colette split.

'2013 Tom and Colette divorce. Colette continues using the name Colette Barry.

'2014 Tom and Isabella marry for the second time.

'Somewhere throughout 2015, 2016 and 2017, Thomas and Isabella's second marriage to each other collapsed but they never divorce.

'Somewhere during these years Tom and Colette start to see each other again but discreetly.

'2018 Thomas and Colette are, to all intents and purposes, an item at this point, but they remain discrete and retain individual residences.

'Feb 14th 2019, Thomas and Colette in a private ceremony, make their vows to each other but Thomas doesn't seek a divorce.

'Thursday 18 July this year, Thomas is found dead. On the night he died he had dinner with the wife he divorced but is no longer separated from, while the wife he is separated from, but not divorced from, was seeing and sleeping with Seamus Buckley, Thomas's Business Partner and the less diplomatic of the Buckley Bros. While the cultured Buckley Brother, Sean, the one Thomas has a much better working relationship with, turns out to have given a false alibi.'

'How do you remember all of the relevant information without a notebook,' Johnson asked in awe.

'He makes mental notes, then has a notebook he writes up each night. Once he writes it into his notebook, he can recall every fact. It's true. He can tell you things like the length and colour of a witness's socks,' O'Carroll offered by way of explanation.

'So, what are we missing?' McCusker continued, wanting to remain in his zone, 'the thing Colette keeps refusing to discuss with me is why she and Thomas split up and then divorced each other shortly thereafter.'

'Okay, what do you think it might be?' O'Carroll asked. 'Why did he leave the woman he loves to re-marry the woman he doesn't?'

'And why did he give up a possible career in politics at around the same time?" McCusker asked but wasn't expecting to be answered.

* * *

On the trip back to Portrush, DS Johnson quickly read through the cards containing the details of the late-night phone calls into the PSNI station house on the night of Wednesday 17th July and the early hours of the morning of Thursday 18th July.

There were five cards in total.

17/7 at 23.30, a Robyn Hode rang in from the harbour end of Kerr Street to say she'd lost the password to her laptop and it was most definitely an emergency. She insisted the PHSI had to crack the code to reclaim the password for her. She was told to ring back in the morning, She said it would be too late by then and the world as we know it would have ended at sun-up the following morning and warning the operator with, "On your head be it, goodbye."

17/7 at 23.58 Someone not realising his telephone details were immediately traceable rang up and belched into the phone for six and a half minutes before hanging up.

18/7 at 00. 47 Ann Mosey rang in to say an ATM machine down by the Town Hall had eaten her credit card and she needed £20 to get back home, to Coleraine. She wanted to know if she could come over immediately and pick it up.

18/7 at 01. 53 a George Hickey at the harbour end of Main Street rang the line to say there was a helicopter flying very low over his roof, and he was worried the helicopter was actually going to land on his roof. He needed someone, the PSNI preferably, to ring through to the pilot of the helicopter and tell them his roof was not secured for landing. A few seconds later, he said, 'Oh, sorry, it appears to have gone.'

18/7 at 02.16, a William Henry Carthy Jr., rang in from a flat in Princess Street. He wanted to know if his son robbed the Northern Bank down on Main Street could his son or his son's family, meaning himself, keep the funds even if his son was caught.

* * *

They dropped DS Johnson off at her apartment on Hamilton Place on route to McCusker's house on Strandmore. They watched a bit of telly as in the highlights of Shane Lowry being awarded the Claret Jug.

JB Holmes, who was in the lead the first day, was still in with a shout on the Friday and Saturday. However, he took a disastrous 87 shots on the final day. To put this in perspective, every player had a bad day on the Sunday, Shane Lowry shot a round of 72 the same day. Shane, however, had battled the elements to finish the competition 16 under par for the four days, six shots ahead of his nearest rival, Tommy Fleetwood. Shane and his caddie, Bo Martin, looked like they were having so much fun all weekend they could have been two mates who had been out for a drink down their local and they'd accidently stumbled onto The Royal Golf club, picked up a set of clubs and joined in the play. McCusker thought Shane Lowry had taken maximum enjoyment from his own playing. McCusker had always felt this was such an infectious quality: the ability of great athletes, or musicians for that matter, to visibly enjoy their own work.

The commentator claimed Shane was the first bearded golfer to win the Open since 1882.

'Your mate Anthony Robertson had £100 bet on him to win, didn't he?' O'Carroll said, as they watched the Irishman pick up his precious award and cheque.

'Not only did he actually put a £100 bet on Shane, but he put it on a few weeks ago, and he got odds of 100 to 1,' McCusker replied.

'Ten grand!' O'Carroll gushed, 'but you're still upset over Rory not doing better?'

'If only he didn't have his disastrous first round,' McCusker offered, through a large audible sigh, 'but you know what?'

'What?'

'They still don't have an "if only" column on the Golf scorecards.'

Chapter Forty-Seven

Monday 22nd July

'I know you said you'd never discuss any relationship you had with Isabella Scott, Lefty, but would you be prepared to comment on a different kind of question on Isabella?' McCusker asked the following morning as Lefty dropped in once more conveniently at breakfast time. So conveniently in fact, to lead O'Carroll to suggest he been outside McCusker's door sniffing by the letterbox waiting for the first aromas from the rasher-wagon to emerge, before he knocked on the door.

'I will if I can ask you a question and state a fact,' Lefty replied, taking his usual seat at the head of the table, before being invited.

'Okay, deal,' McCusker said, 'were yo…'

'No, visitors first,' Lefty interrupted before McCusker had a chance to get his question out. 'Fact: I said I wouldn't discuss any relationship I had, *or didn't have*, with Isabella Scott.'

'Acknowledged,' McCusker said, for the record, and in front of a witness.

'And I was invited to the reading of Mister Barry's Will this morning at 09.00, and the reading was cancelled late last night because some due to attend couldn't make it and the Will reading was delayed indefinitely. Were you the person in question, Brendy?'

'Yes,' O'Carroll admitted on McCusker's behalf, 'Superintendent Ivan Valley felt it might compromise the investigation if a member of the investigating team was seen to be a beneficiary of the will. The Superintendent asked the reading of the Will be postponed until the investigation was concluded.'

'Right,' Lefty said, 'I figured as much, well maybe not Valley's interjection as much as a potential conflict of interest.'

'Lefty, I need you to not betray my confidence in you by sharing this,' O'Carroll said, 'and in return you'll receive this morning's extra rasher, if McCusker ever finishes preparing breakfast.'

'What, I'm only getting one?' Lefty protested. The BLT wingman was turned out spic and span as usual in his regular form of clothing. Today's colours were blue button-down-collar, shirt, green tie, Royal Blue, V-Neck jumper, green cord, trousers, and tan cord jacket.

'As long as it's only one,' McCusker said, 'now it's my turn for a question.'

'Shoot,' Lefty said as O'Carroll winked at him from behind McCusker's back, showing her visitor three fingers.

'Do you know whether or not Isabella was having an affair with Sean Buckley?'

'Warm,' Lefty responded immediately, 'correct family, wrong sibling.'

'Seamus Buckley?' O'Carroll and McCusker uttered in perfect unison.

'But…' McCusker started off again, solo this time.

Lefty Kelly raised his hand in a stop sign to McCusker.

'I'm not going to say another word on this subject, Brendy. On top of which, I will admit I'm quite fond of Isabella. I know a lot of people find her quite…well, let's just say she's not backward about coming forward. For myself, I can only speak as I find. I've found her very uncomplicated, perhaps she suffers from above-average levels of oxytocin, but she's consistently supportive and speaks what's on her mind. This wasn't always the way, I used to think she was very aloof and seemed fixated on her beauty. I think she eventually discovered her beauty wasn't going to bring her happiness.'

McCusker, still preoccupied by yesterday's revelation on Seamus Buckley, now confirmed by Lefty, knew not to push for any more at this stage. More to the point, breakfast was ready, and its arrival silenced the table for a few minutes.

'You're not much older than McCusker, are you, Lefty?'

'Older enough to favour the chemist over the sweetie shop as my priority call.'

'Old enough that the grocer won't sell him green bananas anymore, so he is,' McCusker offered and when the laughter between the three of them died down, McCusker slowly shifted to a more serious tone. 'He's four years older than me. He's…sorry…he was two years older than Tom.'

'So what age were you all when Thomas picked up Isabella's glove?'

'Lefty would have been nineteen, Tom was seventeen, and I was—'

'Still a kid,' Lefty offered.

'I was fifteen,' McCusker admitted. 'Tom and I had been good mates for a while when we met up with our wing man. Little did we know.'

'*Little* did you know,' Lefty repeated.

'What age was Isabella?' O'Carroll persisted.

'Isabella was seventeen, same age as Tom,' McCusker offered.

'So really Isabella should have been more attracted to you,' O'Carroll said, looking at Lefty.

'Lefty has always had a problem with his neck,' McCusker explained, 'he wasn't as quick as Tom was at stooping down to pick up Isabella's glove.'

'Aye, you're not wrong, Brendy, but we could all see what Mister Barry saw in her. Don't get me wrong, it wasn't just her looks, when her looks would have been more than enough for three teenage boys. Isabella Scott had something more. She had an air commanding you to want to get to know her, defied you to ignore her. She was so sharp, so smart, but her main attraction was she didn't go beating you around the ears with her intelligence.'

'If truth was told, I suppose you all fell in love with her the first night when she dropped her glove,' O'Carroll claimed.

'Aye, the woman's not wrong,' Lefty admitted, 'I say, you're not wrong there, Lily.'

'Did youse fight over anyone else other than Isabella Scott?' O'Carroll asked innocently.

'There was no point,' Lefty replied.

'Why Lefty?' McCusker asked, amused by the subject.

'Because it's all mapped out for us in advance; whatever will be will be, so why fret over the small stuff. The only secret of life I've discovered is to smile when you're winning and never cry when you're losing. If it's never going to happen, it's most definitely never going to happen. I've found it's just best to get on with it. There's always some good times around the corner, the only problem we have is we always have to go through some bad times to get there.'

'I remember this little foible of yours, Lefty, so after all these years, you still think no matter how much we would like to meet and marry someone like…say…Barbara Parkins, for instance, we won't?'

'Correct.'

'But I still think you're wrong, I still think we might,' McCusker suggested.

'Yes, we *might*, but in the real world we never will.'

'But we could?" McCusker persisted.

'Technically, we could, but you won't.'

'But we could?'

'In principle, yes, we could, but in the real world you won't.'

'But we could?'

O'Carroll rolled her eyes in exasperation.

'No, it's never going to happen.'

'Lefty, how do you know for certain?' McCusker asked.

'Well, in this particular instance, because when I had dinner with her last night in my hotel room,' Lefty boasted, 'Barbara Parkins assured me, she was not interested in anyone else but me.'

Chapter Forty-Eight

Twenty Minutes later, McCusker and O'Carroll were knocking on the door of Sean Buckley. Just like a minister, but with badly applied fake tan, who had recently lost his portfolio after a shuffle, Sean had been left without an alibi after Isabella claimed she had spent Wednesday night last with Sean's brother, Seamus.

O'Carroll and McCusker had debated which of the Buckley Brothers to interview first. McCusker favoured Sean over Seamus mainly because he was still having trouble accepting Isabella would have picked Seamus over Sean. O'Carroll didn't have a preference one way or the other, so it was Sean who had drawn the short straw, in more ways than one.

It turned out Sean wasn't at home, but they found him over at their portacabin headquarters on the harbour forecourt, close to the Colabella House building site.

Sean was in his office. Seamus wasn't in yet, and Sean didn't know when he'd be in.

'Wouldn't youse normally come into work together?' McCusker asked, as Sean cleared two bucket seats of their files, brochures and samples for the member of the PSNI and the Grafton Agency cop.

'Mostly yes, but he'd already left his house when I called to pick him up.'

'When did you speak to him last?' McCusker asked.

'Yes, just after lunch time.'

'Would that be usual?' McCusker asked.

'Augh, you know, Elaine likes her and Seamus to enjoy their special time on Sundays, so I usually leave them alone,' Sean explained. 'Anyway, what can I do for you both this morning?'

'Well, Sean, we've been checking out your alibi, and I'm afraid we've discovered Seamus was in someone else's company on Wednesday night rather than your own?' McCusker stated for the record, which was recorded in her notebook by O'Carroll.

'Sorry?'

'As relayed to us, Seamus was with someone else the time you said he was with you,' O'Carroll chipped in.

'Which kind of means you no longer have an alibi?' McCusker added.

'You mean he's saying he was with Elaine, his wife?' Sean said, through a grimace, which McCusker guessed was the advance party for the builder's heartburn.

'Well no, actually, apparently someone else altogether,' McCusker said.

'Wow,' Sean Buckley gasped, trying his best to deliver a smile.

'So, with this in mind, do you want to tell us what you were doing last Thursday?' McCusker asked quietly.

'Do you think I need a solicitor before I answer any more questions?' Sean replied.

'Entirely your decision,' O'Carroll advised him.

'That's my decision.'

'Okay,' O'Carroll said, 'here's what we'll do, we'll take you around to the PSNI Station for further questioning, when your solicitor arrives.'

'Are you arresting me?'

'No, we're inviting you to accompany us to the station for further questioning to assist us with our inquiries into the death of Thomas Barry,' O'Carroll stated for the record.

'And if I don't wish to go with you?'

'Well, if you didn't want to accompany us to the PSNI station, we would have to arrest you,' DI Lily O'Carroll replied.

* * *

They dropped Sean Buckley off at the station house on the sun-drenched

Lower Lansdowne Road in the company of DS Melodee Johnson, with instructions to ring O'Carroll the minute Buckley's solicitor arrived.

On the way back into town, as O'Carroll showed how not to change gears, while waking up all the neighbourhood, she said, 'You know I don't mean to upset you, but I think, if only for the balance of our case, I really have to put this out there.'

'Go on,' McCusker replied absent-mindedly.

'Can you please tell me if you have been considering Lefty Kelly for this?'

'On the grounds of?'

'Well, you suspect he was dating Isabella. He just said how much you all loved Isabella.'

'It was you who said how much all the BLT gang loved her; Lefty just agreed with you.'

'Agreed, but I'm starting to consider if, perhaps behind this whole thing, the simple fact is Isabella really only loved Thomas, and all these affairs were just to make Thomas jealous and drive him back to her. So, what if Lefty was also still in love with Isabella, but he knew her heart was elsewhere, as in with Thomas, so he figured out a way to get rid of his competition.'

'Pretty darned good, Lily,' McCusker said very slowly, 'pretty darned good.'

'But?' O'Carroll suggested, sounding like she felt there must be a "but."

'I mean, really, we're not at the stage of ruling anyone out,' McCusker said, 'However, I will admit to you, I do hope it's not Lefty.'

They drove in silence for a few seconds.

'So how do you feel with Sean as our prime suspect?' McCusker asked.

'Well, I'm having trouble with Sean as a suspect, if I'm honest,' O'Carroll offered.

'And this is all because poor Lefty doesn't pull his weight when it comes to washing the dishes?' McCusker suggested.

'No diff to me, man, sure you're house trained, you're happy to do your own dishes,' O'Carroll said, 'I think Sean on paper has much, much, too much to lose by the death of your friend Thomas. I mean, they were on the verge of completing Colabella House, a career-making project. If they pulled the Colabella project off, either together or individually, the sky would have been the limit.'

'Good point…but…'

'But you still have suspicions on Sean?' O'Carroll pushed.

'I did notice he must have left his house in a hurry this morning,' McCusker said, as the Buckley Bros harbour headquarters, four portacabins, two stacked on two, came into view.

'What makes you say that?'

'His left shoe was perfectly polished and shined. His right shoe was just polished.'

'OMG, McCusker, don't be going all Sherlock Holmes on me,' was O'Carroll's immediate reply.

'Okay, Watson,' McCusker replied, not loud enough she would hear, he thought.

'I heard you. Can I just remind you Grace is my sister, and one sisterly word from me would be all it would take to put you on the drawbridge-up mode.'

'Ach sure…'

'OMG I can't believe I just said what I was thinking, it forced me to consider you and my sister…as in togeth…oh, perish the thought. Let's get back to Holmes. What else did he observe?

'Funny you should ask, but did you notice Sean wasn't clean-shaven this morning,' McCusker replied. 'He's always clean-shaven.'

'Yeah, there was something not right about him, but I couldn't quite put my finger on it,' she admitted, 'well done Holmes.'

'Sound,' McCusker replied, pleased as punch.

'Nope, sorry McCusker, but your delivery of "sound" is still not happening for you. You still need a bit of work on to pull it off like a local.'

'Okay, I will,' McCusker replied, surprised at himself for not protesting his localmanship.

'Sound,' she offered through a knowing grin.

Chapter Forty-Nine

They returned to Buckley Brother headquarters at the harbour, and Seamus was still AWOL

'So, do we track down Seamus?' she said, as they returned to the car.

'I don't think so, I really feel like walking around with a hard hat on for a while.'

'Sorry?'

'See those boys up there working on the Colabella House,' McCusker started up, 'they've all got these really wonderful yellow hats. I've always fancied wearing one of those. Do you think if we flash our PSNI IDs, they'd let us wear one of those yellow hats and have a wee dander around the building?'

'Must be worth a try,' O'Carroll replied, 'we might even bump into Seamus.'

'Perhaps, but I seem to remember Sean promising a gentleman by the name of Rowdy the Buckley Brothers would come down to his building site first thing on Monday morning to get the job back on track. Now we know Sean is otherwise engaged, so perhaps Seamus is visiting Rowdy as the sole representative. Anyway, a wee gander at this famous Colabella House, at this stage in the proceedings, could be of interest.'

Ten minutes later, not only did McCusker get to wear the yellow hard hat, with a matching one for O'Carroll, but they managed to find a very friendly site manager, John Duffy, who escorted them into the building and up to the roof, atop the seventh floor. McCusker couldn't believe how wonderful the views were from the top floor. He could see all over Portrush, from the apartment blocks to the north, the roof of the PSNI building on Lower Lansdowne Road and then in the other direction to the Barry's Amusement Arcade building down in the dip to the right of the historic clock-tower. They had to move down to the sixth floor, for health and safety reasons, when the yellow tower crane, which loomed over them, had to deliver a load from the street to where they'd previously been standing on the roof of the seventh floor.

'Did Tommy Barry ever come up here?' McCusker asked the site manager.

'Augh aye, he was never a stranger here,' John Duffy replied, 'he was very proud of this building, sure he named it after his two wives. The Col from Colette and the Abella from Isabella. They were both sisters, you know,' he concluded with a wink.

'I never knew where the name of this building came from,' O'Carroll admitted, 'mind you, I'd never really thought about it.'

Just then, from their vantage point, they could see a cloud of dust rise as a wine-coloured Nisson Navara pickup truck screeched to a halt just by the Buckley Brothers portacabin offices, six floors below. They watched as Seamus Buckley, wearing a red checked shirt, which wouldn't have looked out of place on Bruce Springsteen: denim jeans and a fawn pair of Timberland work boots, dashed out of his vehicle. His look was all topped off with his trademark long, black, curly hair. The same outfit the man who had come calling on Isabella Scott just after McCusker had left her on his first visit had worn. McCusker had patiently sat in wait in the Bob and Bert's gaff just across the road from the old bank building, which housed Isabella's penthouse apartment. McCusker had never equated this look to Seamus Buckley because of his more sophisticated attire when the detective first visited him in his home.

McCusker and O'Carroll reluctantly, particularly McCusker, well, only McCusker really, returned their yellow hard hats to the site manager and made their way PDQ across to the hub of the Buckley Brothers on-site activity.

They bumped into Seamus Buckley at the door.

'Sorry, *I'm* in a hurry,' Seamus bawled. He acted like he was used to bawling people out, and they'd jump out of his way to save themselves.

DI Lily O'Carroll was not one such person. She stood her ground, blocking his exit through the door.

'Don't worry,' McCusker offered, 'we'll give Rowdy a shout and tell him you're running a wee bit late.'

Seamus was taken aback by McCusker's knowledge of his movements, and it was enough of a diversion for McCusker and O'Carroll to step into the neon-lit room and close the door behind them.

'You *better* c'mon in,' Seamus replied as he led them through, clearly annoyed, and with the swagger of a petulant teenager.

'Tell me this, Seamus,' McCusker began, before they'd even had a chance to sit down in his very tidy office, 'how come, if you and Sean were in here stock-taking, last Wednesday night through to Thursday morning, Miss Isabella Scott is also claiming you were in her company during those hours?'

'It's like this, *Inspector...*'

'I'm not an Inspector,' McCusker offered for the record, as he felt he must. 'However, my colleague here is a Detective Inspector.'

'It's like this, Mr McCusker *and* DI O'Carroll,' Seamus said, as he took a seat at his desk, 'on the previous occasion you refer to, if you check your notes I believe *you'll* discover what I actually said was, "Yeah, I believe my brother *told* you we were here working and then kipping." I don't believe I ever *confirmed* his claim as a fact.'

McCusker marvelled at his answer, a wee bit from the content but mostly at the fact it was the longest answer Seamus Buckley had ever offered the Portrush branch of the PSNI.

'Are you now confirming you spent Wednesday night and Thursday morning with Isabella Scott?' McCusker asked.

'Define *morning?*'

'Okay, let's try a different way,' McCusker started, still a wee bit thrown at the way Seamus Buckley over-emphasised one word in each sentence. If the detective was not careful, he found himself waiting for the keyword and trying to figure out why it was a keyword, rather than listening to his answer attentively. 'What time did you and Isabella Scott meet up on Wednesday evening?'

'Just after midnight, *maybe* half past twelve.'

'And where were you before midnight?' McCusker continued, happy they seemed to be making some progress at last.

'I was *with* my wife Elaine,' Buckley started, 'Sean and I *always* try to have dinner with our families, no matter what business we have to attend to.'

'After dinner?" O'Carroll asked.

'Sean and I were in here for a *couple* of hours?' Buckley replied, still delivering his answers to McCusker.

'But not all night?' McCusker asked.

'As I have *already* said, I saw Bella after midnight.'

'And why so late?'

'A *gentleman* never tells.'

McCusker knew O'Carroll was thinking, "And you're no gentleman, so spill the beans." He prayed she'd keep quiet on this subject, and his prayers were answered.

'I'm trying to put a shape on your evening, Seamus, I need you to help me here,' McCusker said through an audible sigh. 'So, you had dinner with your wife, you met up with Sean, to do some stock-taking up here. What time did you leave your wife?'

'Oh, about *eight* o'clock.'

'And did you come straight here?'

'Ah, no, sure I *went* for a pint at the Atlantic.'

'And then you came here?'

'*Aye*,' Seamus grunted, at least McCusker had no problem working out where the Ulster emphasis was with this reply.

'So, you reached here at?'

'Shit, man, you're *worse* than my dentist,' Buckley complained. 'I'd say no *later* than nine.'

'Tell me this, Seamus, did you have a pre-arranged date with Isabella or was it a spur-of-the-moment impulse?'

CHAPTER FORTY-NINE

'Bella rang *me* up and said she needed to see me.'

'I mean, were you seeing each other regularly?'

'None of *your* business.'

'I'm afraid it is Mr Buckley,' O'Carroll chipped in, 'we already have one false alibi from you.'

'Not from *me,* you don't.'

'Well, we're giving you the benefit of the doubt on this Mr Buckley, but in your own best interest you need to give us more detail so we can verify this new alibi.'

'Look, *miss,*' Buckley started up, clearly agitated, and not bothering to try and hide it.

'Detective Inspector will do, thank you,' O'Carroll offered.

'I was going around to see a grown, *single* woman, and just before midnight,' Buckley barked. 'I wasn't going around to discuss how bad *Rory McIlroy* was going to do, now was I?'

McCusker and O'Carroll kept stum. McCusker was hoping Seamus Buckley might continue with his rant, rather than his preferred short answers, and give something away.

'So surely I'm not implying an ongoing *relationship,* am I? Surely the fact I'm *happily* married to Elaine, kinda implies Bella and I are not officially dating, doesn't it?'

'Here's the thing, Seamus, we don't know. So, we are here to try and find out?' McCusker offered in a calm voice.

'Bella *rang* me. She asked me what I was *doing.* I *told* her. She said she'd *just* opened a bottle of red. Asked me if I *wanted* to join her. This was her *code* for: she'd be waiting for me by her front door with nothing on but a...'

O'Carroll cut him off with, 'No need to spell it out in *such* detail, thank you, Mr Buckley.'

'Afterwards, was it usual for you to stay overnight, you know, what with being happily married and all?' McCusker asked.

'I'd a *long* day. I was *tired. We* fell asleep. When I left at *six*-thirty, Bella was *still* sleeping.'

O'Carroll scribbled away in her notebook, recording all these facts.

'So why do you think your brother claimed you, and he had spent the entire evening from Wednesday evening through to the following morning at five o'clock, when you'd a few hours kip, before starting work again?'

'I am not my *brother's* keeper. I don't know what *he* was trying to hide.'

McCusker looked like he was searching for another question, but one didn't come.

'Look, I hate to break up our wee *intimate* get together,' Buckley said through a yawn as he rose from his chair. He walked around to their side of his desk, 'but I've a stack of work piling up, on top of which I understand you've taken my brother away to help you with your inquiries.'

Buckley muttered something under his breath. McCusker couldn't be sure, but he thought it might have been something like, "Good *luck* with that one."

He had no doubt whatsoever about the Ulster emphasis on the word luck.

Chapter Fifty

As they were driving back around Ramore Head to the PSNI station, O'Carroll said, from out of nowhere. 'I suppose we could have our man, you know, McCusker.'

'Sean?'

'Sean,' she confirmed.

'Well, now we know he doesn't have an alibi, and he asked for a solicitor. But we still have to take into consideration the fact Lefty seemed convinced it was Seamus who was having the scene with Isabella.'

'A fact confirmed by Isabella herself when she called in her alibi,' O'Carroll suggested, 'not to mention Seamus himself, who seemed happy to spell the details of his Wednesday night, Thursday morning rendezvous out for us, even though he seemed very reluctant to divulge much other information.'

'But what if Isabella was having an affair with Sean and then switched to Seamus?'

'We'd lose our motive,' she said.

They both looked at each other for ten seconds.

'Yeah, I know you're right,' he announced, 'let's stick with the facts and get back to them. Can you drop me at Colette's, please?'

'Okay, and when I get back to Lower Lansdowne Road, I'll check if we've received the results of those forensic tests Anthony Robertson ordered up.'

'Maybe also check to see if either Donnie McCartney, the accountant, or Michael McKnight, the solicitor, advised DS Johnson what would happen to Thomas's buildings and assets should he die. Particularly if either of the Buckley Brothers would have any involvement, as in: did they benefit by his death?'

***

McCusker saw Colette Barry in her back garden, more like a well-groomed meadow than a garden. She was standing by a chestnut mare that seemed happy in her company and was grazing away to her heart's content. Between mouthfulls of the sweet green meadow, the chestnut would nuzzle her nose around Colette's shoulder. Colette was wearing a light blue denim jacket over a long, flowing, yellow-patterned dress, which reached down to a pair of red Dr Martens. As with the previous time when McCusker ha spotted her on gardening duty, she had her blonde hair bundled up and under (what he'd guessed as being) her father's cloth cap.

She was gently petting the horse about the neck. McCusker always felt horses were the most contented of animals and most certainly a creature of beauty and dignity. Colette, still not aware of McCusker's presence, looked as lonely as a solo diner in 55 Degrees North on St. Valentine's night.

'Ah,' Colette whispered to the mare, as McCusker made his presence known, 'this is a friend of mine, Brendy. Brendy, this is Sandy. Pat her on the neck so she knows you come in peace.'

'Hi, Sandy,' McCusker said, doing as he was bid.

Sandy completely ignored him. McCusker felt there was something so appetising about the sound a horse makes while grazing. They have the ability to make grass sound perfectly tasty.

'She is eating a lot,' Colette whispered, as though Sandy would understand her, 'because she is also missing Tom. He would come out here and talk to her for hours. It was one of his favourite things to do. He sat over there on the gate, and he would comb her mane with one hand while the fingers of his other would be twiddling around in his beard absent-mindedly, as if he was trying to curl it. Did he have a beard back in the BLT days? No, of course not, I remember now.'

'No, he didn't,' McCusker agreed, 'but he did attempt his first moustache the day after he met your sister.'

'I guess you are here for the next round?'

McCusker nodded yes.

'Thank you for being patient with me,' she started, 'Sandy, Brendy and I are going into the house for a wee chat.'

She patted Sandy's neck a few times affectionately. McCusker did the same without thinking about it, and as they walked away, Sandy returned Colette's affection by nuzzling her shoulder again. Sandy totally ignored McCusker once again. Sandy stopped her serial grazing for the first time since he'd arrived and glared after them as if to say, "I thought we were all meant to be grieving together."

There was something about the day, might have been the weather; might have been because of the anti-climax of The UK Open being over; might have been the fact Rory had another bad weekend; might have been due to the fact Grace was back in Belfast; might have been McCusker was disappointed in Isabella's alibi—not the fact she had one, but the one she had – but whatever it was, McCusker felt flat, very flat.

Colette Barry had the perfect antidote: a fresh brew-up of tea and three Paris buns she was heating up in the cosy kitchen Aga, with the promise of, 'two of these wee treasures will have your name on them if you go easy with me?'

'Ah, Colette,' McCusker began, 'I'm not looking—'

'It is okay, Brendy,' she replied, 'I know all you are doing is doing your work…it is just so painful. I just feel so…empty…so empty inside."

'I accept that. I'm just trying to find out what happened to Tom and I have a suspicion you and he breaking up in 2012, divorcing in 2013, and Tom and Isabella remarrying in 2014 and Tom quitting his attempt at entering politics in 2012 might have had something to do with what happened to Tom on Wednesday night through to Thursday morning. I also need to understand what happened between Tom and Isabella. I mean, Lefty and I always thought…thought…'

'Thought they were going to live happily ever after,' she prompted, while wetting the tea.

'Well, yes.'

'Brendy, you really want to know what happened to Tom and Isabella, do you?' Colette said, sounding a tad impatient. 'Well, I will tell you, but first I have to ask you a question?'

'Shoot.'

'Do you remember what it was like when girls first caught your attention, when you found yourself involuntarily attracted to the fairer sex?'

'I do,' McCusker said and couldn't stop smiling at the memory. 'It was Adele Hutchinson.'

'I thought it might have been for some reason, go on?'

'She was older than me by three years, but at an age when three years was a lifetime. She was always very pleasant to me. She was always very friendly to me. One summer's day, a group of us boys and girls were, for some reason, down by the harbour, might have been a church thing. There was a canoeing class, and people were getting paired off to go out in a canoe together. I was just about to go out with Lefty when, from the other side of the group, Adele Hutchinson said, "I want to go out with Brendan." I heard her say this and I didn't register it as my name as everyone called me Brendy. I really thought she was talking about someone else. I remember thinking: he's a lucky bloke. Then she said, "Brendan McCusker will you go out in a canoe with me?" Lefty looked like he was fit to be tied, while I mustered up the courage to say, "Yeah, I'd really like to."

'So, Adele and I selected a canoe, and we were given our instructions about paddling and how to manoeuvre turning. Eventually, we were about to get in the canoe, and Adele noticed one of her mates returning in another canoe, and her mate was soaking wet. Adele said, "I'm not going to soak my new shorts and top." She smiled at me and continued, a little self-conscious and very quietly whispered, "I've got my cozzie on underneath, do you mind if I take my shorts and top off?" And I said, like a fool, "Oh yeah, I'd really like that."

'So, she took off her t-shirt and shorts and gave them to her mate for safekeeping. She was standing there wearing this incredible white bikini, and I couldn't take my eyes off her. I quite literally could not take my eyes off her, what with her blonde hair and her dark eyebrows.

'She hopped into the canoe, took the back seat and then patted on the floor between her legs and said, "You sit in here."'

'I did as bid and our instructor pushed us off, out into the harbour,'

'Not far from the Pilgrim's Steps,' Colette suggested.

'Very close in fact,' McCusker agreed. 'I didn't know what to do. I didn't know how to row. I didn't know where to look. My memory bank kept replaying all the magical, mystical parts of her body, the body I had just witnessed harbour side. It was at the same time, you know, when you were still trying to figure out how all the pieces of the opposite sex's body came together to create your daily preoccupation. I couldn't understand all the thoughts and new feelings racing through my body, but they were so wonderful, I didn't care about not understanding them.

'Adele was so nice to me. She was so close to me I could feel every part of her body. I could drink in all her enticing scents. She whispered in my ear how to row. She insisted I do it slowly, "We're in no hurry," she said, "let's just enjoy ourselves out here by ourselves."

'I don't think I spoke two words to her the whole time we were out paddling around the harbour. But my brain activity was in complete overdrive and it never felt like I wasn't talking. Adele kept whispering away in my ear the whole time we were out.

'She said she picked me because she knew I would react the way I did when I admitted, yes, I really would like to go in the canoe with her. Rather than the "Yeah, okay if I must," one of the other boys would have said, trying to be cool in front of his mates. While on the inside, he would be really busting his gut over the chance. I didn't admit I had noticed the look in all the boys' eyes, particularly Lefty, as we had started out into the harbour. She said my enthusiasm over her getting her shorts and top off might just have been just a bit too keen for our first date, but she loved when she had removed her shorts and top and I was staring at her. She said I was actually looking at her face the whole time and not her body. To be honest, I think she might have been gracious on my behalf with that one.'

'Who knows, Brendy, you might have been looking at only her face while maybe in your mind you were drinking the entire vision in.'

'She was beautiful, it was the perfect, sweet-smelling summer's day during what became the perfect summer.'

'And was there another date?'

'No,' McCusker admitted, 'I mean, there was no awkwardness or anything, and she was always very heartfelt and friendly to me but…' McCusker paused trying to find the correct words, 'well there was no "but" really, because I had my day in the canoe wither her in her white bikini and whispering in my ear. Where's the "but"? There was no downside?'

'None, Brendy, none at all,' Colette agreed very enthusiastically and looking genuinely moved. 'As I suggested to you in one of our chats, Adele Hutchinson had hinted to us she would have liked for you to have asked her out. But you were instinctive enough not to. So, in a way, you have just answered your own original question, "what happened to Tom and Isabella?"'

'Really?' a bemused McCusker said.

'Do you not see the "day in the canoe with a beautiful girl in a white bikini" moment was your "Hi Love, you just dropped your glove" moment? The main difference, the only difference was you had the sense not to spend the rest of your life trying to re-live the special magical feeling. You did not feel a need to chase the rainbow. You were content to be part of the experience. We should not feel the need to try to drink the rainbow again and again. We should be happy to be part of the experience as opposed to trying to covet another experience. Being happy to be part of the experience is how we create romance. On the other hand, when we get all our bits out, if there is no romance, then all we create is a hot, sweaty, self-spectating sport.

'Accept the first time you experience the beauty of the female form is only going to be tarnished by your need to see and feel the experience over and over again. Imagination and familiarity cannot make up for the loss of the first buzz a beautiful girl is capable of inflicting. Savour the first hit, do not tarnish it by trying to repeat it, ever, and most certainly never on a daily basis like our Isabella and Tom tried to do. Humans should not be allowed to mess with this stuff. We really do need to be protected from ourselves.

'Let the mystery truly be,' she whispered, 'if only Tom and Isabella had done so, then perhaps I would be sitting here today talking to Tom and him recalling for me and our children, his own "Girl in a Canoe in a White Swimming Suit, Whispering in His Ear" moment. So many people would have enjoyed happier lives if only that was the case.'

'Tell me this, Colette,' McCusker asked, hoping his own candour might help Colette to talk about stuff she clearly didn't want to discuss, 'the last time we spoke, you kinda admitted to me it was Tom who left you when you split up in 2012. I thought youse were happy together by then?'

'We were,' she admitted immediately, and then poured the tea, while instructing him to retrieve the Paris Buns from the oven, 'use the oven gloves.'

They talked about domestic stuff for a while, McCusker's sweet tooth, the Aga, how hard the dishwasher was on her antique cups and saucers, the simple and utter joy of a strawberry jam and melting-butter-filled Paris bun.

'Was it a requisite of the BLT you had to be fans of Paris buns?' she asked.

'Well, Lefty still loves them as well, even though he now claims the chemist, and not the sweetie shop, or Tom Tom's Bakery, is his priority call.'

'And Tom always loved them,' she said after smiling at Lefty's claim. She looked like she was going to say more but didn't. She stared at McCusker and tried another smile, which didn't work. Her nostrils started to twitch, and her chin contorted, signalling teardrops were on the way.

McCusker resisted asking a question.

She took a deep breath, a very deep breath, kicking the tears into touch.

'One, two, three, four,' she counted and then launched herself. 'Tom and I were in love, very much in love. Everything was going great. We were enjoying our lives together. We were living in his house in Antrim Gardens, and my parents were still living here.

'Then Isabella and Ryan had a series of spats. I mean, I really think all their trouble boiled down to the fact both of them found it impossible to be monogamous. Maybe I am oversimplifying it. Ryan found it impossible to be with one partner. He just could never resist the mystery of other women. Equally, once they traded in their mystery, i.e., slept with him, their attraction disappeared quicker than a reality TV star disappears off our small screens.

'Isabella, on the other hand, had a wee bit of that and a lot of…well…she wanted Tom. I sincerely believe she only wanted Tom because she did not want anyone else, for instance, me, babe, being with Tom. Even though when she had been first married to Tom, she was cheating on him with Ryan, amongst others. You know, if I am being very fair to her, I think she just could not help it. If she was a man, she would have been celebrated and called "one of the blokes." As it was, she was someone's wife, and as an Ulster wife, she was tarred with a different brush.

'So, anyway, Ryan and Isabella had separated and would soon be divorced. When they were married, we would have nothing to do with them, and they would have nothing to do with us. After they split in 2010, Isabella contacted me again directly and contacted Tom again directly. In her words, "To open lines of communication again." She was saying she was hearing all about his political ambitions and wanted to support him. Tom and I fussed to ensure we would not have her back in our lives again, most definitely not. But in the spirit of anything for a simple life, we refused to completely block her out.

'She started to turn up at some of Tom's political Town Hall events and was making herself very busy on his behalf. She would be talking it up with the locals as if she was on the ticket. And not all of her rhetoric was positive, it has to be said.

'I happened upon her by accident at one event and overheard her saying to a local council type, "It is very difficult being the sibling of a saint," she said and paused for a beat when she noticed me walking over to her. "Have you met my sister, Colette?" Tom thought it was getting to be a wee bit much and told her so. Tom did not think having his ex-wife and her sister, his current wife at these things would prove to be good for his political career. It reached a point where he had to tell her to stop coming to his events. He very firmly instructed her to stop meddling in his campaign.

'Our Isabella, as only she can do, went into a complete meltdown. Totally nuclear. So much so, she moved back in here so my parents could look after her.

'True to form, for our Isabella, after a few days, she got into a screaming match with my mother when my mother dared to say Tom was right and Isabella should really stop interfering where she was clearly not wanted.'

Colette looked like she had reached the end of her information. McCusker was still trying to join the dots. When Colette's silences had reached an embarrassing minute, each second ticked off on the noisy antique clock by the kitchen door, he felt he had to try to get her back on track.

'So, how did Isabella forcing Tom to pull out of politics cause you and Tom to split up?' McCusker asked.

'I am building up to that,' she admitted, 'this is where I have got a big admission to make, and I really need you to help me protect the memory of Tom's name and not mention a word of what I am about to tell you?'

'Of course I'll be here to help, but equally I need to advise you if my remaining silent about anything you are about to tell me, gets in the way of justice, or potentially helping someone to get away with a crime, well, my hands will be tied, I'm afraid.'

'And I respect you did not fib to me to get the information out of me,' she whispered, 'let us break for another wee cup of tea, Brendy. This is...I feel like I am reliving the events all over again. I have never discussed this with anyone since it happened. As a result of what I am about to tell you, I never spoke with my mother again in my life.'

Chapter Fifty-One

'Okay, I am ready to continue,' Colette announced twenty-one minutes later. They'd had their fresh pot of tea and discussed Sandy, Grace, Ryan and how great she thought he was as a song-writer, how long Barry's (the amusements arcade family) current owners might remain in charge, how great it had been to see the Town Hall restored to its former glory, everything in fact bar the two topics McCusker had come to talk to her about: Why Tom Barry surprised the community by announcing, "You should never vote for anyone who wants to lead you," and dropped out of politics. This move was particularly surprising because it looked like he was going to win. And, *why*, shortly thereafter, had Tom and Colette split up, divorced, and Tom and Isabella remarried all within the space of two years, specifically 2013 and 2014.

McCusker just nodded for fear of unsettling her again. He followed from the kitchen into the living room filled with all her and Tom's personal bits and pieces, all their collectionwhich served as signposts and prompts to a treasured collection of the memories they'd created and enjoyed across their years together. McCusker hoped she had retreated to this room, this safe cocoon, to help her tell the rest of her story.

'When we stopped for our tea, I really did not think I was going to be able to tell you the rest of this, at least not today,' she started off quietly, then reprimanded herself with, 'Oh Colette, for heaven's sake, stop flipping faffing around and tell the poor man what he needs to know. Okay, Okay, I will...I will, so I will...one, two, three, four.

'The way my mum told me the story, on the last day we ever spoke,

Isabella felt her parents had once again sided against Isabella in favour of me, saying I was right. Isabella screamed back at my mother, "Of course she is. In your and Daddy's' eyes, she's never done anything wrong. Well, I wish I could have been the perfect daughter for you like our Colette always was."

"'Oh, Colette's none too perfect herself," my mother shot back in the heat of the argument.

"'Don't lie to me, in your eyes, she never ever did anything wrong." Isabella screamed at my mum.

"'You clearly don't know about the abortion, then?"

'My mother said she had been so furious at Isabella, the words had just slipped out without her even realising.'

'Abortion?' McCusker said, the word escaping out before *he* even knew it.

'Yes,' Colette replied quietly, 'remember I told you the other day Tom and I had been friends, as in *good* friends as opposed to *just* friends, and we had original got together sexually because I felt I could save my marriage with Ryan, if only I could get pregnant?'

'And Tom had offered, "to donate his body to the cause," were the words I believe you used?'

'Yes, exactly. Well…actually, we-am…he actually…got me pregnant. Sadly, by that time, Tom and I had fallen for each other, and Ryan was straying in the direction of Isabella, and all our lives were a complete and utter mess. I just thought I don't want to bring a child into the world and be responsible for messing up their life even before they had a chance to start. I felt it was just wrong, Brendy. I discussed it with Tom, and he agreed. We both made a decision, I would have a procedure,' she said, and then she whispered, 'an abortion.'

'But you…'

'I never really fully comprehended the impact it would eventually have on my life,' Colette continued, completely ignoring McCusker's attempt at sympathy, her voice so close to breaking. 'I mean you make a decision on a termination, never matter of fact of course, but in a way you discuss it with your partner and you both agree that it's something you need to do…bla…I mean, I don't know…am…physically, secretly, romantically, politically. You think it's something you need to do…have to do. I mean, it's only meant to be a procedure, isn't it? People do it all the time, don't they?'

Then her voice broke. Completely, utterly.

But Colette continued, rambling while sobbing, and McCusker couldn't understand her words. But he could understand her pain.

McCusker reached his hand out to her.

She batted it away aggressively as if he'd the plague.

'Sorry! Sorry! Sorry!' she cried out, but starting to form her words in a decipherable state again. 'That wasn't against you, Brendy, that was against my mother. She was my mother; she was meant to comfort me. She was meant to explain to me that I should forget all the physical, romantic, practical, political reasons and I should think about what I was going to do, again. She should have reminded me that there was no "we" involved in the termination: there was only a "me". She should have warned me that it wasn't a procedure…that it was all me and I was going to be guilty, guilty of…of God bless me, Brendy, guilty of mu…I wanted a child sooooooooo much and I… Brendy, I can't continue with this… I just can't…I just can't deal with this so soon after also losing Tom.'

Colette broke down.

Well, what happened was her sobbing overcame her to the point where it looked to McCusker like she was convulsing violently. She raced like a bat out of Lucifer's Lair towards the bathroom, and McCusker could hear her howling in there. The unhuman noises Colette was hollering in there—greatly amplified by the bathroom's tiled surfaces—sounded, like a banshee on a midnight visit to claim her dead.

At one point, the noise was so scary it sounded like there really was a banshee in the bathroom with Colette.

A chill ran down McCusker's spine like one he'd never experienced before.

He realised he was genuinely terrified.

He was tempted to go and try and comfort her and, in fact, got as far as the bathroom door, which he found was locked. He returned to the sitting room.

About ten minutes later, she came back into the sitting room and said, 'Sorry, Brendy, I am just going out to Sandy for a few minutes, she will calm me down again.'

Seven minutes later, she returned to the sitting room with two glasses of chilled white wine.

'I am sorry, Brendy, I only have white. I never drink red, and so I never have any in the house,' she said, very matter-of-fact, and then sighed very loudly, 'telling you was a lot more traumatic than I thought it would be. I have never admitted this episode to anyone else before in my life. After I had the procedure, I was so ill I came back here so my mum and dad could look after me. My mum obviously knew what had happened, but I never told her any details. She promised me she would never breathe a word to a soul, not even my father. I was so ashamed. But when she and Isabella had their yelling match, it all came out. I didn't realise until later, much later, that I had come to my mum needing her not just to comfort me, but to mother me, to heal me.'

'Are you okay?' McCusker asked, feeling somewhat inadequate while just wetting his lips with the wine, feeling now wasn't the time to suggest, "I never drink while on duty," which he didn't. He felt totally drained. He rationalised that if he felt drained, what must Colette be feeling

'I am okay, thanks,' Colette faux smiled, 'when I get that stressed, when those demons visit me again, a few minutes with Sandy calms me down,' Colette said, her eyes bloodshot but kind again, 'I really don't think I could get through this grieving sickness if it wasn't for Sandy.'

'But you know I've never discussed it with anyone before. I mean, obviously Tom and I talked about it…but I never admitted, even to him, all those things to anyone before. Maybe not even to myself if I'm being very honest. I've always understood all my resentment towards my mother came not from the fact that she betrayed my secret to Isabella but that she didn't have what it took to be a proper mum to me when I needed it most.'

Colette then ruffled McCusker's ruffled hair some more. 'Brendy, I do sincerely believe that I would have opened up to anyone other than you, you poor man, sorry for putting you through all of that. Thank you,' and she rose and kissed him gently on his forehead.

McCusker just smiled back at her when a smile was all that it took.

'So where were we?' Colette said before taking a generous swig of her wine.

'No, no, Colette,' McCusker protested, 'I've put you through enough for one day. We can finish this another day.'

'I'd prefer now that we've started, I'd like to finish, so that I can spend tomorrow with Sandy,' Colette offered, 'now where we? Isabella…of course then…, Well, the long and the short of it was she came to see Tom and myself and she said if he did not pull out of the political race, she was going to take the abortion story to the papers. She thought *Husband cheats with wife's sister, gets her pregnant, forces the wife's sister to have an abortion*, would run very well with the voters. She actually said, "Mr and Mrs Barry have enjoyed their day in the political sunshine; it's now time for them to return to the wintry streets of Portrush."'

'When did this happen?'

'2012.'

'No…not the Tom pulling out of politics but you and he splitting up, I meant the original procedure.'

'Oh, yes, sorry, I see, that was in 2002, just before Ryan and me divorced.'

'Okay, so what happened next?'

'Of course, Tom had to pull out,' Colette said, 'this was when it started to get funny.'

'Oh? Funny?'

'Well, not so much funny as weird, as in extremely weird,' Colette explained. 'After Tom pulled out of politics, Isabella invited Tom to come around to her place and again threatened she would go to the papers with the story if he didn't sleep with her.'

'What? No? Never? She didn't?'

'Yes, you heard me right. Tom was worried she really would go to the papers and so he did as she wished. He did as she had blackmailed him into doing and spent the night in her bed.'

McCusker just whistled in disbelief.

'Needless to say, it drove a wedge between Tom and me.'

'How did you find out?' McCusker asked.

'Why? You won't believe this, but she had rung me before Tom had even got home and took great pleasure in advising me in chapter and verse, of course,' Colette admitted. 'I did not mention this to Tom, but he confessed to me the following morning.'

'Unbelievable.'

'Oh, it gets worse. Next, she told him she would take the story to the papers if he did not leave me and move in with her again. He was all for calling her bluff and telling her to eff off this time, but I figured, she had nothing to lose. I thought she would be happy to just play the wronged-wife card. Having won the first two rounds with her blackmail, our Isabella had decided it was time to totally destroy us. I did not want to risk it. So, Tom moved back in with her.'

'Isabella Scott,' McCusker hissed in a whisper.

'Ah, she was far from finished, Brendy,' Colette continued, clearly out of her earlier troubled waters and looking like she was now driven and seemingly happy to vent her spleen on her sister. 'Next, he had to divorce me, or she was going to the media. This time she expanded her threat to include "the media" and no longer just the papers. The final stab, the vinegar in our wounds, part of her crucifixion of Tom and Colette Barry, was Tom had to re-marry her.'

'Now I see how it all fits together.'

'I also had to move out of the house Tom owned in Antrim Gardens, she had "plans for it." My mum and dad were so embarrassed and worried the whole scandal was going to break at any moment. Finally, they had enough of both their daughters and skedaddled off to the wee retirement cottage they had in Tenerife. As a going-away present, my dad gave me this house, deeds and all, and so luckily enough, I had somewhere to move into.

'I must confess I never found it in my heart to forgive my mother. I knew I should, but I just could not do it, and we never spoke again. God forgive me, but I did not even go to her funeral. I went and stayed with my dad for about a week after the funeral.

'I remember it like it was yesterday. The only thing my dad said to me about my mother during our week together he said, "The thing about being a mother is you have to endure your own suffering and then you also suffer the suffering of your children." He did not apologise for her, and nor did he criticise me. I was shocked that my father had never grasped the vital role of a mother.

'My dad died two years later in 2016 and he left me the cottage in Tenerife. Tom and I visited it a couple of times for winter breaks to escape the bad winters here.'

'So, you and Tom continued to see each other?' McCusker asked.

'Yeah, Tom and Isabella remarried in August 2014, and by December, he brought me around a Christmas present. It was very strange; here he was married to my sister again and yet continually declaring his love for me. Tom said he had found a way out of our situation. I had kept the name Barry. I point-blank refused to give it up, so he knew where my heart lay. Tom told me he had recorded Isabella's two final blackmail conversations with him, the one where she blackmailed him into divorcing me, and the one where she blackmailed him into marrying her. He said he had told her he was going to leave her, and this final time, if she did anything about it, it would be his turn to hand over the tapes of her two blackmail demands, not to the media but to the police, pointing out blackmail was illegal, a criminal offence rather than a civil one.

'Tom said Isabelle agreed not to fight it. Apart from anything else, they were both back to their original ways of not getting on with each other and, he claimed, the marriage was a complete farce. She said her only condition was, she would never divorce him…'

'Which is why Tom and you didn't remarry?'

'Which is why Tom and I did not marry a second time,' she agreed, 'and then she added a second condition, which was Tom and I could not officially "live" together…'

'Which is why he moved back into Antrim Gardens?' McCusker

suggested.

'Exactly,' Colette agreed, 'and we also had to refrain from rubbing her nose in it by prancing around in public as "the happy couple." She made him agree we would be discreet. So, I enlisted my good friend Ellen DiVito to be Tom's go-to "plus one" when needs must. We enlisted Ellen to our cause, mainly as a result of Tom and I being a little careless and flaunting ourselves at this year's North West 200.

'When she saw us together on the TV at the North West 200, she told Tom she was going to throw me out of this house. Tom had to advise her that our parents, well, my dad really, had gifted me the freehold to this wonderful haven. She was not best pleased by the news, I can tell you.'

'You and Tom never had any children?'

'Well, we wanted to, but the by-product of the procedure was I could not conceive. My punishment for my sin.'

Here she paused for at least a minute as she appeared to dwell on her confession,

'At the time, I felt it would eventually break Tom and me up, but if anything, it made us closer as a couple. As you saw, I dote on Sandy. Luckily enough, Tom did as well.'

Chapter Fifty-Two

As luck would have it, Sean Buckley's solicitor, a middle-aged gentleman by the memorable name of Colin Collins, was entering 21 Lansdowne Crescent as O'Carroll and McCusker were pulling up in front of the building. Although neither of the two parties knew this to be the case at the time. It was only when Colin Collins announced himself at the reception desk did the penny drop.

The solicitor requested a private half an hour catchup and briefing with his client.

DS Melodee Johnson was waiting for McCusker and O'Carroll by her treasured notice board, which she'd just updated.

'Anthony Robertson said the forensic report proved some of the fibres found about Mr Barry's person were similar to those found in a carpet, most likely a blue carpet, but if not a blue carpet, then a predominantly blue carpet. Discovered in Mr Barry's hair were a few very small pieces of material similar to those found in a white bath towel. The other traces found on Mr Barry's person was, as he originally advised you, particles of sand and particles of cement.'

'I also contacted Mr McKnight and Mr McCartney, and both said as far as they knew neither of the Buckley Brothers had any benefits to come from Mr Barry's estate.'

'Excellent, DS Johnson, brilliant work, thank you so much,' McCusker gushed, 'in the next transfer season we'll have to see if we can do a direct swap, no money to change hands, of course. But I would propose Customs House United will get you, and Ramore Head Wanderers will get DI Jarvis

Cage in exchange.'

'I don't think a DS for a DI is a fair swap,' Johnson said, through a hearty laugh, 'On top of which I've no desire to leave the Port, and neither has Dawn, my girlfriend.'

She winked at O'Carroll out of McCusker's line of vision; O'Carroll nodded, whole-hearted approval.

'I suppose the only other way we could tempt you,' O'Carroll continued after a prolonged wink of her eye, 'would be for us to send Cage *and* McCusker to Portrush and you and Dawn Leng come to Belfast.'

'Now you're talking,' Johnson said, and chuckled just as the phone rang, she lifted it quickly, 'DS Johnson here, how can I help you?' Silence. 'Yes, they're here.' Silence. 'Okay. Thank you. I'll tell them.' She returned the handset to its base and said, 'Mr Sean Buckley and Mr Colin Collins are ready for their interview.'

* * *

Collins and the younger Buckley brother were already in the interview room when McCusker, O'Carroll and Johnson arrived. McCusker had insisted Johnson be part of the interview.

Colin Collins was around fifty. Either he was poor, or he was preoccupied with his work because his clothes, while clean, were certainly showing the signs of wear. He was overdressed for July due to wearing a traditional Donegal Tweed jacket, with brown leather elbow patches; a Fair Isle, V-neck, sleeveless, sweater, aka a tank-top; a white shirt; a green woollen tie, a pair of grey flannels, so old they actually shined in places, and a pair of black leather sensible shoes. His hair was black, tidy, but not combed with a parting. He was just this side of overweight with a farmer's tan, a weather-beaten face beneath a pair of thick-framed glasses, the ones usually only worn by an older generation of schoolteachers. He opened his brown leather shoulder satchel, took out a yellow legal pad and two pencils and set them out neatly on the table in front of him. He then proceeded to drum out beats with the fingers of both hands on the wooden table and only stopped when he appeared to force himself to clasp both his hands together in front of him as though he was about to commence praying. McCusker figured O'Carroll was clocking the fact the solicitor's hands and fingernails were spotlessly clean.

O'Carroll switched on the audible and visual recordings and announced the date, time and those present, for the record. She also cautioned Sean Buckley in accordance with the Police and Criminal Evidence Order.

Surprisingly, Colin Collins was the first to speak.

'My client, Mr Sean Buckley, is the joint MD of Buckley Brothers, a successful local firm of builders.' Collins offered in an accent which was more Northern England than Northern Ireland. 'He wishes to apologise because he feels he might have misled you somewhat when he told you what he was doing on the evening of Wednesday 17th July and the early hours of Thursday the 18th July this year.'

Nothing but the gentle purring of the air-conditioning was heard for a few seconds until Sean Buckley eventually, seemingly reluctantly, spoke up.

'I have to advise you I wish to change my original statement as to my whereabouts on the night of the 17th of July.

'In point of fact, I was where I claimed to be at the time in question; however, my brother was not with me for the entire time.

'Seamus arrived at nine-thirty, and at around midnight, he received a call. A few minutes after the call, he left the offices, and I concluded the work by myself, which is why the work took so much longer than expected. Consequently, I had to work through the night finalising the stock-checking. I caught a few hours' sleep in the office before starting back up again.'

'Have you any idea who made the call to Seamus?' McCusker asked.

'I do.'

'Yes and?' O'Carroll pushed.

'The call came from Isabella Scott.'

'Were you aware your brother was in a relationship with Isabella Scott?'

'Yes, I was,' Sean admitted, betraying signs of heartburn again.

'Was Thomas Barry aware your brother was having a relationship with his ex-wife?'

'I suspected he did, but I never discussed it with him. His priority was Colette Barry, his other ex-wife, and they seemed happy, but kept low-key. To be honest, I didn't really have that kind of relationship with Thomas. We never discussed each other's personal lives.'

'Why did you tell us Seamus your brother and you worked the whole way through the night?' McCusker asked.

Sean Buckley looked at his solicitor. Colin Collins closed his eyes and nodded to his client to continue.

'When you came calling, I started to worry about Seamus…' Sean paused, McCusker looked at the tape running and knew he couldn't prompt him so four sets of eyes focused on Sean Buckley, eager for his next words. Eventually, they came. 'I was worried he might be involved, even though I couldn't work out how. I figured if I gave him an alibi, well then it wouldn't come out while someone had been murdering Isabella's husband, my brother had been in bed with her. I figured such a revelation wasn't going to do anyone, particularly my brother and Isabella, any good. I didn't think I was doing anything wrong.'

'Did you discuss with your brother the fact you had given him a false alibi?' McCusker asked.

'Yes, of course,' Sean admitted, 'I wanted to let him know I had protected him and Isabella. I didn't want him coming up with a false alibi.'

'You mean you didn't want him coming up with another false alibi on top of yours?' O'Carroll suggested.

'He assured me he wasn't involved,' Sean said, ignoring O'Carroll's comment, 'so what was the harm?'

'It's never advisable to bear false witness to the PSNI,' the only Northern English voice in the room was heard to say. Three heads nodded in agreement; one head shook in shock at his solicitor for chastising him in front of the very same PSNI. 'I'm just saying for your own good, Sean,' Colin Collins said, raising his hands, palms upwards, to the ceiling in surrender.

'When you saw Seamus the following morning, how did he look?' McCusker asked.

'He looked like he hadn't had much sleep,' Sean replied, with a nudge-nudge, wink-wink, kind of grin, seeming to forget there were two ladies present.

'When Seamus left your harbour offices on Wednesday night around midnight, did he leave on foot?' McCusker asked.

'No, he drove away.'

'Do you know what vehicle he drove away in?'

'Why yes,' Sean admitted, seemingly amused, 'he drove away in his Nissan pick-up.'

'Is this Nissan pick-up the property of The Buckley Brothers or the personal property of Seamus?' McCusker continued.

'It's a company truck,' Sean confirmed.

'Sean, do you as an officer of Buckley Brothers agree the PSNI can take this truck in for examination?' McCusker asked, surprising everyone at the table.

Sean's brow wrinkled in concern, 'What, you don't still think Seamus is involved?'

'Just routine investigation procedure, Sean,' O'Carroll offered.

'But he already has an alibi,' Sean protested, 'Isabella has admitted they spent the night together, surely her word is enough?'

'Sean, here's the thing,' O'Carroll started to explain, 'this part of our investigation is purely an elimination process. Bit by bit we rule people out. We must check everything out. Let me give you an example. You had already confirmed to us you had spent the night with your Seamus...'

'But I already explained why.'

'Yes, yes,' O'Carroll continued patiently, 'but you just proved, no matter the justification, people can, and will, lie if they think it's going to keep them, or, in this case, their brother, out of trouble. So, in this instance, we have a dilemma. You have already proven you are capable of lying, and if we follow that example to the extreme, then Isabella could also be lying, and equally, Seamus, himself, could be lying...'

CHAPTER FIFTY-TWO

'But why would he?'

'I don't know,' O'Carroll admitted, 'we now know, or at least you claim, he wasn't with you, perhaps he wasn't. Perhaps he wasn't even with Isabella Scott? Could Isabella be lying? Or, could it be Seamus's lie? Or could you be lying to us yet again?'

'The point is, Sean,' McCusker offered in conclusion, 'we don't know, and it's our job to find out.'

Sean exhaled air from his lungs in a long and loud gasp and sat upright in his uncomfortable fold-away wooden chair. The poor light in the basement interview room was served only to take the look of his poorly applied fake tan to the nth degree in the embarrassment stakes. Still, McCusker thought, Sean didn't come across as self-conscious as he felt he would. McCusker knew O'Carroll would have claimed Sean was the only one who didn't have to look at himself.

'What do you think?' he asked his solicitor.

'Here's the thing, Sean, it's really a moot point, you could refuse if you decided to,' Colin Collins offered his client. Sean seemed relieved. 'However, the PSNI have the right thanks to PACE, which is the Police and Criminal Evidence Act of 1984. In short, they can take away your vehicle, anyway, to continue the lines of their investigation. My advice to you would be to cooperate with them. You've explained to me you've done nothing wrong,' Colin Collins continued, and turned at this point, and looked at the PSNI side of the table, 'and I do believe you, so why not agree and let them get on with their elimination process and get this sorry mess behind all of us.'

'Okay,' Sean said, nodding his head up and down several times to confirm he was accepting his solicitor's advice and agreeing to McCusker's request to impound the company pick-up. 'You have my permission to take the company vehicle.'

'Thank you, Sean,' McCusker said, when he really wanted to thank Colin Collins. Solicitors who didn't go out of their way to protect their clients at any cost these days were as rare as showbands without a brass section.

'One last question, Sean,' McCusker started, before the recorders were switched off. 'Was it you, or was it Seamus, who first slept with Isabella?'

Colin Collins, DS Melodee Johnson, and DI Lily O'Carroll looked more in shock at the question than Sean Buckley, who proved sibling rivalry was still alive, well and thriving on the streets of Portrush. He only managed to get as far as, 'Me...' before he'd really digested the question properly.

Chapter Fifty-Three

'I fancy a wee bit of fresh air,' McCusker offered, as the three of them stood in the reception area of 21 Lansdowne Crescent. McCusker had his hands deep in the pockets of his chinos. He looked like a farmer trying to count the change in his pockets before deciding whether or not to buy an ice-cream cone.

'Count me in,' O'Carroll agreed.

'I'll organise picking up the Buckley Brothers' truck,' Johnson volunteered.

McCusker and O'Carroll walked over to the bench seat by the rocks on Lower Lansdowne Road, where O'Carroll and Johnson had interviewed James Lamb.

They sat in silence for several minutes, McCusker with legs stretched out, hands still in pockets. McCusker had always felt the ocean views down here and around Ramore Head were life-affirming. There was just something about the waves continually crashing, or even gently lapping, against the rocks below them, confirming, no matter what was happening in people's lives as they busily darted from one shop to the next, from one joy to the next, from one disaster to the next, yet through all of this the world and its waves were still prepared to roll on and on without them.

'So, where do you think we are?' O'Carroll said to break their silence.

'I think I believe Sean, but then I think because he sounds so believable, he might still be lying to us.' McCusker said, in a voice he had to raise to make himself heard above the sound of the crashing waves and the seagulls squawking as they dive bombed the ocean waves, seemingly just for the fun of it. 'I think after what Colette told me, Isabella might be involved, but I can't figure out how. But then I wonder if Colette wanted me to think along those lines, just because she was trying to hide something herself.'

'And Seamus Buckley?'

'I still can't figure out his motive,' McCusker claimed, 'he had nothing to gain, and, with his brother, he'd a heck of a lot to lose.'

'You're not wrong,' O'Carroll conceded. 'And what about Lefty Kelly?'

'You're still not going to give up on poor Lefty, just because he didn't do the breakfast dishes,' McCusker said through a laugh, 'or could it be you can't forgive him for giving up on you?'

'You caught me out,' she jested, 'great detecting. Seriously, though, have you ever thought of becoming a proper detective? Oh no…I remember now, Yellow Packs like yourself can't become proper members of the PSNI, can they?'

'And then the big question still is,' McCusker continued, completely ignoring her, 'how did whoever murdered Tom manage to place his body by the Pilgrim's Steps? No matter how late at night, the murderer was always going to risk either a car driving past and catching our culprit in the act, or someone out for a latenight walk or walking the dog, like the grumpy old man, Hugh Costello, who discovered Tom's remains in the first place. There was always going to be a chance someone was going to come upon our murderer in the commission of the crime. No one who has just killed another human is going to risk being caught red-handed in such a public place.'

'Or being caught on CCTV,' O'Carroll offered.

'Or being caught on CCTV,' McCusker agreed.

'Then why not dump the body somewhere else?' she continued.

McCusker froze in this thought.

'*Then why not dump the body somewhere else?*' he repeated, as if O'Carroll had just turned on a light bulb. 'Exactly. Exactly. Why not take him out to the country and dump him in a sheugh by the roadside? Our murderer didn't dump the body in a sheugh because it, eventually, would have been found there. The body was dumped by the Pilgrim's Steps because the murderer thought it would be washed out to sea and…*and* as a failsafe, if the body was ever subsequently washed up, people would think Tom had drowned, fallen into the sea by accident, walked into the sea to end his life. Or, as most likely the plan, Tom Barry's remains would never ever be seen or heard of again.'

'Which means?'

'Which means the murder wasn't premeditated. Maybe our murderer didn't mean to kill Tom, but when they did, they needed to find a way to dispose of the body.'

McCusker felt an indeterminable connection to the case, but he could feel it slipping away. The more he tried to chase the connection, the faster it disappeared from his thought process. He eventually conceded it was gone with a large sigh, a sigh he turned into a whistle. He started to whistle *Yellow Submarine*, perhaps unconsciously showing where his thought pattern had been leading him.

Without discussing it, they stood up and walked off towards town, passing all the campervans with their wee moveable steps up into the accommodation section. Needs must, McCusker thought, as he figured the built-in, slide-out steps were compromised due to the height of the footpath they were parked against. Hence, the reason for the mobile, foldable steps.

Even though Portrush's facelift was meant to have been completed in time for last week's UK Open Golf Tournament, there was still a lot of rebuilding, refurbishing, and new builds springing up all around the town. Most of the new builds were signposted by large yellow tower cranes dotted here there and everywhere around the skyline. A lot of the older buildings out of the town centre, where most tourists would never see, were still in a bad state of repair, and it looked like a loving lick of paint wouldn't have gone amiss.

'Why did you start to whistle *Yellow Submarine* there?' O'Carroll asked, as they hit Antrim Gardens.

'*Yellow Submarine?*'

'Just now, when we left our bench?'

'That wasn't *Yellow Submarine*, my song was called *Stork Margarine*,'

McCusker confessed, 'all the kids, back in the day, used to wander around singing:

> *'We all eat Stork Margarine, Stork Margarine,*
>
> *'We all eat Stork Margarine, Stork Margarine,*

'To the Beatles' tune.'

'Do you know anything at all from this Millennium,' O'Carroll posed, and not really as a question, 'and I hope you never use the term, "back in the day," when my sister is around.'

'So, you call it Yellow Submarine, do you?' McCusker asked, distracted again, '*Yellow* Submarine…I think you might have hit on something there, Lily. Let's head back to 21 Lansdowne Crescent. We can take our walk later.'

Chapter Fifty-Four

McCusker spent the remains of the daylight hours checking his paperwork, reviewing his notebook, and working out a plan. From seven o'clock onwards, he kept going to the window and looking out over the ocean, checking, waiting and calculating how long it would take for the sun to go down. He wasn't convinced the sun had actually bothered to come up on that particular miserable Monday. He really needed to be up on Ramore Head to witness the sun setting on the west. Without making a fuss, he slipped out of the station, turned left, passed Tracey's Diner, with only the slightest of regret, and proceeded up and around to the peak of Ramore Head. It was worth it. The big skies were angry and bloodshot. He had to lean into the wind for fear of physically being blown over. He stood there from 21.30 until the sun had disappeared at 21.47.

He returned to the PSNI headquarters at 21 Lansdowne Road, checked all his plans were in place, picked up O'Carroll, and briskly walked down to Isabella Scott's million-dollar apartment in the old bank building.

Isabella was far from pleased to see them, nonetheless she invited them in. McCusker wouldn't have bet money on it, but he thought he heard someone in the spare bedroom.

'You'll be pleased to know we're nearly done,' McCusker began, when they were safely inside the brochure-furnished apartment.

'Really?' Isabella said as she sat down on her sofa, folding her legs under her and comforting herself by hugging her favourite cushion. She looked like an incrediblly small person in this position. She was dressed in her black tracksuit top and bottoms.

'Yes, but before we get started, would you mind awfully if I visit the wee boy's room. Nothing serious, just caught short,' and McCusker wiggled around a bit as if to amplify the point.

'It's marginal,' she replied sourly, 'I suppose, but better my toilet than my carpet.'

As McCusker rushed into the open plan toilet and master bedroom—carefully locking the door behind him—he could hear O'Carroll and Isabella laughing.

McCusker put the stopper in the posh sink, turned the tap on, so the water was running slowly, hoping the sound of the water running into water would accurately recreate the sound of someone sitting on the toilet leisurely going about their number one. Then he took a pair of blue evidence gloves from his pocket. He had great difficulty finding his fingers' way into them. He only succeeded after he blew into them one by one. He knelt on the predominantly blue speckled thick pile rug beside the deep, large bath. He removed from his other pocket a small pair of scissors, a pair of tweezers, and two evidence bags. He snipped a few tufts from the carpet, let them fall into the carpet and then lifted them from the carpet using the tweezers, placed them in the evidence bag and then sealed the bag. Next, he lifted one of the white towels from the side of the bath and once again repeated the process securing towel fabric in the other evidence bag. Next, as per O'Carroll's prior instructions, he used her spare phone to take photos of the blueish rug in situ in the bathroom and then the target area of the rug he had removed the specimens from and the same with the white towel, while at the same time flushing the toilet to hide the sound of the mobile at work.

He snapped off his gloves, washed his hands using her soap dispenser, emptied the sink, unlocked the door, and returned to the lounge, as casually as he knew how, while smelling one of his hands.

'Isabella, what's the soap in your bathroom? There's a beautiful smell from it?' McCusker said, taking a seat next to O'Carroll.

'It's Suede Hand Wash from Byredo,' she replied, looking all puffed up with herself as if it was an item she had personally developed.

'Yeah,' McCusker said, smelling his hands again, 'I figured it was either that or Palmolive.'

Isabella Scott and Lily O'Carroll shared a moment by rolling their eyes in sync.

'So, Brendy, to what do I owe this late-night pleasure?' Isabella announced, 'and for the record, I wasn't offering either a come-on or an invitation.'

'And none taken, Isabella,' McCusker declared, still feeling a bit of a rush from his James Bond manoeuvres in the bathroom. 'As I mentioned at the door, we're nearly there on this case. We've not yet discovered anyone who took Thomas's life. Still, I think we'll be on our way back to Belfast in the morning, maybe lunchtime at the latest. But one wee thing I needed to check with you before we wrap this all up.'

'Oh yes?' she said, sounding like she didn't know whether to feel relieved or worried.

'Yes, Tom's diamond ear studs…'

'Yes?'

'Well we only found one of them and we have to assume there were two,' McCusker admitted, 'so, we have an idea where the second one might be but to save ourselves a bit of trouble, you know, dredging the harbour and all, I thought you would know whether or not he wore one or two diamond ear studs?'

'I see,' she replied, appearing to give the matter, some thought, 'yes… now I come to think of it I only remember ever seeing one. In the right earlobe I believe if my memory serves me correctly.'

O'Carroll made a point of writing this into her notebook. She then closed her notebook and placed it, along with her pen, in her inside pocket. Signifying, McCusker hoped, they'd concluded their investigation. The inference being—McCusker also hoped—Thomas Barry's demise was by misadventure.

As if to show how grateful Isabella Scott was, she offered them coffee, she had a fresh brew going, she claimed and suggested she might even find some suitable nibbles for them.

'Coffee at this time of the night,' McCusker said, rising up out of the sofa, 'it's already past my bedtime, if I have a coffee, I'll be up all night. But thanks for the offer.'

'So, I won't see you now until the wake,' she said, as she was leaving them to her front door.

'Yeah I'll come back up from Belfast when the Coroner releases Tom's remains,' McCusker said.

* * *

'Only one flaw in our visit to Isabella,' O'Carroll said, as they rushed across the deserted Main Street and up the narrow Church Pass crossing over the residential Mark Street Lane.

'And what was our… sorry my, what was my flaw?' McCusker asked as they continued along Church Pass, crossing the prime real estate of Mark Street and down the steep steps onto Kerr Street, the last street before the ocean.

'I don't think, in all your history,' she started as she had to add an inch to her step to keep up with McCusker, 'well at least not in all the time I have known you have you ever turned down an opportunity to enjoy some nibbles.'

'I think we'll be okay,' McCusker replied, as they took a right into Kerr Street, up past Ryan Shannon's ivy clad house and arrived at the harbour. 'Isabella would have been thinking only of herself,' McCusker concluded as they met up with DS Melodee Johnson, Superintendent Ivan Valley, Constable Albert Blundell and Constable Billy Traill.

Chapter Fifty-Five

The six were connected by SFR (Static Free Radio) and all went to the pre-planned positions. Because of the complicated one-way system in Portrush the only legit way to get to the Harbour area by vehicle was to drive down Kerr Street from Barry's Amusement Arcade, past Finn McCool's lost bicycle wheel on the left, past the public toilets on the left, past Ryan Shannon's grand house on the right, past the Lifeboat House on the left and finally down to the Harbour. Constable Billy Traill, in an unmarked car, was parked opposite the Lifeboat House on Kerr Street. He would act as the advance look out. Constable Blundell was positioned on the public viewing platform on North Pier. He was right beside the Harbour Master's Office, which Superintendent Ivan Valley had persuaded Harbour Master Melvil Edwards to allow them to use as their headquarters. Edwards had even turned up in person to supply them all with fresh tea and coffee. Valley, citing rank, based himself in the temporary command centre. Next to the Harbour Master's office in the landward direction was The Harbour Bar building, next was the popular tourist attraction Water World and next to Water World a large four-story building with massive RAMORE spelt out in single white letters on the top floor. The letters were base lit, in an obvious homage to the legendary HOLLYWOOD sign, 5077 miles away to the west in California. The building beneath RAMORE lettering housed: Coast Pizzeria, Ramore Wine Bar and the

Mermaid restaurant. DS Melodee Johnson knew the manageress of the Mermaid and so enjoyed the perfect fourth floor view of the Harbour, the Colabella House, the work-in-progress between Kerr Street and Main Street, and the Buckley Brothers four-unit portacabin mobile headquarters in the Harbour forecourt. McCusker and O'Carroll sat in an unmarked car on the U-turn from Kerr Street up into Main Street.

Midnight came a lot slower than any of the team had anticipated. The late-night Monday night was so boring in Portrush even the seagulls had scarpered, most likely over to Ballycastle for a bit of late-night action.

At 02.21 Valley radioed McCusker.

'At what point do we call this off and go home?'

McCusker's first instinct was to give a funny reply along the lines of: "Do you mind sir, we're trying to sleep in here." He thought the better of it and was formulating a civil reply when Valley repeated his question.

'McCusker, at what point do we call this off and go home.'

McCusker was just about to reply when the team received a message from Constable Traill on lookout.

'Target vehicle travelling down Kerr Street.'

'Okay here we go,' McCusker announced over their SFR system.

Within thirty seconds, first Blundell and then Johnson offered confirmation of target vehicle. Johnson confirmed the target vehicle was the wine-coloured, Nissan Navara. The pickup truck was turning from Kerr Street up the steep incline into Main Street.

'Okay,' McCusker declared to O'Carroll, slinking down in his seat, as the Nissan came into view.

The Nissan pulled in beside the right-hand pavement. The lights remained on and the engine kept turning over. After three minutes the Nissan pulled away from the pavement and drove slowly away down Main Street.

'Not okay,' McCusker said to O'Carroll and announced to the team, 'Target moving back into town.'

McCusker sunk even further into his seat. O'Carroll kept quiet while glaring down the street after the Nissan.

McCusker felt his hunch had been totally off the mark and he had wasted all of these people's evening. His stake out had been a flop and he knew within seconds, a minute at the max, Valley would be on the radio again asking if they should all go home. Perhaps they should but…but he didn't feel as disappointed as he felt he should. He wondered what the reason behind his lack of disappointment might be.

Valley, to give him his due, was not on the radio immediately or even three minutes later.

The next radio message came not from the Superintendent but from Constable Traill.

'Target vehicle heading back down Kerr Street again,' Traill announced, to the team.

Blundell and Johnson confirmed the same from their locations and Johnson announced the target vehicle was turning in from Kerr Street to Main Street.

This time the Nissan pulled into the left-hand pavement and repeated its process from last time. The difference on this occasion was, after four nail-biting minutes, the vehicle's engine and lights died.

Nothing happened for another nine minutes.

At 02.55 the driver's door of the pick-up opened and a man, with black curly hair, a red checked shirt, blue denim jeans and tan Timberland boots stepped out.

Seamus Buckley walked across Main Street. He was carrying nothing but an unlit industrial torch.

Thomas Barry had obviously bought a house and garden at this end of Main Street and raised it to the ground to facilitate an entrance to his prime site for his latest, and he hoped, greatest project. Colabela House was a seven-story building and was located on a green patch between Main Street and Kerr Street. It was right behind the Neptune and Prawn Restaurant. Its seven-story height dominated the area and most probably the entire town.

There was only one higher structure in the area.

'Now what?' O'Carroll asked.

McCusker felt she was happy his plan had worked…so far.

'Sit tight,' he replied.

'Why did you not panic when he drove back off into town earlier?' she asked.

'You know,' he replied, 'a mouse will rarely dart straight into a trap to try to collect the cheese. The mouse, if it is clever, will case the joint first.'

'In other words,' she suggested, 'you were bricking it.'

'Exactly!' McCusker admitted.

The only structure which dominated the skyline more than Colabella House was a yellow tower crane, which was so tall it seemed to reach the whole way up to heaven.

Johnson was first to report the next sighting.

'Suspect is climbing the ladder up the tower crane,' she reported.

Blundell was next, with a similar report, followed closely by Valley.

Eventually when the suspect had cleared the roof height of the terrace houses in Main Street McCusker and O'Carroll spotted him.

McCusker felt the scene was quite eerie due to the fact Buckley was so far away from them they couldn't hear him, yet they could still see him as he climbed on and on into the darkness.

When he reached the yellow cab of the yellow crane he turned and looked back down to the ground and McCusker noticed Buckley flashed his light on and off three times in the direction of the Nissan.

The passenger door of the car opened and out stepped Isabella Scott. She was immaculately dressed head to toe in all black, i.e. tracksuit, trainers and baseball cap. She too was carrying a similar torch to Buckley. McCusker hated to be cynical but before he'd even voiced his thought O'Carroll beat him to the punch with: 'I bet she went out specially to buy a designer outfit for night-time manoeuvres.'

Isabella Scott ran up Main Street towards them, disappeared around the corner, down the slope, to the top of Kerr Street. She was directly below Johnson who immediately radioed the team to report, 'looks like she's checking for traffic or pedestrians. She signalled the suspect by switching her torch on and off three times.'

Above them they could all hear the engine in the cab spoil the silence of the light as it spluttered into action.

'The reported helicopter?' O'Carroll suggested.

'The reported helicopter,' McCusker agreed.

'Do we move in now?' Valley asked over the radio.

'Not yet, Sir, please?' McCusker replied, 'let's play it out a wee while longer.'

McCusker feared Seamus Buckley, so far, could claim to be guilty of nothing more than showing off to his lover.

Above them they could hear the cranking of pullies and cables swishing over and around them. Then they noticed the large bucket rise from its position up into the sky. The bucket had been parked as an anchor on a fifth-floor annex which was accessible only, at this point, from the sky. Once the bucket had cleared the roof level of the terraced houses on Main Street and the Neptune and Prawn Restaurant on Kerr Street, Buckley moved it out towards the end of the jib and then, on another three flash signal from Isabella Scott, who had ran back up on Main Street again, he started to lower it down to street level.

'Okay, let's move in now,' McCusker announced to the team.

Isabella Scott was waiting for the bucket by the time it hit the tarmac on Main Street. Another quick three flashes and Buckley stopped lowering.

McCusker couldn't believe how quickly Isabella Scott effortlessly scampered over the five-foot dinted and damaged side of the circular bucket. Even for a tall woman, it was a bit of an ask.

They could see brief bursts of shadows and light from her lamp as she appeared to be scouring the bottom of the bucket.

'Is this what you're looking for,' McCusker asked, as he looked over the edge of the bucket with a diamond ear stud proudly between thumb and forefinger. He was happy to note the insides and drop-bottom of the bucket was generously speckled with bits of cement and a generous stash of grains of sand had escaped as the bucket came to rest on the tarmac of the sleepy end of Main Street.

'What the f…' she gasped, 'what are you up to now?'

'Get her out of there before he hauls the bucket back up again, and with her in it,' McCusker said.

If anything, Isabella came out willingly, perhaps preferring the security of terra-firma versus ending up adrift over the harbour.

While on solid ground DS Melodee Johnson arrested Isabella Scott, read her, her rights and Constable Blundell removed her to a cell in the basement of 21 Lansdowne Crescent. The constable was back on the scene within ten minutes. Meanwhile, Seamus Buckley had not moved from the overhead cab of the crane. McCusker risked life and limb by climbing up on the rim of the bucket and detaching the two cables from the crane. The bucket was secured and covered with tarpaulin for forensics to start their work in the morning. McCusker had secured the keys to the Nissan truck from Isabella O'Carroll. PSNI Portrush already had permission from an officer of Buckley Brothers to impound the truck for forensic examination.

An hour later the other Buckley brother was still fifty metres high above street level and he showed no signs of descending.

'Should I climb up and trying bring him down,' Constable Traill offered.

'No thanks, constable' McCusker replied, through an uncontrollable yawn, 'nothing to gain, and a lot to lose with you, and possibly him, falling. You don't need to go up, but he will need to come down.'

The stalemate lasted until 10.00 am. It lasted until 10.00 am because McCusker felt 10.00 am, the first tea break of the day, was a socially acceptable time to use a megaphone to scream up to Buckley the PSNI were going nowhere anytime soon and would be waiting for him when he returned to mother earth. McCusker, on O'Carroll's prompt, also advised Seamus without food he was going to grow weaker and the weaker he became, the more dangerous would be his strenuous task of scaling down the crane's ladders.

Two minutes later Buckley was seen to leave his cab and five minutes later he was safely on the building site. Quite a crowd had gathered around the harbour and on Main Street, mostly tourists with a few locals and the majority with their mobiles focused on the top of the tower crane and then in ever decreasing angles until McCusker and Blundell arrested Seamus

CHAPTER FIFTY-FIVE

Buckley and read him his rights at the foot of the crane.

McCusker didn't even admit this to O'Carroll but up until he and Blundell took an arm each of the Buckley brother, he wouldn't have been surprised at all if Seamus had turned out to be Sean disguised in his brother's trademark work gear and with a curly wig. He couldn't work out exactly why he felt this. The closest thing he could suggest to himself, the only thing he could come up with was how affectionately Sean Buckley always pronounced the name Isabella.

Chapter Fifty-Six

The team retired to their various locations for a couple of hours of catch-up sleep.

McCusker and O'Carroll returned to his house. O'Carroll retired to her bedroom and an hour later after McCusker had showered and shaved he could hear her up walking about her bedroom and then the sound of the shower pump in her room being turned on. By the time she walked into his kitchen twenty minutes later, McCusker served the both of them an Ulster Fry.

By one o'clock they were sitting in the interview room of the Ramore Head, PSNI nick, and DS Melodee Scott was announcing for the benefit of the recording equipment, herself, Isabella Scott, her solicitor, Cliff Webb, DI O'Carroll and Mr McCusker were all present. Her cautioning Isabella Scott was also caught on the recording devices. She didn't mention Superintendent Ivan Valley was monitoring audible images from next door.

'Huh,' Isabella began, 'I'm afraid you've dropped yourself in the smelly stuff on this occasion Brendy, there'll be no way back from this one.'

'Do you think so, Isabella?'

'Of course,' she boasted, baring her protruding top two teeth, 'all you have is me and one of my men friends out for a night where he started to show off to me about how he's brave enough to climb up and operate the big crane himself. He probably thought I'd go all weak at the knees, and he'd end up in my bed.'

'Just like he did on Wednesday night?' McCusker replied.

'We both know only very special men get invited into my bed, don't we?'

she replied seductively.

She turned to look directly at O'Carroll at this point.

'Okay Isabella, here's how we're going to do this,' McCusker stated for the record. 'I'm going to tell you how all of this happened. I promise not to ask you any questions and then at the end you can say what you and your solicitor feel comfortable saying, okay?'

'This should be interesting, shoot Brendy.'

'First the motive,' McCusker said, knowing the end of his journey and which islands he needed to visit along the way, but not entirely sure which order he should be visiting them in. 'You and Thomas Barry met in 1976, a rainy Sunday afternoon.'

'Phew,' Isabella gasped, 'I thought for one moment there you were going to start back in 1959 on the days we were born.'

'You met, something clicked. It was a fairy tale romance and you married six years later. As with every fairy tale, there's always the morning after the camera stops rolling and our hero and his princess wake up and have to start to deal with each other's faults. You both start to think: "Jez is this it, for the next sixty or so years if my life?" You both individually start to doubt your decision. You've never been with anyone else, so how do you know if he (or she) really is the one for you.

'Temptation minus experience equals adultery and the problem is you cannot rewind the clock. You once told me it's better to cheat than to be cheated on. Your logic was, you had tried both and there was no competition. It was the being cheating on, you couldn't take. Not so much from the loss of love but from being shown up in public. You and Thomas split up. You took up with and married Ryan Shannon and Tom fell in love with Colette and eventually they married. The problem was Colette and Tom were in love and you and Ryan weren't. And when you and Ryan divorced you set about finding a way to destroy Tom and Colette's marriage. You successfully wormed a piece of information out of your mother and you used it initially to blackmail Tom into withdrawing from his promising political career.'

Isabella dropped her top lip over her teeth, she sat upright in her chair and the grin melted from her face. But she said not a word.

'When you saw the power this information gave you over Tom and Colette,' McCusker continued, while noting her reaction, 'you took it a stage further and blackmailed Tom into leaving his wife, moving back in with you and, finally, your ultimate goal, remarrying you.

'Things didn't turn out the way you hoped, and you and Tom drifted apart again. You took solace in other men's arms and what you didn't know was Tom and Colette never ever stopped loving each other.

'Eventually Colette and Tom drifted back together again. Once more you threatened blackmail if Tom defied you and dared to move in with Colette again. You knew they were together, but you just didn't want your face rubbed in it. You didn't want everyone knowing, Tom had ultimately chosen Colette over you. He moved into his own house in Antrim Gardens. And he and Colette continued their relationship discretely.

'A few years pass, Tom and Colette grew less careful about being discrete and this May you saw them on TV at the North West 200. They were flashed across the TV screens together and all loved up.

'Again, you threaten blackmail. Tom started to be seen in public with a beautiful young lady called Ellen DiVito. Initially you were happy with Tom's new situation. But only until you discovered it was a ruse and Ellen was in fact Colette's best friend and their sham only served to rub your face in it more, because everyone else seemed to know about it except you.

'Your spies told you Tom was at the UK Open practice rounds on Wednesday night and he was with Ellen DiVito. You demanded via Ellen, to see him that evening. You threatened him by advising him he better call on you or you would go straight to the press. After leaving The Royal Golf Club at 18.30 on Wednesday evening, Ellen and Tom drove to Colette's house and enjoyed dinner with her. Tom enjoyed a glass of white wine with his dinner. Ellen and Tom left Colette's house at 20.45 and Ellen dropped Tom outside the 55 Degrees North restaurant and he walked to your apartment in time for your 21.00 appointment. Tom had a glass of red wine with you. Colette only ever has white wine in the house, and you told me you drink nothing but your special red. Tom advised you he and

Colette didn't care about your threats anymore and invited you to do your worst to them. He advised you he and Colette refused to be blackmailed any longer.

'Tom was getting ready to leave. You endeavoured to seduce him, as you had done many times in the past by playing the innocent girl card. You ran a bath. You invited him into your bathroom where you were waiting in your seductive gear. Only this time, he refused to succumb to your playacting. You grew angry. You caught him by surprise and pushed him into your bath. You grabbed him by the heels of his shoes and lifted his feet up so his head was underwater. Your vice like grip on the heels of his pumps were so strong you left bruises on the sides of his heels. He struggled, he couldn't get a grip, on anything to raise his head out of water.

'Eventually he drowned.

'Your big problem now was you had a dead body in your apartment. There were no obvious solutions. Then you remembered the man, Seamus Buckley, you were currently having an affair with, was a builder. He had a works pickup truck. You figured he'd know how to get rid of a dead body. You ring him. You were in luck. He was working late with his brother over at their temporary offices at the harbour. He nipped over, arriving at your apartment just before midnight. He suggested you throw Tom's remains in the back of his pickup and drive somewhere and dump it. You had a chance to think it all through by this point. You felt this was just delaying the inevitable of Tom's body either being discovered, or people starting to ask why, where and how of Tom's disappearance. You felt it's better if it appeared he drowned. You discussed where you could both leave the body where it would be washed out to sea, making it appear Tom drowned without any suspicion of foul play. Yet at the same time you needed to avoid being caught in public disposing of the body.

'Seamus had just spent months working down in the harbour area. He knew it very well. He suggested leaving Tom's body by the Pilgrim's Steps and the tide would wash him out to sea.

'You were probably concerned someone would see you dump him there. He told you not to worry as he had already worked out a plan.

'You carried Tom out of the building. Just in case you happened upon anybody on the way from your apartment to Seamus's truck, you both propped him up between you, pretending he'd too many drinks and was just the worst for wear. You got him out of the building and put him in the back of Seamus's Nissan pickup truck. You threw something, like the white bath towel you tried to dry him with, over him in the back of the truck. You drove down Kerr Street and turned around into Main Street. Seamus parked his truck up by the entrance to his work site. He scampered up the tower crane. He lowered the bucket to the same position in the street as he did tonight. He had to come back down again and help you lift Tom from the back of the pickup and deposit him in in the bucket from the crane. He scooted back up to the cab of the crane, hoisted the bucket up and outwards to the far end of the jib. He swung the jib around, so it was extended over Kerr Street. According to my pacing out earlier today, this would have placed the bucket just over the Pilgrim's Steps. He lowered the bucket down, guided by you and your torch, and once it was in position, close to the Pilgrim's Steps, you would have signalled him to open the bucket, the same way he would have done if he'd been depositing a load of cement somewhere on the site. Tom would have fallen through onto the rocks, just by the Pilgrim's Steps.

'The main problems with your plan were:

1. 'You severely bruised the sides of both Tom's heels when you were grasping them tightly while you were unbalancing him and using your grip on them to keep him submerged until he had drowned.
2. 'The tell-tale stains of red wine on his teeth and residue in his stomach betrayed where he'd enjoyed his last red.
3. 'When you and Seamus removed Tom from your empty bath, you placed him on your blue speckled bathmat and some of the fibres from the same mat were found about his body. When you tried to dry him off and cover him in the back of Seamus's pickup with one of your white towels some fibres of your towel were found on Tom's person.

4. 'The pathologist reported the water in Tom's lungs wasn't sea water but in fact tap water.

5. 'High tide on the morning of Thursday 18th July was 08.00, so when Tom's remains were discovered at 5.50, the water was nowhere near high enough on the rocks to wash the body out into the harbour.

6. 'Traces of sand and cement were found on and about Tom's person. There is no evidence of either sand or cement around the Pilgrim's Steps. There was however evidence of traces of both sand and cement about the sides and in the bottom of the bucket of the Tower Crane you dumped Tom's body in. I should warn you each builder uses their own individual mix of sand, cement and water to achieve their ideal solution of concrete. Samples have been taken away from the bucket and I bet you anything you want when the results are returned, they will match up exactly with the traces found on Tom's body.

7. 'You thought your movements on Wednesday night had been unde-tected, however one of the neighbours in Main Street reported sounds overhead which matched perfectly with your escapade.'

O'Carroll turned to McCusker with a look, a look, which suggested she wouldn't have been any more impressed with him if he'd just invented penicillin.

Whereas Isabella Scott merely said. 'You daft apeth you, Brendy, would you ever cop yourself on. With such vivid imagination you should be writing murder mysteries, not trying to solve them.'

'You've just had your first strike, the evidence,' McCusker said, 'and in this room today, two strikes and you're out.'

He asked DS Johnson to announce the termination of the interview and got up and left the interview room.

On the way out he overheard Isabella say to her solicitor, '"Two strikes and I'm out," what did he mean?'

'I don't think he was referring to your liberty,' Cliff Webb replied.

***

Isabella Scott was removed to her cell and was replaced in the interview room by Mr Seamus Buckley and his solicitor Mr Colin Collins, who was dressed exactly as he had been the day before.

McCusker laid out his evidence chapter and verse as he had for Isabella Scott and Cliff Webb.

'Can I confer with my client, please?' Colin Collins asked, when McCusker had concluded his report.

DS Johnson once again announced the end of an interview and when they were called back in again twenty minutes later, she announced the fact the interview was about to continue, those present and the times.

'My client would like to say something,' Colin Collins announced, once they were up and running.

'I admit to my part in this. I had no part whatsoever in the drowning of Thomas Barry, though. As you know he was a business associate of mine and his demise will be a disaster to my business. I would also like to admit I was having an affair with Isabella Scott. On the night in question she threatened to tell my wife she was having an affair with me if I didn't help her. It's not common knowledge but my wife is the money behind Buckley Brothers, she owns the house she and I live in. She also owns the land where we have our works-yard and where Sean built his house. My wife and I have had our troubles in the past and if my wife divorced me the Buckley Brothers would be finished. I just couldn't let that happen.'

'My client is prepared to give and sign a statement of the above if you agree he will not be an accessory to murder or manslaughter,' Colin Collins announced.

McCusker looked to O'Carroll, O'Carroll out of respect deferred to DS Melodee Johnson who, left the tape running, excused herself, stepped outside. She returned two minutes later and reported, 'Superintendent Valley said he feels the NI Public Prosecution Service would agree to this on condition no further incriminating evidence comes to light.'

* * *

Fifteen minutes later, following a quick chat between Superintendent Ivan Valley, McCusker, DI O'Carroll, DS Johnson and Colette Scott, proceedings started back again in the interview room with Seamus Buckley and Colin Collins being replaced by Isabella Scott and Cliff Webb.

'Isabella, I have to advise you Mr Seamus Buckley has pleaded guilty to his part in helping you dispose of the remains of Mr Thomas Barry,' McCusker announced, there was no joy, no victory apparent in his voice. 'We are now charging you with the murder of Mr Thomas Barry and you do not have to say anything but anything you do say will be taken down and may be given in evidence.

'You do not have to say anything. But it may harm your defence if you do not mention when questioned something which you later rely on in court. Anything you do say may be given in evidence.'

* * *

'It was an accident,' Isabella Scott claimed, making it perfectly clear from the get-go what her defence was going to be.

At the end of her statement as she was being led away down the corridor, back to the cells, Valley said, sounding genuinely regretful, 'she had everything, looks, money, men who loved her, where did it all go wrong?'

'Isabella feels she was wronged when she was cheated on by Thomas Barry,' McCusker said equally quietly, 'her only problem was she went over the top while trying to balance the books.'

Chapter Fifty-Seven

The rest of the day positively flew past, what with writing up the reports and following up on the various forensic reports. Superintendent Valley insisted every aspect of the case and reports were finalised before McCusker and O'Carroll headed back down to Belfast.

The plan was DI Lily O'Carroll would head back down to Belfast later in the day, citing privately to McCusker, DS Melodee Johnson had fixed her up with a University friend of hers who was working for the BBC down in Belfast. They had spoken once on the phone and according to O'Carroll, 'he seemed okay. It's very early days so I'm not going to get my hopes up, at least not just yet.'

'Have you written up one of your wee five by threes for him yet?' McCusker asked.

'I have,' she replied proudly.

'Hit me with it.'

'Okay, I will,' she took it out of her inside jacket pocket, 'Name: Shane Mac Droucherty, I'm not sure of the exact spelling. Age: thirty-two. Hair: bit of a mess but clean. Teeth: all present and correct and clean and his own. Fingernails: short, tidy and clean. Hands: Clean. Dress: he doesn't wear dresses… Sorry…sorry, I couldn't resist doing a McCusker in front of McCusker. Dress: borderline traditional but always well turned out. Car: doesn't drive.'

'Doesn't drive?'

'It's okay, I do, he likes to cycle, so we can work something out.'

'And you asked him all these questions when you were on the phone with him?

'No, of course not. Melodee helped me fill in all the details.'

'Well he's a lucky man, Lily, I hope he doesn't blow his chances.'

'That makes two of us,' O'Carroll admitted, visibly moved by McCusker's remark, 'that makes two of us.'

'Sorry I forgot to ask you something, McCusker.' She started back up again after a few moments where the both of them were lost in their thoughts of O'Carroll and her next date.

'Yeah?'

'Well you know last night when we found Isabella Scott hoaking around in the bottom of the crane bucket?'

'Yeah?'

'And you produced a diamond ear stud and said, "Is this what you're looking for?"'

'Yeah, and?'

'Well, I was just wondering where you found the second diamond ear stud and when did you find it.'

'Did I ever actually claim it was *the* second diamond ear stud?'

* * *

As O'Carroll was re-packing both her suitcases, he knocked on the door of her room. She opened the door for him, and he presented her with her present, still in its brown paper bag. She seemed at first confused and then she rescued Otis Redding's album from the bag and immediately flipped it over to the back, scouring the credits and titles.

'Yes, yes, yes, *Mr Pitiful*, ah McCusker,' she gushed, and then started to well-up. 'I…I…' she attempted but couldn't get the words out. She eventually put the record down on the bed and rushed over to him and just hugged him.

McCusker felt O'Carroll had obviously reached a point with him where she didn't need to use words to express what she was feeling.

Ten minutes later McCusker waved O'Carroll off. The house felt empty without her.

He had another duty to perform. He walked out the scenic Bushmills Road to Colette Barry's wonderful cottage. He knew he was going to see her the following morning in Michael McKnight's office for the reading of Thomas Barry's Will.

Although she was in a more sombre mood, dressed all in black, she looked like she was happy to see him.

'It is finished,' she said, 'I can tell by the look on your face.'

He looked surprised and impressed by her powers of deduction.

'Oh, go on then, I will admit the fact Michael McKnight just rang me up a few minutes ago to say the case was solved, and he will read Tom's Will tomorrow morning, might have helped me a bit in my assumption.'

Colette didn't seem to take any pleasure from her sister Isabella either being responsible for Tom's death, or that she had been assisted, after the fact, by Seamus Buckley.

'How did you solve it?' she asked.

'With a great team,' McCusker admitted. 'My last chat with you helped me a lot and I didn't have to repeat the info on your termination.'

'Thanks, Brendy.'

'But it was enough info to supply the basis of a motive and once we have a creditable motive, then all we need is a bit of luck.'

'I'm sure there was more than luck involved,' she said, sounding like she was thinking about something else. 'What will happen to our Isabella now?'

'Well, she'll remain in custody. She won't get bail. She'll go to trial at the soonest February, possibly March next year and she'll be sentenced and go to prison.'

'How long will she be in prison?'

'The fact she's pleaded guilty will act in her favour, although she's claiming it was an accident as in, she pushed him and he fell and hit his head, she actually…'

'No…no…Brendy, I don't want to know the details,' she interrupted.

'Sorry, yes, okay, I see. I'd say she could get anything from 10 years to life.'

Once again Colette didn't appear to take any joy from this news, nor did she appear sorry.

'It's just I'm still trying to come to terms with this all,' McCusker admitted, 'I remember how excited, possessed even, Tom was the Sunday night he met her. You know I'm finding it difficult to accept she's Isabella.'

'I can sympathise with you. At the same time I should tell you, you would be even more shocked how the sweet wee girl who made you feel all warm and gooey on the inside when a wee boy came up to her and said, "Hey love, you just dropped your glove," could turn into an absolute monster. I witnessed it several times when she saw another girl try to move in on her man. Even though the girl might only have been flirting mildly with Tom, Isabella metamorphized into a fouled-tongued, blood- spitting, screaming, punching, hair-pulling, fishwife in a matter of seconds.

'What we have to remember here is, it was *this* sweet young girl who first took a lover other than her husband. What did she think was going to happen? Did she really think Tom was going to put up with that carry-on? Of course, he was going to stray. What partner in a marriage could remain faithful after the other had betrayed the marriage bed? But our Isabella, well she wanted her man to be faithful to her, she wanted her man to pick her and to keep picking her, particularly in front of everyone else.

'Yes, she could flirt with other males. Yes, she could take other lovers and she would even flaunt them in public. Everyone would know and I think part of it was a show and the other part of it was, well put bluntly, our Isabella really loved the sexual side of a relationship. But she still wanted *her* man, Tom, to keep confessing she was the absolute love of his life, and that he would always be there for her. The public humiliation of anything other than such a commitment would have been unbearable for Isabella.

'Then when Tom publicly cheated on her she just could not take it. But even more humiliating for Isabella it was like rubbing vinegar in her wounds when Tom was seen to be cheating on her with her very own sister, as in me. She blackmailed him into leaving me, divorcing me and re-marrying her. Then Isabella made a very big fuss over the fact she had "won" Tom back again. She was as proud as Rory McIlroy's parents, when she and Tom had their second wedding. She was incensed when I refused to stop using Tom's family name as my family name.

'I think beneath it all, she did not really want him back again. She knew they had lost the magic. She seemed to be really enjoying her single life, with all her men friends drooling over her. At the same time, she wanted to show everyone she, despite everything, could have Tom back if she wanted to.

'Then when she realised Tom and I did not care about her blackmail threats anymore, and we did not need to get married, but because we were happy just to be reunited, it all kicked off again.

'You know when we were younger, I had *always* wanted to be close to Isabella. She was my older sister. I loved her. I saw how tight the three Hutchinson sisters were, including Adele by the way,' Colette said nodding to McCusker in acknowledgment of his admission at their previous chat. 'Yeah, the Hutchinson sisters were always there for each other, they really loved each other. I wanted to have a similar relationship with Isabella. But no, it was like she always had to be competing with me. It took me a good few years to figure out it wasn't really her fault; it was our mother's fault. Don't you see, my mother was always competing with Isabella for attention, so Isabella in turn felt she had to compete with me. I guess what I'm saying is, our mother was the genesis of all our family problems. I admitted as much to you , yesterday evening. On top of which, as I mentioned, our mother was the one who gave Isabella the information to blackmail Tom and me. I know I broke my father's heart over it, but I just could never find it in my being to forgive my mother. I know now the betrayal was really just a cover up issue, clouding over my real problem with my mum. Perhaps if it had been a few decades later and I'd benefited from independent counselling and my mother and I would not have been estranged when she passed away.'

Chapter Fifty-Eight

Wednesday 24th July

McCusker met Lefty Kelly and Colette Barry at Michael McKnight's functional offices.

Donnie McCartney, clearly having postponed his trip to Lanzarote, was also in attendance. Tea and Kit Kats were both plentiful and welcome.

Thomas Barry addressed both McCusker and Lefty Kelly at the beginning of the Will, fondly recalling their BLT days.

McKnight continued reading out Barry's words, 'I often think of those days and what great friends we all were. Really, I don't think I've ever had better friends. I believed, I think we all believed, we were going to be best friends forever. One of my main regrets, okay, okay, maybe my second biggest regret is, for my part, I didn't do enough throughout the intervening years to keep in touch. Colette once told me regrets are bad for the soul. So, she suggested I focus on something positive about the BLT days. Remember when we all used to walk around the streets of Portrush in the miserable rain saying if only we could find someone to blag a fiver each from, we could scoot down to Belfast for a night where there would be some real action. Well, Brendy and Lefty, you're in luck. Recently I came across two fivers (old ones I'm afraid) and Mr McKnight is going to hand these across the desk to you now,' which he did, with a smile on his face, as he continued to read Thomas Barry's words, 'may the sauce be with you.

Oh, he's also going to give you another envelope with a wee note in it from me, save it for when you're both out for a Paris Bun and a cup of tea.'

There were no other surprises in the Will. Everything but everything, including Isabella's penthouse pad at the top of the old Northern Bank building in Main Street, went to Colette. Michael McKnight was the executor of the Will and Thomas Barry recommended Donnie McCartney remain accountant for the estate, reporting to Colette Barry.

Lefty and McCusker walked Colette home. They offered to keep her company for a while. She politely declined, saying with all the whoha going on, she and Sandy had to grieve for Tom. She said she felt she was now ready to start her mourning. They both voiced concern about her being alone.

'I'll be alone, but not lonely,' she said, 'besides Sandy and I will keep each other company.'

Lefty and McCusker popped into Tom Tom's Bakery on the way back and stocked up with Paris Buns.

McCusker was shocked to see what he believed to be some activity in his house as they walked up Causeway Street. He wondered if O'Carroll had second thoughts about returning to Belfast, or if she'd left on the lights in her bedroom when she was packing her stuff.

Neither proved to be the case.

'So, I had such a fun time on my first visit to the legendary Port,' one of the O'Carroll sisters announced enthusiastically from the sitting room, 'I really felt at home here, and as I had my own key, I took a few days off work, and I booked you a couple of days off as well so I could pop back up here for a long weekend.'

She ran straight into McCusker's arms. At the last possible moment, she noticed her lover wasn't by himself.

'Why, hello Lefty, great to see you again,'

'Oh, hello Grace, and brilliant to see you again as well. While youse two are getting reacquainted, I'll get the auld kettle fired up for tea to go with our stash of Paris buns.'

Over tea and hot Paris Buns they chatted away, the conversation never dipping for a second.

Lefty was first to remember the letters from Thomas Barry. McKnight had handed over to each of them.

They both opened their identical envelopes simultaneously.

Lefty looked to McCusker and nodded in Grace's direction as in, "Is it okay to discuss the contents in front of her?"

McCusker immediately announced, 'Yes, of course.'

Lefty read out his letter. McCusker assumed it was identical to his letter as it started off with, "Dear Brendy and Lefty."

'Dear Brendy and Lefty,' Lefty started aloud,

'Sorry about the wee joke about the old fivers.

'I've included another bit of paper in the bottom of this envelope, I hope you find them a bit more appropriate.

'I also wanted to ask a wee favour of you both.

'I wanted to ask you to keep an eye out for Colette (not the auld glass eye joke, please Lefty). Times are going to be tough for her for a wee while and Isabella is going to be cranked up to Mach Ten when she finds out she's not included in the Will.

'I also hope you'll both be prepared to council Colette and give her business advise on running the Ramore Investments, which I have passed on to her. She's cute enough (no, "but not as cute as Barbara Parkins" jokes, please, Brendy.) Colette's more capable than she's aware, but just knowing she would have you two to depend on would be a great comfort to me and to her.

'I've also suggested this to her in her letter, and we did discuss this, but she wasn't 100% confident either of you would outlast me.

'So, this is it. Are either of youse two, even still around? If you are and I'm not, what got me in the end? (No, "woodworm in my false leg," jokes please, either of you, behave!)

'Take good care of each other.

Cheers

'T. Barry (still no relation to the amusement arcade people. Now Barry's might be an investment the three of you should look at?)'

And there at the bottom of his official letterhead they found in his distinctive neat handwriting their original (unused) BLT motto:

Life is a beach and then the tide goes out.

The other "bit of paper" they found in the bottom of their envelopes was a banker's draft made out to each of them for the sum of £99,999.99!

'Holy smokes!' Lefty cried out, turning it over to see if there was anything on the other side with might declare or reveal Thomas Barry's final joke!

'Well bring on the bleedin' elephants!' McCusker shouted as he handed it to Grace.

Grace examined it calmly and said, 'Yep yours is real.' And handed it back to McCusker.

Lefty automatically handed his to Grace for approval.

'Whoa Lefty,' she whooshed, 'yours is dated two years ago. Tom must have forgotten to update it.'

Lefty's head and neck bolted back upright to a position they hadn't been in for the fifty odd years McCusker had known him. He wheezed so drastically, McCusker worried it sounded like a death rattle.

'She got you Lefty, she really got you!' and they all fell into convulsions of laughter. McCusker felt there was a good chance Lefty's chuckles were just as much from relief rather than humour.

'We should go out and do something fun to celebrate Tom's life,' McCusker suggested.

'I've got the perfect thing for us to do,' Lefty announced, 'the Rainey Players are doing The Last Dance tonight in the Town Hall. It's a musical about the showband scene!'

'I'm game,' McCusker enthused, 'Grace?'

'As long as it doesn't make me cry,' Grace replied, slowly.

'It won't be that bad,' McCusker wise cracked.

'I really hope this doesn't make me cry,' Grace repeated, as they headed out to the Town Hall.

'It's not that type of a musical,' Lefty replied, being the adult, he turned out the lights and shut the door after them.

'Oh, anything can make me cry,' Grace said, as she interlinked her arms with McCusker on her right and Lefty tactically on her left.

'*Anything?*' Lefty asked.

'Oh yes anything,' Grace gushed, 'sometimes I even cry over the fact I can't find anything to cry over.'

'Oh,' Lefty said, grinning largely at McCusker, 'she can join our gang any time she wants to.'

No one mentioned the fact they were currently one member down.

Gone but never forgotten.

Acknowledgments

Martin Edwards, who is always over-generous with his support; Fraser Kennedy for always being there. Christina Czarnik, who always keeps a steady steer on the good ship Asgard, not to mention keeping the proverbial rattles in the pram; to Shawn and Deb at Level Best Books for always being on the case and for offering shelter from the storm to myself, Kennedy, Starrett, and McCusker. To Catherine for always being Catherine.

About the Author

Paul Charles managed his first group, The BLUES by FIVE, when he was fifteen years old and his business card listed the number of the local telephone box in his native Magherafelt, Northern Ireland.

He moved to London in September 1967 when he was seventeen years old and studied to be a civil engineer, but the music business was his real distraction and he was more interested in writing about the London scene for Irish music papers than surveying, planning and drawing.

His real education began when he took on the multiple roles of manager, lyricist, roadie, sound-engineer, agent and the last one to be paid for the Belfast band FRUUPP. Fruupp signed to Dawn Records and worked touring around the UK and Europe for several years in the early seventies. Sheba's Song, with one of several sets of Paul Charles' lyrics from that period (the fine music was from band member John Mason) was sampled and recorded with the original lyrics as Soon The New Day by American Rap artist Talib Kweli with Nora Jones guesting on vocals for Talib's Warner Bros album, Ear Drum.

The album entered the Billboard USA top 200 at #2 on 2nd September, 2007. Norah Jones also featured Soon The New Day on her "Featuring" album, released on Nov 16th 2010 on Blue Note Records which was also a USA Billboard Top 20 album. The same song was used for a Kendrick Lamar cut on his Dot K worktape Training Day.

Fruupp eventually spilt up after four albums but by that point Paul Charles had met Paul Fenn and they became firm friends and, eventually partners in the Asgard Agency where, over the last 30 years, Paul Charles has been agent for a wide range of quality music acts including: Tom Waits, The Kinks, Jackson Browne, Crosby, Stills & Nash, Ray Davies, Lonnie Donegan, Gerry Rafferty, The Blue Nile, Christy The Essential Beatles Book 123 Moore, Paul Carrack, Don McLean, Lisa Ekdahl, Elvis Costello, John Lee Hooker, Sonny Terry and Brownie McGhee, Rory Gallagher, Gordon Lightfoot, Nick Lowe, Ry Cooder, Robert Plant, Planxty, Van Morrison, The Waterboys, The Undertones and the Buzzcocks. He's also programmed the Acoustic Stage at Glastonbury Festival for the last 25 years.

Music has always been a major force in his life: "I have a need for the music of The Beatles, Hank Williams, Nick Drake, Otis Reading, Bob Dylan and the artists we've been lucky enough to work with." But as well as all of that he's also a committed book reader—and collector—particularly British Detective fiction.

"I have always loved writing, anything really, shopping lists, lyrics, sleeve notes, short stories, etc., so in 1996, inspired by Colin Dexter (the creator of Inspector Morse), I attempted my first Detective Inspector Christy Kennedy Mystery, *I Love The Sound of Breaking Glass*, which was published the following year." November 5th 2019 saw the publication of *Departing Shadows* the 11th mystery in the critically acclaimed Christy Kennedy series.

October 25th 2025 marks the beginning of a multi book relationship with Level Best Books with the publication of *Hi Love, You Just Dropped Your Glove*, the third in the McCusker Mystery series. This mystery is set in Portrush, the sleepy seaside town, on the north coast of the island of Ireland.

AUTHOR WEBSITE:
www.paulcharlesbooks.com

SOCIAL MEDIA HANDLES:
  (Instagram) @paulcharles

Also by Paul Charles

Detective Inspector Christy Kennedy Mysteries:
I Love The Sound of Breaking Glass
Last Boat To Camden Town
Fountain of Sorrow
The Ballad of Sean & Wilko
I've Heard The Banshee Sing
The Hissing of the Silent Lonely Room
The Justice Factory
Sweetwater
The Beautiful Sound of Silence
A Pleasure To Do Death With You
Departing Shadow

Inspector Starrett Mysteries:
The Dust of Death
Family Life
St Ernan's Blues

McCusker Mysteries
Down on Cyprus Avenue
A Day in The Life of Louis Bloom

Other Fiction:
First of The True Believers
The Last Dance
The Prince Of Heaven's Eyes (A Novella)
One of Our Jeans is Missing

Factual:
(The Complete Guide to) Playing Live